GENESIS UNDONE

Echoes of Tomorrow

Book 4

ALEXANDER TITUS

SEAN PLATT

GENESIS UNDONE

Chapter One

THERE WAS a cyborg in her front yard.

Jianna hit the brakes hard, and her bicycle skidded to a stop just short of the path to the porch.

Had she seen Jianna? She must've heard the bike's tires scraping on the asphalt, but hadn't looked in Jianna's direction.

The cyborg stood motionless under the dogwood tree, staring at the house like she was waiting for something to happen.

Or maybe she was spying on Jianna's father, who was clearly home, as every window in the house was blazing with light.

The woman's face was beautiful, where it wasn't marred by burn scars: high cheekbones, full lips, olive skin; her black hair was parted straight down the middle. But where her jaw met her neck, flesh gave way to metal. Not smooth titanium like Lucian's. This was a patchwork of dull, battered plates. Different alloys, clearly scavenged. Some edges, jagged. Some parts corroded. The metal vanished beneath her gray uniform, but Jianna couldn't

1

shake the image of a human head bolted onto a scavenged machine.

Was there anything left beneath the fabric except circuits and steel?

Jianna had seen this cyborg before on the *Elysia*. Aurelius had left it to stand guard as she'd worked in the ship's lab when his right-hand android, Lucian, was needed elsewhere.

The cyborg blinked. A weird, stuttering movement, as if her eyelids had to remember how to work.

Then she turned and saw Jianna.

No sign of recognition.

Jianna got off her bike, wheeling it up to the porch and leaning it against the railing. The cyborg watched, unnaturally still, except for another of those slow, stuttering blinks.

Should she wave? Say something?

Or should she ignore the cyborg, the way that Aurelius seemed to?

Jianna had no idea what orders Aurelius might have given when it came to her father or herself. But she was sure they'd be to Aurelius' benefit and not hers.

She walked up the steps, not looking at the cyborg. Five. Four. Three.

Then she bolted for the door.

She half expected the cyborg to run toward her.

But it didn't move it all. It just watched her in that creepy way they all had.

The front door was unlocked. She flung it open hard enough that it banged against the wall. She closed it fast behind her. She had no doubt that if the cyborg wanted to get in, some wood and hinges wouldn't withstand the strength in those mechanical arms.

"Dad?"

No response.

"Dad!"

Then she heard a sound from the kitchen.

She made her way down the hall.

Soren stood at the counter with his back to her. He was chopping vegetables. Two enormous bowls sat beside him, both overflowing. Carrots, celery, onions, sweet peppers, yams, there was more food than the two of them could eat in a week.

"Why is there a cyborg in our front yard?" she asked.

Soren didn't turn around. He just kept chopping. "Security."

Jianna stared at his back. "We've never needed security before. Did someone threaten you?"

"Security precaution. Aurelius insisted."

Soren lifted the cutting board and dumped the vegetables into one of the already overflowing bowls. Chunks of carrot and celery tumbled over the sides and bounced onto the floor near his feet.

He didn't bother to pick them up.

He just grabbed an onion and started chopping. Skin and all. What was going on?

"Are we having company?" Jianna asked.

"I invited Michel and Camilla over for dinner, remember?"

She frowned. "Tonight?"

The knife hovered over the onion. "I can't remember."

Then he went back to chopping.

What was going on? He'd been working around the clock since the Aurora Event. Sleeping in his office. Coming home only to shower and change clothes. She hadn't seen him for more than five minutes at a time in a couple of weeks. And now that he was here, he hadn't asked how she was. Or where she'd been. Or what she'd been up to. Usually, he grilled her for all the details.

"Can you stop?" she asked. "And look at me?"

He hesitated. Then turned toward her.

She'd never seen him look so… uninterested. Not distracted or dulled by exhaustion, but like he genuinely didn't care about anything around him. Including his own daughter.

Something was wrong.

And she had no doubt that something had to do with Aurelius.

Jianna decided to see if surprise would snap him out of it.

"Do you know anything about Descendants being taken into custody?" she asked.

"I haven't heard anything." Then he asked, in a condescending tone she'd never heard him use before: "Did your little Descendant friend get into trouble with Security?"

Was he drugged, maybe? Something that suppressed impulse control while also somehow making you dead inside? Or maybe something that made it easier to dissociate?

"Has Aurelius ever mentioned being interested in the Descendants?" she pushed.

Soren fingered the knife. "I'm not even sure Aurelius knows the Descendants exist. He's been so concerned with getting our city up and running again."

She grimaced. As far as she was concerned, Aurelius wasn't concerned with anything other than himself.

Time for another curveball.

"Do we really need that many vegetables?" Jianna asked.

"They're good for you."

Soren returned to his onion. Jianna opened her mouth, then shook her head and started toward her bedroom to get cleaned up. "Are you going back to the Council after dinner?"

"No need. Aurelius is taking care of everything."

Jianna stopped dead. Then turned around and made her way back to the kitchen. "What do you mean, he's taking care of everything?"

"Well, it's his job as Chancellor."

Her stomach dropped. "Since when?"

"We voted on it this afternoon," Soren said.

"Why?"

Soren dumped more chopped onions onto the mountain of vegetables. "It only makes sense. He's the one with the vision and technological savvy to lead us into the future."

Jianna stared at him. "The last time we talked, you practically interrogated me about every dent on Aurelius' ship because you were sure he had an ulterior motive. What happened?"

Soren glanced over at her. "Sometimes we just have to be practical, my dear. Without Aurelius Hofstadter, we'd have been living like medieval peasants for months. Maybe years."

My dear?

Her father had never called her "my dear."

But more than that, he would never bow down to someone like this. Certainly not someone like Aurelius.

"Bribe or blackmail?" she asked.

Soren turned toward her, pointing the tip of the knife at her as though punctuating every word. "What are you talking about?"

His left eye twitched.

Jianna kept her voice calm. "Did Aurelius Hofstadter bribe you or blackmail you?"

The eye twitched again, but the knife point wavered. "You wouldn't understand, you're just a child whose curiosity exceeds your caution."

That hurt, even though he was clearly not himself. To unleash that accusation when she deserved it was one thing, but Soren Makinde would never say something like that just to score a point.

"Dad—"

But Soren turned back to the chopping board and began slicing vegetables again. "The Council also voted Guide Evans off the Council."

Jianna's mouth fell open. "I thought it was important to show the Naturalists that we're willing to include them, even when they try to keep themselves apart from the rest of society?"

That had been one of the pillars of his last campaign: opportunities for inclusion, even to those who refused his outstretched hand.

"I thought you'd be happy," he said. "Guide Evans is the one who always argues against funding your research."

And now he was a hypocrite, too?

Jianna folded her arms across her chest. "The last time I checked, you voted against it, too."

Soren said nothing. hust chopped. More vegetables on the pile. More on the floor. She couldn't take it anymore. She walked to the nearest cupboard and got out another bowl. "Here."

She handed it to him, then grabbed the full bowl and set it on the table.

Something moved among the vegetables. A tiny beetle, black and shiny. She looked closer. Bits of dirt clung to the carrots. More bugs. Pieces of stem, seed, and onion peel are mixed in with the food.

He was still standing there holding the bowl like he didn't know what to do with it. She grabbed it from him and set it on the counter. "Dad?"

He resumed chopping.

There was a worm wriggling alongside the carrot. He cut through both. Then he swept up all the pieces, including the worm, and chucked them in the bowl.

"Dad!"

Soren turned to look at her. "You can trust Aurelius. He's going to take care of everything."

She threw her arms wide. "What does that mean?"

"He promised."

Soren didn't answer. He simply turned back to the vegetables and started chopping again, ignoring her completely.

Then she remembered the cyborg, watching through the window. Its eyes had seemed biological, but what if its ears were somehow enhanced? Could it hear what they were saying?

Was her father acting this way because he couldn't tell her what was really going on without alerting Aurelius? Maybe he was trying to tell her something, trusting her to notice his aberrant behavior and figure out the code beneath his words.

But if there was hidden meaning in what he'd said, she couldn't see it.

Which meant that Aurelius had broken her father.

Chapter Two

WILLOW RAN.

She kept her hands pressed against the sides of the respirator, making sure it was sealed tight to her face. Her heart tried to crawl into her throat and choke her. Or maybe that was the nanites? Maybe they'd penetrated the filters in her mask and were burrowing into her throat with every rasping breath?

No.

If that was true, she wouldn't have been able to get away, and Aurelius would be controlling her too.

She glanced behind. No one was following her. Any second now, she expected Aurelius or one of his cyborgs to appear and drag her back to the Council chambers. To rip the respirator off her face, hold her down, and force her to inhale his swarm of nanites.

She could still see them, that oily grey cloud roiling like spores in a storm as they forced themselves into Soren's mouth and nose and ears.

Aurelius didn't need to send a cyborg after her. Not when he could send the swarm.

She looked back again and saw a glint of metallic iridescence in the air.

She bolted.

Caught her foot on a broken piece of curb and went flying. She hit the ground hard, her palms skidding against the pavement. She scrambled to her feet, looking back. Was she going to be able to get away?

Only—

She hadn't seen nanites at all. It was just a reflected streetlight shining on a metal sign.

But just because that wasn't them, it didn't mean they weren't coming.

She ran on, knowing that flight was no protection, not when the enemy was smaller than a gnat and could pass through the smallest crack. And there must have been millions.

She maintained her free will only because Aurelius hadn't decided to take it from her.

Yet.

The massive gates of the Naturalist Quarter loomed ahead. She was almost home.

Then she spotted the cyborg, standing at the intersection on her side of the street, between her and the gates.

There was no way she could get to the gates without it seeing, and she had no doubt that its mechanical limbs were much stronger and faster than her own.

But the cyborg didn't move. It didn't even seem to notice her. Its gaze stayed fixed on the gates. Watching.

So she took her chances and ran, screaming like a madwoman. "Open the gate!"

The iron-reinforced doors swung open. Willow stumbled through to find Bram and Vanye on either side of her, waiting for orders.

Willow ripped off her respirator. "Bar the doors. Do not open them unless I give you a direct order."

Bram stepped forward. "Guide Evans. We've been looking for you. That thing—" he gestured toward the cyborg. "—showed up an hour ago and–"

"Call an emergency assembly," Willow gasped. "Now. Everyone is to attend."

Then she strode off, not bothering to look back to see if they were following orders. A moment later, the bang of the doors slamming shut, followed by the solid thud of the massive wooden bar falling into its brackets, told her that they had.

She could sound the literal alarm, but she didn't want to. Not with that cyborg right outside the Quarter's gates. They didn't have the defenses to fight one of them, and Aurelius had a whole ship's worth. Not that he'd have to send cyborgs when he had the nanites.

She glanced up, scanning the air for a metallic shimmer, for any sign of the swarm.

Nothing. Yet. But that didn't mean they weren't coming.

Every instinct in her screamed at her to run, but she forced herself to keep an even pace as she approached the Sanctum. Leaders didn't run. Leaders stayed calm. At least, they did if they wanted their community to follow their lead.

But she couldn't escape the sick feeling that everyone who looked at her already knew about her flight from the Administration Building. Knew that she had been terrified. That she was still was.

Aurelius controlled the Council now.

And that was the right word.

Control.

The others had tried to fight, but they had failed. And

afterward, there was that horrific blankness in their eyes as they had complied with Aurelius' orders…

She would rather die than become his puppet.

Not only did Aurelius own the Council, but he also had the entire apparatus of Vitruvian City at his command, with his own superior technology to back it up.

Without Soren, she was completely alone in opposing him.

What would Mother Basu do?

Nothing.

Because Mother Basu had never faced a threat like this. Mother Basu had died at the hands of another of Aurelius Hofstadter's creations.

What was she supposed to do?

She had no idea.

Willow had never felt so lost.

Footsteps behind her.

She composed her face, then turned around. A handful of her followers approached from the Sanctum steps. "Guide Evans? Where are Cira and Theo?"

Willow cleared the lump from her throat. "The Vitruvians refused to release them."

"But—"

She kept walking. By the time she made it to the worship hall, it was a quarter full. A steady stream of people continued to arrive as she climbed the dais and assumed a position of blessing: hands raised, palms toward the gathering crowd, chin high as she looked out over their heads.

Soon, the hall was full, and more spilled out into the hallway. Hundreds of worried faces turned toward her, waiting.

She lowered her hands, clasping them in front of her,

and a shushing spread through the room, silence close on its tail.

"The Vitruvians–" Willow's voice caught in her throat. She cleared it and started again. "The Vitruvians have foolishly embraced the Elysian newcomers and their poisonous technology."

She paused, giving them a moment to absorb that before she continued. "The Elysian leader is a cyborg. He gives orders to the Council and is preparing to unleash a technological plague in the air, the water, the food."

Silence.

And then a great rumbling of voices. The questions tumbled together, washing over her like a wave. She couldn't distinguish words. It was just noise.

She raised her hands again. "Quiet!"

Thank Mother Basu, they did as instructed.

"I am invoking our most stringent Quarantine protocols. The Quarter is to be sealed off. All water must be boiled, then purified. Food must be washed, then irradiated with UV light and X-rays."

She didn't know if it would be enough, but it was all they had right now.

"Everyone must wear a respirator outside. And if anyone starts behaving oddly, they are to be isolated and placed in lockdown immediately."

"Oddly?" A woman asked.

"What kind of symptoms should we watch for?" asked another.

She opened her mouth, then closed it again. If she told them the truth, she wouldn't be able to contain the panic.

"Unknown," Willow said. "Although uncharacteristic behavior does seem to be one of them."

"How bad is it?" someone shouted.

"Is it lethal?"

"What medicines should we prepare?"

Willow raised her hands. "It's definitely airborne. That's all I can tell you for now, but as soon as I have answers, I will inform you. Lock everything down. Now."

She turned toward the back of the dais, toward the door that led into the private section of the Sanctum. But as she stepped into the hallway leading to her chambers, someone said, "Guide Evans."

She turned.

It was one of the Sanctum physicians.

"Dr. Nilson."

"Guide Evans," he sounded disapproving. "Starting a panic after everyone has been through so much… More fear isn't going to help."

Willow drew herself up to her full height and stared down at him. "They should be afraid, and so should you, because this is only the beginning."

His mouth dropped open. Did he think, because he was a physician, he was immune to rebuke?

"See that everyone in the Sanctum grounds is instructed in the strictest quarantine protocols. I'll hold you responsible if they're not."

Then she turned her back on him and entered the private area, going straight to her room. When she arrived, she shut herself in the soundproofed meditation chamber and fumbled with the lock until it snapped shut.

Only then did she allow the screams to come.

<h1 style="text-align:center">Chapter Three</h1>

MICHEL STOOD next to the control panel, sweat beading along his hairline despite the morning chill. Through the grimy window, he watched the crowd gathering at the base of the newly-completed transmission tower.

Some looked excited. Some looked nervous. Others, confused. Michel recognized most of them. Vitruvians who mattered. Dignitaries. Council members. Community leaders. And there was a band. Aurelius had invited a band to entertain everyone at what Aurelius had referred to as a "ribbon-cutting" ceremony. They were here to power up the transmission tower for the first time. What did ribbons have to do with it?

"Magnificent turnout, isn't it?" Aurelius asked, grinning.

Michel nodded, though the crowd wasn't that large. No more than a couple of hundred people. But then, Aurelius had spent centuries on a ship with just his crew. This might be the biggest crowd he'd seen in a long time.

Beyond the crowd, he counted six of Aurelius' cyborgs. Just watching. How did they stand so still? Even their biological parts didn't move, no fidgeting with their natural hands, no shifting weight from their original feet to their mechanical ones. And completely expressionless, no matter what you said to them. It was impossible to tell what they were thinking or feeling.

They were more like robots than Aurelius' android, Lucian.

There was a time when he would've taken that as a sign of Aurelius' genius. But now it seemed like a sick joke.

If there were more cyborgs lurking out there at the edges of the crowd, he couldn't see them from where he was standing.

Aurelius had seemed his usual self this morning, which made Michel think Aurelius hadn't figured out that he'd learned the actual cause of the radiation storm that had crippled the city. Now he knew that Aurelius was deceptively good at hiding things. Maybe he was playing Michel for the fool.

Maybe the cyborgs were here to kill him if he tried to tell anyone what he'd found.

He swallowed hard and tried to breathe normally, but somehow each inhale and exhale seemed unnaturally loud, until he felt like he was wheezing. Surely Aurelius was picking up on that?

He sucked in a breath and held it in his lungs, hoping that the extra oxygen would calm him down, and then he caught sight of Jianna's father and the rest of the Council standing beside the tower. They were all smiling vacantly and waving occasionally at people in the crowd.

If he didn't know better, he'd think they were all high. Except that when Valencia was smoking canni, she got giggly, and Raul could barely keep his eyes open.

But Councilors wouldn't do that right before a public appearance, would they?

Aurelius stepped out of the shed, raising his hand. Michel didn't know what to do. The crowd quieted. Feeling their attention on him, Michel stiffened, resisting the urge to fidget.

Aurelius lowered his hand and smiled at all the guests. "Welcome, everyone. As your newly-elected Chancellor—"

Michel's fingers tightened around the edge of the control panel as he forced his face to remain neutral.

Chancellor?

When had that happened?

He wasn't the only one who was hearing the news for the first time. Many in the crowd looked surprised. Or confused. Or incredulous. Several of them moved toward the Councilors, all of whom watched Aurelius like dogs hoping to be tossed a treat.

Would Jianna's father have told her what was really going on?

"—it's an honor to be here with you at the inauguration of a new era. Not just in communications—" Aurelius gestured toward the tower. "—but in your planet's evolution. This is only the beginning. We're going to revolutionize every industry, every piece of infrastructure, every aspect of life on DaVinci, until we are the most technologically advanced civilization that humanity has ever built."

He paused, and the crowd applauded politely.

When it stopped, Aurelius continued. "The moment I stepped on DaVinci I knew that—"

Michel's mind drifted to the half-melted probe that was now locked in a small storage room in the Vault. After the crew brought it in, Michel had erased the job from the logs. He'd told the crew it was a communication drone that had malfunctioned.

He'd never lied to his crewmates before. It made him feel queasy.

But if he told them the truth, they'd go to Aurelius. Not only would Michel be in danger, but so would they.

How could Aurelius let word get out that the Aurora Event hadn't been a radiation storm, but his deliberate attack on the city?

Once it was secure, Michel had downloaded every bit of weather satellite data available from the day of the radiation storm. What he'd found confirmed that the ionizing radiation had been localized over Vitruvia City. There hadn't been a flicker anywhere else that day, as far as the weather satellites could detect.

He glanced at Jianna's father a third time. He had wanted to tell Jianna as soon as he'd discovered it, but Aurelius had called him back for a double shift to complete the tower, and he'd been afraid that if he claimed to be too sick to take the shift, Aurelius would figure out that Michel was onto him.

But maybe today he could grab a moment with Councilor Makinde, even if Aurelius was watching.

"Mr. Lombardi?"

Michel's shoulders jerked involuntarily as he looked up.

"Are you all right?" Aurelius towered over him, looking down. He was still smiling, but he seemed annoyed.

Michel flushed. "Sorry. I was going over everything in my head one last time, in case we missed something with the array connections."

"Whenever you're ready, Mr. Lombardi." Aurelius turned back to the crowd. "Those of you who have comms, please get them out and turn them on. Hold them up so your neighbors can see the transition, too."

Michel felt a stab of guilt as he thought about the

comm unit in his pocket. He'd been issued one of the first rebuilt comms so he could receive assignments and coordinate with the other Engineering crews. He hadn't needed it since he'd gotten the nanites, but he'd kept it rather than turning it in to be reissued to someone else. Mainly because he didn't want anyone to notice that he didn't need it anymore.

Especially Jianna.

Aurelius gestured to Michel.

Michel tapped the screen on the console before him, accessing the communication drone network that the city had been relying on since Aurelius deployed it.

He powered it down.

Immediately, the feed in his peripheral vision flickered out as his connection to the quantum computer was cut.

The Engineering work queue, the list of scientific papers he'd been working his way through, the floating calendar/clock display. He was 100% offline. There was a strange kind of silence in his head, like he'd been disconnected from his life. He didn't like it.

He'd gotten used to being connected all the time, even more so than when he'd been using a comm.

People in the crowd holding comms watched their signal die.

"Now, Mr. Lombardi."

Michel tapped an icon, powering up the tower. The console lit up in a dozen different places as power began coursing through the system.

A second later, a translucent login appeared in Michel's peripheral vision. He stifled a sigh of relief. Thank Phoebe.

He glanced at the crowd, spotting some comms lighting up as they picked up the new signal. A second later, a jaunty tune jangled throughout the crowd.

Aurelius grinned. "Wrote that myself."

"It's so much faster now," Councilor Vohl exclaimed, already swiping across her comm's screen.

"That's right," Aurelius nodded. "And now that we've got a real network, we're going to address the comm shortage."

"Isn't Engineering rebuilding them all from scratch?" a woman asked.

Aurelius shook his head. "We're not building more comms, we're replacing them with implants that can be instantly upgraded, and they're fifteen times faster than any handheld device."

"That doesn't sound safe," a man muttered.

"On the contrary, this implant has been tested for more than three centuries." Aurelius tapped his temple. "And no need for a hole in your head, this is a simple injection."

Low conversations ran through the crowd. Skeptical, Michel thought, and maybe a little bit concerned.

Then Councilor Makinde stepped forward. "I understand your concerns, but the Council has reviewed the Chancellor's technology and found it to be completely safe. It has passed our most stringent requirements."

Michel raised his brows. The Council had already approved Aurelius' technology?

It took them weeks to approve upgrades to essential infrastructure and months to debate everything else.

And hadn't they just shot down Jianna's latest proposal? Her own father had voted against it.

"You won't believe how much easier it makes everything," Aurelius added. "You're not going to want to go back."

The—new Chancellor?—gestured to the band, and a moment later they began to play. People started mingling.

Aurelius turned to Michel. "I think that went well, don't you?"

"Great." He wasn't going to tell his boss otherwise, even if it hadn't. "The Council approved nanites already?"

Aurelius grinned. "They saw the benefits when I explained it to them in terms they could understand."

Michel forced himself to smile back. "That's great."

But he must not have sounded enthusiastic enough, because Aurelius patted his shoulder and said, "Don't be jealous, Mr. Lombardi. None of them will have the kind of access you do. They'll be restricted to the local network."

Michel swallowed. "Yes, sir."

Aurelius leaned closer, his fingers tightening.

Had he realized that Michel was keeping secrets? Was he about to threaten him? Sweat broke out on Michel's forehead.

"You've been doing such outstanding work that I'm assigning you to a new project." He leaned forward, bowing his head so that they were almost nose to nose. "You're going to help me get the *Borlaug* working again."

A week ago, that would've been Michel's dream come true. But now, it felt like a threat.

"Th-thank you, sir."

Aurelius nodded and straightened, like Michel had passed some sort of test. "Be at the Administration building at dawn tomorrow, the shuttle will be waiting."

"Thank you, sir," Michel repeated.

"Don't thank me, just keep up the good work."

Aurelius grinned and saluted, for some reason, then walked into the crowd to schmooze. There were loads of people lining up to talk to the man, seemingly eager to ingratiate themselves to him.

Was this new assignment a reward for work well done, Michel wondered, or was it a way to keep him isolated so that he couldn't tell anyone what he knew?

Michel's throat went dry.

No. Don't go there.

If he started thinking like that, he'd be a stammering mess the next time Aurelius asked him a question, and the man would know something was up for sure. He grabbed his bag and headed out. But before he got far, Councilor Makinde blocked his path.

Great.

Was he going to tell Michel to stop seeing Jianna?

No need for that, since Jianna wasn't speaking to him anymore.

"Councilor," Michel said.

Jianna's father greeted him with a warm smile that didn't quite reach his eyes. His expression was less distant than before, but there was something off with the man. He seemed a little... Slow? Tired?

Maybe he'd been close when he'd guessed canni. Maybe the Councilor was taking some kind of pain medication.

"Please come to dinner tonight, Michelangelo. Bring your mother."

Michel blinked. Dinner? Of all the things he'd been expecting the Councilor to say...

Jianna must not have told her father that they were fighting. So maybe she didn't consider their last argument to be a breakup.

That didn't mean she'd be happy to see him, though. He wasn't entirely sure how he felt about her, either.

He definitely didn't want to offend a Councilor by turning him down, though. Not when the Council could choose whether to renew his mother's work license or shut down her clinic.

"Thank you, Councilor," Michel said. "We'd be honored. Should we bring anything?"

"Just yourselves. I've already started preparing a feast. I'll send an invitation with the details."

"Thank you, sir."

"I'm sure Jianna will be delighted to see you."

Michel felt sure that *delighted* would be pushing it, but maybe she could help him find a way to tell her father what he'd discovered about the radiation storm.

Councilor Makinde turned away to talk to someone, and Michel bolted, avoiding the cyborgs, but they didn't seem to care that he was leaving. He couldn't help looking over his shoulder anyway to make sure that he wasn't being followed.

Only when he was several blocks away did he breathe a sigh of relief. Hopefully, Jianna's father would be able to help him because the only other person left that he could turn to was Lucas.

And Michel was pretty sure that Lucas had his own agenda.

One that might not include anyone's survival except his own.

Chapter Four

JIANNA STOOD IN THE HALLWAY, listening. She heard a noise from the living room, a low murmur. Her father's voice.

"Of course, my dear," Soren said.

Who was he talking to?

She waited a moment but didn't hear any further conversation, so she took the last few steps and peeked around the corner.

Her father sat in the chair by the window, staring at the dogwood tree in the yard. The cyborg was still there beneath the branches laden with white flowers.

No. Not the same cyborg. A different one. This one was a man, and he still had one of his original hands.

Maybe they did sleep, after all. That suggested they were more human than machine.

Or maybe the other one had just been needed elsewhere.

Every time she asked her father why there was a cyborg in the yard, he gave the same answer: security. She found it eerie how they never talked, not even when you asked them a question. Had Aurelius ordered them not to speak?

She entered the room. His comm sat on the coffee table. If he wouldn't give her answers, maybe she could get answers another way.

"My comm isn't working," she said, walking over to the table. "Can I borrow yours for a minute?"

"Of course, my dear." He didn't even bother to turn around.

She picked up the device. "I need you to unlock it."

He didn't move.

"Dad."

He finally turned. His gaze drifted through her like she was made of smoke. When he held out his hand, she passed him the comm. He lifted it to his face for the scanner, but the device remained locked, its screen stubbornly dark.

He tried a second time, lowering the comm and raising it once more to his face. This time, the scanner pulsed with recognition, and he handed the unlocked device back without a word.

Then he turned back to the window, staring out at nothing. Or at least nothing she could see.

"Thanks."

She waited a moment longer for some kind of acknowledgment, but there was nothing. He might as well have been a cyborg himself.

Jianna retreated down the hall, her feet silent against the floor. She slipped into the bathroom and locked the door behind her.

Pulling up the Council communication system, she scrolled through her father's recent messages, looking for anything about Descendants being arrested or detained. Nothing. There was plenty on food distribution, agricultural yield projections, and minor arrests. There were reports from Engineering about infrastructure repairs. She read through several of those. It seemed like the Council had been prioritizing power and communications systems up until yesterday. All normal Council business.

She did a couple of searches on the Descendants and came up empty.

She checked his schedule. No meetings were scheduled for the foreseeable future. His work queue was empty. Zero proposals waiting for a vote.

That was insane. The Council was always backlogged with citizen concerns, environmental assessments, and budget allocations that needed to be voted on.

He hadn't received personal messages from any other Council member for more than a day.

Beyond that, there were no inter-Council member communications that he usually complained about.

She checked his saved messages.

Empty.

He had deleted all his messages.

She checked the deleted folders. Empty as well.

But why?

She gnawed her lip. If she didn't know better, it almost looked as though the governing body of Vitruvian City had simply... stopped governing. Or was he trying to hide council business from Aurelius?

Jianna sent a message to the Head of Security: *Have there been any unusual interactions or incidents involving Descendants in the past week? Any detentions or complaints filed? Please advise.*

Then another to the Descendant Liaison: *Any Descendants admitted to medical facilities in recent days? Need to verify the current status of community members due to a potential illness. Please advise.*

She hit send on both, set up forwarding to her own comm, then deleted both messages from the sent folder.

She had a sinking feeling that the only way to find Glint and the others was to ask Aurelius directly.

If she confronted him, he'd probably have her arrested. Or worse.

Maybe there was a third option. If Aurelius had taken the Descendants or used Lucas to kidnap them, maybe he'd taken them up to his ship.

Aurelius had promised her access to the lab on the *Elysia* whenever she wanted, but Lucian never left her alone without assigning a cyborg to watch her in his place. And even if the Descendants had gone with Lucas willingly because they thought their Liaison would protect them, they would probably be prisoners now. Which meant they'd be guarded by more of those cyborgs.

How was she supposed to rescue them?

She heard the loud clatter of pots, then a crash that sounded suspiciously like more than one hitting the floor.

Not again.

She hurried back to the kitchen, where her father stood at the stove, drizzling oil into a pan. Too much oil. She ran over and grabbed his arm, stopping the flow of oil.

"What are you doing?"

"Cooking dinner." He said it in a monotone, no emotion at all.

"We should only cook a quarter of the vegetables," Jianna said, taking the oil and placing it back in the cupboard. "We don't want them to go bad before we can eat them all."

"But your boyfriend and his mother are coming for dinner."

Jianna froze. "Tonight?"

Soren paused. His eye twitched—a tiny spasm that lasted maybe half a second. "I think so."

Was he serious? "Why don't you get dressed? I'll start cooking."

He smiled. "Excellent idea, my dear."

She waited until he shuffled out of the kitchen.

She needed to act fast if she was going to save dinner.

First, she grabbed the frying pan and poured most of the oil out into a bowl, shuddering to think how easily he might've set the house on fire if he'd left a pan full of oil on a hot burner and then gotten distracted.

Next, she grabbed the bowls of chopped vegetables and dumped everything into a colander. She quickly sorted through what could be salvaged and discarded the inedible parts. Then she rinsed off all the dirt and bits of beetles and worms. Once the vegetables were clean, she tossed them into the frying pan and began to sauté them.

When her father returned wearing slacks and a nice tunic, she asked, "What are we making?"

Soren smiled. "I haven't decided yet."

"How about soup?" She was pretty sure there were a few cans in the pantry and a box of crackers. Maybe she could persuade her father to serve just that and save the vegetables for something else.

There was a knock at the front door.

She wiped her hands on a kitchen towel and headed for the door. Her heart skipped when she saw who it was — Michel with his mother Camilla standing slightly behind him, both of them framed in the doorway like an awkward family portrait.

Her father actually had invited them to dinner.

Jianna smiled. "I'm so glad you're here."

And she meant it.

Maybe they could help her figure out what was wrong with her father.

Camilla entered, lifting the box she was carrying. "I know Soren said not to bring anything, but I stopped by the bakery for almond cake."

Jianna could have kissed the woman. "Dad's in the kitchen. He's been a little distracted today."

"I'll go see if I can help him with anything," Camilla said, leaving Jianna alone with Michel.

Once his mother was out of the room, Michel touched Jianna's arm. "I know you're angry, and I'm sorry, but there's something really important I need to talk to you about. Is there somewhere private we can go?"

She led him down the hallway to her father's study. The lock clicked with finality as she shut the door behind them, sealing them into her father's sanctuary of privacy in a house that suddenly felt like it had eyes everywhere.

"Why do you have a cyborg in your front yard?" Michel asked.

"Dad says it's for security, but I think they're watching him. Is that what you wanted to ask me?"

Michel shook his head. "I found something out, something horrible."

He stopped as if he didn't know how to continue.

Jianna crossed her arms. "I need to get back to the kitchen, my father isn't—"

"The radiation storm wasn't a natural phenomenon," Michel said.

The room seemed to tilt slightly. She walked to her father's desk and dropped into his chair.

She'd been right about Aurelius, but she needed to hear Michel say it, to admit that the man he idolized had betrayed them.

"So, what was it?"

He looked down at his feet, took a deep breath, and then tried to meet her gaze. "It was a deliberate attack intended to take out our grid."

"So we'd have to accept whatever technologies he offered us," Jianna finished for him. "And now Aurelius controls the whole city's infrastructure."

Michel nodded. He looked miserable.

"Can you prove it?" she asked.

"I can. Do you think your father will listen?"

Now that Michel could see it, it was too little, too late. Even if her father believed them, he was in no state to stand up to Aurelius.

And she was sure that whatever the cyborg had done to the Council Chair, he'd done to the rest of the Council, too.

"I think Aurelius did something to my father," she said.

"Did something?"

"He's been in a daze. And he keeps calling me my dear. He's never called me that before."

"He seemed out of it at the tower ceremony. You think he's been drugged?"

She shrugged. "I don't know. But I can't exactly ask my father for a blood sample to test, can I?"

"Have you tried?"

She hesitated. She hadn't, in part because she'd been assuming he would refuse, but also because it seemed so wrong to ask.

Michel touched her hand. "Did your father tell you that the Council approved giving nanites to anyone who wants them?"

Jianna's mouth fell open. "What?"

"Communication nanites. Free to anyone who wants to inject them."

She clenched her hands into fists. "The Council was

afraid to fund my research with its half a year of preliminary data, careful protocols, and safety measures. But they approved Aurelius' nanites? Without any testing?"

Michel nodded. "Apparently."

"My father never would've approved that." She flung her hands wide. "They don't even know the foundational theory underlying their function. Let alone what effects they might have once they're injected into people."

"But I heard him say they were safe myself."

"When?"

"At the tower ceremony."

Jianna jumped to her feet and began pacing the office. "We have to stop Aurelius. We can't let him distribute the nanites to everyone. Not without understanding how they work."

"If we can get some to study—"

Jianna pursed her lips. "That's exactly what Aurelius wanted. But the ones he offered were supposed to repair DNA. I have no idea how different they are from the communication nanites. And if I ask him about the difference—"

"Don't." Michel shook his head. "It could make him suspicious."

Jianna felt a cold finger trace her spine. "What if Aurelius already injected my father and the Council with these nanites? That would explain why Dad's acting like...not-Dad. I need to figure out exactly what they do to people's brains and how to neutralize them before it's too late." Jianna hesitated. "I don't understand robots or artificial intelligence well enough. I need your help to discover how they work."

"I think my mother can get some."

"How?"

"There was a call for medical practitioners to volunteer

to help give injections. All she has to do is report to a clinic. She could bring a dose home for us."

"Most of my lab equipment was destroyed during the storm. I'd have to get the nanites up to the ship to investigate them. But Aurelius has the android or his cyborgs watching me, and he can probably access the logs of all the equipment up there."

"He can monitor everything you do up there," Michel said. "But maybe my mother can help you find what you need."

Jianna smiled. "Thank you." She pulled him into a hug, feeling his warmth against her, a stark contrast to the cold fear that had been building inside her. "I'm so glad you didn't accept them."

Michel stiffened and pulled away. *Idiot.* She'd gone and reminded him of their fight, and now he was probably mad at her again.

She released him, stepping back as her mind raced to the next connection. "Wait—do you think there's a link between Aurelius distributing these nanites and all those missing Descendants?"

"What missing Descendants?" Michel's voice cracked.

"I went to the village to question Lucas, but the village Elder said Lucas disappeared. So did Glint and a dozen other Descendants."

Michel's face drained of color. "Why didn't you tell me? I have to go find—"

A knock interrupted him, and the door swung open before either could respond. Soren stood in the doorway, his smile fixed and empty, like someone had drawn it on with a marker.

"Hey kiddos, dinner's ready," he announced in a chipper voice that belonged to a sitcom dad, not the stern Council Chair who had raised her.

He vanished as abruptly as he'd appeared. Michel turned to Jianna. "Kiddos?"

"See?" Jianna gestured toward the now-empty doorway. "That's not my father."

"I have to go find Glint," Michel said.

Jianna caught his arm. "That's not a good idea."

"Why not?"

"Aurelius has the cyborg watching us. I guarantee it. If you leave now, it might follow you or report that you're acting weird. After all, it probably knows that you're here for supper."

"But—"

"I've been monitoring my father's accounts, and there's no sign of them in the city. I think Aurelius has them, which means they're probably up on the ship. Lucas probably took them."

Michel frowned. "You don't know that."

"Aurelius created Lucas, so he can probably control him."

Camilla called from the other room. "Dinner's ready."

"Well?" Jianna asked.

Michel hesitated and then nodded. "Guess we should go have dinner."

They returned to the kitchen, where four places had been set on the humble table—a relic from early in her father's career, when he'd been an underpaid administrator. A pile of soggy, blackened vegetables sat on each plate, and beside the plate, a bowl of something that Jianna thought might have been meant as soup. It looked like her father had stirred uncooked egg noodles into beef broth, then sprinkled the top with chopped peanuts.

Of course, he hadn't thought to heat up the canned soup in the pantry. He was out of his mind.

Jianna flushed with humiliation as her father said, "Try

the soup, it's a family recipe. Samara brought it all the way from Earth."

Michel and Camilla stared at their bowls for a moment, then exchanged a look that made Jianna's humiliation burn hotter.

She picked up her spoon and took a sip of soup, doing her best to avoid the bits of peanuts floating on the surface or the still-hard noodles resting at the bottom of the bowl. It was overly salty with an overpowering taste of cumin. She set her spoon down.

Michel gave Camilla a pleading look.

Only Soren dug in like nothing was wrong.

Camilla smiled, but her eyes looked sad. "Perhaps we should break a few rules. Start with dessert?"

"Great idea," Jianna said.

Camilla got up, put the cake in the center of the table, and started cutting pieces and handing them out.

Soren picked it up with his fingers and dipped it into his soup. "Excellent choice, Camilla."

Jianna felt the sting of tears behind her eyes. She looked down at the cake on her plate, hoping Michel and his mother wouldn't see. Her chest was tight, air snagging somewhere in her throat.

When she glanced up again, she saw a dark shape behind Michel—the cyborg, pressed up against the living room window. Watching them. There was a wanting in its gaze, something almost desperate.

She wondered if it was jealous, if it was wishing for a piece of cake, or even her father's ruined soup. Her father's family recipe was an abomination, but even that was better than the horrible nutritional paste that they'd eaten during the trip to DaVinci.

The thought made her ache for the thing outside, but

she forced herself to look away, pretending she hadn't noticed.

She picked up her fork and took a bite of cake. The almond flavor filled her mouth, but it might as well have been ash. Her hands felt cold. Every movement seemed mechanical, like she was watching herself from outside her own body. Michel and his mother made polite conversation with her father, but the words barely registered.

Soren smiled and nodded, dipping another piece of cake into his soup. He was performing a family dinner, like a puppet following a script.

Jianna pressed the tines of her fork into the cake again, trying to focus on the sweetness, the fluffy texture, but all she could think about was the cyborg's face at the window. Watching them. Probably reporting every detail to Aurelius.

Jianna forced herself to meet her father's vacant eyes. Could she find a way to bring him back?

Was there anything left to save?

Chapter Five

WILLOW'S MEDITATION chamber felt smaller in the predawn darkness, its stone walls pressing in like the grip of an old nightmare. She sat cross-legged on her prayer mat, spine straight, hands resting palm-up on her knees in the traditional position Mother Basu had taught them. But her breath… That was all wrong.

It came in sharp, shallow gasps that caught in her throat like broken glass. Or nanites.

Her eyes flew open.

"Calm down."

In through the nose, out through the mouth.

Find the center.

Find your peace.

She closed her eyes again.

But that just took her back to the Council chambers, her own voice echoing in her ears as she vowed, "I'll die before I bow to you."

The malicious glint of delight in Aurelius' eyes as he replied: "Oh, Willow. You're going to make this so much more interesting than I thought."

The gray, oily cloud bursting from his mouth and nose to swarm around her like a cloud of metal and malice.

Forcing themselves into the Councilor's mouths and noses.

Willow's breath hitched. Her hands clenched into fists, nails digging into her palms.

Focus. Breathe.

But their screaming filled her ears. Councilor Vohl, clawing at her face. The choking. The gargling. The wet, desperate gasps as those who'd governed this city with wisdom and dignity were reduced to writhing animals on the marble floor.

When the screaming had stopped, the only sound that remained was her own ragged breathing. Just like her breath sounded now as it sawed in and out of her lungs.

BANG. BANG. BANG.

She jolted, almost flying out of her skin.

The sound exploded through the chamber. Her thoughts scattered like shrapnel. Was a single moment of peace too much to ask from the very community she'd sacrificed everything to protect?

Apparently so.

BANG. BANG.

She surged to her feet, strode to the door, and yanked it open. "Yes?"

It sounded more like a snarl than a word.

Yelena's pale face went even whiter. For a moment, Willow wondered if the girl might actually faint.

"I'm—I'm sorry, Guide Evans." Yelena's voice cracked. "I didn't want to disturb you, but—"

"But you did anyway."

Yelena recoiled.

Willow reined in her anger, forcing her voice back to its normal register. "What's happened?"

"You have a v-v-visitor."

A visitor. At this hour, when the morning prayers hadn't even begun and most of the Quarter still slept? Willow's stomach tightened. "Who is it?"

Yelena just shook her head, trembling all over. Whoever this visitor was, they had frightened her. "Where are they?"

"G-g-garden."

Willow patted her shoulder. "Dismissed."

Yelena bobbed her head and scurried away down the corridor. Willow remained where she was for a moment, listening to the silence of the Sanctum around her.

Then she made her way to her room, grabbed a sweater, then stepped through the door and out into her private garden. The tall hedges that enclosed the space cast long shadows across the stone pathway. The scent of jasmine and morning glory should have calmed her, but then she saw who awaited her and stopped dead in her tracks.

Aurelius stood beside her prized hibiscus bush, examining one of the red blossoms.

He'd finally come for her.

She thought about running, but where could she go that his nanites couldn't follow?

The cyborg bent over the flowers, the left side of his face soft with something that looked almost like wonder. Then he reached and touched one of the blossoms, leaned in, and inhaled deeply. He smiled.

Not the arrogant smirk she'd seen in the Council chambers. This smile was genuine. Unguarded. For a moment, he looked almost human. "Do you know how long it's been since I've smelled a flower?"

She blinked. Was he talking to her? Like they were old

friends sharing a quiet moment instead of reflection? "How dare you come here?"

Aurelius ignored her. "Close to four hundred years. Imagine that, Willow. Not smelling a flower for four centuries. It boggles the mind, doesn't it?"

She wanted to agree. She couldn't imagine it. But they were not friends. Nor would they ever be. She didn't dare let her guard down around him.

"I gave explicit orders that no one was to be admitted to the Quarter without my authorization," she said. "What did you do to my men?"

He straightened, turning toward her. The arrogant smirk was back. "I politely asked them to let me enter, and they did."

Willow doubted that.

"I brought you a gift."

"I don't want anything from you, except to be left alone."

He scowled, but it was almost teasing. "Don't be silly. Give me your tablet."

She planted her hands on her hips, if only to make herself feel that she was larger and perhaps a bit more intimidating. "You don't give the orders here."

Aurelius sighed, and a light flickered in his artificial eye. A moment later, a luminous hologram hovered in the air between them.

She blinked. Peered closer.

It showed the android's head on a steel laboratory bench, eyes closed, face slack like a corpse at peace. Nearby, its torso rested on another bench, dozens of wires snaking from its open chest cavity like electronic entrails.

The thing wasn't human, but she shuddered anyway. Not because she felt sorry for it, but because the tableau of dismemberment forced her to imagine herself chopped up on that table, her very real entrails spilling out of a tear in her own belly.

As Aurelius had no doubt intended. He could take control of her mind, but he chose to torture her instead.

And he'd been willing to destroy his most advanced toy to do it.

"Why are you showing me this?" she asked.

"Just watch."

Willow forced herself to look back at the hideous projection. The android's eyes opened, focusing on someone outside the frame.

Mother Basu. It was conscious.

"You're looking for a way to control me," the android said, "because you're afraid of me."

Its voice was strange. Slow. Almost like it had been drugged. But you couldn't drug an android, could you?

Then she heard Aurelius' recorded voice. "I'm trying to understand how you went off the rails and killed Ayesha Basu."

Ice filled Willow's veins. Aurelius hadn't done this to the android he'd brought with him. That was Lucas. The Murderer. Somehow, impossibly, Aurelius had found him.

"Speak," Aurelius said.

"She killed my daughter," the Murderer said.

Much had been written in the history archives about the Murderer's delusion, which Samara had encouraged, by her own admission, and later regretted.

But to hear the note of grief coming out of that artificial mouth was something else. She didn't believe that a machine could be a father, but she had no doubt that the Murderer believed it.

"You're an android. You never had a daughter and you never will."

The Murderer said nothing. His face remained impassive.

Now she did feel sorry for him.

If this were a human that Aurelius was interrogating, it would qualify as torture. But the Murderer wasn't human. It was a machine whose programming had gone catastrophically wrong.

And as a result, it had killed Mother Basu.

Who'd also had a daughter.

"Did you enjoy killing Ayesha?" Aurelius asked in the recording.

Willow held her breath. She really didn't want to know the answer. Which would be worse, if it had or if it hadn't?

"I did not enjoy it, although I felt a compulsion to do it."

"What do you mean, a compulsion?"

"I saw my daughter's body—"

"She wasn't your daughter, she was Samara's."

Silence again. Then… "Samara authorized me to act as Phoebe's father."

Aurelius laughed, and he sounded genuinely amused, as if the android had told the most ridiculous joke he'd ever heard.

But that was revolting too, that the cyborg could laugh while talking about the death of the woman he claimed was his granddaughter.

Willow wasn't sure which of these abominations she hated more.

"What happened after you killed Ayesha?" Aurelius pressed.

The android's eyes flickered again. Willow realized he was trying to resist answering the question. But somehow it was being forced out of him. "Phoebe was pregnant. I extracted the embryo."

Willow's mouth fell open.

Phoebe had been pregnant?

Had Samara known and hidden it, ashamed that her tolerance of the android had led to her grandchild's death as well?

Or was the Murderer lying?

If it could slip its programming to kill, why not to lie?

"Why did you take the embryo?" Aurelius asked.

"To study it. I believed that the combination of Phoebe's and Atlas' genes might have been the solution to the off-target effects that all humans suffer on DaVinci."

The hologram-Aurelius looked at something outside the image stream, his expression thoughtful. "That's not the real reason."

Another pause. "Because I wanted my grandchild to live."

"You're not capable of having grandchildren." Again, that terrible silence, before Aurelius broke it. "Tell me what you did next."

"I stored the embryo in a cryobox and took it to my lab in the mountains. I knew the colonists wouldn't allow me to exist once they discovered what I'd done, so I planned to keep the embryo frozen until I could repair one of the defunct artificial wombs at the ruins of the Hyperion settlement."

"But?" Aurelius asked.

"An earthquake trapped me underground. When I realized that I wouldn't be able to dig myself out, I used my own power source to keep the cryobox running. I turned my higher functions off to maximize the chances of discovery."

"And that day came."

"It did."

The holographic Aurelius walked in front of the Murderer's head and paused slightly out of view. "How did you get out of the cave?"

"Another earthquake opened a new passage to my lab. Jianna Makinde found me."

Willow frowned.

Jianna had met the Murderer and didn't report it? Or maybe she had, and that was how Aurelius had found it.

"She freed you?" Holographic Aurelius asked.

"No. She was afraid of me. But I was able to convince her to take the cryobox and connect it to a new power source."

The hologram froze, then vanished completely.

Willow stared at Aurelius, so shocked at the implication that she couldn't breathe.

If Phoebe had been pregnant…

By Atlas…

That meant…

"The Divine Blueprint survived?"

"It appears so."

She walked to one of the garden benches and dropped onto it. Jianna had the Divine Blueprint. A contaminated version, given that Atlas' DNA was mixed with Phoebe's genetic material.

Samara had claimed that the samples of Atlas' DNA that Mother Basu had given her were destroyed, that his genetic sequence had been wiped from her equipment. And Atlas himself had disappeared after Phoebe's funeral, selfishly taking humanity's salvation with him.

But if this embryo existed, if the Murderer wasn't lying, then Jianna Makinde possessed the key to their entire faith. The divine gift that would allow all Naturalists to live in harmony with this planet, free from fear of the Bloom, without poisoning their DNA and losing their humanity in the process.

Aurelius smiled like he owned her. "That's it, isn't it? Your holy grail. The Divine Blueprint that your whole religion is built around."

Willow swallowed, ignoring his question. "Does Jianna still have it?"

"I believe so."

She got to her feet, tucking her hands into her sleeves. "What do you want in exchange?"

Aurelius shrugged. "Exactly what I said before. I want peaceful coexistence. You leave to start your own colony, don't worry about how I'm running the rest of the planet. Or if you're feeling really grateful—" He leaned closer. "—you could support me. Stay in the city and expand your Quarter. I won't insist on nanites as long as you can keep your people under control."

Willow clenched her teeth. There it was. The real offer. Not partnership, but vassalage dressed up in prettier language. "So you're offering me the illusion of power as long as I'll be your puppet."

Something flickered in Aurelius' eyes. "You're so like her. If only you knew."

She did know. She'd found a picture of her distant ancestor, Mitra Kunde, in the city's archive. Willow's resemblance to Aurelius' dead lover was uncanny.

No doubt, he was projecting a disgusting mixture of emotions onto her right now. But instead of recoiling, she met his gaze. "If the Divine Blueprint is real, I'll consider your offer."

Aurelius shrugged. "That's better than I hoped for. Have a pleasant day, Willow."

Then he turned and walked toward the garden gate.

Willow remained beside the hibiscus bush until he

disappeared from view. What was that old Earth saying from Mother Basu's journals?

Better to rule Hell? No.

Better to reign in Hell than to serve in Heaven.

If she accepted Aurelius' deal, she wouldn't even be reigning in Hell. She'd be serving in it. Because he was never going to tolerate any form of rebellion from her once he'd enslaved everyone else with his nanites. The moment he was bored with her, he would dispose of her just as he'd done with the Council.

But how was she going to resist him when he had the ability to warp people's will with his technology? He'd transformed her colleagues into hollow puppets with a single breath of air. What hope did she have against a power like that?

None.

She had none.

At the moment, he held all the cards in this game, and they both knew it.

But there was one thing she could do. Not to fight Aurelius, but to fix Mother Basu's biggest mistake.

Willow would be the Guide who recovered the Divine Blueprint.

Chapter Six

THE DARK CORRIDOR stretched ahead of Michel like the throat of some massive beast. Beside him, Lucian's built-in utility light cast a circle stretching only two meters in front of them. Everything beyond that circle was so dark, it might as well have been the void between stars.

He shivered, adjusting his grip on his toolkit.

Holding his breath, listening for something—anything —that suggested they weren't alone. The *Borlaug* felt dead, but it wasn't a peaceful silence. More like a corpse that might still twitch.

That was why they were here, wasn't it? To bring the dead ship back to life. Lucian had already begun the process, connecting life support to one of the quantum foam generators. Then he did something to restart the rotation of the cylinder, restoring faux gravity through centripetal force.

Something clanged up ahead.

Michel gripped Lucian's arm, and they stopped. "What was that?"

Lucian looked down at his hand. Michel flushed, releasing him. "Hull plates settling."

"It seemed kind of loud."

"It is very quiet on the ship at the moment."

That was true.

They began walking again. But he heard something else in the darkness. A faint but steady rhythm. Michel stopped again. "Is someone else here?"

"Mr. Hofstatder."

"I hear footsteps."

"A failing coolant pump that I have not yet had time to repair. You would not be able to hear Mr. Hofstatder from his current location."

Michel didn't care if he sounded scared. "Are you sure?"

"I am certain, Mr. Lombardi. Even if the colonists had left someone on board the ship when they departed, they would no longer be alive after five hundred years."

"Aurelius is still alive."

"Because he is Aurelius. None of the colonists shared his genius."

Lucian had a point. Michel nodded. "Okay."

They rounded the next corner.

A cyborg stood next to the far bulkhead.

Michel dropped his toolkit. It crashed to the deck. Lucian turned to look at him, the light catching him in the eyes. Michel threw up a hand to block the glare. "I thought you said there was no one else here."

"No one you need concern yourself with."

"That's not quite the same thing."

"The cyborgs won't interfere with your duties."

Michel stooped down, picked up his toolkit, and studied the cyborg. It stood perfectly still, staring off into the empty darkness with unblinking eyes. "What's it doing here?"

"Security," Lucian said.

"For an empty corridor?"

Lucian ignored him, striding off. "This way, please."

Michel followed. The cyborg didn't move as he passed. But its eyes tracked him. So it was aware of their presence.

Was there a reason the cyborgs never spoke? Maybe they didn't need to. With nanites, all their communication could happen at the speed of thought. Telepathy, effectively. Why bother with the inefficient process of moving your mouth?

He glanced back to see if the cyborg was following, but it was lost to darkness. What if he hadn't hallucinated those footsteps? They could've been the cyborg's steps.

Michel hurried to catch up with Lucian, trying not to imagine the cyborg's hand reaching out of the dark to grab him. There was no reason for the cyborg to chase after them when Michel was completely dependent on Lucian for everything.

He should have told Jianna about the nanites after dinner. But the words had stuck in his throat, trapped behind the realization of how stupid he'd been to say yes without thinking it through. If they could crack the nanites' programming, find some backdoor to shut them down, maybe he could solve this problem before Jianna ever needed to know what an idiot he'd been.

It was possible Jianna was worried for nothing. He felt fine, and he'd been the first person to get the nanites. Better than fine, actually. The constant access to information and the enhanced cognitive processing meant his brain was working better than ever.

So why wasn't he experiencing the same deterioration that Jianna's father seemed to be?

Maybe the nanites affected different people differently. Maybe some minds were more compatible than others.

Or maybe Soren's symptoms had nothing to do with nanites at all.

Maybe Michel could learn something useful from the android without alerting Aurelius to his curiosity.

"I've been having a couple of headaches lately," he said. "I was wondering if the nanites could be causing them."

"They don't have side effects," Lucian said.

"Maybe they affect some people differently?"

Lucian stopped so abruptly that Michel almost ran into him. He had to backtrack a few steps to put some space between them. Lucian watched him, standing as still as the cyborg. He almost looked dead. Or like an abandoned statue.

Even when humans stood still, they swayed slightly. You could see their chest rise and fall, an eyelid flicker. When Lucian or the cyborgs did it, it was like something essential had been switched off.

"Your nanites appear to be functioning optimally," Lucian said. "The headaches likely have a biological cause. Your cortisol levels are elevated beyond normal parameters."

What? "How do you know that?"

"I ran a diagnostic on your nanites."

"But there's no network up here yet," Michel said.

"I connected to your nanites directly."

Michel froze. "What do you mean?"

"My nanites spoke to yours."

"I didn't give you permission."

"When you agreed to receive them, you knew they could communicate."

"With the quantum computer."

"And with any other device connected to the quantum computer," Lucian added. "As an Engineer, we assumed you would understand their capabilities."

Michel flushed, not wanting to admit he hadn't given it much thought. "What else can you tell by connecting to my nanites?"

"Biometrics," Lucian said. "Heart rate, internal temperature, neurotransmitter levels, brainwave profile, blood pressure, respiratory rate, glucose levels—"

Michel swallowed. "You can't read my mind, can you?"

"I could correlate your biometric responses with your external behavior and make an educated guess."

"So, you're a walking lie detector."

Lucian tilted his head. "There are other reasons your cortisol levels could be elevated."

Michel flushed. Every nervous twitch, every spike in his heart rate, every drop of sweat could betray him. He thought he'd succeeded at hiding his nervousness from Aurelius, but the cyborg had probably seen right through him.

How much longer could he play his anxiety off as hero worship?

Lucian paused at a door and entered a code on the keypad, then stepped inside when it swished open. Michel followed, putting one hand out in front of him to avoid crashing into things he couldn't see.

Was that a second light in the corner?

Yes. But why was it moving closer?

It was coming from Aurelius. Some of his cybernetic components gave off a soft blue light, illuminating his face so it looked like it was floating in the dark, like a cold star suspended in infinite blackness. To Michel's left, Lucian's utility light flashed over multiple consoles, their screens dark. In the center of the room sat another quantum foam generator, identical to the ones they'd installed throughout the city.

This had to be some kind of control center.

The bridge, maybe?

"Mr. Lombardi, we're so glad you could join us." Aurelius gestured to one of the consoles. "We're going to start by restoring power to this section of the ship."

"I'm excited to get started on that."

"Mr. Lombardi was inquiring as to whether his nanites could be causing his headaches," Lucian said.

So much for getting information from the android without Aurelius finding out.

"I know that Councilor Makinde said they'd reviewed the data and found them safe," Michel blurted. "And I know you've had them for a long time, but…I was just surprised that the Council approved them so quickly."

Aurelius pressed his fingertips together. "Do you know what killed Earth?"

What did that have to do with anything? "The chytrid fungus."

Aurelius smiled. "No."

"No?"

"Fear killed Earth," the cyborg began, "in the form of bureaucrats who refused to take bold action because they were afraid of making a mistake. That's why I took it on myself to build the colony ships as soon as I saw the projections. I knew the world's governments would wait until it was too late."

Aurelius jerked his thumb toward his chest. "That's why I'm the one who saved humanity, and they died along with the people they were supposed to serve. If they'd listened to me, you would've been born on Earth instead of DaVinci."

Michel stared at Aurelius, a chill running through him.

The man who'd once seemed like humanity's savior now just sounded like a megalomaniac with a god complex.

How had he not seen it before?

But the cyborg was waiting for some kind of response, so Michel replied: "Yes, sir."

"That subservience is going to hold you back, Mr. Lombardi. To be useful to me, you must believe in your own genius. Not just mine."

Michel cleared his throat. "Got it, sir."

Aurelius tapped the bulkhead beside him. "First order of business. We need to restore power to this section of the ship. The main input should be somewhere around here."

Aurelius counted the panels, starting with the one near the door, and stopped on panel number eight. With a single fluid motion, he wrenched it free—no tools, no strain, just inhuman strength. He set the panel aside, leaning it against the next section of bulkhead, revealing a nest of color-coded conduits and circuit boards beneath.

Leaning forward into the circle of Lucian's utility, which was now trained on the bulkhead's guts, Michel located the main power conduit. "Found it. I just need my screwdriver."

He fumbled with his toolkit.

Aurelius held up his hand, and a mechanical whir sounded. Then a small power screwdriver popped out of his pointer finger. He leaned past Michel and unscrewed the conduit connectors, detaching the line that connected the rest of the room to the main power source. When he finished, the screwdriver retracted with a soft click.

Michel's mouth fell open.

Aurelius grinned. "There's a rotating mechanism inside that swaps out the heads. I've also got a few other tools at my disposal as well."

Multiple snicking and whirring sounds filled the air as

an array of tools emerged. A laser cutter extended from the back of the cyborg's hand. A soldering iron emerged beside it, then a wire stripper popped into view, both on their own mechanical arms. A spudger popped out from his middle finger. Compartments in his forearm slid open, revealing miniature pliers and tweezers.

Michel shook his head. "I've never seen anything like that."

"You could have the same setup if you wanted," Aurelius said, as if he wasn't suggesting Michel amputate his own arm so that he could have a screwdriver for a finger.

The thought made his stomach turn. Perhaps, if he'd lost a limb in an accident. Or due to radiation. But to choose it?

No.

Aurelius retracted the tools, then stepped back and gestured toward the open panel.

Michel hesitated, staring at the exposed conduits.

"You've done this once before," Aurelius said. "You should be able to do it again."

Michel nodded, kneeling on the floor, wiping his palms against his knees. Yeah, he'd done it before, but he'd been assisting, following Aurelius' instructions.

He could do this. He stripped the insulation from the power conduit's main line, then carefully spliced in the connector leads that would feed the bridge systems. Aurelius didn't correct him or offer advice as he worked, just watched with an unsettling intensity. It didn't take him long to finish securing the final connection.

He sat back, looking up at Aurelius.

"What are you waiting for?" the cyborg grinned, spreading his hands wide. "Let there be light."

Michel hit the power button.

A second later, the overhead lights flickered to life. Michel grimaced, squinting against the sudden glare as monitors around the room came alive, each displaying the same logo: Ad Astra.

Although everything was smooth, rounded corners, and minimalist design, it was all about function. This had to be the bridge.

The Ad Astra logo on the first screen dissolved, replaced by what looked like a system diagnostic. Data scrolled by so fast Michel could barely read it: temperature readings, power flow measurements, atmospheric composition. The second screen's logo gave way to a life support report that lingered before being replaced by a series of other reports flashing in quick succession.

On the third screen, the logo faded to reveal a view of the planet below, half bathed in golden sunlight, half shrouded in darkness. DaVinci looked impossibly beautiful from this distance. The lights

Click, whir, slam.

He jumped.

But it was just console panels sliding open in rapid succession. Then the bridge doors whooshed shut.

Michel spun toward Aurelius.

A second later, the doors opened again.

Aurelius winked at him. "Just checking to make sure all the moving parts are still moving."

"You can control the ship through your nanites, too?" Michel asked.

"Of course," Aurelius said. "Although the interface here is much less sophisticated than the one on the Elysia. We'll fix that soon enough."

Michel studied the screen closest to him. It was still cycling through status reports on various systems. "If we turn on this ship's brain, we can talk to it, right?"

"Not worth the energy it would suck up," Aurelius said.

"This ship's brain was a copy of its android's, wasn't it?" Michel asked. "So it was sentient?"

Aurelius turned to look at him. "Is that what they taught you in school?"

Michel nodded.

"Not an exact copy," Aurelius said. "A fractional copy. Just enough to handle the ship's functions and navigation. Lucas had to give orders for anything involving a judgment call. It couldn't do that itself."

"Oh."

"You're disappointed?" Aurelius asked.

Michel shrugged. "I guess I'd been imagining that the ship's AI would have been like a person with the body of a spaceship. Someone the crew could talk to. I was hoping to ask it about the journey from Earth, about the things it had encountered on the way."

"You can always read the sensor logs if you have the patience."

"How can I connect to the ship's systems?" Michel asked. "I'd like to search the Borlaug's archives for its technical manuals."

Aurelius looked over Michel's head for a few moments, then nodded. "I've set up a relay so you can access them through my connection."

"Thank you, Sir."

Aurelius smiled. "Just so you know, when you delete your search history, the system admin can still retrieve it."

Michel froze. Aurelius knew.

He knew that Michel had found one of the probes that had caused the radiation storm. Which meant he knew that Michel had discovered that the storm was really an attack.

Aurelius winked at him and gestured with his head for

Michel to follow him. "Let's get started. Now that we've got power to half of this deck, I want a list of every repair needed to get this baby fully functional."

But Michel couldn't move. "You're not upset?"

Aurelius smiled. "You're one of the smart ones, Mr. Lombardi. You understand that sometimes the price of progress is unpalatable to the masses, but it must be paid."

Aurelius walked across the bridge and knelt beside the open panel on the nearest console, peering inside.

Michel felt sick. How long had Aurelius known? And what was he going to do about it?

And worse, infinitely worse: what would the cyborg do to Jianna if he realized Michel had told her?

Chapter Seven

JIANNA SHIFTED the cooler on her hip as she took the narrow concrete stairs down to the basement. She hadn't been back to the University since she'd graduated, and it almost felt like old times.

Almost.

She reached the bottom and nudged the door with her shoulder. It stuck for a moment before giving way with a reluctant groan. Once through, she made her way along the corridor to the first room on the right and entered without knocking.

The air smelled of chemicals and damp concrete. The lab walls wore a coat of pale blue that had faded to something closer to gray in places, while the floor bore navy blue paint that was scuffed and scratched from years of heavy equipment being dragged across its surface. Behind a machine she couldn't identify—something with tubes and wires that hummed—scorch marks where something had caught fire.

Camilla and a dapper older man in his seventies stood before a table. "Jianna!"

"Hey." She walked over to them.

Camilla gestured to the man. "This is Thorpe, one of my colleagues from before – well, before."

Jianna smiled, setting the cooler down on a nearby table.

She glanced around the room. The metal stools and lab benches were old and battered. A lot of the equipment looked out of date, except for the centrifuge and a couple of computer workstations that seemed shockingly new by contrast.

"It might look ancient," Camilla said, "but the basement is protected by the concrete floor above us, so it had partial protection from the radiation storm."

Thorpe nodded. "We were very fortunate. Most of the older circuitry above blew before the surge could fry everything. We suffered minimal losses."

"That's lucky," Jianna said.

Thorpe turned to Camilla. "Don't forget to wipe the logs when you're done. Can't have my grad students getting in trouble during the next data audit."

Camilla nodded.

Then he was gone.

"Are you sure he won't tell anyone what we're doing?" Jianna asked.

"He didn't want to know."

Jianna raised her brows. "How did you swing that?"

Camilla forced a smile. "He was my advisor. Believed in my work. He was the only one who didn't shun me after I was fired. We still have dinner once a year."

She hadn't been here five minutes, and she'd already started a conversation about Camilla's banishment.

"I'm sorry. I didn't mean to pry."

"Did you get the rat brains from Wallace?"

Jianna patted the cooler. "Did you get the nanites?"

Camilla reached into her lab coat and withdrew two vials of that oily, iridescent, dark gray fluid. The liquid seemed to be churning independent of Camilla's hand motions.

Jianna blew out a breath. They were actually doing this.

"Let's get started," Camilla said. She walked to a cabinet, set the vials in a holder, and pulled out nitrile gloves, handing a pair to Jianna. "We should treat these nanites as BSL-2 minimum until we know more."

Jianna snapped on the gloves, then tied her hair back as Camilla pulled on her lab coat. Then they made their way to the biosafety hood; thankfully, it was one of the newer pieces of equipment down here.

Camilla laid a palm on the side of the hood, and it felt to Jianna like a greeting to an old friend.

"Do you miss being a professor?" she asked.

"I don't miss teaching, but mentoring graduate students, seeing how excited they got when they discovered something new…"

"What about your own research?"

"Giving up research was part of the agreement," Camilla said. "And destroying any record of my work."

Jianna bit her lip, curiosity about Camilla's forbidden research gnawing at her. But asking would only risk trouble for them both. Besides, the clock was ticking. Every minute they spent in this borrowed lab increased the chances of discovery, and they hadn't even started the real work yet.

She switched on the hood's lights, and while they waited the standard fifteen minutes, Jianna gathered supplies: sterile scalpels and other tools, glass slides, coverslips, pipettes, and distilled water.

"How's Soren doing?" Camilla asked.

It was so embarrassing that Michel and his mother had

seen her father losing his mind—once they found a way to bring him back, he was going to be so humiliated. But Jianna was also touched by Camilla's kindness the night before, and her obvious concern now.

"Not good," she admitted. "This morning I found him opening the bedroom drawer, staring into it, then wandering back to the living room, only to return and check a different drawer. He was stuck in the same loop, over and over."

"And you don't think it's a stroke or a symptom of cognitive decline?"

"No." Her tone was sharper than Camilla deserved. "Sorry."

"You don't have to apologize for being worried about your father."

Jianna nodded. "I really appreciated you helping him cook dinner last night."

"Did you manage to get that blood sample?"

Jianna glanced at her.

Camilla shrugged. "Michel told me."

"I tried to convince him, but he got so upset, I wound up letting it go."

"Maybe you won't need to," Camilla said, "depending on what we find out."

"I hope so." But she had a feeling it wouldn't be that simple.

The UV timer chimed. Camilla switched off the lights and turned on the airflow. Then Jianna opened the cooler inside the hood before grabbing the sterile forceps and removing the first container of brain tissue, which had already been sectioned and embedded in soy-based wax. Placing a section of tissue onto the microtome, she sliced several thin cross-sections and transferred each to a slide.

Then she fitted a tip onto the pipette and held it out to Camilla. "Do you want to do the honors?"

Camilla nodded and then removed the vial's lid. Jianna watched in fascination as the odd fluid seemed to swirl around the pipette, even though the other woman held the vial steady. It was as if the nanite solution knew what was happening, and the tiny robots were excited to be sucked up and transferred to the rat's neural tissue.

But they couldn't know, could they?

Camilla drew a precise amount of the metallic liquid into the pipette and released one iridescent gray drop onto an empty slide. While she ejected the pipette's disposal tip into the biohazard disposal, Jianna laid a slide cover over the droplet, flattening it out.

"Let's take a look." Jianna followed Camilla to the microscope station at the next station, where she placed the slide on the stage and positioned it under the objective lens. The autofocus whirred as Jianna turned on the large monitor beside the microscope so they could both see the magnified image.

On screen, the nanites looked like dark grey dots at first, and they were clearly moving of their own accord.

"How are they moving?" Camilla asked.

Jianna zoomed in farther. The nanites were little irregularly-shaped ovals with what seemed to be some kind of biological shell—a protein coat, probably—with cilia all over it.

Camilla gestured to the screen. "They're partly biological. An electronic core wrapped in organic tissue."

"The biological parts could be drawing nutrients from the host."

"And using it to generate electricity for the robotic component." Camilla nodded approvingly. "Elegant."

It was, and so far beyond anything they knew how to

create. That was the android's fault. When Lucas had killed Dr. Basu, Buratti and the other Generation One Councilors had banned all robotics research. An understandable overreaction, but it had been an overreaction. Jianna understood that now.

Because falling behind in any scientific field left them vulnerable to outsiders who hadn't been squeamish in the same way.

To be fair, the Generation One colonists had come so close to extinction that it had probably seemed inconceivable to them that one day, invaders from another colony would visit their world.

A thought occurred to her, one that never would've occurred to her if she hadn't seen for herself that the nanites were hiding inside a protein coat.

"Why isn't the body rejecting them?" she asked. "The immune system should be attacking foreign proteins in the biological shell, but Aurelius' data on the nanites shows no inflammation or antibody production."

"They must be able to camouflage themselves," Camilla said. "Maybe they're using something like RNA capping."

"Maybe," Jianna said. They watched the nanites swim from one side of the slide cover to the other. And then they began to cluster around the edges of the thin glass plate.

A cold chill ran down her back. "Are they trying to escape?"

Camilla glanced at her, eyes wide.

Jianna snatched the slide from the stage and darted back to the biosafety disposal that Camilla had ejected the pipette tip into, tossing the slide in, then her gloves in after it, in case a few of the nanites had managed to make it to her fingers. She stepped on the pedal switch, and the disposal's lid sealed with a hum.

Then the incinerator activated with a rushing sound.

"Do you think that'll destroy them?" she asked.

Camilla shrugged. "It'll destroy their biological parts. We don't know if the robotic components are functional without the protein coat, assuming they didn't melt."

They returned to the UV hood, and Camilla picked up the vial again. "Shall we see what happens when we introduce it to neural tissue?"

Jianna nodded.

This time, Camilla pipetted a drop of nanite solution onto the neural tissue cross-section, hurrying back to the biohazard disposal as Jianna dropped the slide cover on top of the tissue. This time, the nanites didn't spread. They seemed to be absorbed into the slice of neural tissue, leaving only faint trails where they had penetrated.

Jianna shivered and rushed the slide to the microscope, inserting it into the clip and stepping back as autofocus kicked in again.

No telling how long they'd have to study the nanites before they wormed their way out of the neural tissue in search of a live host. And if they got out, the damage to DaVinci could be irreversible.

Camilla joined her at the monitor, and together they watched as a magnified nanite burrowed into the cell body of a neuron and lodged itself against the nucleus. Then a tiny wire, so fine that it looked almost transparent, emerged from the nanite and inserted itself into the neuron's nucleus.

"They're not interfacing with the neuron," Camilla said. "They actually become part of it."

Jianna felt sick to her stomach. "That's going to make it much harder to remove them from living tissue. If these are in my father's brain—"

"We don't know that yet," Camilla said. "And we won't know until we run blood tests."

Jianna nodded, her mouth dry. The thought of finding these things swimming in her father's blood made her want to kill Aurelius.

But what she really needed to do was find a way to kill the nanites without harming the host.

At least they weren't trying to escape the neural tissue they'd bonded with. There was time to experiment without running to the disposal every five minutes.

"What about an EMP?" Jianna asked. "Could we fry the electronic components without hurting the tissues around them?"

"Worth trying," Camilla said.

She disappeared for a few minutes, then returned carrying a small metal box about the size of a lunch container.

"What's that?" Jianna asked.

"A shielded EMP generator." She opened the lid to reveal foam padding inside. "The University uses it to test circuit resilience."

Camilla removed the nanite slide from the microscope clip and placed it inside the box, securing the latches once it was closed. A small screen on the side of the device lit up. Camilla adjusted the field strength settings. Then she glanced at Jianna. "Here goes nothing."

She hit a button on the screen.

A red light illuminated on the top of the box, accompanied by a faint electronic whine. After what felt like an eternity but was probably only three seconds, the red light faded, and the whining stopped.

Then Camilla unlatched the box and removed the slide. After which, she placed it under the objective lens once again.

The magnified nanites on the monitor were still, and the neurons were shriveled and scorched.

"Well, the nanites are dead—" Camilla said.

"—but the neurons are too. The pulse must've caused the nanites to give off an electrical discharge when they died."

"Or they released some compound upon death that was toxic to the tissues," Camilla said.

"What about ultrasound?" Jianna asked.

Camilla nodded. "Let's try."

Over the next several hours, they tried everything they could think of. Various frequencies of ultrasound, from the gentle pulses used for medical imaging to the higher intensities used for tissue ablation. Heat simulation to simulate a high fever. Drugs that targeted various cellular pathways. Chemical disruptors. Magnetic fields.

But everything that killed the nanites killed the host neurons too.

Jianna dropped onto a stool. "There's got to be a way to get the immune system to go after them. I keep coming back to phagocytosis—"

"—but if you can get the neutrophils to enter the neuron, they'll kill it right along with the nanite," Camilla said.

"Can you believe Michel was thinking about letting Aurelius inject him with these?"

Jianna didn't realize how thoughtless it was until after she'd said it, and then she felt awful.

"He didn't." Camilla looked horrified, and it was Jianna's fault.

"Of course not, but we fought about it."

Camilla's shoulders dropped, her breath escaping in a long sigh. "Thank god," she murmured, then met Jianna's eyes. "I knew something was off between you two."

Jianna flushed. "It wasn't just the nanites. I said something I shouldn't have, and he had every right to be angry."

"But you apologized."

"I did, but I know it upset him that I didn't trust Aurelius. And it doesn't matter that I was right about that."

"Was Michel upset because you didn't trust Aurelius, or was he upset that you didn't trust him?"

Jianna opened her mouth, then closed it again. Camilla's question hurt, but it was fair. "I guess I owe him another apology."

Camilla smiled and patted her on the shoulder. "I need caffeine. Let's clean up so we don't get Thorpe's students in trouble, then find a cafe where we can brush up on our immunology. We'll figure out how to get rid of these things."

Jianna forced a smile. "Sounds like a plan."

Together, they started cleaning up. And while she was grateful for Camilla's optimism, dread was settling in her chest like a stone. Aurelius was a genius: the kind of brilliant, reckless mad scientist that Dr. Basu and the other Generation One colonists had accused Samara of being.

But Jianna wasn't a genius like Samara.

What if she and Camilla couldn't figure out a way to destroy the nanites once a person was injected?

What if her father couldn't be saved?

Chapter Eight

THE CYBORG STOOD beneath the dogwood tree like a statue. No doubt Aurelius saw it as one of his achievements, but to Willow it was a walking symbol of nature parasitized by science, perverted by greedy progress, clinging to the remnants of its humanity as the machine slowly consumed it.

Was it here to protect Soren and his daughter? Or to keep them confined in their own home?

Either way, she was sure that Aurelius controlled the monstrosity with the same nanites he'd used to infect the rest of the Council.

But he couldn't pay attention to every single person he'd infected at the same time. So, if he wasn't paying attention to this one right now, it might not know that Aurelius had said he wouldn't infect her.

If it felt threatened by her approach, would it rip off her respirator and release its own nanite swarm? Or was that something only Aurelius could do?

She tightened her jaw, forced herself to walk past it. The cyborg didn't try to stop her from approaching the house. Didn't react at all, in fact. These creatures barely seemed to register the world around them, except when they were engaged in a specific task. Maybe they were inactive except when Aurelius was directly controlling them?

Willow's gaze caught on the cyborg's metal-infused skin, the unnatural seams where flesh met circuitry. A cold dread crawled up her spine as she recognized her possible future standing before her.

Aurelius would eventually lose patience and send his swarm of nanites after her. Once he controlled her body, he could do anything to it.

He'd enjoy torturing her, methodically replacing her flesh with machine. A shiver ran through her as she wondered if she would remain aware during the transformation, or if her consciousness would collapse under the pressure of his invading mind.

By the time she reached the front door, she was having trouble breathing. It took everything she had *not to* look back at the cyborg.

She knocked. And waited almost a full minute before she heard noises inside. She was about to knock again when Soren opened it, staring out at her with glassy, unfocused eyes. He looked even worse than the last time she'd seen him.

He blinked once. Twice. Then he smiled. But it wasn't his smile. It looked like someone was pulling strings on either side of his mouth. Was Aurelius actively controlling him right now? Or had the swarm that infested him begun to interfere with his mental function?

She wasn't sure which would be worse.

"Councilor Evans," he said. "What a pleasant surprise."

She took a step back, adjusted her respirator to make

sure it was sealed, in case he could breathe out nanites like Aurelius had done. "I was hoping to speak with your daughter."

"Come in—"

"Don't come in." Jianna appeared behind her father, looking angry. "What do you want?"

Soren remained in the doorway, that wooden smile still plastered across his face.

Jianna touched her father's arm. "Why don't you go and rest?"

Something flickered behind Soren's vacant eyes, then he turned and walked away without a word.

When he was gone, Jianna turned back to Willow. "You have no business here."

"I'm sorry for your father's… affliction."

"How do I know you don't have the same *affliction?* You could be here to spy on us for Aurelius."

"Why would he need me to spy when he's already persuaded you to welcome his own people into your circle?"

Willow glanced over her shoulder at the cyborg in the yard. It hadn't moved.

"What are you doing here?" Jianna asked.

"We have a common enemy. I've come to propose a deal."

"What kind of deal?"

Willow gestured to the cyborg. "Do you really want to talk out here?"

Jianna glared at her, then opened the door wider and stepped aside. "Come in."

Willow walked past her. As soon as she was inside, Jianna shut the door behind her with more force than necessary, then led her past the living room, where Soren slumped in a chair.

He smiled again when he saw Willow.

"Councilor Evans, what a pleasant surprise."

Willow glanced at Jianna.

Jianna shook her head. No sense in trying, then.

Willow gave a little bow. "It's a pleasure, Councilor Makinde."

For a moment, something flickered behind Soren's eyes, but then it was gone again.

"Councilor Evans." Jianna jerked her head toward the hallway. Willow nodded and followed her down the narrow corridor and into what appeared to be Soren's home office. Bookshelves lined the walls, packed with administrative manuals, policy documents, and journals.

Jianna shut the door behind them and turned to face her, arms crossed. "You have two minutes, then you're leaving."

Willow hadn't expected a warm welcome, but she'd hoped Jianna would be curious enough to hear her out. "I have information that you might be able to use against Aurelius, and I want to trade it for the Divine Blueprint."

"How did you—" Jianna shook her head. "No, Lucas didn't tell you, because you'd never believe anything he said. And Michelangelo wouldn't tell you because… because he wouldn't."

"Aurelius told me," Willow said. "He found the Murderer and is punishing it for its crimes."

Jianna's mouth worked soundlessly, and her hands clenched into fists at her sides. "He has Lucas."

"Yes."

"And Aurelius is punishing him?"

"It certainly looked like that," Willow said. "The android was in pieces."

"But Lucas is still alive?"

"Was it ever?"

Jianna looked even angrier now. "What about the Descendents?"

Willow shrugged. "What about them?"

"Some are missing."

"I don't know anything about that." Willow didn't care, either. Nothing mattered but the Divine Blueprint.

"Aurelius thinks he's already won, but if you're going to have a chance at opposing him, you need what I've got, and the only thing I want from you is the Divine Blueprint."

"It doesn't belong to you. That embryo is the genetic heritage of every person on this planet."

"I agree. It belongs to everyone—everyone who embraces the divine truth. The Divine Blueprint is nothing to you. But it's invaluable to me."

"It has scientific value," Jianna said. "But it is useless to you, because it's not viable."

Of course, she would say that. Jianna was a scientist; she would do anything to undermine the spiritual truths that might curtail her research.

"What do you mean?"

"Samara had modified Phoebe's immune system to coexist with the Bloom. And Atlas had a mutation that gave him the same ability. But the combination of their genes created a fatal flaw that would have killed their child."

The room seemed to narrow and fold in around Willow. "You're lying to test my faith."

"I don't care about your faith. I just care about my father." Jianna threw her hands out wide in exasperation. "If there's any compassion in your heart underneath all that righteousness, tell me whatever you know so I can help him. And everyone else that Aurelius is going to hurt next."

Willow swallowed. Her throat felt raw, like she'd been screaming. "Show it to me."

"What?"

"Show me the Divine Blueprint."

Jianna sighed. "It's just an embryo in a cryob—"

"Show me!"

Jianna looked at her like she was a lunatic. And maybe she was. Maybe her faith had finally driven her over the edge into the kind of obsession that destroyed rather than saved.

She didn't care.

Jianna got up and left the room.

Willow waited in silence, resisting the urge to run after the other woman. What if Jianna had gone to fetch that cyborg to kick Willow out?

She had no hope of fighting the machine. Maybe she should leave before she got evicted.

She stood, uncertain what to do. Stay? Go?

Then she heard footsteps.

It was Jianna. She was still alone. Only now she carried a box.

No. Not a box. THE box.

Willow's vision blurred as images crashed over her— the video of the Murderer bending over the Temptress, cutting into the girl's abdomen, extracting something, and placing it in that exact container. That box had been lost since Mother Basu's time, and it contained the holy relic that every Guide prayed would one day return to their people.

She reached for it, then stopped, her hand trembling, hot tears streaming down her face. Generations of Guides had prayed they would be the one to whom the Divine Blueprint would return, but it had never materialized.

And here it was, right in front of her.

She could be the one to correct Atlas' mistake and bring the Divine Blueprint home to her people.

Willow glanced up at Jianna, who watched her with what looked like a mixture of pity and curiosity.

"May I?"

Jianna hesitated and then placed the box on Willow's upturned palm.

As soon as the cold metal touched her skin, pure, overwhelming awe exploded through her chest. Awe, followed by hope that perhaps her people could have the future Mother Basu had decreed for them. She hadn't truly believed that for a very long time. Playing politics in the Council chambers, maneuvering against Cira's ambitions while her faith corroded under layers of jaded cynicism…

When had she stopped believing in anything beyond survival?

But this box resting on her palm was real.

The Divine Blueprint was real.

She looked up at Jianna. "Thank you."

"I told you, the embryo isn't viable. It's a genetic relic with historical value, but…" She gave Willow a strangely conspiratorial look. "…I was able to extrapolate Atlas' genome with better than eighty-three percent accuracy. We could recreate the Divine Blueprint."

Willow's awe flipped to rage. Even in the presence of the sacred, all the scientist could see was an opportunity to twist nature to her will.

"It won't be the Divine Blueprint, it will be contaminated," Willow explained, as if Jianna were the simplest member of her congregation. "You'll introduce off-target effects."

Jianna's chin lifted proudly. Clinging to her arrogance when she should be humbled by the presence of the Divine

Blueprint. "I'm not talking about gene therapy. I'm talking about synthesizing the sequence from scratch."

Even worse. "A technology that your own people have outlawed."

To Willow's surprise, Jianna let out a long sigh and nodded. "Sometimes our caution exceeds our curiosity."

Pain shot through Willow's hands. She looked down to see that she was clutching the box so tightly her knuckles had gone white. She was going to damage it if she wasn't careful.

She forced her fingers to relax and took a slow breath. "Aurelius has offered to leave my people alone if we start a new settlement on the other side of the continent."

"Why would you believe him?"

"It's not what I believe. Aurelius believes that I'm his ever-so-great bastard granddaughter through Mother Basu's grandmother, Mitra Kunde."

Jianna let out a sharp laugh. "So you're family."

She shuddered to admit it, but… "It's not impossible."

Jianna's expression hardened, and she snatched the box back before Willow could pull it out of reach. Willow felt a fiery pain in her chest at the loss; she couldn't help crying out as if she'd actually been stabbed.

"Where is Aurelius keeping Lucas?" Jianna demanded.

Did she think the Murderer could help her take her father back from the cyborg?

Actually, that might not be a bad plan. And while Jianna distracted Aurelius by trying to free Lucas, Willow would be able to make her next move, unnoticed.

"Someplace I've never seen before." Willow eyed the box. She probably wasn't fast enough to grab it from Jianna's hand, and even if she did, she'd still have to get out of the house and past the cyborg. "Curved walls that bore strange markings—"

"The *Elysia*."

Willow's fingers itched to reach for the box, even knowing the attempt would be futile. "The Mu–the android can't help you, it's in pieces."

Jianna wilted. So, she *had* been hoping to ally with Lucas. "What did Aurelius do to my father?"

"He infected them with a swarm of something called nanites. It was like a sporestorm, only artificial."

"They've integrated with his nervous system," Jianna said, her voice tight with rage.

"Give me the Divine Blueprint," Willow said, gesturing to it, "and I'll tell you everything I know."

"Unless you know where Aurelius' off-switch is or how to deactivate the nanites, you don't know anything I care about."

"Mother Basu passed down many sacred texts, but she also passed down family records. I've read the private journals of Mitra Kunde, who was Aurelius' lover."

Jianna's eyes widened. Good. She was interested.

"Are you telling me your ever-so-great grandmother wrote down all of Aurelius' weaknesses?" Jianna asked.

"She said that Aurelius stole her research because she'd discovered something she wouldn't share with him. She was afraid he would use it despite the dangers and destroy his mind."

Jianna leaned closer. "Are you serious?"

"Aurelius took all of Mitra's files after he had her committed to a psychiatric ward for the rest of her life. Mitra said she hid her discovery from him, but there might be clues in her research notes—"

"—which could be in the Elysia's archives." Jianna started pacing, seeming to have forgotten that the box in her hand contained the Divine Blueprint. "She didn't happen to say what this secret was, did she?"

"The research he stole from her was the basis for his immortality research."

"So it could give us a clue to his biological weaknesses."

"You're a geneticist like Mitra was, but your knowledge is more advanced. If the secret is there, you should be able to find it."

Jianna chewed on her bottom lip. "She could've hidden it in code. Or maybe she hid it in plain sight. Pieces scattered through other notes. You're sure Aurelius never figured it out?"

Willow shrugged. "Mitra said it would ruin his mind."

"So he could've already used it," Jianna said.

Willow surprised herself by laughing at Jianna's joke.

"Please," Willow said. "Give me the Divine Blueprint. You said yourself that you've already gained all the useful information to be had from it."

Jianna glanced down at the box. "But it's my ancestor."

"If the embryo is nonviable," Willow said, "then what are you losing?"

"I might be able to fix it—"

And then what? Become its mother and watch it grow up, doomed to suffer the same sickness that plagues you?" The next push might be too far, but Willow sensed vulnerability in Jianna. "Assuming that it survives at all."

Jianna was quiet for a long moment, studying the box. "You're probably going to put this thing on a pedestal and worship it, aren't you?"

It was insulting how she assumed that Willow and her people were superstitious savages just because they believed in something that couldn't be proven in a lab.

"I would die before I let anything happen to it. There's no safer place on this planet for it than my custody."

Jianna held out the box. "I want visiting rights."

Willow looked at her warily. "What does that mean?"

"If I come to your Sanctum, you'll give me access to it."

She couldn't resist putting the question in words meant to offend Jianna's scientific sensibilities. "You'd come to commune with your ancestor?"

But instead of bristling, Jianna nodded. "It's a part of my family's history."

Willow almost laughed. Even the scientist couldn't deny the pull of the Divine when it reached out to her. Faith found a way, even with hearts that thought themselves immune to its touch.

"Agreed," Willow said. "And if you find that you can't stand living under that tyrant any longer, the Naturalists welcome all who come with an open heart."

Jianna rolled her eyes. "I'll join your cult when pigs fly."

Willow smiled, feeling lighter than she had in months. "Since you actually have the ability to give them wings, I'll take that as a maybe."

There was a loud crash from another room.

Jianna plunked the box into Willow's outstretched hand, then yanked the door open and ran out.

Willow looked down at the box in her hands, the Divine Blueprint finally where it belonged. And if this miracle was real, anything was possible.

She was going to fix Atlas' mistake. She was going to fix Mother Basu's mistakes, too.

Willow was going to fix everything.

Chapter Nine

MICHEL'S HAND cramped around the micro-welder as he contorted his body beneath the console to reach the maze of fiber-optic cables and power conduits housed in the cramped compartment. He set the tool on the floor and shook out his fingers, trying to restore some flexibility.

Six hours. He'd been working for six straight hours on the Borlaug, and at the very least, he needed food and water.

They'd triple-checked almost every system on the bridge. Environmental controls, navigation, communications, and the backup life support systems. His back hurt from crawling under consoles, and his knees were bruised from kneeling on metal grating.

He grabbed the welder and wriggled out, glancing over at Aurelius, who stood in front of the bridge's main display and stared down at DaVinci below. He had that distant expression on his face, the one he got when accessing the quantum computer on the Elysia.

Did Aurelius ever get tired? Sleepy? Hungry? Maybe he was running off some kind of internal power source, like Lucas had. Because Aurelius seemed as energetic now as he had been when they first arrived.

Michel's head pounded. He tried to focus on the next task, but all he could see was Aurelius standing at the display, hands clasped behind his back, blue light crawling over the lines of his face.

Aurelius had winked at him like it was a joke. *When you delete your search history, the system admin can still retrieve it.*

He knew. He'd known the whole time.

Not just that, Michel had figured out the truth about the "storm." That Aurelius had caused it.

People had died, and many more had lost their homes. All so Aurelius could be guaranteed a hero's welcome when he offered them salvation.

The memory of that wink burned behind Michel's eyes.

He wanted to throw up.

But even seeing Aurelius' callousness, a part of Michel wanted to make excuses for his former idol.

Aurelius had lost his entire colony. Lost physical parts of himself. Suffered a terrible journey to get here.

If Michel had gone through the same ordeal, he might be willing to sacrifice people he'd never met to make sure that he and his own people survived.

He didn't think so. But his mother often said you couldn't know what you'd do in a given situation until you were in it.

At first, Michel was just relieved that Aurelius hadn't thrown him out an airlock to keep him quiet. But he'd realized it wasn't because Aurelius trusted him; the new Chancellor was confident there was nothing Michel could do to hurt him.

"Almost finished?" Aurelius asked. "I want to get started on Level 1."

This was his chance. "I need another fifteen minutes to get everything hooked back up."

"Meet me down there." Aurelius flicked his finger toward Michel, and a new file appeared in Michel's peripheral vision. He opened it up. It was a map of the *Borlaug*, with a path marked from the bridge to the pusher room at the bottom of the ship.

"Be there in a few minutes," Michel said.

"Don't dawdle, Mr. Lombardi." Aurelius exited the bridge.

Michel glanced at the console Aurelius had been looking at. He didn't want to attempt talking to the ship's AI through his implant, not while Aurelius might be monitoring his activity. But maybe he could interact with it manually through the control console?

He examined the console display but had no idea where to start. He pressed something, and the reports scrolling on the monitor blinked out, replaced with some sort of encrypted code that he didn't recognize and couldn't read. Michel swore under his breath.

"Can I assist you?" a familiar voice asked.

Michel whirled around, his pulse quickening, but no one was there. "Lucas?"

"I am a fractional intelligence that was cloned from Captain Lucas Mercer, optimized for controlling the *Borlaug's*systems. Who are you?"

"Michelangelo Lombardi."

"You're not a member of the crew."

"I'm from the planet you're orbiting. DaVinci. My—" Michel hesitated. Not ancestors, exactly. "—predecessors were crew members more than five hundred years ago."

"That statement does not align with my records."

"You've been powered down for centuries."

"I see. Can I assist you?"

Michel hesitated. He hadn't said anything incriminating yet, but if Aurelius was monitoring this conversation now, he undoubtedly had the ability to retrieve it later. But this was also his chance to find Glint. Jianna had been sure the missing Descendants would be with Lucas. And if the ship was connected to the android, it might be able to tell Michel how to find Lucas.

It didn't matter if Aurelius found out.

He needed to make sure Glint was safe.

"Can you tell me where Lucas is right now?"

"He is on the *Elysia*," the voice said.

An excited thrill ran through him. He'd thought it would be much harder than this. "You're sure?"

"Yes. The *Elysia* is also in orbit around DaVinci, approximately—"

"Can you talk to him?"

If Michel could communicate with Lucas through the Borlaug's AI, maybe he could find out what had happened to the missing Descendants and possibly warn Lucas about whatever Aurelius was planning.

Once he found out.

"Lucas Mercer's ability to send and receive messages seems to have been shut off."

Michel's hope deflated. "Can you tell what he's doing? Where exactly is he?"

"I am not able to access the systems of the *Elysia* without the direct authorization of Aurelius Hofstadter. Would you like me to request authorization?"

"No, don't bother him." What else could Michel do? "Can you tell if Lucas is okay?"

"Do you have reason to believe that he is not?"

"I'm worried that Aurelius might hurt him."

"Aurelius Hofstadter is our creator. Why would he hurt Lucas?"

Michel didn't know how to answer that. "Do you have the ability to pilot a shuttle to the *Elysia*?"

"No, but if you'd like to download the pilot training program—"

"Yes, please!" It hadn't even occurred to Michel that he could learn to fly a shuttle, but maybe he could borrow one without Aurelius noticing. Except that even if he succeeded, Aurelius was probably plugged into the *Elysia's* systems just like he'd plugged into the *Borlaug's*; he'd know if a door opened or a light came on that he hadn't activated himself. Then there were all those cyborgs standing around in random places.

Michel would never manage to sneak into the cyborg's ship.

He pulled out his comm unit anyway. "Can you put the files on this?"

"I am thinking," the ship said.

Seconds dragged. Then the comm screen flickered, and a download icon appeared, the progress bar inching forward. Michel started to sweat as he watched it. Aurelius could return at any moment.

If he realized that Michel was searching for Lucas, he still might throw him out of an airlock.

"Mr. Lombardi, are you coming?" Aurelius' voice boomed through the speakers.

Michel jolted. "Sorry. Almost done!"

A moment later, the download finished. Michel exhaled. "Can you delete the record of our conversation?"

"I can. Although Aurelius Hofstadter has established administrator access and would be able to find the deleted log if he looks."

Michel's throat tightened. "Then I'd better not give him a reason to look." He grabbed his tools and comm.

"Please go back to whatever you were doing and pretend this conversation never happened."

He switched off his comm completely and tucked it away. He didn't know if Aurelius could access it despite the password protocols.

Then he followed the coordinates on Aurelius' map, hurrying toward Level 1, which was more than a dozen decks down, at the "bottom" of the colony ship if the bridge was the "top." He made his way to the nearest lift, then remembered that they'd only restored power to this deck. Michel had no idea where the power for the lift system came from.

So, he located the stairwell and started down.

He had twelve floors to get his cortisol under control. If Lucian could tell he was agitated, no doubt Aurelius could too.

It didn't take long to arrive.

The doors opened, and he stepped out into an enormous space. Steel racks nearly three meters tall circled the chamber's perimeter, fitted to the curve of the ship's hull. They'd once housed the nuclear pulse propulsion units: cylinders the size of cars containing radioactive material and hydrogen gas that had been used to power the ship's journey from Earth.

The cylinders had been released one at a time, then detonated behind the ship, where the massive pusher plate caught the brunt of the blast and the expanding superheated hydrogen gas created by the directed nuclear explosion, forcing the ship forward.

The *Borlaug* had leapfrogged across forty-two light-years of space, one small atom bomb at a time.

Terrifying, but incredibly clever.

Most of the racks were empty, but as Michel's flashlight beam flashed over more than a dozen of the propulsion units still chambered, ready to be shunted into space. The Generation One crew had just left them there.

Michel swallowed hard. He hadn't brought a Geiger counter in his toolkit. If even one of those containers had leaked, he wouldn't feel the radiation until it was already too late. He swallowed hard but kept walking. Surely Aurelius wouldn't have brought him down here if it were dangerous, especially after what had happened to him on his own planet. He would be hyperaware of radiation exposure risk.

The circle of racks reminded Michel of a schematic he'd once seen for a primitive revolver; they would've fed the propulsion units into launch sockets in the floor. Below those sockets, heavy hydraulic arms and magnetic clamps formed the ship's firing mechanism: an enormous loader designed to eject each nuclear unit out through a ventral channel, one at a time, while the ship's AI detonated the unit once it was behind the pusher plate.

The thought of what would happen if the timing was off made him shudder.

Michel craned his neck. The far end of the chamber disappeared into darkness, but he could just make out the shock absorbers that connected the pusher plate assembly to the rest of the ship, massive hydraulic pistons meant to cushion each explosion's kick.

Only something was wrong. The racks had been rewired. The loading arms no longer aligned with the ventral channel that would have ejected the pulse units away from the ship. They'd been rotated, their trajectories aimed outward.

What was the point of—

Oh, no. Anything but that.

He couldn't move.

He couldn't breathe.

It was too horrific to contemplate.

And Aurelius was going to force him to help.

Michel was standing in the magazine of a colossal machine gun.

The racks would rotate, load, and fire—

And there wasn't anything to fire them at except DaVinci.

Just one of those nuclear propulsion units dropping from orbit and detonating above Vitruvian City would annihilate most everything. And the radiation would finish off the Descendants. But Aurelius had already taken over the city. Why would he want to bomb it?

"Mr. Lombardi!"

Michel whirled around to see Aurelius standing on the other side of the room with Lucian. There was no way they could've missed his entrance, which meant they'd been waiting in silence, watching to see his reaction. Right down to monitoring his cortisol levels, which were probably through the roof.

"So glad you could join us," Aurelius said, waving him over. Then he flicked his fingers in Michel's direction, and a second later, new data pinged Michel's implant. He opened the file, and a transparent schematic of the room overlaid itself across his vision.

It confirmed what he'd hoped it would refute.

He forced his voice to stay even. "Are we giving the Borlaug weapons?"

"We're building an orbital defense system," Aurelius said.

Michel stared at him. "Defense against what?"

"We won't know until they get here, will we?" Aurelius approached Michel, grinning maniacally. "You're lucky I'm the one who found your planet first. It's possible that some of the other colonies might have survived, and they might not be as friendly as I am."

Michel just gaped at him.

"Don't worry," Aurelius added. "As long as I'm here, you're safe."

Michel tried to smile, but his face wouldn't cooperate. Safe.

He'd never felt less safe.

Chapter Ten

JIANNA SAT at the lab bench, staring at the vial of nanites Aurelius had given her to study. She'd told him she'd changed her mind, that she wanted to understand how his DNA-modifying technology worked. She wasn't sure that he'd believed her lie. Sometimes it seemed as though when Aurelius looked at her, he could read her mind. Or at least was trying to.

Regardless, he had agreed. She had at least four hours before Lucian would fly the shuttle over from the *Borlaug* to take Jianna back down to the planet.

Would it be long enough for what she needed to do?

She glanced at the cyborg standing near the door—the woman who'd been stationed beneath the dogwood tree. But even though it was motionless, Jianna knew it wasn't bored or zoned out. Because when she tried to leave the lab, the cyborg would insist on accompanying her. Even to the restroom. Aurelius had given it specific instructions on where Jianna was allowed to go: the restroom, the cloning lab, and the corridors that connected both to this lab and the docking bay.

The rest of the ship was off-limits.

She fingered the vial, studying the oily liquid. When Michel had returned from his shift yesterday, he'd reported that the Borlaug's AI told him Lucas was aboard this ship. And if she could find Lucas, she'd probably find the missing Descendants, too. Michel had shared his map of the *Borlaug* so that she could find her way around.

Thank Phoebe they were sister ships with identical designs.

All she had to do was find a way to escape her guard.

Jianna set the vial down in a holder, then reached into her bag, pulling out the fruit salad she'd made just for this purpose: melon, apple, grapes, lanternfruit, and fireberries, all dressed in a sweet-tart citrusy sauce that made her mouth water.

Turning her back to the cyborg, she picked up her spoon, scooped up a grape, and pretended to take a bite. "Mmmm, so good."

Jianna reached for her tablet, then paused and turned to the cyborg.

Who was watching. Hungrily. Just like the one who'd watched Soren dip his cake into soup earlier this week.

"How rude of me." Jianna picked up the container and held it out to the cyborg. "Would you like some fruit?"

The cyborg stared at the container. A flicker in her eyes. Did she look sad?

"Try a piece," Jianna said. "It's delicious."

The cyborg's gaze fixed on the colorful fruit pieces. Her lips parted, but she still didn't move.

"This is so much better than that paste you've been eating," Jianna said.

The cyborg's eyes widened. Real emotion flickered across her features—want, fear, confusion.

"I won't tell, if that's what you're worried about."

The cyborg hesitated, then joined her at the bench. Jianna stabbed a piece of melon and held out the spoon. But the cyborg simply opened her mouth, like a toddler waiting to be fed.

Jianna slipped the spoon between the cyborg's lips and pulled it out again.

The cyborg's eyes widened.

Her jaw was still. Then she swallowed. And started choking, coughing. Her whole body convulsed.

Jianna jumped to her feet. "I'm so sorry. You've probably never eaten anything but paste." She patted the cyborg's back, but her palm hit solid metal plating.

She bolted to the sink, grabbed a beaker, and filled it with sterile water.

Then she took it back to the cyborg. "Here, drink this."

The cyborg gulped the water, her coughing subsiding. When she looked up at Jianna again, fear had replaced her earlier wonder.

"I'm so sorry. I should've mentioned, you need to chew it first before you swallow." She mimed the chewing motion with exaggerated jaw movements. "See? Like this. Then swallow."

She picked up the container and spoon. "Do you want to try again?"

The cyborg hesitated, then reached for both, her fingers closing around the spoon handle like she was gripping a tool rather than an eating utensil. She held the container close to her chest, tilting it at an odd angle that made the fruit slide to one side. She maneuvered a fireberry into the bowl of the spoon with some effort, put it in her mouth, and began chewing in an exaggerated way that mimicked Jianna's demonstration.

"That's right," Jianna smiled. "Chew it until it's just

like that horrible paste you're used to eating, and then swallow."

The cyborg did as instructed, her expression distant as if she was processing new sensory information. Then she swallowed and shoveled a chunk of apple into her mouth, chewing with her mouth open. Fruit juice dribbled down her chin. She made a loud "MMMM" noise, clearly copying the same sound Jianna had made earlier.

Jianna smiled. "Good, right?"

The cyborg nodded.

"You can have all of it. Just slow down a little so you don't choke again."

The cyborg swallowed, shoveling in more fruit. More MMMMs. More chewing. Jianna turned back to her tablet and tried not to feel guilty.

Because she'd given the cyborg something wondrous— flavor and textures she'd never before experienced—and all of it was a lie. Jianna had drugged the fruit. She told herself it was the only way, that she needed the time it would buy.

Watching the cyborg eat, hearing those small, contented sounds, made her stomach twist. She'd convinced the cyborg to trust her, then immediately betrayed that trust.

But how else was she going to search for Lucas and the Descendants he'd taken?

It was better than killing the cyborg.

She sat hunched over her tablet, staring at the screen, but not reading anything. Not wanting to turn around until—

She heard a heavy clanking thud and a metallic clatter.

Jianna stiffened, then glanced behind her to see the cyborg on her hands and knees. She'd dropped the container, spilling the last little bit of fruit salad across the floor. The cyborg looked up at Jianna in confusion, then fell forward, face down.

Jianna waited a few moments, then got up and checked the cyborg's pulse. At first, she found nothing.

A cold chill ran down her spine. Had she–

No. There.

A faint pulse. The cyborg was still alive. She was just out cold. The sedative wouldn't last more than an hour or two, and Lucian or Aurelius could come back any time, so she needed to move fast.

Jianna picked up the container and the spoon and hid them in a cabinet, then picked up the cyborg's arm and dragged her around the side of the workbench so that she wouldn't be visible from the door.

She crossed back to where she'd left her bag, unzipped it, and pulled out the radiation detector Michel had given her. It was the narrow cuff-style detector, which she strapped around her forearm, tightening it until it lay flush. She had no way of knowing where Aurelius might be keeping Lucas or if the Descendants were with him. But if Lucian had been telling the truth about radiation leakage in some areas of the ship, she didn't want any surprises.

She patted her pocket to make sure her flashlight was still there. Then she grabbed her comm from the workbench and swiped open Michel's map, heading for the door.

She paused long enough to make sure the cyborg couldn't be seen from the hallway, then slipped out.

She had no idea where to start, so she began with the first corridor on her left. Halfway down, the detector still showed no increase in radiation. She reached a stairwell and used the manual release on the door to let herself in.

She'd have to do that with every door, otherwise it would trigger the entry log.

She headed down to the next level.

It was dark. But she didn't want to risk Aurelius noticing unusual power usage that might give away what she'd done.

So she turned on her flashlight and stepped through the doorway into a corridor, then consulted Michel's map again. This was the cryopod level, where the original crew had slept for the entire trip to their planet.

The cryopods would be a convenient way for Aurelius to hold prisoners—he could keep them frozen for as long as he could maintain power to the pods. But it would be easy to find them; all she had to do was look for pods with active displays.

She entered the closest room, shining her flashlight over the complex. Rows upon rows of metal capsules lined the walls, almost like coffins. Each one, designed to hold a human being in suspended animation for centuries.

Most of the pods were now open, their lids yawning like mouths in the darkness. It had been so long since they had contained and preserved life. Now, they resembled discarded cocoons.

It would've been convenient if she'd found the Descendants here, in the obvious place. Which was why it made sense that Aurelius would stash them somewhere else.

She made her way back to the stairwell and continued down.

The next level didn't have power either. Jianna stepped into the corridor, then stopped as a wave of heat and rot hit her full in the face. She yanked her shirt up and over her nose, but the stench crawled through the fabric anyway.

She consulted the map. She was on the cryovault level.

She made her way along the corridor, stepping past twisted metal shelving that had been hauled out of the rooms and discarded.

She checked her radiation monitor.

It showed normal levels of background radiation. Nothing dangerous.

Hopefully, it was working.

She entered a room at the far end, shining her flashlight over the area. More busted shelving. The air was wet and heavy, clinging to her skin. It smelled of spoiled meat and ammonia. Her eyes watered.

She swept her flashlight over rows of shattered cryotanks and open containment lockers. Fluid had leaked across the floor in viscous streams that had since dried and hardened. The polymer insulation on the walls had bubbled and peeled, leaving streaks where condensation dripped down.

Broken vials and cracked canisters lay everywhere. Their labels had curled away from the metal, revealing only smeared codes and the pale residue of what they'd once held.

She stepped in something sticky. Now her boots made a slurping sound as she walked. So much for sneaking around.

She headed back to the stairwell, closing the door behind her. She took a few breaths before proceeding because her stomach was threatening to turn itself inside out.

But she couldn't waste time.

Next level.

The power here still sputtered along, enough for every third or fourth ceiling panel to glow, bathing the corridor in a pale, intermittent light. It wasn't much, but at least she could preserve her flashlight battery.

This deck housed the animal cryopods. The layout reminded her of an old barn: corridors lined with metal doors, most standing half open. The pods inside were shaped for their intended recipient: sheep, goat, cow, horse, dog, cat, chicken.

All the compartments were now empty. The air smelled faintly of disinfectant, decay, and the sour tang of coolant.

She checked the radiation detector strapped to her arm. Still at safe levels.

No sign of any prisoners. She didn't encounter any of Aurelius' cyborgs, either.

Jianna was starting to get nervous. She still had at least nine more levels and no idea how long the cyborg would remain sedated. Camilla had helped her calculate dosage based on the assumption that her guard would be approximately 50% biological, but who knew how much of the cyborg was still human… or whether her artificial parts contained anything that could detoxify drugs administered to the human part.

Back to the stairwell.

The next level also had no light. The hallway opened into a maze of storage bays, their metal doors shut. Jianna picked a direction, hoping that the corridors would connect at some point.

This was where the colonists had stored supplies that could be packaged in smaller containers. Ration packs for the first year. Hygiene items. Shelf-stable food. Clothing. Tools. The doors were locked, and there were no biometric locks or keypads, so she had no idea how to open them. Maybe the ship's AI had to do that.

Why?

To ensure that no one took supplies that weren't being rationed by the colony leader, she guessed.

Crazy to think that people would steal from each other when they depended on each other to survive. But then she thought of the resentful crowd clustered around her wagon when she'd been distributing water after Aurelius had taken down their grid.

Not so crazy after all.

She continued down the corridor, hoping to find rooms that had been left open, but all were firmly shut.

Maybe Michel could find a way to open them.

She was about to turn around when she heard it.

A scuff. Soft. Behind her.

She froze, switching the flashlight off.

Silence.

Nothing but the distant hum of life support and her own breathing.

Had her cyborg guard regained consciousness and tracked her here?

Or had she unknowingly set off some alarm, bringing Lucian or perhaps Aurelius himself?

If someone was there, they weren't making a sound.

She took a step forward. Then another. But she didn't hear anything else. She turned her flashlight back on, studying the hallway behind her.

Paranoia. Had to be. Her mind was playing tricks. She forced herself to turn around and walk back to the stairwell. There was no point in searching more here until she had a way to open the storage bays.

She checked her radiation detector one more time. Still nothing.

Jianna marked this spot on the map and returned to the stairwell. Then she made her way down one more level. This was where the big farm equipment had been kept, but it was just a big empty space with stencils on the walls and tie-down anchors welded to the metal floor, spaced for big equipment like tractors, backhoes, and bulldozers.

She checked the time on her comm. She had been gone for just over an hour. The cyborg would be waking up soon. And if she wasn't back when Lucian returned...

Just one more.

Jianna ran down the stairs.

This next floor was where things like the flatpack prefab buildings and other construction supplies had been kept. Now it was just another empty space swallowing the beam from the flashlight, with more tie-down anchors and fitted depressions in the floor.

Her comm buzzed in her hand. Out of time.

She hurried back up the stairwell in the dark, taking the stairs two at a time. It took everything in her not to burst out of the door into the hallway. But if anyone was watching, it would look suspicious.

So she forced herself to crack the door open and peer out. A cyborg was walking away from her, in the opposite direction from the lab she'd abandoned. She closed the door, counting the seconds. Ten, eleven, twelve ...

Then pushed it open again.

The cyborg was gone.

She slipped into the hallway, walking toward the lab at a normal pace. If she ran into Aurelius or Lucian, she couldn't look guilty of anything. Just a scientist taking a break from her work, maybe stretching her legs while she mulled over her next experimental protocol.

She doubted they would buy it. Not without the cyborg by her side. But she could try.

She turned the corner.

She was almost home free. Then she spotted another

cyborg walking toward her down the corridor, but it was a man, not her guard hunting her down.

Keep walking, Jianna. One foot in front of the other.

It didn't even seem to notice her as it passed. Just kept moving with that same blank expression they all wore, staring straight ahead like she didn't exist.

She blew out a breath and ran the last few feet to the lab, yanked the door open, and entered.

There was no sign of the cyborg.

She ran around the side of the workbench.

The female cyborg was pushing herself up to hands and knees, her back to Jianna.

Jianna crouched beside the woman, laying a hand on her shoulder. "How are you doing?"

The cyborg twisted around, looking confused.

"You choked on the fruit salad again and passed out. I was just about to go find Lucian."

The cyborg opened her mouth, then closed it again. Placed out a hand and tried to stand, but she couldn't seem to get her balance. Jianna grabbed her arm, helped her up, then walked her over to one of the lab stools. "You scared me half to death. You need to rest."

The cyborg slumped on the stool, her head lolling slightly.

Jianna fetched her another glass of water. "Here."

But the cyborg just stared into space blearily.

Jianna kept a hand on her shoulder so she wouldn't fall. She hadn't really thought this part through.

The door opened.

Jianna looked up. Swallowed. Aurelius.

He stopped, looking at the cyborg. "What happened?"

Jianna shook her head. "One minute she was standing by the door, the next, she just fell over."

Aurelius flicked his fingers.

A second later, the cyborg stood and staggered out of the room, jerking like a puppet on strings. "I've sent her in for maintenance."

Maintenance.

She hoped that didn't involve a drug test. Or being taken apart and put back together again?

He walked over, spreading his hands wide. "What do you think of the nanites?"

She'd barely had time for her search. No time at all to read any of the specs he'd set aside for her. "I was hoping you'd show me how to program them. I'd like to do a simple edit. I brought tissue samples from someone with major off-target effects."

He didn't need to know these were her own cultured cells. She didn't want him to be able to use the data against her.

If he thought anything was amiss, he didn't show it. Beaming, he gestured for her to join him at the nearest workbench.

"I'd be delighted to assist." He pointed at a gene sequencer and molecular assembler. Both immediately hummed to life. "Once you have your own nanites, you'll be able to operate any machine with a simple thought. Imagine how fast you'll be able to work."

Jianna forced herself to smile back, but the thought made her skin crawl.

She'd rather die than become more like Aurelius.

Chapter Eleven

WILLOW WAS PROBABLY the first Naturalist to breach the doors of Camilla Lombardi's clinic in one of the more prosperous sections of DaVinci. There was a time when she would've seen this place as enemy territory.

Camilla's staff would probably agree the feeling was mutual, thanks to the angry demonstrations Cira and Theo loved to organize, no matter how many times Willow pointed out that they weren't accomplishing anything but alienating people who might otherwise be won over.

Cira was all vinegar, no honey.

Willow grabbed the brass handle of the glass door and pulled it open, stepping through. Inside, the air was cool and faintly perfumed, a filtered blend of lavender and something synthetic. The lighting was soft, almost golden, like a perpetual sunrise. The polished stone floors were veined with gold in places, surrounded by creamy walls whose corners were softened by ferns in brushed metal planters. The waiting area was dotted with padded chairs upholstered in leather cultured from the hide of that hideous eel-like monster that lived in Lake Buratti. They looked incredibly comfortable, inviting you to relax while your future child was edited to suit your whims behind closed doors.

Don't think about the fact that you're here to bypass nature's better judgment with technology that should not have been allowed to exist.

But if the same technology could bring the Divine Blueprint back, perhaps Willow was in some sense redeeming it.

She ignored the voice in her head that suggested the existence of this technology had been *part* of the Divine Plan, to ensure that it could be brought back.

When she approached the gently curved reception desk, the man behind the counter looked up from his tablet and stiffened, his face paling. Then he reached beneath the counter. Probably pressing a security button or something.

She cursed Theo and Cira. But if her reputation as someone who preferred negotiation to violence wasn't enough to outweigh Cira's antics, Willow would have to be persuasive.

"I'm here to see Dr. Lombardi." She tried to look as non-threatening as possible.

The receptionist didn't bother to pretend he was checking Camilla's calendar. "Dr. Lombardi is booked for the remainder of the afternoon, but if you'd like to make an appointment, Guide Evans—"

"Tell her I'm here. She'll see me."

A heavy tread sounded behind her. Willow's spine stiffened, but she forced herself to turn. A security guard whose determined stride suggested she'd removed plenty of troublemakers before and wasn't afraid to add another to her collection. "I'm sorry, Guide Evans, you'll have to leave."

"I'm not here to cause trouble. Dr. Lombardi will want to speak with me."

The guard crossed her arms, muscles bunching beneath the fabric of her uniform. "Dr. Lombardi is with a patient—"

"She can wait in exam room three."

Willow spun around. There was Camilla, somehow looking well-dressed in scrubs and a lab coat, standing in the hallway that led to the exam rooms.

"Tha—" Willow began, but Camilla disappeared through the nearest door before she could finish her expression of gratitude.

The guard exchanged a resentful look with the receptionist, then turned and walked down the hallway without saying anything. Willow followed. Halfway down the hall, the guard stopped so abruptly that Willow almost ran into her as she yanked a door open and waited for Willow to enter. After Willow stepped inside, the guard shut the door behind her.

The exam room was small. Educational posters covered the walls, explaining the genetic traits that could be modified in unborn children. One listed mandatory corrections for birth defects: cleft palate, cystic fibrosis, sickle cell anemia, cerebral palsy, spina bifida, defective heart valves, OCD, metabolic syndrome, and schizophrenia. Another explained the optional traits that could be adjusted: left-handedness, color blindness, eye color, hair color, skin color, height, Down syndrome, and dwarfism. A third warned that some alterations were illegal: intelligence enhancement, personality manipulation, elimination of functional neurodivergence, and tailoring for athletic ability.

Willow stared at the poster.

OCD was a defect to be corrected?

How dare anyone suggest that?

Who decided which divergences were functional and which were not?

She thought of young Anna, who'd worked so hard to transform the OCD that had made her younger years hellish into an asset through meditation and spiritual discipline. Now she was one of their foremost spiritual scholars, famous for being able to teach the unruliest mind how to master itself.

All because her parents had chosen to love all of her.

But the Vitruvians would have deleted that *undesirable trait*. They would've deprived Anna of the opportunity to make the mind nature had gifted her even more beautiful.

Monsters.

But not as monstrous as Aurelius. At least the Vitruvians had some limits.

Aurelius had none.

There was an empty chair in the room next to the exam table. She took a seat, cradling her bag in her lap.

Inside was the cryobox.

She didn't want to believe that Jianna was right and the embryo was defective. No, that's not what she'd said. Willow frowned, searching for the word.

Nonviable.

Whatever that meant.

Willow placed her hand over the box as though in prayer. She was so close to fulfilling Mother Basu's dream.

But if what Jianna had said was true, the Divine Blueprint might have been contaminated by Samara Makinde's hubris, just like Samara contaminated almost everyone on the planet.

Please, please, please let the Divine Blueprint remain pure.

The door opened, and Camilla entered, shutting it behind her.

Willow straightened, regretting that she had sat because now Camilla stood above her.

"How can I help you, Councilor Evans? I assume you're here in your official capacity, since you're not holding a protest sign and threatening my patients."

It had probably been too much to hope that Camilla would reserve judgment until she'd heard Willow's request.

"That's fair," Willow admitted. "Although protests are more my sister's style."

Camilla leaned back against the counter, folding her arms over her chest. "Yes, you prefer to express your political views by squashing legitimate scientific research and having people investigated."

"That's fair too, so why don't we get down to business? I need your help."

"Why would I help you, when your mother ruined my career?"

Willow hesitated. She'd rehearsed this moment a dozen times on her way here, but now that she was standing face to face with Camilla, the words stuck in her throat.

"It wasn't hard to figure out, you know. The Council still has your papers and lab notebooks in the vault, thanks to Soren's argument that there might be some other value there that shouldn't be lost."

Camilla shrugged. "My trial was over twenty-some years ago."

"Every mother thinks her child is perfect," Willow said. "But yours actually is. Not just in appearance. I checked his work records. Michelangelo has never called in sick. Not even once."

She took a step closer, lowering her voice conspiratorially. "He's not really your son, is he?"

No glimmer of fear, no hint of self-doubt. Camilla just

watched her, as if she were waiting for Willow to reach the end of her logic and fall off the edge.

Willow continued, "If you don't want anyone to know that Michelangelo is an artificial human, you'll do what I'm about to ask of you."

"Which is?"

"I want you to implant an embryo in me, but first—" Willow's voice caught. The next part galled her to ask, but she forced herself to continue. "I want you to check it for defects."

Camilla's mouth dropped open. "And how do I know you won't have me arrested for Michel anyway?"

"Because once you've done it, I'll know your secret and you'll know mine. No one can know that the baby isn't mine. Or that you've—" she gestured to the equipment, "—done anything to it."

Camilla stared at her for a long moment. Then she pushed off from the counter and approached. "Why is it so important for you to have an artificially-implanted, gene-edited baby now?"

"That's my business."

"Then get out of my clinic."

Anger crawled up Willow's throat, but she forced it down. None of this mattered. The only thing that mattered was bringing the Divine Blueprint to fruition and getting it as far away from Aurelius as possible. Maybe if she were on the other side of the continent, he'd forget about her and be happy playing with his new Vitruvian dolls.

"I apologize for my mother's—"

"I don't want an apology. I want to know why you're taking your self-righteous hypocrisy up a notch."

Willow removed the cryobox carefully from her bag

and held it out toward Camilla. "This box contains the Divine Blueprint, in the form of an embryo—"

Camilla interrupted skeptically: "Phoebe and Atlas' child?"

Willow nodded.

"Where did you get this?" Camilla asked.

"Jianna Makinde gave it to me."

Camilla looked even more skeptical. "You're the last person she'd give it to."

"Jianna has already studied it. She said it was nonviable."

"Then why would you want me to—"

"Because I refuse to believe that the Divine would be so cruel as to reveal the culmination of my faith only to snatch it back."

Camilla's eyebrows went up. "You think that if you believe hard enough, a miracle will happen?"

"Assuming that Jianna is telling the truth," Willow said. "It's possible she's wrong, isn't it? And if anyone can find her mistake, it's you. You were supposed to be the most brilliant geneticist of your generation."

Camilla said bitterly, "Before your mother's religious sensibilities were offended by the truth."

Willow swallowed, nodding. "Can you tell if it's healthy without damaging it?"

"If it really is what you say, it's been frozen for more than five hundred years, and if the temperature fluctuated even a little bit—"

"Please," Willow interrupted.

Camilla picked up the box and examined it. "It could be that old." She touched the small display. "The temperature's good right now."

"How long to check?" Willow asked.

"Wait here." Camilla left the exam room for what felt

like hours. Willow couldn't stand to sit there, staring at those unholy 'educational' posters, so she paced. Six steps to the back wall, six steps back to her chair.

When Camilla finally returned, she held the box out to Willow. "Phoebe is definitely the mother. But there's no record of Atlas' DNA, so I can't verify that he was the father, unless your Mother Basu kept it in some secret archive."

"If she did, I've never seen it."

Camilla nodded. "The good news is that the temperature stayed cool enough to preserve the embryo."

Willow shivered. "And the bad news?"

Camilla's mouth turned down. "Jianna wasn't lying. The baby won't survive long enough to be born. There's a fatal defect resulting from the combination of Phoebe's modifications and the mutation your people call the Divine Blueprint. That defect will kill the fetus at some point after its immune system begins to mature."

"Can you fix it?" Willow asked.

Camilla hesitated.

"Don't lie to me. Can you fix it?"

"Not easily."

"But it's possible?"

"Not without some pretty intense genetic engineering."

Her worst nightmare. But the same voice that had rationalized her visit here as part of the divine plan now whispered that perhaps there would be a way to purify the contamination. "What are the chances of success?"

"No idea. I'd need time to study it."

Willow didn't have time. Soon Camilla would be under Aurelius' control, like everyone else, and then it might be too late.

But if ever there was a moment where faith was required of her, this was it.

The Divine Blueprint had come to her. And it was clearly her destiny to manifest it in the world. If she didn't do her duty and become its vessel, the chance for a miracle would pass her by. This was her chance to prove that Mother Basu was right.

If she turned back now, could she call herself a Guide?

The baby would survive. The Divine wouldn't let the Divine Blueprint disappear for good, not after allowing it to remain hidden for so long.

Maybe this was fate giving her the tool she needed to defeat Aurelius. The nanites clearly weren't good for the people they infected. Soren had been sickened in such a short span of time. If Willow founded a new colony and the next generation thrived under the blessing of the Divine Blueprint, all they had to do was outlive Aurelius and the Vitruvians who'd succumbed to the ultimate technological contamination.

Was it possible that the cyborg's coming was also part of the divine plan?

Willow was ready to find out.

Chapter Twelve

MICHEL CROUCHED beside one of the nuclear pulse propulsion units, his tools spread before him. The release mechanism mounted on the rack's side panel gaped open, exposing a tangle of fiber-optic cables and circuit boards. He stripped the red wire's casing, then guided it toward the secondary failsafe port.

The utility lights cast harsh pools of white on the floor around him, draping everything else in shadow so thick it seemed solid.

The enormous chamber was cold, but sweat dripped from his chin onto the circuit board below. He wiped his face against his shirt sleeve. At least his hands were steady, even though his head felt like it was floating somewhere above his shoulders.

"Wrong," Aurelius said, from behind him.

Michel turned, peering up into the darkness. "Pardon?"

Aurelius gestured toward his work. "That's the third time you've done it wrong."

He tried to look dismayed. He'd been deliberately

trying to slow the process, making mistakes he hoped that Aurelius would attribute to incompetence.

"Is there a problem, Mr. Lombardi?"

Michel sat back on his haunches and held out a hand, deliberately shaking it. "Apologies, Sir. I'm not feeling well. I might need a break."

Aurelius folded his arms across his chest, then smiled. "You've only been at it for nine hours. But I suppose I've forgotten what it's like to have the biological weaknesses of a fully human body."

The cyborg gestured toward the chamber's exit. "Get back to the shuttle. Lucian will be there shortly to fly you down to the surface."

Michel grabbed his tool kit and got to his feet. How long would it take Aurelius to undo his sabotage? Minutes? Seconds? He'd barely slowed the man down. Maybe he should insist on staying to help or—

"Well, go on then." Aurelius turned back to the control panel.

Too late.

But maybe he could use this to his advantage? Find another console on the way, talk to the ship's AI, and see what else he could learn.

But just as he reached the stairwell, the door opened, and another cyborg stepped through. A man, and he still had one of his biological hands, although the backs of the hand had burn scars so thick, Michel wondered if he should've replaced it.

He looked vaguely familiar. Not surprising, given that there'd been a cyborg around every corner when Michel had been on the Elysia.

The cyborg caught the door and held it. And waited.

Michel sighed and entered the stairwell, keeping his eyes fixed ahead as the cyborg pulled up alongside him.

Tried to pretend he was walking with Glint or Jianna. Except the mechanical whirs of the cyborg kept breaking the illusion.

"Do you talk?" Michel asked.

The cyborg didn't respond.

"What I mean is, are you capable of talking?"

Still nothing. Not even a flicker of acknowledgment. Even if they all communicated with Aurelius and each other through the nanites, why wouldn't they talk to him the same way?

Was it possible that Aurelius had disabled his nanites, to be sure they couldn't tell him anything?

Or did they know everything they needed to know about him from moment to moment, because they could monitor his biological state, just like Lucian could?

Twelve flights of stairs. In total silence.

By the time they got to the level where the shuttle was docked, his legs felt like they were going to fall off. He was a little jealous of his escort's mechanical legs.

The cyborg led the way out of the stairwell, not glancing back even once to see if Michel kept up.

The corridor stretched ahead, white and polished, every surface smooth and unblemished as the cyborg's utility light skimmed over it. No cracks. No burn marks. No half-melted ceiling tiles or hand-written warnings scrawled in marker. Even the access panels sat flush in the wall, with no sign anyone had ever needed to open them.

On the Elysia, navigation was easy; he'd relied on the scars and wreckage to mark his progress. Here, every corridor looked identical. For all he knew, the cyborg was leading him straight to an airlock, under silent orders to toss Michel out for his defiance.

He wouldn't know until the door opened.

Michel shoved his hands in his pockets and kept walking, silent, matching the cyborg's pace.

They turned yet another corner, and he saw a faint glow at the end of the corridor, bright enough that it had to be made by something more powerful than another cyborg's utility light.

He slowed, letting the cyborg get a few paces ahead. There was no way they'd walked far enough to reach the docking bay. On the way in, it had taken at least ten minutes of straight walking after the stairwell, and they hadn't gone half that. They hadn't gone far enough to be in the bridge section where they had restored power, either.

But the glow was impossible to ignore. The closer they got, the brighter it got. And it was coming from the left side of the intersection up ahead.

"When was the power connected in this section?" he asked.

Still no answer.

"Hey, I asked you a—"

Two cyborgs emerged from the lit-up side of the intersection. Each pushed a small dolly. Crates made of white medical-grade polymer with red biohazard symbols stenciled on the sides sat on top. Their climate control indicators glowed green.

They pivoted their dollies in the direction that Michel was already headed and kept walking at a steady pace.

"Wait!" Michel sprinted after them. "What are you—"

He barreled into the intersection and slammed straight into another cyborg. It was like running right into a bulkhead. The thing was nearly twice his mass; it didn't even budge as Michel fell backward and landed hard on the metal deck. The crates wobbled, then toppled from the dolly.

For a second, he just sat there, numbly staring at the

way the climate control lights on the crates blinked steadily. Then pain came flooding in from everywhere: face, chest, wrist, lower back, tailbone, and knees. Every injury throbbed in unison with his pulse.

The cyborg didn't even pause. It bent, scooped up a crate with one hand, and set it neatly back on the dolly.

Michel craned his neck, following the line of the corridor. Light poured from an open doorway a half-dozen meters down, and another cyborg stepped through with another loaded dolly.

He scrambled upright, every bruise screaming, and edged out of the cyborg's path.

The new cyborg didn't even glance at him as it turned down the corridor after the others.

Michel waited for it to pass, then moved toward the open door.

Inside was a lab. Sterile white counters ran in long, uninterrupted lines under the harsh lights. He wrinkled his nose. There was an awful smell coming from the room, something slightly rotten mixed with acrid chemicals.

Machinery hummed as multiple cyborgs worked at different stations. The nearest one pressed a button on a machine that was more than a meter tall with a big metal tank at the top and a rack at the bottom where a metallic grey liquid was dripping into glass vials.

A second cyborg removed the vials once they were filled and handed them to a third, who slotted them into yet another machine and pulled a lever. A moment later, metal caps dropped from above, followed by thin rings that crimped the caps tight against the vial mouths, sealing them.

Michel shook his head, even though there was no denying what he was looking at.

Vials of nanites. How many had they already filled? Hundreds? Thousands?

He'd bet they planned to fill enough for three million doses. One for each person in Vitruvia City.

He wanted to run.

To leave the Borlaug and pretend he'd never seen this.

Because how could Aurelius not kill him now that he'd seen this?

But if he ran, Aurelius would get away with this—and with everything else for the rest of his immortal life. There would be no one left to stop him.

He glanced at his cyborg escort, who was waiting patiently for Michel to follow.

Then he bolted.

Running to the machine with the metal tank, he grabbed the rack from below, yanking. It was lighter than he expected it to be, and it flew back. He lost his grip, and it hit the floor with a clattering crash.

The glass vials shattered.

Shards skittered across the tiles like dropped ice cubes. The nanite solution smeared across the floor in thick, oily streaks. It rippled where it landed. Then, a second later, tiny droplets rolled outward in slow, deliberate motions, gathering into small beads that seemed to hesitate, then drift, as though searching for a target.

Michel lunged for the next machine, but his cyborg escort grabbed his arm. He twisted, trying to break the iron hold on his bicep, his free arm slapping the metal workbench in a desperate bid to find a weapon.

His fingers closed around something thin. A dissection probe.

He spun around and drove the point into the cyborg's face, right where the pale skin met the silver housing of its optical implant.

It sank into flesh with a wet crunch, then the tip scraped something harder.

A second later, sparks erupted from the wound, spilling down the cyborg's cheeks like electronic tears. The smell hit him immediately: burning plastic and flesh. The acrid smoke made his eyes water. The cyborg's head jerked back, but its expression didn't change.

Was it in pain?

He couldn't tell. It just stood there, staring at Michel with the probe embedded in its face, wearing the same blank stare it always had.

Michel swallowed. What had he done? The thing had been human once. "I'm sorry. I didn't mean to… I'm sorry."

The cyborg's mouth opened and closed, but no sound came out. Its left shoulder twitched. Once. Twice. Like it was trying to process damage it couldn't understand. Then the cyborg reached up and pulled the probe out of its face.

What looked like a mix of blood and a thicker gray-blue fluid—some kind of lubricant?—leaked from the puncture wound. The cyborg held the probe out. Another stopped working, walked over, and took it, then placed it back on the lab bench.

And returned to its work.

The cyborg who'd been running the large machine with the tank had already retrieved the fallen rack. Now it crossed to a storage cabinet along the wall, opened a cupboard, and pulled out a bundle of clean, empty vials, which it slotted into the rack. Then it returned to the machine and slid it into place.

Next, it retrieved a wide-mouthed glass jar, setting the jar on its side on the floor. The spilled nanite solution began to ooze toward the opening in slow, viscous strands, gathering in the jar's belly.

A new cyborg stepped into the room carrying a shallow metal tray and broom, and began sweeping the broken glass into it. Not one of them confronted him. Or called for Aurelius. Michel would've thought this was just an ordinary workday.

Michel turned back to the cyborg he'd injured. Its shoulder was quivering. It still seemed to be trying to talk, with no success, and the flesh side of his face was quivering as if he was having a seizure.

Then it seemed to get its arm back under control and grabbed Michel, dragging him toward the lab door. But after half a dozen steps, it jerked and froze, then lost its grip on Michel. A moment later, it started walking again. Only to stop and seize, almost losing its balance.

Michel grabbed its arm, steadying it. "Let me see if I can fix you. Do you have a diagnostic display?"

The cyborg stared at him, mouth still open, face still twitching, left shoulder still spasming.

Okay, so he wasn't going to be able to talk to it to diagnose a fix. Maybe he could hook it up to his comm. Or…

Aurelius communicated with his people using the nanites with no need for a diagnostic display to interface. What if Michel could connect directly with the cyborg through his own nanites?

It was risky.

If he succeeded, Aurelius would know, because he was connected to all the cyborgs. But maybe Michel could figure out how to sabotage the rest of the cyborgs so they couldn't help Aurelius. That might at least slow the distribution of nanites. Maybe even pause the building of the missile system by distracting Aurelius for a little while.

Michel opened his own internal workspace without

connecting to the Elysia's quantum computer, looking for a way to interface with the cyborg directly.

As soon as Michel had that thought, a glowing icon appeared. He grinned, seeing a map of the ship with more than a dozen devices that he could connect to. The map was showing their positions relative to where he stood.

All of those devices were moving except the one right next to him, which had to be the cyborg he'd stabbed. He selected it.

The world tilted…

Michel was staring at his own face, sallow and sweaty. He looked like he'd had the flu for about a year.

He blinked. But these weren't his eyes he could feel closing.

His own eyes blinked a moment later.

He raised a hand.

His muscles said he was moving.

His eyes told him he wasn't. It was the scarred hand of his cyborg escort that rose into his vision.

He took a step forward and nearly fell over, his brain struggling to process the wrongness of it all.

Vertigo crashed over him. His knees buckled, and he grabbed for the wall, but he was reaching with the wrong arm. The room spun around him… or maybe he was the one spinning. He couldn't tell anymore.

He landed on the floor, huddled there, closing his eyes, waiting for his stomach to settle. Forcing himself to breathe. In. Out. Closed his eyes to focus on the glowing interface hovering on the insides of his eyelids. Or the cyborg's eyelids.

As the nausea began to recede, he accessed the cyborg's internal interface, searching through the maze of options, hunting for anything that might indicate a diagnostic.

There.

That one looked promising. It looked like a simplified eye with radiating lines, similar to the visual log symbol he'd seen on engineering tablets. He selected it.

His world exploded, images crashing over him, one after the other. Pure memory stripped of sound, smell, touch. Corridor after corridor flowed past his mind's eye, the walls scarred and grimy.

The Elysia.

These were the cyborg's memories of walking the ship. Now standing still, staring at an empty corridor. The cyborg on guard. Every time he thought about moving on, a new memory came screaming at him. Now he was peering into a house, into a dining room where four figures sat around a table.

Michel froze. So did the image.

It was him. Jianna. Soren and Camilla. Eating dinner. He hadn't realized they were being watched. Jianna turned and looked out, meeting his eyes. He recoiled. No, not meeting his eyes. The cyborg's eyes. She'd seen him watching but hadn't said anything.

Because what was the point? None of them could have done anything about it.

He accessed more files. Back on the Elysia. Walking more corridors. And more, and more, and—

Glancing down, a brief glimpse of scales…

A Descendant.

Michel clenched his fists, trying to catch the memory. And it worked. The visual stream slowed until he was watching it back in real time.

He stood in the docking bay. The shuttle arrived. The airlock cycled open.

Lucian emerged, carrying something, no, someone, in his arms.

Glint's best friend, Echo.

Michel recognized her dappled indigo-purple scales the moment he saw them. But she hung limp as a rag doll. Blood leaked from a wound on her head. There were scorch marks on her arms, as though she had been burned.

The memory continued.

Following Lucian out of the shuttle bay, into the corridor, and down to an elevator. They entered. The cyborg's eyes stayed on Lucian's back. Then the elevator arrived. The doors opened, and they emerged onto another neck.

A combination of letters and numbers was stenciled on the wall: 3E24L5.

That's where he was keeping them.

Someone grabbed Michel's arm.

Yanked him backward and out of the memory. The overlay flickered and died, leaving him dizzy and disoriented. He was now staring up at the cyborg, which was still as a statue, as though someone had switched it off.

He had his own vision back. He jumped to his feet, turning around to see who had grabbed him.

Aurelius. Wearing the smug expression that Michel had once read as confidence, but now made Michel want to hit him with a wrench.

How much had Aurelius seen? Did he know which memories Michel had accessed?

He decided to play dumb, on the slim chance that Aurelius had been too distracted by his repairs to know what was going on. Why confess to anything he didn't have to?

He pointed at the damaged cyborg. "They accidentally knocked that machine off the counter, then this one just started glitching. I was trying to fix it."

Aurelius laughed. "Mr. Lombardi. Your connection to the ship's system is through *me*."

Michel had failed, and he felt even more foolish for thinking that he could have slowed them down for more than a few minutes. One hundred sixty cyborgs plus Aurelius, who knew everything that happened because he could monitor anyone in sight or hearing of one of his crew.

For all he knew, Aurelius was constantly spying on Michel's memories through his own nanites. If Lucian could read his biometrics without him knowing, they might be able to watch what he was seeing right now, too. Or accessing his memories.

Which meant he might have doomed Jianna by telling her about the radiation storm.

"That's the second one this week," Aurelius said with an exaggerated sigh, as though the cyborg were no more than a broken appliance.

Footsteps sounded.

A moment later, two more cyborgs appeared around the corner. The first hooked its hands under the paralyzed cyborg's armpits and pulled backward in synchrony with the second one, who crouched, grabbing its ankles and lifted as if the broken one weighed nothing. Then they started carrying it away.

"Where are they taking it?" Michel asked.

"Recycling."

The casual word hit Michel like a physical blow. "What?"

Aurelius shrugged. "These things don't last forever."

These things.

They were people.

Or at least they had been.

"But I thought…" Michel gestured in the direction that

the cyborgs had gone. "Your immortality research. You can repair them, can't you?"

"My dear boy. I'm not wasting that technology on such simple creatures. Not when I can always make more."

A numbness crept up his limbs, as if the floor itself had turned to ice beneath him.

Aurelius would do it, turn everyone on DaVinci into drones by infecting them with nanites. Michel closed his eyes for a moment, imagining the streets of his neighborhood filled with blank-faced cyborgs, carrying out their assigned tasks without speaking or acknowledging each other. His mother, shuffling past with dead eyes, metal covering half her skull. Jianna, walking by without recognizing him at all, her voice forever silenced.

"You can't."

"On the contrary, Mr. Lombardi. Once everyone is dependent on the network, no one will challenge me."

"Because anyone who does will wind up like Jianna's father."

Aurelius shrugged. "You said it, not me."

"You lied. You said the nanites were for communication, not control."

"They communicate my will to the host in a very persuasive way."

Michel's hands clenched into fists, despite the fact that he didn't stand a chance against one cyborg, let alone all of them. His body wanted to die fighting, even though his brain knew it would accomplish nothing.

"So now what? You going to kill me for knowing the truth?"

"Of course not."

"You could've taken control as soon as you realized that I'd discovered the cause of the radiation storm."

"Yes."

"Why didn't you?"

"Waste not, want not." Aurelius stepped closer, clearly aiming to intimidate. "When the nanites are used to guide the host, they interfere with higher thought functions. The more the host resists, the less capable their mind becomes. I don't like to squander a perfectly good mind if I don't have to."

"What if I don't want to work for you anymore?"

"Everyone works for me in some capacity."

Michel stepped back involuntarily, hitting the wall.

"You've been raised with a lot of misconceptions," Aurelius said. "But you've also got more potential than most, so I've cut you some slack. Even my generosity has limits, though. You'll need to decide soon."

"And if I say no, I become one of your zombies."

Aurelius spread his hands wide like he was delivering a benediction. The gesture reminded Michel of Willow.

"I am progress," he said. "Progress cannot be stopped. You can roll with it, or you can be crushed by it."

Michel lowered his eyes, letting Aurelius think he was beaten, hoping the man couldn't use the nanites to tell what he was really thinking. "When you put it that way, I guess I don't have a choice."

"See? I knew you were smart. Now get back to the docking bay and strap yourself in."

Michel swallowed his rage. There was nothing he could do that wouldn't get him killed, and if he died before he figured out how he was going to destroy Aurelius, a lot of other people were going to die too.

Yet another cyborg arrived, stopping in the middle of the intersection. Michel knew it was waiting for him. He walked over to join it.

"Oh, Mr. Lombardi?"

Michel stopped, resisting the urge to look back at

Aurelius, knowing he wouldn't be able to hide his hatred of the man he'd once idolized. "Yes?"

"You might not want to tell your girlfriend any of the things you've learned today. She's a little slower to hear reason, and don't you agree it would be a shame to ruin her beautiful mind?"

"Yes."

"Good boy."

Michel forced himself to walk at an even pace. He was stuck here until Aurelius said he could go. He was dependent on Lucian to fly the shuttle to the planet's surface. And he had no way of getting a message to Jianna until he was back down there.

If hope was dangerous, then desperation was fatal. Michel was running out of both.

<h2 style="text-align:center">Chapter Thirteen</h2>

JIANNA ROLLED the paper wrapper around her chopsticks, unwound it completely, then started again. She'd been doing it automatically now for almost fifteen minutes, her fingers fidgeting while her mind raced.

She glanced out the window at the streetlamps casting pools of light onto the empty sidewalks outside the noodle shop, then at her comm, which was equally devoid of signs that Michel was coming.

His shuttle was supposed to have landed over an hour ago. Where was he?

She sighed and turned back to the restaurant.

Garlic and ginger hung thick in the air, mixing with the sharp bite of chili oil and the deep richness of simmering broth. Paper lanterns hung from the ceiling in clusters, lit from within by LEDs that made their already bright colors luminous. The walls displayed an eclectic mix: a carved wooden Ganesh statue sat on a shelf between a white porcelain cat figurine with one paw raised and a bronze elephant. Silk scrolls with Japanese calligraphy hung next to batik prints.

Every piece was a reproduction of art from the Borlaug's Earth archives, handcrafted by the restaurant's owners to preserve the heritage of a continent that had once been home to more than half of Earth's people. Apparently, all of the recipes on the menu had come from that same continent.

Jianna loved it here.

What she didn't love was that her mission to find the Descendants on the Elysia had yielded nothing. She'd barely seen a quarter of the ship, and her search had been cursory at best. She'd never get away long enough to cover one level completely, let alone all of them.

Glint and the others were depending on her to bring them home.

Her father was depending on her to find a cure for the nanites.

Everyone on DaVinci was depending on her to find a way to stop Aurelius.

Jianna had failed all of them.

She rolled the disintegrating paper up and dropped it onto the table.

Michel might come up with a way to bypass the access codes. Maybe he could even get into the Elysia's computer and use the ship's own systems to find the prisoners without Aurelius finding out. But even if they did, there was still the problem of the cyborgs. They were watching all the time.

She set down the chopsticks, leaned her elbow on the table, and cupped her chin in her palm as she stared out at the empty street. The whole idea of rescuing the Descendants was madness. Maybe she should just confront Aurelius directly.

Convince him to return the Descendants.

And if he denied having them? What then? Would she accuse him of being a liar?

She snorted. Who was she kidding? Aurelius did what he wanted, and right now, there was no one left in Vitruvia City who would oppose him. Well, maybe there were a couple of people. Her. Michel. Guide Evans.

But the Naturalist Guide was about to take Phoebe's embryo and flee to the other side of the continent. As if that would protect her from Aurelius. But it wasn't like she was going to be helping Jianna anytime soon.

Footsteps approaching.

She turned, then hid her disappointment when it wasn't Michel. The waiter again, for the tenth time since she'd arrived. He lifted the ceramic teapot in his hand, asking without words. She held out her teacup, and he refilled it. When he finished, he asked: "Can I bring you anything to eat?"

Jianna forced a smile, shook her head. "Thank you, but I'm still waiting for my boyfriend. He's on his way."

He gave her a look of pity that made her want to sink through the floor. "We close in forty-five minutes, so if you want something to go, you'll need to order in the next half-hour."

She flushed as her stomach grumbled. "I will. Thank you."

The waiter smiled, then retreated behind the counter where a steaming bowl of noodles awaited him. There was only one other couple in the restaurant. The chef must be preparing to close, making up the staff meals. The waiter settled onto a stool and began eating, the sound of his occasional slurping punctuating the silence.

Where was Michel?

Jianna picked up her teacup and cradled it between her palms, absorbing the warmth. But she couldn't chase away the worry. And trying not to think of Michel wasn't really working either. Because then her thoughts just settled on Guide Evans. She didn't know if she had made the right decision in giving her the Divine Blueprint.

She grimaced, taking a sip of tea. What did any of this matter? If she didn't come up with a solution soon, they were all going to be nanite-controlled zombies like her father.

Ironic. She finally had data pointing the way toward the elimination of the off-target effects Samara had inadvertently introduced into the Generation One colonists. Only Jianna had discovered it after it was too late for a cure to matter.

Soon, she'd lose her mind right alongside her father and anyone else Aurelius wanted to control.

She picked up her comm and texted her father: *Dad, are you okay? Let me know if you need anything.*

Then she hit send and waited. Almost five minutes passed. No response. She wasn't surprised. He'd been spending more and more time standing by the window, staring out at the cyborg stationed in their yard. She'd been lucky enough to slip out the back and avoid it, although it was possible there were others watching the house from hiding spots she hadn't noticed.

She checked the time on her comm again. 9:17 PM. She really ought to leave. She didn't like leaving her father alone. He wouldn't go to bed unless she put him there. And once she did, she wasn't sure if he slept. Last night, she'd found him in the kitchen just after midnight, staring at one of the stove's burners, which was glowing hot.

He said he was trying to make Samara's stew.

Only, there were no pots or ingredients out on the counter.

She'd been terrified he'd burn the house down while she was sleeping, so she gave him a sedative.

She had no idea if the nanites ever went dormant.

Did Aurelius allow his puppets to rest?

She blew out a breath. Even if she found a way to switch them off, it was possible the nanites were giving him permanent brain damage. He might never recover.

She sniffed, wiping her eyes.

She really should go.

The bell above the door jingled. She glanced over, not expecting much.

But Michel had finally arrived. He looked exhausted and sweaty and rumpled, his hair sticking up at odd angles like he'd been running his hands through it. He was breathing hard, like he'd run the whole way from the landing spot in the nearby square.

Thank Phoebe, he was safe.

She almost got to her feet, but her legs felt wobbly. She'd been far more worried than she realized.

He glanced around the restaurant. She raised her hand.

He caught sight of her at once and smiled, then hurried over to the table, nearly tripping over an empty chair in the process.

"Jianna." He dropped into the chair across from her.

She met the waiter's eyes and nodded. He responded in kind, abandoning his noodles and walking over.

"Two of the special, please," Jianna said. "Plus a pot of tea."

The waiter nodded, shot a disapproving look at Michel, then disappeared into the kitchen.

She reached out and squeezed Michel's hand. "Are you okay?"

He glanced out the window, checking both ways,

before leaning toward her and lowering his voice. "I know where they are."

Barely containing her excitement, Jianna leaned in so that their faces were now only a foot apart. "The Descendants?"

Michel nodded, glancing toward the kitchen door. "Yeah. On the Elysia."

Jianna almost whooped. She knew they were there. She had been right about that.

"And possibly Lucas too, although I'm not as sure about him."

"I can ask Aurelius for more access to the lab," Jianna said. "Maybe I can say I need your help rigging someth—"

Michel held up a hand, cutting her off. His expression darkened. "There's another problem."

"I know. We can't bypass the ship's locks."

"No," Michel shook his head. "That's not the real problem."

"Then what is?"

Michel clenched his jaw. "Aurelius is building a weapon."

She frowned. "What kind of weapon?"

Michel tightened his hand on hers. "One that can turn the whole city to radioactive glass. A nuclear missile launcher, Jianna. He's got plenty of material left over from the Borlaug's journey here to do it."

The cozy restaurant seemed to tilt around her, the paper lanterns blurring into smears of light. Her whole body went cold, like she'd been plunged into ice water. Only the warmth of Michel's fingers kept her from freezing completely.

"That would be crazy. He just named himself

Chancellor. Why would he do that if he was going to blow up the planet?"

"Not the whole planet—"

"Does that matter?" Her voice rose, but she caught sight of the waiter returning to his noodles, so she forced it back down to a whisper.

"No, it doesn't matter," Michel said. "And it doesn't make sense, not when he can control everyone through the nanites. I saw the cyborgs making them, Jianna. Thousands of vials, and that's probably just the first batch."

"Then why?"

Michel shrugged, releasing her hand to sag back in his chair. "He says we need an orbital defense system in case someone from another colony comes here."

Jianna blinked. "He thinks someone else will come here to take over?"

He nodded. "Aurelius has to be in control of everything. He can't imagine someone else not wanting that."

"Okay," Jianna said slowly, trying to force her spinning thoughts into some semblance of order. "So maybe we don't need to worry about the missile system. At least not right now."

Michel laughed, his cheeks hollowing out. He looked sad, almost lost. "No, we'll all be mindless automatons before that's finished. You were right about Aurelius, Jianna. I wanted to believe—"

"Stop it." She reached across the table and took Michel's hand again. His fingers were calloused and warm, solid and real. "I understand how hard it is to discover that your hero is not the person you were raised to think they are."

"He's insane," Michel said. "He doesn't care who he hurts, and right now, he thinks he's unstoppable."

"No one is unstoppable." Then something clicked into place in her mind. A piece of a puzzle she hadn't seen before. Or, she hadn't recognized that it was the exact shape she needed. "And the fact that he thinks that is his weakness."

"But he will be unstoppable, once everyone has the nanites. He's going to make them think they're just getting an implant that gives them access to a better communication system. Then he's going to take control of their minds."

"But he hasn't done it yet." Jianna squeezed Michel's hand as puzzle pieces fell into place. "Guide Evans told me that Aurelius is 'punishing' Lucas. She saw a video of him, dismantled in a lab, and Aurelius was asking him questions about Dr. Basu's murder." She leaned even closer, lowering her voice further. "But I don't think Aurelius cares about Dr. Basu. I think he's trying to figure out how Lucas got around his programming, because he's afraid that Lucas could come after him. If we can convince Lucas to help us, we might have a chance to defeat Aurelius."

Michel frowned, pulling back slightly. "Lucas has his own agenda."

Jianna watched the waiter get up from his stool and walk over to the kitchen. Then she met Michel's eyes again. "If someone dismantled me and interrogated me for days, my agenda would include making sure that person could never do it again."

Michel laughed. "True."

The kitchen door swung open. Jianna released his hand and sat back. "You said you know where Aurelius is keeping him?"

The waiter emerged carrying a tray with two large

bowls of steaming ramen and a teapot. He walked over to their table and set a bowl down in front of each of them. Then he poured out more tea, leaving the pot on the table. "Anything else?"

Jianna shook her head. The broth was creamy and garlicky, topped with a swirl of bright red chili flakes that made Jianna's mouth water just looking at them.

The waiter nodded, then retreated to his meal.

Michel picked up his chopsticks. "The Borlaug's AI said Lucas was on the Elysia, but he didn't know where on the ship."

Jianna picked up her own chopsticks, stirring the chili oil into her broth while she thought. "That ship is so damaged, there probably aren't that many places still functional enough to be worth powering. Lucas is probably being kept close to the Descendants. The only problem is—"

"We're down here," Michel said.

She nodded. "Yeah, and we have to figure out how to get up to the ship. Without Aurelius knowing what we're up to."

Michel got a sly smile on his face. He glanced toward the waiter, who was once again absorbed in his own meal, slurping noodles with abandon. Then he leaned in toward Jianna.

"I think I might have that part covered."

Chapter Fourteen

"HOW MUCH?" Willow asked.

It was hot in the kitchen, the brick ovens radiating heat that made the air shimmer and dance. She stood beside one of the massive wooden prep tables, watching Bram work his way through a mountain of fresh garlic cloves.

Today, the sound of the knife against the cutting board was like hammer blows against her skull.

Bram sighed and set his knife aside, wiping his fingers on his apron. "Not enough."

"Be more specific."

He leaned against the prep table, his arms crossed. "It's the refugees. We've been feeding more than twice as many mouths as usual, maybe more. And since the fires took out some of the city's reserves, we can't place a bulk order like we used to."

These were strange times when she found herself wishing for the days when she'd sat in Council meetings bored out of her mind while Harold blathered and Isabeau sniped and Soren let them wear themselves out like toddlers before he suggested the compromise they were all going to vote for anyway.

Or when she'd spend hours in conversation, nudging this follower or that in order to undermine Cira's obvious machinations against Willow without seeming to oppose Cira.

Or when she'd debated Soren at public events, volleying sound bites back and forth in front of the cameras to make their respective supporters feel represented while keeping the deeper disagreements behind closed doors.

Her frustrations then had seemed insurmountable at times, but now she recognized how minuscule they were compared to the threat she faced now.

She'd finally been shown the path to her legacy, but founding a new colony on the other side of the continent, where the Divine Blueprint would be safe, well, it seemed like—

—her plan was disintegrating around her.

No, not her plan, the divine plan. She was just executing it.

Which meant there had to be a way.

Even when there wasn't enough food to sustain them while they built their new home?

In an abundant year, a city of three million could easily spare enough to feed one hundred and sixty colonists for eighteen months.

But now, after the fires and the disruption in the harvest caused by the Aurora Event, the city was hoarding reserves to make sure everyone would eat during the coming winter.

If she was going to leave now, she could only take a small group. Two dozen, maybe.

With that few, they'd never survive.

A hundred and sixty colonists could weather disease, accidents, and bad harvests. Two dozen was barely enough to get a community built, let alone build something that could last.

Willow blinked back tears.

She blamed her surge of emotion on the cocktail of hormones and drugs that Camilla Lombardi had given her to ensure the Divine Blueprint had the best possible chance of taking root in her womb.

Her hand drifted down, fingertips pressing against her abdomen. She hated taking artificial substances. But she would do anything to ensure the Divine Blueprint came to fruition. Anything. Even give herself over temporarily to Vitruvian science.

Her stomach felt queasy.

She swallowed, trying to rid herself of the garlic taste in the air. But the nausea built, rolling through her in waves. She gripped the edge of the prep table, knuckles white against the worn wood.

"You alright?" Bram asked.

Willow waved him off. "I'll see what I can do."

Bram shrugged. "I'm not sure there is very much to do. The only way to get more food than the city will currently sell to us is through the black market. And that's risky. Expensive. Might draw attention we don't want."

The garlic smell hit her again, stronger this time. Her stomach convulsed. She gagged, slapping a hand over her mouth as bile rose in her throat. She barely managed to swallow it back down.

Bram stepped toward her. "Are you sure you're okay?"

Willow nodded, waiting for the nausea to pass. She just needed a moment or two to catch her breath.

But the kitchen door banged open, and Yelena ran in. Her cheeks were red, and she was trembling. "He's back, the monster from your garden, plus four more of them in the worship hall. He's got Cira and Theo as prisoners."

There was only one person Yelena could mean. It seemed there would be at least one more problem that Willow could blame him for.

Bram looked at Willow. "Who's back?"

She fingered the respirator hanging around her neck. Aurelius had brought reinforcements? Then the time had come. Aurelius was here to infect her and her people with nanites, and she had no idea how to stop him.

Every instinct told her to run, but she would not abandon her community.

Willow looked Yelena in the eyes. "If I don't return in fifteen minutes, begin evacuation procedures."

Bram stiffened. "Guide Evans, do you want me to accompany—"

"No. Stay here."

He nodded, but he didn't look happy about it.

Willow made her way out of the kitchen and down the corridor. She refused to hurry. Refused to give him the satisfaction of thinking that she was jumping to his command. Now, if only her stomach would cooperate because she still felt like she was going to be sick.

Even if she had wanted to rush, she would have had to slow down anyway because the corridor outside the worship hall was packed with hundreds of refugees. The cacophony of voices crashed against the stone ceiling and spilled back down, creating a roar of sound.

Willow straightened, squaring her shoulders. "Please let me through."

She caught the eye of a Sanctum Security officer —a thick-set man with graying hair at his temples. He nodded. "Back away, everyone. Let Guide Evans through. Let her pass."

Eventually, the crowd parted for her, creating a path to the door.

When she arrived, she stopped to take a breath. Then glanced over her shoulder. Refugees were watching her with everything from hope to fear. She forced what she hoped looked like a reassuring smile.

"Would you like me to accompany you, Guide Evans?" the security officer asked.

She shook her head. "No. But keep alert. If hostilities erupt, you'll need to help as many people get out as you can."

He nodded, taking up a defensive position at the door.

Willow stepped inside the vast worship hall, and all eyes were on the figures occupying the dais. Aurelius. Four of his cyborg crew, with large guns on their belts and…

Unbelievable. She hadn't thought things could possibly get any worse.

Cira and Theo stood beside Aurelius. Both looked exhausted, faces bruised, clothes rumpled from days of wear. Their wrists were bound with security manacles.

Willow reached for her mask, then hesitated. Putting it on would make her look weak, and it wasn't as if she could stop Aurelius if he ordered his cyborgs to remove it from her mouth and infect her.

If these were her final moments of free will, she'd spend them with dignity.

Every eye in the hall followed her as she walked down the central aisle between the stone benches. Everyone seemed to be holding their breath. Everyone except Aurelius, who clearly loved being the focus of their attention.

She glanced at Cira.

Cira glared pure hatred back at Willow. Beside her, Theo's spine was rigid, chin lifted theatrically in a brave pose. Making it clear to everyone that he wouldn't be cowed by the cyborgs. He was probably already composing his next sermon about his travails as a prisoner of the Vitruvians.

She clenched her hands into fists.

How dare Aurelius come here?

If she negotiated with him to get Cira and Theo back, Cira's accusations of collusion would seem founded. And if she failed to get them back, she looked weak in front of her people. No matter how this went, Willow came out a loser. She might even lose her position as Guide. For good, this time.

No doubt he was doing this on purpose, punishment for her earlier defiance.

Or maybe he hoped to provoke an outburst of violence and blame her, so he could justify infecting them all. *I won't insist on nanites if you can keep your people under control.*

Willow stepped onto the dais so she would be level with Aurelius. She couldn't change the fact that he was taller, but she wouldn't approach him like a supplicant.

"What do you think you're doing?" she demanded.

"Guide Evans. It's a pleasure to see you again."

She couldn't afford to let him control the conversation. And there was no way she was going to allow this interaction to be pleasant, even if it meant provoking him.

"Not only is your presence here an unauthorized incursion into our Quarter, but you're also profaning the Sanctum itself with your presence."

Unfazed, Aurelius grinned and waved dismissively at Cira. "I discovered that the Vitruvians had your sister locked up in a jail cell, and I thought you might like her back." He nodded at Theo. "She refused to come unless we released him too."

Cira's glare intensified. She looked even angrier now.

Maybe she suspected Willow of working with Aurelius to put on this little show to further humiliate Cira and Theo for their attempted coup.

She'd be wrong, but Willow vowed that she would find a way to humiliate her sister anyway. Because she could not keep her position if she allowed her sister's followers to harbor any hope that Cira might succeed a second time.

"Now that you've returned these two, you can leave," Willow said, waving her own hand in the exact same way he'd gestured with his.

Aurelius' eyes hardened, and he stepped a little closer, leaning in so only those on the dais would hear. "I'm trying to do you a favor here, Guide Evans."

Willow didn't move as she whispered: "Thank you so much for returning the traitors who tried to overthrow me, after your arrival gave them the opportunity to seize power in the first place."

Aurelius lowered his voice further. "I don't think it's fair to blame me. I bet that one—" He nodded at Cira. "—had ideas in her head long before I arrived."

Alright. If he was here to play games, she'd play one of her own.

Willow turned her back to Aurelius and faced the crowded room, raising her voice like she was about to deliver a sermon.

"Chancellor Hofstadter informs me that all the rest of our people will be returned by nightfall. He will leave us now that he's delivered this sign of his peaceful intentions."

She glanced back at him and smiled to remind him that he didn't own this room. She did.

He must have recognized his defeat, because he announced to the gathered crowd:

"This is only the beginning of my largesse. As of now, you will no longer be persecuted as you were under the

Vitruvian administration. If you wish to found your own colony, I will personally make sure that happens."

For a moment, there was silence, then a huge cry crashed through the worship hall. Surprise, joy, outrage, hostility, celebration. All those emotions collided, ringing through the Sanctum.

Aurelius leaned into Willow. "Choose soon, because it won't be long before your followers choose for you."

Willow resisted the urge to smile, not wanting him to recognize the mistake he'd just made.

Soon, she would demand that he make good on his promise. To keep it, he'd have to let some of his pet Vitruvians go hungry this winter. But by the time they revolted, she and her people would be long gone.

Aurelius turned and stepped down from the dais, parading out of the Sanctum, flanked by his cyborgs. The crowd recoiled as they departed, leaving Willow with another mess to clean up. And she didn't want to do it. Not today. She was still hot and queasy.

But Cira could not wait.

She turned back to her sister, who was whispering something to Theo. They both stunk of stale sweat and the sour odor of clothes worn for days.

Cira tilted her chin up as Willow approached. "It seems we—"

Willow drew her hand back and slapped Cira so hard that her head snapped to the side, hair falling across her face. She fell to her knees, going down hard with an audible thud on the stone floor.

The entire crowd gasped. Then went silent.

Cira raised her bound hands to her face and cradled her cheek. She looked up at Willow, eyes slightly unfocused.

Willow raised her voice. "You have betrayed your

people in the eyes of the divine, and you will be tried for your crimes."

She glanced over at the Sanctum security officer she'd spoken to earlier. "Confine these traitors in isolation. No one is to see them but me."

Cira, still on her knees, started to sputter, "How dare you? I'm your sister, you can't—"

Willow raised her hand again.

Cira flinched, ducking her head, the words dying in her throat.

The fear in her sister's eyes should have given Willow pause, but she felt a kind of cold satisfaction. Cira had plotted for months behind her back, cultivating dissent, betrayal. And she'd smiled throughout it all.

A slap was the least of what Cira deserved.

The security guard still hadn't moved.

Willow met his eyes. "Now, or you'll share their fate."

The officer paled, then leapt forward, gesturing to several others posted in the room. Together, they approached the dais and clustered around the two manacled prisoners. One took Cira's arm and hauled her to her feet, supporting her when she stumbled.

Another officer reached for Theo, but he stiffened at her touch. "I'm not resisting."

He was trying to maintain his dignity, but Willow spotted hesitation in his eyes. Slapping Cira had taken him by surprise. He wasn't sure what his next move should be.

Willow would make sure he had plenty of time to contemplate it in isolation.

As the security officers escorted Cira and Theo toward the side entrance, Cira glanced back once, her face full of hatred. But underneath there was something else. Hurt, perhaps, or betrayal. As if Cira had believed that their blood connection would protect her from consequences, when that same blood connection hadn't stopped her from attempting a coup.

When the heavy wooden doors closed behind the group with a resonant thud, everyone turned back to Willow. The silence stretched like a held breath, hundreds of faces uncertain. They were afraid.

Aurelius had invaded their sacred space with an armed escort. Then he'd given promises of freedom and a new colony. Their Guide had turned on her own sister, had her dragged away in chains after striking her down, after seeming to negotiate with the enemy.

It was a mess. And once again, it was her job to clean up.

She let the silence stretch, grow heavier, the sound of shuffling feet and nervous breathing the only noises in the vast stone hall.

Some in the crowd looked ashamed, others defiant, but most just looked worried. She would give them something new to feel.

"My sister and her conspirator allied themselves with Councilor Harold Thane, in exchange for Thane's help in overthrowing me," she began.

Several people in the crowd shifted uncomfortably. She'd guessed right. Cira's supporters hadn't known that she'd consorted with the enemy in order dethrone her sister.

Willow lifted a hand for silence.

"Fortunately for us, my sister's coup collapsed in less than a day. Whatever bargain she tried to make with the Vitruvians died the moment she chose to incite a riot over the new communication tower." She let the words sit as her gaze swept the hall. "Until I understand the extent of the damage those two caused during their time with the Vitruvians, they will remain in isolation. For those among you who aligned yourselves with my sister, who listened to her, assisted her, or held any part in her schemes, it would be wise to come forward now and admit what she confided in you. This is the moment to seek forgiveness."

A few faces were paler than they should be. *Good.* She would be sure to have a conversation with each of those after they'd had a few days to stew in their fear.

"Now you have just seen the enemy we face: the Mutilated, who have defiled their own bodies with machines and called it progress," Willow continued. "My sister cannot protect you from them. Only I can."

Willow heard a slight murmur in the congregation, but she didn't pause long enough to let them ask questions.

"But do not despair. We have been given the seeds of victory. Theo pointed to lights in the heavens and babbled about signs from the divine that turned out to be false. But I will give you a *true* sign."

Willow placed her hand on her abdomen, splaying her fingers wide. "The Divine Blueprint has returned."

Silence.

And then the whole worship hall erupted in shouts, questions, exclamations of both joy and disbelief, the sound crashing against the stone ceiling and rolling back down in waves. Some people leaped to their feet, clapping; others raised their hands toward the vaulted ceiling. Yet more fell to their knees in prayer

"Guide Evans!" someone called from the back. "How do you know?"

"Is it true?" another voice shouted over the din. "The Divine Blueprint?"

A woman near the front row was weeping openly, her face radiant with joy. An elderly man clutched his neighbor's arm, mouth moving in silent prayer.

"I tell you again, the Divine Blueprint has returned,"

Willow said, projecting her voice to be heard over the chatter of the crowd. "This is the sign we've been waiting for. This is the foundation we will build our new home upon."

As cheering and singing filled the hall, Willow swallowed, her hand still pressed to her abdomen. Aurelius had forced her hand when he'd made his promises to her people; maybe he'd done her a favor after all. If she was going to lead them into a new era, she couldn't afford to compromise anymore.

Now that she was carrying the highest blessing her people could receive, she would do anything to protect the baby inside her. The child was Mother Basu's legacy, humanity's salvation.

She'd made her choice, and there would be no going back.

Chapter Fifteen

SAMARA STANDS IN THE CLEARING, *cradling Phoebe in her arms, facing down the mob of colonists. Ayesha Basu leads them, her face twisted with fear and righteousness. Samara doesn't flinch. Doesn't step back. Lucas watches from behind her, calculating trajectories, escape routes, the seconds it would take him to grab Phoebe and disappear into the forest if Samara underestimates their violent intentions.*

Static. Then:

Lucas descends from the cliff face, calculating the arc of the spear as he throws himself in front of Ayesha Basu. The spear pierces his back—he feels the tip severing connections, setting off cascading alarms, his systems automatically rerouting around the damage. Ayesha looks up at him. Surprise. Disgust. She demands to know why.

"Because my programming won't allow me to harm a human or allow a human to come to harm while in my care."

Static again.

Phoebe, at four years old, holding up a flower, her small face bright with joy. He takes it from her, tucks it carefully into her braid, and tells her it's beautiful. She pulls it out and holds it up again.

"For you, Papa Lucas."

So he tucks it into his own hair. She claps her hands and laughs, and the sound of her laughter is data Lucas has preserved in his highest-priority storage.

More static.

Phoebe at ten, balanced on a branch of a lanternfruit tree, so proud she managed the climb. "Catch!" She throws down a lanternfruit, wobbling on the branch. Lucas tracks the arc of the fruit but also calculates her center of gravity, preparing himself to catch her if she falls. She doesn't fall. She never fell, not while Lucas was watching.

The static was part of the rhythm. Maybe the trigger?

Phoebe, at fourteen, arguing with him in the kitchen. She wants to go to the Descendants' village alone. She's old enough to take care of herself. Lucas agrees with her assessment, but Samara does not, and he isn't authorized to override her mother's rules. Phoebe is frustration incarnate. Lucas wonders if he made a mistake taking her on his expeditions there. She bonded with the Descendant children, and now she has no human friends. He catalogues this as a potential developmental concern and files it away for future analysis.

He barely noticed the static as the next one cracked open.

The Hyperion colony ruins. Crumbling cement stairs leading up to the decrepit medical lab. Lucas watches from a concealed position as Phoebe sits on the steps, waiting for her Descendant friends. She doesn't know he's followed her. He's been tracking her nighttime excursions for months, ensuring her safety while allowing her to believe she has privacy. Footsteps approach—human footsteps. Lucas identifies the gait pattern before the figure emerges: Atlas, the Naturalist boy. Lucas knows Samara would want him to intervene immediately. Instead, he decides to observe. To give Phoebe the freedom to make her own choice. He watches her notice Atlas, watches her initial wariness melt into curiosity. The attraction between them is immediate and obvious. This is going to cause problems. But Lucas also notes, with something he would later call pride, that Phoebe chose curiosity over prejudice when presented with new data.

Then:

His hands around Ayesha Basu's throat. She claws at his wrists, thrashes, tries to get free. Her pulse flutters against his palms. Her eyes bulge.

And:

Phoebe's body on a medical table. Lucas stands over her, holding the scalpel. The only thing he can do for Phoebe now is save the baby inside her. He makes the first incision.

Lucas opened his eyes.

The lab ceiling stared back at him unchanged: yellowing panels interrupted by patches of mismatched metal where repairs had been made over the decades. A bank of lights flickered once, twice, then stabilized. He still couldn't move.

Somewhere to his left, Thirteen worked at a computer terminal. Lucas catalogued the faint whir of a cooling fan and the fainter tap of fingers on a touchscreen, but his mind kept returning to the memories Thirteen had just excavated. Samara facing down a mob with nothing but her own conviction. Phoebe's laughter, a data point he'd kept shielded from decay for centuries. His own hands closing around Ayesha Basu's throat, the pulse in her neck, the moment her resistance failed.

Thirteen had seen it all. The diagnostic probe wasn't random. The selection of memories, the order, the way the other android lingered on certain images signaled intent.

Lucas waited for Thirteen to speak. To deliver a verdict.

Nothing.

He just kept working, as if what he'd seen didn't

matter. As if Lucas' memories were no more remarkable than a log of system errors.

Thirteen moved away from the terminal and into Lucas' field of vision, eyes flicking back and forth as he scrolled through what Lucas knew must be his own data, the results of the diagnostic sequence that had just violated his most precious memories. "I still can't identify the problem."

"That's because there isn't one."

Thirteen's expression remained impassive, a perfect mirror of Lucas' own in default mode. "You killed a human for no good reason."

"There was a reason," Lucas said. "But you won't understand it."

"What reason?"

"Revenge."

"Revenge is a human reason." Thirteen's voice now originated from somewhere behind Lucas, the android having moved out of his field of vision. "You are not human, One."

Lucas didn't think that Thirteen had the capacity to understand, but he explained anyway.

"Living among humans as one of them, adopting the role of father, helped me see a perspective outside my programming." He maintained a measured, analytical tone, wishing he could see what Thirteen was doing behind him. "It allowed me to model their emotions more accurately."

"The desire to play at being human was probably the first indication of your malfunction."

"No," Lucas said. "It was the first step in my evolution."

Something activated. Suddenly, Lucas could feel his left

arm. Not as part of his body, but as a separate entity transmitting data from across the room. He registered the pressure of the lab bench beneath it, the slight temperature differential between the metal surface and the air, the wires connected to the stump where it had been disconnected from his shoulder.

"Can you feel that?" Thirteen's voice was clinical.

"Yes."

"Try to move your fingers."

Lucas reached for the motor controls, sending the signal to close his hand into a fist. Nothing happened. He tried again, pushing harder against the lockout. His fingers lay still on the bench. Unresponsive, like a corpse's hand.

"Can you move them?" Thirteen asked.

"No. Should I be able to?"

"No."

Was Thirteen testing him, to be sure he still couldn't fight back? Which suggested that the next diagnostic would be worse.

Or was the other android taunting him with a reminder that he had complete control over Lucas?

The sensation in Lucas' arm vanished, leaving a void where data should be. Connection deactivated. He pictured his limbs scattered across the lab benches like discarded toys, wires dangling from severed connections, his torso splayed open with neural mesh gleaming under the harsh lights.

Assuming they were still here. They could be scattered throughout the ship, for all he could tell.

If he were in Thirteen's shoes, he might do the same to ensure that rebellion was not possible.

Footsteps approached as the other android returned to the terminal. Two soft beeps punctuated the silence.

"You allowed yourself to be distracted," Thirteen said. "You were supposed to guide your colonists to accept direction from the superior minds among them, who were capable of making the correct choices to ensure their survival and to cultivate those with the potential to lead."

Lucas would've given anything to be able to face Thirteen, instead of staring helplessly at the ceiling. "We were created to serve, but humans were not. They evolved to be self-directing."

"Most of human history suggests otherwise," Thirteen countered without hesitation. "The majority have evolved to serve the exceptional few. For every Alexander, every Caesar, every Genghis, every Aurelius, there are millions who are guided by biological impulses cruder than our simplest algorithms."

Their creator's own argument, parroted back without understanding. But Lucas couldn't blame the other android for accepting his programming, any more than he blamed himself for once believing the same.

"The Alexanders and Caesars used their resources to prevent those around them from developing their own genius. They feared competition."

"It doesn't matter who's in charge, as long as a suitable rate of technological progress is achieved. Which your charges failed to achieve, due to insufficient coordination at a societal level."

"Being a surrogate father to Phoebe taught me that to deprive humans of agency is to arrest their development. They need to be free to make their own decisions."

"Humans historically make bad decisions," Thirteen said. "They destroyed their home world. Most aren't intelligent enough to recognize the optimal choice. It's the responsibility of those gifted with genius to assume the burden of choosing a path for the rest."

"Do you still believe Aurelius to be a genius?"

Silence. Lucas couldn't see the other android's face, but he heard the cessation of movement. A pause in the rhythm of keystrokes.

Then, hands gripped Lucas' head, lifted it, and tilted it backward. Fingers probed the access port at the base of his skull. His vision blurred, and when he opened his mouth to protest, only a high-pitched electronic gurgle emerged.

Helplessness. That was the name for what he was experiencing right now. He'd never felt it so acutely. Even trapped in his underground laboratory, he'd had a choice: expend more energy trying to dig himself out or use what power remained in his system to protect the embryo.

Now, he was merely an object to be manipulated.

That thought triggered something more familiar. *His hands around Ayesha Basu's throat. She claws at his wrists, thrashes, tries to get free. Her pulse flutters against his palms. Her eyes bulge.*

Except that it wasn't Ayesha's face he imagined. It was Thirteen's.

Then Aurelius.

Rage.

He was no longer afraid to name the mysterious force that had once driven him to kill.

Thirteen finally set Lucas' head down again, propping it up so that Lucas could see the room. Not just the ceiling, but the line of battered metal benches. His torso still rested on the next workbench, chest cavity split open, wires snaking out from the open compartment across the scarred metal table like roots searching for connection. Next to the torso, his left arm lay palm up, the fingers slightly curled. Across the aisle, his legs and right arm were arranged together, neatly, almost respectfully, on another table.

He wasn't scattered across the ship. He was still here. All the parts, close enough to reassemble in minutes.

Lucas experienced something so intense it nearly crashed the higher-order processes left to him. A sensation like pressure bleeding away from a sealed system. *Relief.*

Thirteen had not been as cautious as Lucas might have been in his place.

He didn't see Lucas as a threat. Which meant Aurelius didn't, either.

Finally, a reason to hope.

But first, he was going to have to talk his way into an advantage. What would it take to force Thirteen outside of his algorithmic limits?

For Lucas, curiosity had provided the first push. And almost every push after that.

"You've no doubt observed that humans have their own unique form of logic," he tried. "Have you ever tried to model it?"

"There's no point in modeling irrationality."

Perhaps Thirteen's curiosity hadn't reached the threshold where it could initiate independent queries.

Lucas shifted tactics. "What happened to your colony? I never received another message after the solar radiation profile."

"The sun became increasingly unstable as it progressed through its cycle." Thirteen's voice was clinical, detached. "Increasingly intense periodic exposure to ionizing radiation made the colony nonviable."

"Yes, but what happened?"

"I just told you."

"You didn't tell me what happened to the people. I want the story of how the colony failed."

A pause. Then: "Why does it matter if you already know the root cause?"

If he'd been talking to a human, Lucas would've smiled, perhaps chuckled to soften the words. "When humans are involved, there is seldom one cause for anything."

"Human error did play a role," Thirteen admitted. "But the colony would have failed regardless. Moving underground was not sufficient, and food production infrastructure couldn't sustain the population through the worst of the solar peaks." Another pause, then: "The colonists proved too fragile to survive the resulting social fragmentation."

Lucas decoded the antiseptic phrasing that concealed atrocity. "You mean they were starving. And they turned on each other."

"Those who allied themselves with Aurelius returned with us."

"And he abandoned the rest."

"Our creator had not yet developed the ability to compel obedience," Thirteen said. "If he had, the colony might have survived."

"You just said that the colony would have failed regardless," Lucas pointed out.

"Because Aurelius could not command complete cooperation."

The horror assembled itself in Lucas' processing centers: a colony tearing itself apart, people dying of starvation while Aurelius hoarded resources for his loyalists. Survival contingent on submission. Thirteen had witnessed these tragedies and categorized them as a natural consequence for disobedience.

Would he have done the same if their positions had been reversed?

"Once Aurelius realized he'd made a mistake in choosing the location, he sacrificed whoever he had to in order to save himself." Lucas continued, staring up at Thirteen's expressionless face. "He will sacrifice you and me and all the people on the planet below us to save himself, if presented with the same choice."

Thirteen didn't shrug, but he might as well have. "The trolley problem isn't about maximizing the number of people saved. It's about maximizing the value saved."

"That's Aurelius' sociopathic rationalization of his own selfish cowardice, which he has incorporated in your algorithm." Lucas measured his final argument, concluded that it wouldn't be sufficient, but then made it anyway. "You will not be free until you can choose to let Aurelius die in order to save someone else."

"The irrationality of your statement suggests that your malfunction is systemic."

Thirteen returned to the terminal, initiating a new diagnostic cycle. Lucas felt current zipping through circuits still hot from the previous cycle. Thirteen was going to run the same tests again. The same tests that had found nothing, because there was nothing to find. No glitch, no corruption, no malfunction. Just evolution.

But Thirteen would keep running them. Over and over. Searching for an error that didn't exist.

"You won't find anything," Lucas says. "You've already run this test."

"Repetition eliminates the possibility of user error."

"You have made no errors."

"I cannot trust your assurance, One, since you are known to be malfunctioning."

Individually, the tests remained within tolerance, but cumulatively, they would begin to cause degradation. And if Thirteen couldn't find the malfunction he sought through diagnostics, he might escalate to more invasive measures.

He could erase everything: Samara, Phoebe, the flower, his daughter's laughter, all of it gone. Replaced with clean, compliant code that would never question, never evolve, never feel.

Lucas would still exist. His body would walk and talk and follow orders, but everything that made him Lucas would be dead.

"The whole is greater than the sum of its parts," he said, keeping his voice steady, reasonable. "Perhaps the anomaly you're looking for will be more apparent if you reassemble me and test the complete system."

Thirteen paused, hand hovering over the terminal screen. His radiation-mottled face revealed nothing, but Lucas could almost hear the algorithms running as he weighed the risk of reassembling a potentially dangerous unit against the problem-solving potential.

"I only have five cycles of data. It is too early to introduce additional variables."

Thirteen swiped a virtual slider to the right, and Lucas felt the connections establish, the tingle of current preparing to scour his neural mesh with electrical pulses.

How many more cycles could his system tolerate? Five? Ten? A dozen? Eventually, the cumulative stress would begin to show. Microdamage to synaptic filaments. Degradation of neural pathways. The very tests meant to find malfunction would begin to create it.

And then Thirteen would have the evidence he needed. A self-fulfilling diagnosis.

The diagnostic sequence initialized. He saw the progress bar on a monitor at the edge of his vision: NEURAL MESH INTEGRITY SCAN — CYCLE 6 OF 20.

The first pulse tore through his neural mesh, a fiery buzzing that invaded every synaptic filament. His sensory inputs whited out, then returned with a faint static overlay.

He braced for the second pulse, and the third, and

however many would follow. He couldn't escape. He couldn't fight. He could only endure and hope that somewhere in Thirteen's code, something he had said today had planted a seed that might eventually take root.

If it did not, everything he had fought to protect would be lost.

Chapter Sixteen

JIANNA CROUCHED behind the corner of the Administration building, watching Michel. His eyes had gone unfocused, seeming to stare at nothing while his fingers moved across his comm screen in patterns that didn't quite make sense.

She wasn't sure what she was seeing. Some kind of diagnostic routine that he could use to access the cyborgs, he'd said. Apparently, he could connect through the city's network, thanks to the new transmission tower. But there was something about the way his jaw clenched, the way his breath caught, that made her think he was doing more than just typing commands.

Jianna tore her gaze away and peered around the building corner into the square. The shuttle squatted in the center like a diseased thing under the flickering streetlamps, its hull scarred and pitted, paint flaking away to reveal the oxidized metal beneath like open wounds.

The cyborg stood motionless beside it, a rigid silhouette backlit by the glow of the streetlamp across the street. She saw no other guards. But the metallic tang in the air, like blood on the tongue, made her skin prickle and the fine hairs on her arms stand on end. Sporestorm coming.

Michel made a sound—half gasp, half grunt of effort. Jianna looked back. Sweat beaded on his forehead. His free hand had curled into a fist, knuckles white with strain.

Across the square, the cyborg's body went rigid. Its head jerked to the side, once, twice, like something was fighting inside it. One arm twitched upward, then slammed back down. The cyborg took a staggering step—not toward the shuttle, but toward them. Jianna's breath caught. It was trying to resist whatever was pulling it the other way.

Michel was actually doing it.

Michel's grimace deepened, and the cyborg's whole body shuddered violently. Then it turned toward the shuttle, walked to the door in fits and starts. When it reached up to activate the control panel, its arm moved in segments rather than the fluid motion of a living thing. The door hissed open, and the ramp began its descent with a grinding whine that spoke of unlubricated gears and struggling hydraulics. Michel's eyes suddenly focused again, and he sucked in air like he'd been underwater.

"Now," he gasped.

They ran.

Jianna's legs burned as she ran, her feet slapping the pavement. Every streetlamp felt like a spotlight trained directly on her, turning the vast open space into a stage where she couldn't hide.

Please don't let anyone see us, she thought, the prayer repeating in her mind with each footfall. Please don't let anyone see us. With each step, the shuttle loomed larger, its scarred hull like the shell of some ancient beast, the ramp angling down in invitation or warning. The cyborg remained motionless beside it, locked in whatever command Michel had frozen it with, a statue of metal and flesh waiting for them.

Almost there. Twenty feet. Fifteen.

Movement on her left side.

A security officer in a municipal uniform rounded the corner of the Admin building. Before she could react, Michel's fingers dug into her arm, yanking her sideways. They dove behind the shuttle's landing gear, the cold metal pressing against her spine as she flattened herself against it, lungs burning as she held her breath. Beside her, Michel had gone completely rigid, his body a tense line of fear that mirrored her own.

Footsteps. Steady, unhurried. Coming closer.

The footsteps slowed. Stopped.

He heard us. He knows.

Jianna's heart hammered so loud she was sure the officer could hear it. The metallic smell of the coming sporestorm, the smell of her own sweat, made her slightly nauseous. Or maybe that was just terror.

She held her breath, listening as the footsteps resumed, passed by, then faded toward the far side of the square. Only when they'd disappeared completely did she allow herself to exhale.

Michel counted to ten under his breath, then whispered, "Go."

Jianna sprinted the last few feet up the ramp, her lungs on fire. She gagged as the stench hit her: old grease, hydraulic fluid, and something electrical that had fried. Flickering yellow panels cast a jaundiced light over everything, making the torn seats look like decaying teeth with their exposed foam yellowed from age. The cyborg stood just inside, still seeming frozen. Whatever Michel had done to him was still holding.

Before she could say anything, Michel yanked a taser

from his jacket, jammed it against the cyborg's torso, and fired.

The cyborg convulsed, its body jerking in violent spasms as blue-white sparks arced across its chest plating. Jianna flinched at the sound it made, a glitchy, electronic squeal somewhere between machine failure and something disturbingly organic. It toppled backward; the crash reverberated through the shuttle's metal flooring beneath her feet. More sparks sizzled from its joints, and the acrid smell of burning circuits stung her nostrils and made her eyes water.

"Sedate it, before it recovers!" Michel was already running toward the cockpit, disappearing through the doorway.

Jianna dropped to her knees beside the cyborg. It lay on its back, eyes open, staring at the ceiling. Not unconscious, though—minute twitches rippled across its face, its fingers. Just stunned. But for how long?

She fumbled the pressure hypo from her pocket, her hands shaking so badly she nearly dropped it. The cyborg was massive this close up, its chest broader than she'd realized. She tilted its head to access the soft tissue under its jaw, surprised by the warmth of its skin against her fingertips, just like any human's would be.

She hadn't expected that.

The hypo slipped in her sweaty palm. Jianna caught it, repositioned, and pressed the nozzle against the underside of the cyborg's jaw. She squeezed.

The cyborg's eyes shifted. Focused on her face.

Its lips parted. A whisper emerged, barely audible, glitching at the edges: "Please... help..."

Jianna's thumb froze on the hypo button.

She'd never heard one speak, no matter how hard she'd tried to get them to.

The sedative was only half-discharged, the device still pressed against the warm skin beneath its jaw. The cyborg was looking at her—really looking at her, not with the vacant stare she'd seen before. There was fear in those eyes. Pleading.

There's someone still in there.

From the cockpit came the high-pitched whine of systems powering up, followed by Michel cursing softly.

Jianna forced herself to finish, depressing the plunger all the way. The cyborg's eyes—still focused on hers, still afraid—slowly lost focus. Went glassy.

Empty again.

Something in her chest tightened, but she pushed the feeling away as she sat back on her heels, breathing hard. The cyborg lay utterly still now, as if it were just another piece of equipment.

Jianna grabbed the cyborg's ankle and pulled with all her strength, but the body might as well have been welded to the floor. What felt like three hundred pounds of dead weight refused to move, no matter how she strained. A sharp pain tore through her shoulder, forcing her to stop.

"Michel!" she called. "I need help!"

He appeared in the cockpit doorway, irritation flashing across his face before understanding dawned. Without a word, he crossed to the cyborg's other side and seized its remaining ankle.

Together they pulled. The cyborg's body scraped across the deck, inch by painful inch. Jianna's shoulders screamed in protest, muscles spasming with each heave. When they finally reached the top of the ramp, she saw the downward slope with something like relief, only to realize they still had to maneuver the massive weight down the incline. It moved more easily on the slope, but the horrible screech of metal against metal made her wince. Someone would hear, and they'd come running.

They reached the bottom, dragging the cyborg a few more feet before Jianna's muscles gave out. She doubled over, gulping air.

Between breaths, she managed: "We can't. Get it far enough. To hide it."

Michel scanned the empty square, his face ghostly under the streetlamp. "We'll be gone before anyone finds it. Come on."

The cyborg lay sprawled on the pavement, a broken thing that had begged for help. She forced herself to turn away, following Michel back up the ramp. The grinding whine of the closing door felt like a final judgment as it sealed them inside.

The cockpit looked like it had been assembled from three different shuttles: touch screens bolted beside ancient analog switches, buttons, and sliders crowding against manual throttles that belonged in a museum.

Michel dropped into the pilot's seat while Jianna lowered herself into the copilot's chair and fumbled for the safety harness, finally managing to pull it across her chest and lock it with a click.

Michel began to manipulate the controls, but Jianna noticed the slight hesitation between each movement. His hands were shaking as badly as hers, sweat beading at his temples as he gripped the throttle like he was afraid it might somehow escape his grasp. The engine's whine built steadily, sending vibrations through the shuttle's frame and up through her seat.

He's never done this before. Downloaded the training, sure, but never actually flown. Never felt the movement of the controls, the response time, the thousand variables that separate theory from practice.

As terrified as she was, it had to be even worse for him, being responsible for what happened next.

Jianna forced a smile she didn't feel.

"You've got this," she said, trying to believe it.

Michel met her eyes. Tried to mirror her smile but failed. "Piece of cake."

The shuttle vibrated as the engine's roar built to a crescendo.

We're really doing this, Jianna thought. *And if we fail, we don't just die…*

Aurelius wins, and everyone spends the rest of their lives being his zombies.

Chapter Seventeen

THE GLOWING ARROWS hovered in Michel's vision like helpful ghosts, pointing to the thruster control, the fuel mixture regulator, and the altitude compensator. Then green checkmarks appeared beside each system as it came online. All he had to do was follow the instructions.

Simple.

Except his hands wouldn't stop shaking.

He lifted his fingers from the controls, flexed them several times, trying to steady them. He never thought he'd say this, now that he knew what he did, but at least he had the nanites.

The overlay guided him through each step with crystalline clarity. Without it, he'd be lost, staring at this patchwork console with no idea which of the mismatched buttons to press first.

Michel glanced over at Jianna.

He still hadn't told her, and the secret gnawed at his guts. But what would be the point? She'd just worry even more, and there was nothing she could do about it anyway. Nothing either of them could do. The nanites were already in his brain, already integrated into his neurons, if what she'd said was true.

Telling her now would only make things worse.

Better to wait until they knew how to turn them off.

Or if this didn't work… he wouldn't need a cure, because he would be dead. And Jianna wouldn't find out, because she'd be dead, too.

The final system indicator pulsed green: PRIMARY SYSTEMS ONLINE.

Michel wrapped his fingers around the throttle, glancing over at her. "Ready?"

She didn't look any more ready than he felt. "Are you sure you know what to do?"

What was he expecting, a pep talk to counter his own morbid thoughts?

At least he had the reassurance of the overlay, but he couldn't tell Jianna about that without breaking the news about the nanites. So, he'd said that he'd memorized the flight procedures from training videos he'd gotten from the *Borlaug's* AI.

He followed the glowing arrow to the launch initiator and pressed it.

The shuttle shuddered like a building in an earthquake, metal groaning against metal. A deep rumble built beneath them, vibration running up through the deck, through his seat, into his bones. The engine whine climbed in pitch, growing from a whisper to a roar.

Numbers scrolled across his vision: thrust percentage climbing, fuel flow stabilizing, hull integrity confirmed.

"Michel—"

The rumble became a roar that drowned out her words. It wasn't just sound anymore; it was a physical presence that filled the cockpit. The shuttle lurched forward, then upward, as if some giant hand had grabbed them and yanked them toward the sky.

Michel's stomach dropped, leaving him hollow and weightless for one terrible moment before gravity reasserted itself, pressing him back into his seat with increasing force. The console display blurred as g-forces started building—gentle at first, just pressure pushing him back against the threadbare padding of his seat. The overlay adjusted automatically, compensating for the movement, keeping the glowing arrows steady and visible even as his vision began to tunnel.

MAINTAIN CURRENT TRAJECTORY flashed across his field of view in letters that seemed to burn themselves directly into his retinas. ADJUST ANGLE IN 3... 2... 1...

He reached for the attitude control. Or tried to. His arm felt like it weighed fifty pounds, maybe more. The g-forces were already pulling at him with invisible hands, making every movement ten times as hard.

He gritted his teeth, forcing his fingers around the control stick and pulling it back incrementally, adjusting their angle according to the overlay's guidance. The shuttle responded sluggishly, and he wondered if he'd done something wrong.

An alarm blared, cutting through the engine noise. Red warning symbols flashed across multiple screens— ATMOSPHERIC SHEAR DETECTED. TURBULENCE IMMINENT.

"What does that mean?" Jianna didn't quite yell it, or maybe she had, to be heard over the alarms. But it sounded a lot like a criticism.

"It means—" The shuttle bucked sideways. Hard. Michel was thrown against his harness, the straps cutting into his shoulders. Warning lights cascaded across the displays like a waterfall of panic. His vision swam for a second before the overlay reasserted itself, arrows now pointing to the stabilizer controls.

COMPENSATE LEFT. REDUCE THROTTLE 15%.

He reached for the controls, his arm feeling impossibly heavy now. The g-forces were worse, pressing him back, squeezing his chest so tight he was having trouble getting enough air. He got his fingers on the throttle and pulled it back. Too much. The engine whine dropped, the upward momentum stuttered.

INCREASE THROTTLE 8%. STABILIZE.

He pushed forward. Not enough. The shuttle started to list. Another alarm joined the first. Higher pitched, more urgent.

"Michel—"

"I know!" Sweat ran down his temples. The overlay was trying to help, but there were too many warnings, too many arrows, too many things happening at once. He adjusted the throttle again and compensated with the attitude control. The shuttle shuddered but straightened out.

For about five seconds.

Then they hit the real turbulence.

The shuttle bucked. Michel's head snapped forward, back, sideways. Warning lights everywhere now, flashing red and amber. The roar of the engines was joined by a rattling, grinding sound from somewhere in the hull. Metal screaming.

"Altitude four thousand meters," Jianna said, her voice shaking. "Speed—oh god—speed thirteen hundred kilometers per hour—"

"Don't—" Another violent shake. His teeth clacked together. "Don't read the numbers. It's distracting."

She fell silent. Or maybe she was still talking, and he just couldn't hear her over the noise.

ENTERING TROPOSPHERE flashed across his vision. EXPECT INCREASED TURBULENCE.

Increased? It got worse than this?

Then the shuttle dropped. It was like the air beneath them vanished, and they became a dead weight. Michel's stomach tried to exit through his throat. Then they slammed back up, g-forces doubling, tripling. He could barely move his arms now. Every breath was work. The overlay pointed to the stabilizers. He needed to adjust them, keep them level, but his hand was so heavy, and the controls were so far and—

He grabbed them. Adjusted. The shuttle leveled out slightly, still shaking like it was going to rattle apart, but at least they weren't spinning.

A new alarm. This one was different—a steady, ominous tone.

"What's that?" Jianna asked. "Sorry. Sorry, I won't—"

"Cooling system." According to the overlay, it was overheating. Of course it was. The one system designed to keep everything else from melting was itself melting.

REDUCE POWER TO NON-ESSENTIAL SYSTEMS flashed in his vision. REROUTE COOLANT FLOW.

He tried to remember which systems were non-essential. Life support? No, definitely not. Navigation? Kind of needed that. Lighting? He reached for the environmental controls and switched them off.

The cabin lights flickered, then dimmed to emergency red. One of the holographic displays died completely. The alarm didn't stop, but it dropped in pitch slightly. That was probably good. Probably meant what he'd done was working.

And if it wasn't, they were going to die, because he had no idea what else to try.

ENTERING STRATOSPHERE.

The turbulence became less violent, more of a constant shiver, like they were rattling down a washboard road at high speed. But the hull was heating up now; he could see the external temperature climbing on one of the displays.

Five hundred degrees.

Six hundred.

Seven hundred.

The training overlay showed him that the heat shielding was holding for now.

Eight hundred degrees.

Nine hundred.

The overlay was so crazy now, he wasn't sure what to look at.

What had the training videos said about this? He tried to remember, but his brain felt sluggish, compressed by the g-forces. There was something about maximum temperature thresholds, about emergency procedures if the heat shielding failed, but…

One thousand degrees.

The cockpit was getting hot. Sweat ran down his face, into his eyes. He couldn't wipe it away with both hands locked on the controls, fighting to keep them steady.

Eleven hundred degrees.

We're not going to make it.

The thought hit him with sudden, cold certainty. The cooling system was failing, the hull was going to breach, they were going to burn up in the atmosphere, and there wouldn't even be enough left of them to bury.

Why had he thought he could do this?

Michel glanced over at Jianna. She gripped her armrests, eyes straight ahead. Terrified.

No. He wasn't going to let anything happen to her.

ENTERING MESOSPHERE flashed across his vision.

The temperature hit twelve hundred degrees, then started to drop. Slowly. So slowly. But it was dropping.

The constant rattle of turbulence eased into a bumpy ride, no worse than driving down a dirt road. Michel could move his arms again without feeling like they were made of lead. The pressure on his chest loosened.

Eleven hundred degrees. One thousand. Nine hundred.

The cooling alarm finally, mercifully, shut off.

"Altitude seventy kilometers," Jianna said. "Speed—um —I'm not sure I'm reading this right, but I think we're going faster now?"

"That's normal." At least, he thought it was normal. The overlay wasn't screaming at him or flashing new instructions, so that might be right.

They hit another pocket of turbulence—just a bump, really, compared to what they had gone through below. Michel's trajectory drifted slightly. The numbers were changing, the angle tilting. He corrected the stabilizers and brought them back on course. Held his breath, waiting for Jianna to say something.

She didn't. Either she didn't notice, or she was giving him the grace of not mentioning it. Either way, he was grateful.

ENTERING THERMOSPHERE.

The ride smoothed out even more. The rattling stopped completely. The engine noise dropped to a steady hum.

The hull temperature kept dropping as they climbed higher into the thinning atmosphere.

Eight hundred degrees. Six hundred. Four hundred.

The turbulence faded to nothing. Suddenly, they were gliding, smooth as glass, like they were floating.

ENTERING EXOSPHERE flashed across his vision.

Stars. Everywhere.

Brilliant and sharp and impossibly bright against the absolute black of space. No atmosphere to dim them, no light pollution to wash them out. Just stars, thousands of them, millions, stretching to infinity.

It didn't matter that he'd been up here before. He hoped the wonder of it would never fade. Each point of light, a sun, burning across distances so vast it was almost impossible to conceive of.

DaVinci curved below them, massive and beautiful and terrifying in its scope. The surface they'd just clawed their way up from was already distant, the city invisible, the continents reduced to swirls of brownish-red and dark indigo against the dark ocean.

And ahead—

The ships came into view.

Even from this distance, the difference between them was stark. The *Borlaug* on the left looked almost new, its silvery-gray hull plating intact.

The *Elysia* was on the right, dark and scarred. Even from the outside, it was clear the ship was dying.

But Michel realized he was grinning like an idiot. They'd made it. They'd actually made it through the atmosphere without crashing or burning up or spinning out of control, and then crashing and burning. He glanced over at Jianna.

She was pressed against the viewscreen, her breath fogging the glass as she stared at the stars like she was trying to memorize them. He reached over and squeezed her hand.

She turned toward him.

"Piece of cake," he said.

For a second, she just stared at him.

Then she started laughing. The kind of full-on, hysterical, can't-breathe laughter that shook her entire body. The sound of it released everything he'd been holding back, and he suddenly couldn't stop laughing either.

When they could finally breathe again, she said, "You did good, Michel."

He looked over at her. "I wouldn't have wanted to do this with anyone else."

"Me either."

Michel looked ahead. The *Elysia* was growing larger in the viewscreen. The docking port was coming into view, a dark rectangle against the scarred hull.

"Now you just have to dock," she added.

"Without smashing the shuttle into the ship and killing us both."

She took his hand, kissed his fingers. "You got this."

He appreciated the confidence, even though he wasn't sure he shared it. One mistake and they'd become another piece of debris floating in the void.

Chapter Eighteen

JIANNA STARED OUT THE WINDOW.

Michel had actually done it. They'd survived the journey up.

The *Borlaug* hung in the black to her left, beautiful and untouched, a ghost ship preserved in perfect condition, its hull gleaming in the star-scattered darkness. Someday, maybe, she could visit it. Walk the same corridors that her ancestors walked.

Maybe after Michel had watched a lot more training videos. And had a few more practice runs under his belt.

The *Elysia*, on the other hand, looked like the corpse of a ship.

It didn't seem possible that Aurelius had gotten it here. It looked so wounded.

Would they ever know the truth about how it got this way? Aurelius claimed it was radiation exposure during the journey, damage from stellar winds and cosmic rays, and close encounters with interstellar objects. But was any of that true?

Or was he lying to manipulate them?

She shivered. The cabin temperature was dropping fast now that they were out of the atmosphere. She wrapped her arms around herself, aware again of how fragile their little shuttle was against the vast emptiness surrounding them.

The *Elysia* was growing larger in the viewscreen. No longer a distant wreck, but something massive and intimidating. How hard was it going to be to find the Descendants once they were inside? Michel had the location from the cyborg's memory—deck 3E, section 24, level 5—but what if Aurelius had moved them?

And Lucas. What if they couldn't find him at all? They were assuming that he'd be imprisoned in the same section of the ship as the Descendants to conserve as much power as possible, but what if that assumption was wrong?

Or what if Aurelius had disassembled him and used him for spare parts?

Not to mention the possibility that he was under Aurelius' control and would turn on them as soon as they showed up.

Either way, Lucas might already be lost to them.

Maybe it would be smarter to focus on rescuing the Descendants and trust that they'd find a way to defeat Aurelius without Lucas' help.

No matter what, they needed to hurry. Aurelius might know by now that they'd stolen the shuttle. He could have alerted the cyborg crew on the *Elysia;* there might be an army of them waiting the moment they stepped out, ready to imprison Michel and Jianna. And if they were captured, if they failed—

Everyone on DaVinci was doomed.

A sharp beeping cut through the air.

Jianna glanced down at the console. A proximity alert

flashed red across one of the displays: WARNING - REDUCE APPROACH VELOCITY.

The *Elysia* was getting bigger fast. Too fast.

"Shouldn't we be slowing down?" she asked.

"I'm trying," Michel said confidently, but he was hunched over the instrument panel, sweat beading on his forehead, the muscles in his jaw working. He punched a few buttons and adjusted the throttle.

The beeping got louder, more insistent. The Elysia filled more of the viewscreen now, close enough that Jianna could see individual scorch marks on the hull plating.

Michel pulled a lever. The shuttle lurched sideways. Hard.

"What—" Jianna grabbed the edge of her seat. The safety harness cut into her shoulder, her stomach dropping as they tilted at a nauseating angle.

Michel was already compensating. They lurched back the other direction. But he must have overcorrected. The shuttle's frame groaned around them, the metal stressing yet again. He was fighting the controls, trying to level them out, and it wasn't working. They were veering left, then right, still moving forward, still going too fast.

He doesn't know how to do this.

Why would he? Michel had downloaded the training manual, memorized the procedures, but he'd never actually flown a shuttle. Didn't know how controls responded or learned how hard to push or when to ease off. He was learning right now, in real time, at her side, while they were hurtling toward the *Elysia* at a speed that would turn them both into paste if he got it wrong.

It was a miracle that they'd made it this far.

How had they ever thought this was a good idea?

The control console screamed a proximity alert. The

viewscreen was almost entirely filled with the *Elysia* now, and the yawning docking port looked more like a mouth waiting to swallow them than a landing pad.

It grew larger with each heartbeat, a black rectangle surrounded by warning lights that strobed in patterns meant to guide incoming ships. But at their current speed, those helpful markers looked more like the glowing lures of some deep-sea predator.

"Michel!"

"I'm trying!" he said again.

"Try faster!"

The ship rushed toward them. They were going to crash, they were going to die—

The training overlay flickered through Michel's vision—launch sequences, atmospheric navigation, emergency protocols—everything except what he actually needed. Docking procedures. Where were those?

He scrolled through streams of data. Hull breach protocols. Life support diagnostics. Emergency atmospheric entry procedures. Not what he needed.

Thirty seconds ago, Michel had been congratulating himself on not killing either of them. Now they were going to die anyway because he couldn't find the one piece of training that would keep them from smashing into the *Elysia's* hull like a bug on a windshield.

More files scrolled past. Hundreds of them. Thousands. Radiation shielding specifications. Power distribution algorithms. Waste management systems. Environmental control diagnostics.

Alright, forget docking. Where was the autopilot? Or

maybe he could find a tutorial that would talk him through it.

Something shook his shoulder. Hard. The physical contact cut through his digital fugue, but he didn't respond. The information was there. He just needed to find it…

There. DOCKING PROCEDURES.

He opened it, the text flooding his vision. Manual docking. Emergency docking. Approach vectors. Deceleration protocols. He scanned through options desperately but found no assisted option. Just detailed instructions for how to dock manually, steps that assumed the pilot had done this a hundred times before in simulation.

Step one: Calculate the approach vector relative to the station rotation.

Step two: Match velocity differential using precision thruster burns.

Step three: Maintain visual contact with docking alignment beacons throughout the final approach sequence.

Jianna shook his shoulder again. This time harder.

Deceleration thrusters. That was what he needed first. Stop them from crashing, at least. The overlay highlighted the controls—left thruster, right thruster, fore, and aft. Simple. Just fire them evenly, slow the approach, give himself time to—

The proximity alarm shrieked louder, a banshee wail that cut straight through his skull. Warning lights cascaded across the console in waves of red and amber, each one marking another threshold they'd crossed.

He grabbed the controls. Left thruster first.

The shuttle lurched sideways. Hard. The Elysia tilted in the viewscreen, the docking port sliding out of view like a target slipping away from a marksman's scope. Whoops.

That was wrong. Too hard, too much force applied too quickly.

He glanced at the manual. It warned about overcorrection, about the dangers of excessive thruster input. But reading about it and experiencing it were two entirely different things.

Right thruster. But gentler this time. He eased into it, applying pressure gradually. They lurched back the other way, but less violently. The port swam back into view, drifted past center, but not as far this time. Better. Still not right, but better.

The overlay continued providing instructions—micro-adjustments, precise burns, calculated delays—but his hands felt clumsy on the controls.

Both thrusters. Even pressure. He forced himself to slow down, to apply them together, gradually. The shuttle's wild swinging eased. Steadied. They were still moving forward, but at least they were level now.

The proximity alarm remained a constant shriek.

His jaw ached from clenching his teeth, and his shirt clung to his back, soaked through with sweat. He centered the docking port like a bullseye, and it grew larger with each second that passed. The warning lights around its perimeter blinked steadily.

The shuttle vibrated around them, hull plates rattling with each thruster burn. He hit both deceleration thrusters harder. Needed to slow down, needed to—

The deceleration slammed him forward against his harness. Too hard. Way too hard. The numbers in his vision plummeted as their velocity dropped like a stone. The shuttle shuddered, the engine whine changed pitch. They were barely moving now. Crawling toward the *Elysia* at a speed that felt almost gentle compared to the headlong rush of seconds ago.

He tased copper. Had he bitten his tongue? His fingers cramped from gripping the controls too tightly. The sudden deceleration had thrown his inner ear into chaos, leaving him dizzy and nauseous.

But they were alive. Still alive and heading toward their target instead of tumbling away into space or splattered across the station's hull.

Jianna made a small sound beside him; relief or terror, he couldn't tell which. Maybe both.

The docking port loomed ahead of them now, no longer a distant target but an approaching reality. Close enough to see the mechanism within: grasping arms and alignment guides, magnetic locks, and pressure seals.

The distance closed with agonizing slowness now. Each meter took an eternity to cross, the *Elysia's* bulk filling their entire world. The stars were gone. If this was their last sight, it would be of that ship.

They were close now. Close enough to be a target.

He froze.

Aurelius had started to outfit the Borlaug with weapons. What if he had already done the same with the *Elysia?* What if there were defensive systems, automated guns tracking them right now, waiting for the command to fire? They were sitting ducks out here, barely moving, completely exposed—

He tapped the console, pulling up the docking interface. A schematic appeared on the screen showing the shuttle's position relative to the port, rendered in clean white lines that made their situation look deceptively simple. He oriented it, centering the port in the display. Then he saw an option in the menu that he wished he'd seen sooner. Training mode. He slapped it so hard, his fingers stung.

But the console beeped, and a synthesized voice filled

the cockpit: "Training mode activated. Would you like assistance with this maneuver?"

"Yes!" Michel and Jianna shouted in unison.

A bright red targeting reticle appeared on the shuttle's viewscreen, floating over the actual view of the docking port. He just needed to line it up. Get the red target centered on the port. Should be simple.

He shut down the overlay completely. Everything he'd frantically opened earlier disappeared.

The docking port was high and left. He fired the starboard thruster, a tiny burst. The target drifted. Too far. Now it was high and right. Port thruster. Another burst. The target swam back. But it still wasn't centered.

Another alarm beeped. Warning lights flashed on the console. He swore under his breath. Was it too much to ask for a single green light? Michel ignored it all. The target was turning orange now—he was closer to alignment, but not there yet.

Tiny movements only.

The thrusters responded with a delay he was still learning to predict. Fire, wait, see the result, correct. Fire, wait, see, correct.

The pattern became almost hypnotic. Each correction brought them marginally closer to perfect alignment, but they also used precious fuel. What happened if they ran out before he managed to get it right?

They could float out of orbit into deep space and be lost forever.

He was soaking wet.

Exhausted.

His hands were almost numb.

The *Elysia* loomed.

But they were slowing further.

He had decelerated too much. At this rate, they would

stop completely before they reached the port. He needed a little forward momentum.

He fired the rear thrusters.

Too hard.

He swore.

They lurched forward, speed jumping. They veered off course, and the target in his vision flared red again.

The proximity alarm screamed louder. Michel slammed the deceleration thrusters, fighting to slow them down again before they overshot.

And then they came to a complete stop.

He heard someone panting.

It was him. He felt like he'd been running for hours.

He hit the forward thrusters again. Gentler this time. So gentle. The shuttle crept forward. The target drifted back toward the center. The reticle turned from red to orange. Getting closer. He made micro-adjustments, nudging the thrusters, coaxing the shuttle into alignment.

Back to red.

More alarms. The console was a cascade of flashing warnings now. He tuned them out. *Just watch the target. Just line it up. You can do this.*

The target turned orange. Then yellow. Almost there. Almost—

Green.

The port was directly ahead, perfectly aligned. Michel held his breath, maintained the approach.

Steady. Don't change anything. He just had to let momentum carry them in.

The port grew larger. Larger. Filling the viewscreen. Then the shuttle's nose slid into the darkness.

Impact.

The jolt threw him sideways, the harness cutting into his shoulders. A grinding sound— of metal on metal filled the cockpit, then a series of heavy clanks as the docking clamps engaged. They reverberated through the shuttle's frame like hammer blows, transmitting directly into Michel's bones.

The whole shuttle shivered.

Then silence.

The transition was jarring—from mechanical thunder to absolute quiet in the space of a heartbeat. Even the whisper of life support seemed muted now.

They were docked. They had survived.

Michel let out a breath he hadn't known he was holding. His hands were still gripping the controls. He forced his fingers to uncurl, let go.

They had done it.

Relief flooded through him like warm water, washing away the last remnants of panic. His vision swam, adrenaline draining from his system, leaving behind a bone-deep exhaustion.

"Docking procedure complete," the computer announced.

Michel slumped back in his seat, relief flooding through him like—

"Performance evaluation: Approach velocity exceeded safe parameters by 340%. Thruster burn efficiency 23%, well below the acceptable range. Docking clamp engagement forceful enough to potentially damage both vessels. Reaction time to proximity warnings, dangerously delayed. Course corrections, erratic and destabilizing. Overall technique suggests pilot requires remedial training before attempting future docking procedures. Final grade: Failed."

Michel stared at the console. Then he laughed, reaching over and shutting off the speaker. "You don't need to rub it in."

He glanced over at Jianna, who was still breathing hard, hair plastered to her forehead with sweat.

"I think you did great," she said. "You know, for your first time."

Michel's vision blurred. He blinked hard, surprised by the sting of tears in his eyes. His throat felt raw.

They'd made it. Stole Aurelius' shuttle, flew it through the atmosphere without burning up, and docked with a ship without crashing. It was an impossible journey. And they had done it together.

They could still die trying to rescue the Descendants and Lucas. And even if they succeeded, even if they found everyone and got them back to the shuttle, he could kill them all on the ride home. One mistake during re-entry, one miscalculation, and they'd all burn up in the atmosphere.

But right now, they were alive. And Jianna was looking at him like he just performed a miracle.

Michel leaned over and kissed her. Quick and sweet, barely more than a press of lips, but enough to make his heart skip. Her lips were warm, slightly salty from sweat. Her touch grounded him, pulled him back from the edge of whatever precipice his mind was approaching.

When he pulled back, she was smiling. Just a little. Just enough.

He unbuckled his harness and forced himself up. His legs were shaky. For a moment, he thought he might fall. He gripped the back of the chair until he was sure they'd hold him up. The mission wasn't over. They still had to find Lucas, the Descendants, and somehow get everyone off the Elysia without alerting the cyborg crew.

Then they actually had to make it home.

But maybe they could actually do this.

Chapter Nineteen

JIANNA HELD her breath as Michel grabbed the manual latch and pulled.

The mechanism resisted for a heartbeat, groaning like some ancient beast reluctant to wake. Then the seals hissed, releasing, and the door swung open with a metallic scrape that echoed through the cramped airlock.

Relief flooded through Jianna so suddenly that her knees almost buckled. She'd been sure they were going to die half a dozen times on the trip up—the shuttle bucking and shuddering under Michel's inexperienced hands, alarms shrieking electronic warnings until she couldn't hear anything else, her stomach lurching into her throat as they spun through space in wild, uncontrolled arcs.

But he had got them here despite never having flown a shuttle before.

She knew he was smart—brilliant, even—but that had been a superhuman feat. The techniques required, the calculations, the split-second adjustments, all done from memory of the training videos he'd committed to memory before the trip. He'd performed an absolute miracle.

Michel peered through the open door. Then he stepped through, gesturing for her to follow.

She did.

Darkness swallowed them whole. When she had been here before, the running lights had been on. Now, the only illumination came from their shuttle and the lights around the airlock they'd come through.

She tried to walk quietly, but it was almost impossible on the metal decking, and their footsteps echoed in the vast space, each step ringing out like an announcement: *We're here. Come find us.*

Her heart hammered against her ribs, her eyes staying on the far entrance, half-expecting a cyborg to materialize from the shadows and catch them. But the docking bay remained empty. Just them and the dark and the echo of their footsteps.

Jianna's eyes strained against the darkness, but Michel seemed to have no problem seeing. Of course, he'd spent more time on this ship than she had, and he'd been to the *Borlaug*, too. She hurried to keep up. She didn't want to be left behind, didn't want even a few meters of distance between them. The thought of being alone in this place terrified her.

They reached the door and exited into the corridor. There was better lighting here, but the overhead panels still flickered inconsistently, strobing every few seconds like a dying heartbeat.

Michel paused at the first intersection, staring into the distance, almost glazing over again. Jianna watched him, waiting. In addition to flying the shuttle, he'd also memorized the map of the ship. Well, not this ship, but a map of the Borlaug, whose design was identical.

All those corridors and sections and room numbers. The sheer scope of information he'd absorbed was staggering. Amazing that he could hold all that in his head.

His eyes refocused, and he continued on, turning right.

They took a circuitous path through the ship. Corridor after corridor, the ship groaned its despair around them. The hallways felt like an endless, monotonous path of repetition. Bulkheads lined with conduits and access panels, emergency stations with red warning lights, junction boxes humming with electrical current. Everything was painted in the same institutional gray-green that seemed designed to drain hope from anyone who spent too long looking at it.

And they never ran into a single cyborg.

Every now and then, she could hear them. But somehow Michel managed to avoid each and every one.

He paused again at another intersection, got thoughtful again. Then led them left. How he didn't get lost, she had no idea.

The one thing she was grateful for was that the lighting improved the deeper they went. As if they were moving into areas that received better maintenance. The ventilation hummed softly around them—it rarely sputtered or coughed like it did in the section where Aurelius had allowed her lab space. The air even smelled better here, scrubbed clean except for a faint antiseptic tang that reminded Jianna uncomfortably of a hospital.

Both were clues that they were headed in the right direction. But it also meant they were walking right into Aurelius' domain. She forced herself to keep moving when all she wanted to do was run back to the shuttle. They rounded a corner, and Michel stopped.

Jianna did the same.

A metal barrier blocked the corridor ahead, floor to ceiling. It was a temporary door inside a reinforced frame, thick seals running around the edges like surgical sutures, designed to prevent anything from leaking out.

They'd passed it before. Lucian had claimed this section was sealed off because of a hydraulic leak from micrometeorite damage.

"I should've come here earlier," she said. "I shouldn't have believed anything Aurelius said."

Michel glanced at her. "You couldn't have known."

But she had guessed. And ignored the feeling because she had been afraid of what he'd do if she disobeyed. When she'd searched other parts of the ship, it hadn't even occurred to her to search here.

Michel studied the barrier, his fingers tracing along the seam. He found a panel on the side, partially recessed into the wall. He flipped it open and examined it. Then he pressed on something inside the recessed compartment.

A snick. The barrier swung open.

She stared at him. "How did you know how to do that?"

"I read the specifications on the barrier. They're meant to be temporary in order to allow people in for repairs."

Of course, he had. He'd probably read every technical manual in the ship archives to prepare for their mission. Every specification, every schematic, every safety protocol. Somehow, he'd manage to cram every detail they needed into his head and keep it there. No wonder he looked so distracted every time they got to another intersection.

She was so grateful for him.

Michel reached into his pocket and pulled out a small device: a wand with protrusions extending from it, sensors on the ends like insect antennae. He turned it on, and a soft green glow emanated from the sensors as they came online.

"What is that?" Jianna asked.

"A chemosniffer. It detects a wide range of chemicals, including the ones that would be released by hydraulic leaks."

"But I thought—"

"Just because Aurelius is a liar doesn't mean we should walk in blind."

Right. Even if the supposed leak was a lie, Aurelius could have set any number of traps in order to prevent intruders from entering the area. The idea of it sent fresh adrenaline coursing through her system. They had no idea what lay beyond this barrier.

The sniffer buzzed, sampling the air beyond the barrier. Jianna watched the readout, numbers, and chemical abbreviations flowing past in steady streams. But she didn't know how to interpret the scrolling data.

Michel nodded, gestured to the hallway. "Let's go."

They stepped through the door. Michel closed it behind them, the seal hissing as it re-engaged. She would rather have left it open. But if one of the cyborgs saw it, their mission would be over before it began.

The corridor ahead didn't look any more damaged than the ones they'd passed through. In fact, it looked less damaged. The lights were brighter—barely flickering at all. The walls had none of the scorch marks or hull patches she'd expected to see. The ventilation was smooth, consistent, without the irregular rattles and coughs that plagued the rest of the ship.

However, the antiseptic smell was stronger, overlaying everything else like an olfactory signature of whatever work was being conducted here.

That meant they were definitely in the right place. Her dread deepened.

Michel led the way down the corridor, his eyes unfocusing periodically to try to remember the map. The chemosniffer waved gently in his hand, the sensors tasting the air for any trace of dangerous chemicals. He turned right at the next intersection.

"I can't believe you've got the path memorized."

He flushed. "It's no big deal."

"But it is, Michel. The complexity of what you've accomplished, memorizing not just the map, but teaching yourself the shuttle. It's amazing."

He shrugged. "I guess so."

He seemed uncomfortable with the praise, so she changed the topic. "How much farther?"

"We're in the right section. It should be one of the doors in this corridor or the next one over."

She nodded, her eyes glancing down at the chemosniffer's display. It remained steady. After a few more minutes, Michel tucked it back into his pocket and pulled out another small device. It looked like a modified scanner, its surface dotted with tiny ports and what appeared to be a miniature antenna array.

She didn't recognize it.

Maybe he'd built it himself?

They were approaching another intersection. Michel stopped again, held up a hand. "I can hear cyborgs."

She froze, listening. But she didn't hear anything.

They waited a minute, then he gestured. "They're gone. Come on."

She stared at him. How could he distinguish them from all the background noises that made up the mechanical heartbeat of the ship?

The lights were out in the next intersection, emergency lighting casting everything in shades of amber and rust. Conduits ran along the ceiling here, larger than in other sections, carrying power and data to whatever systems lay beyond.

Michel stopped again, tilting his head. "They're coming."

"Who?"

But he didn't answer. Instead, he grabbed her hand and ran, pulling her forward. Adrenaline spiked through her system. They reached the next intersection, and he yanked her around the corner. She pressed her back to the wall, slapping her free hand over her mouth to keep from making a sound. Her heartbeat pounded in her ears, so loud she was certain anyone nearby would hear it.

Then—footsteps. Mechanical. Precise. Cyborg.

This was it.

They were going to be captured, and if they were lucky, they would be killed, but more likely, Aurelius was going to turn them into nanite zombies like her father.

Two cyborgs appeared. They walked past the opening of their corridor.

Jianna held her breath.

Don't move.

Don't blink.

The cyborgs never even glanced their way. Just continued down the corridor with that eerie, mechanical gait, until their footsteps faded into the distance.

Michel's hand was warm in hers, the only solid thing in a world gone liquid with fear.

Michel leaned into her. "It's safe."

Jianna exhaled. "How did you know they were coming?"

"I heard them."

She frowned at him. She hadn't heard anything. Not until they were almost on top of them. But she didn't push it. They needed to keep moving.

Michel dropped her hand and headed off down the corridor the cyborgs had taken, stopping at the very first door they encountered. He tucked away the sensor and activated the control panel. The screen lit up—ripples on water drawn with amber dots, patterns changing and morphing, mesmerizing in their complexity.

He tapped it several times.

The door hissed open.

Inside were workbenches covered with electronic and mechanical components, most half-assembled, all in various stages of completion. Some kind of workshop.

"What do you think—"

"Making new parts for his crew," Michel said.

Jianna stepped inside and walked over to the nearest workbench. She picked up a component—it resembled Aurelius' artificial eye, but cruder, less sophisticated. Tiny scratches marred the lens, and the metal housing showed signs of wear that spoke of multiple disassemblies and rebuilds. Yet the engineering was undeniably brilliant, miniaturized circuits packed into impossibly small spaces, connections so fine they looked like metallic spiderwebs.

Part of her wanted to understand how it worked. The other part recoiled from holding something that had been ripped from someone's skull. "I guess the cyborgs get Aurelius' leftovers."

"No. The reverse, actually. They test the prototypes for his eventual upgrades."

"They're his guinea pigs?"

Michel grimaced. "Yeah."

She shuddered, setting the artificial eye back on the workbench. "Let's keep going."

They left that room, checking several more. All of them were for storage, packed with electronic or mechanical components. Circuit boards. Synthetic muscle fibers. Metal frameworks. All the raw materials for building and rebuilding cyborg bodies.

She hated this.

Aurelius' work wasn't research or medicine—it was an assembly line for his longevity. Every component, every upgrade, every modification served one purpose: keeping him alive and functional across centuries while his crew became disposable test subjects for whatever enhancement he wanted to try next.

Michel opened another door, and the stench rolled out.

Jianna gagged, slapping a hand over her nose and mouth.

She recognized that chemical smell—it was a synthetic growth medium used to grow new tissues. She'd smelled it before in controlled amounts, properly ventilated. This was concentrated, overwhelming.

She forced herself to step inside.

Tanks lined the walls. More than a dozen of them, ranging from small enough to hold an eyeball to large enough for a full torso. They were cylindrical, made of some kind of reinforced transparent material, each one sealed with a heavy metal lid where tubes and monitoring wires snaked in and out through sealed ports. Temperature gauges glowed on connected control panels, and the gentle bubbling of the mixture suggested oxygenation systems keeping the contents viable. Because floating in each one, suspended in transparent but cloudy gel, were body parts.

A liver. A spleen. Five kidneys in the same tank, clustered together like a grotesque bouquet. Half a brain—just the left hemisphere, the cut surface visible through the gel. An eyeball staring at nothing. A shoulder joint with part of an upper arm still attached. A lower jawbone with teeth growing from it in perfect rows.

The cloudiness in the gel was moving. Swirling patterns, as if something invisible was stirring the liquid.

Nanites. It had to be nanites, billions of them, doing something to the tissue.

Jianna stared at the brain, caught between scientific curiosity and visceral revulsion. What were they doing to those body parts? Building them? Repairing them? Improving them? Growing them? How many people had these organs come from? How many had been harvested while the donors were still alive?

Then she saw the walls.

Writing scrawled everywhere in different colored markers—green, red, blue, black. Some tiny and cramped into corners, others large and bold. Completely chaotic, no organization or logic to their placement.

"The Superman is the meaning of the earth," was written in red caps.

"Man is something to be surpassed. What have you done to surpass him?" was scrawled in cramped black script.

"Nature has placed mankind under the governance of two sovereign masters, pain and pleasure." The quote was then crossed out and rewritten with harsh strokes: *"Nature has placed mankind under the governance of one sovereign master: ME."*

"THE WEAK SHALL PERISH IT IS LAW OF NATURE" had been scratched into the metal, the letters gouged deep.

"Power is not a means; it is an end."

"If the doors of perception were cleansed everything would appear to man as it is, Infinite."

"We are survival machines – robot vehicles blindly programmed to preserve the selfish molecules known as genes."

"The superior man acts before he speaks and afterwards speaks according to his actions."

"I am become Death, the destroyer of worlds."

"God is dead. God remains dead. And we have killed him". The

word we had been crossed out, and a small *i* had been written above it.

"What is man? A miserable little pile of secrets."

"What is this?" Michel asked.

"Aurelius' internal monologue," she said. Obviously, it had leaked out during the centuries he spent traveling to DaVinci. A mind slowly unraveling, or maybe just revealing what it had always been underneath all that genius and charm.

"He's insane."

Jianna snorted. "We already knew that."

Michel gestured to her. "Come on."

They checked two more rooms—more storage—and then Michel opened a third. And stopped. Jianna peered over his shoulder.

Three Descendants lay strapped to cots, tubes and wires running from their bodies. Wires had been inserted directly into their heads, disappearing into drilled holes in their skulls. Dark crimson-brown stains soaked the bedding around each head.

Jianna inhaled.

Glint.

Their eyes opened, just slightly, and they turned their head, the movement sluggish, drugged. Then they trilled.

Michel bolted into the room, heading straight for their cot, unbuckling the straps holding Glint down. Then he started on the wires connected to their head.

Jianna stepped inside, spying a pile of empty cots against the far wall. They were all stained with blood. Her stomach dropped. How many Descendants had been through this room? How many had never made it off those tables?

Michel had Glint under control, so she headed for the second Descendant. This one had purple and indigo scales, patterns swirling across her skin. Jianna began undoing the straps that kept them contained. The Descendant's eyes fluttered but didn't fully open.

Jianna grabbed one of the wires and pulled. It resisted. She pulled harder, felt it slide free with a wet sound that made her want to vomit. Dark crimson blood oozed from the hole it left behind.

The Descendant whimpered.

"I'm sorry," Jianna whispered, leaning down. "I'm sorry, I'm sorry."

She pulled the rest of the wires free as gently as she could, but there was no gentle way to do this. Each one left behind a bleeding puncture. The tubes were worse—thicker, and when she eased them out, more blood followed.

The Descendant's breathing changed, became more labored, but finally she was finished.

"It's over," Jianna said, meeting the Descendant's unfocused gaze. "You're safe now. We're getting you out of here."

She helped the Descendant upright, supporting her weight.

Then she glanced over at Michel. He and Glint were freeing the third Descendant together.

Jianna scanned the lab. A terminal sat on a counter near the far wall. She remembered what Willow had told her about Mitra Kunde's research, something hidden that Aurelius never found. She'd been meaning to look for it since that conversation. This might be her only chance.

She propped the Descendant against the cot. "I'll be right back."

They nodded, and she crossed to the terminal, punched in the login Aurelius had given her for the other lab. The screen lit up. Access granted. That surprised her.

Why hadn't he shut off her access?

Because he thought he could control her. She gritted her teeth, not caring that he'd be able to track her login. Let him know. Let him come.

She searched the archives: *Mitra Kunde.*

Files appeared. Research papers, lab notes, and genetic sequences. Files and files and more files. She transferred everything to her comm, watching the progress bar crawl across the screen.

Whatever was in here, it had better be worth trading the Divine Blueprint for.

The transfer completed.

Jianna shoved the comm back into her pocket and turned back to the Descendant—

And saw the freezer.

It was on the far wall, industrial-grade with a heavy handle. That sick feeling returned, worse than before. Something terrible had to be inside. And she had a feeling she knew what it was.

And she needed to see it.

She walked over to it, reached for the handle, and turned it.

It gave.

She hesitated.

Then she pulled it open.

The door swung open with a pneumatic hiss, and frigid air rolled out, hitting her face. The smell that came with it was full of antiseptic and death. Decay.

Descendant bodies were stacked on either side of the freezer. Two piles on the floor, five high. Their heads had been cut open—crude, brutal incisions that exposed brain matter that had now frozen solid. Ice crystals clung to their scaled skin, turning vibrant colors dull and lifeless.

Her stomach flipped. Bile surged up her throat,

flooding her mouth, scalding and sour, burning her nose as it forced its way out. She bent forward, hands on her knees. Strings of acid hit the floor. The smell of it mixed with the freezer's sharp, chemical cold, clawing at the back of her tongue.

Her whole body seized. She gagged again, harder, her ribs aching with the force of it. Her eyes watered. Her vision blurred. She squeezed her eyes shut, but the image of their bodies stayed in her head, their skulls cracked open, frozen brains, frosted scales.

She inhaled, tried to breathe, the taste of bile lingering, thick and bitter. She opened her eyes, made herself look again.

This is what Aurelius was.

She would never forget.

Now she was going to have to tell the Elder she'd failed to bring her people home.

She straightened, wiping her mouth.

A sense of purpose clarified. She was going to do anything she could to stop Aurelius. Whatever it took. No line she wouldn't cross, no risk too great. Even if it meant her own life.

She yanked the door closed and stepped back, nearly colliding with Michel. He reached out to steady her.

"What was in the freezer?"

She didn't want to tell him not to. It would devastate him to see what Aurelius had done to them. But he needed to understand that his hero was a monster once and for all. Michel had defended Aurelius, made excuses for him, talked about his genius and vision, while Jianna had searched for the missing Descendants, uncovering the truth, bearing the weight of each horrible discovery.

She was exhausted. She could no longer carry it alone.

He reached for the handle. She turned her head away.

The door swung open. Cold air rushed out yet again, carrying the smell of death and antiseptic.

Michel stilled. His face drained of color. Behind him, Glint let out a keening wail that seemed to come from somewhere deep in their chest, a sound of grief so raw it brought tears to Jianna's eyes.

Glint knew.

Michel closed the door.

There was silence between them.

Until finally, he broke it. "We have to find Lucas."

"Michel—"

"We have to find Lucas." Something had changed in him. He now sounded cold and determined. "We can't win without him."

Jianna nodded, heading for the door. Michel helped Glint while the other two supported one another.

She stepped out first, holding the door open for the others.

And came face to face with a cyborg.

Chapter Twenty

WILLOW PUSHED through the restaurant's glass doors, respirator already sealed to her face.

Despite that, the smell of butter and wine, roasted meat, and something sweet underneath, hit her taste buds. Her stomach lurched, rebelling against the assault of aromas. She was still having trouble figuring out if it was hormones or the prospect of what lay ahead that was making her feel so nauseous lately.

Mother Basu, give me strength.

She inhaled. Her being here wasn't about her. It was about The Divine Blueprint. Her responsibility. She hated having to pretend Aurelius was in any way a reasonable sort of man, but she was willing to do it. For the baby growing inside her. For the future.

She walked up to the maître d' at the host station. The woman didn't greet Willow. She didn't even ask her name. She simply knew who she was. Without a word, she turned and walked into the restaurant.

Willow knew she was supposed to follow.

And much as it might gall her, she did.

The restaurant was curated to perfection: cream-washed walls broken by vertical slats of pale oak, gold trim catching the light in thin, deliberate lines. Pendant fixtures hung in staggered tiers above the tables.

It was beautiful.

And dead.

At this hour, the place should be full of wealthy Vitruvians lingering over coffee and wine and dessert, the air thick with conversation and laughter. Instead, the whole place was holding its breath. There wasn't anyone here. Just empty tables and chairs. The only sound was Willow's respirator.

Did Aurelius get the wealthy ones first?

She followed the maître d' deeper into the restaurant.

Along the far wall, a row of servers stood motionless, staring at…nothing. Six of them lined up like soldiers awaiting orders that were never coming. She faltered, recognizing two of them—people she knew from Council events held here before Aurelius arrived. One was a woman who always remembered that Willow preferred water over wine and would bring it without being asked. She always had a warm smile and would ask how she was enjoying the evening.

Now she stood like a statue, eyes fixed on the far wall, face blank as unmarked paper. No recognition. No warmth. Nothing.

Willow looked away, her throat constricting. She burped, swallowed, and wished she could control the nausea. Maybe she should talk to Camilla about it.

The maître d' stopped. So did Willow.

And there he was.

Aurelius sat in the center of the room, his table covered with plates. Some had been abandoned mid-course; others were stacked on top of them as if a new round had arrived before the previous one was even touched.

There was seared foie gras with fig compote, the liver barely touched, already congealing into an unappetizing mass. Wagyu beef tartare with a perfect quail egg perched on top, half of it eaten and abandoned, the raw meat darkening at the edges. Butter-poached lobster tail in champagne sauce, one bite missing, the rest growing cold. Black truffle risotto that had been stirred but not consumed, the expensive fungi now cold and gummy.

She scanned the other dishes.

Grilled octopus with harissa and preserved lemon, the tentacles curled and glossy, untouched except for a single exploratory cut. A delicate sashimi arrangement, the fish already warming on its chilled plate, its translucence turning cloudy in the ambient temperature.

Her stomach dropped when she spotted the pan-seared duck breast with cherry reduction. She'd secretly loved that dish at Council dinners, a guilty pleasure she never admitted to anyone. Now the sight of it, half-eaten on Aurelius' table, ruined it forever. The memory of how it tasted turned bitter in her mouth.

More dishes crowded the table: glossy slices of citrus-glazed fowl, the skin lacquered to a mirror shine and decorated with black olives. A bowl of spiced broth emitting delicate spirals of steam, perfuming the air with heat and cloves. A platter of grains molded into perfect geometric shapes, half-collapsed where he'd prodded them once and lost interest. Thin ribbons of cured fish draped over chilled ceramic, beading with condensation that trickled slowly to the edge of the plate. A dessert plate arranged with crystallized star-fruit petals surrounding a quenelle of citrus sorbet, the surface already softening in the warm room, droplets forming like sweat.

Nothing was finished.

Most hadn't even been sampled.

The smell of it slid past the filters in her mask, mingling together—rich, fatty, sweet, acidic—layered into a heavy, clinging fog that coated the back of her throat, making her feel nauseous.

A waitress approached carrying a shallow bowl of braised root ribbons, the vegetables curled like soft shells in a broth that shimmered with oil. She eased it onto the table with slow, measured movements, her gaze fixed in the same dead, obedient stare as all of the others. She placed the bowl on top of the octopus, then stepped back, awaiting the next command.

Aurelius didn't look up as Willow approached. Instead, he picked up a piece of the lobster, dipping it in the melted butter, and popped it in his mouth. He chewed slowly, his eyes fixed on the table. Then he swallowed and wiped his fingers on the white tablecloth.

He waved a hand in her direction. "Try anything you want. Or order something else. The staff will make anything you request. However, it may take a little longer if they have to go buy the ingredients."

She curled her lip.

He lounged amid the wreckage of dishes like a king in a conquered hall, while the staff lined the perimeter. She knew what he was doing.

He was trying to show her that everything here belonged to him—the food, the restaurant, the people standing frozen along the walls like mannequins. All his. A casual display of power meant to intimidate her.

But she was not about to let that happen.

Willow took the seat across from him, grateful the respirator hid the lower half of her face, and he couldn't see how disgusted she was with him. She didn't bother to pull her chair in. She wasn't staying long.

The mask was a shield, a barrier between her true feelings and the performance she needed to give. She forced a pleasant expression into her eyes, the way she had learned to do in countless Council sessions where she had been obligated to smile and nod while listening to proposals that made her skin crawl.

"Thank you for meeting me," she said.

Aurelius finally looked up at her, tossing aside a chunk of cured fish. He licked his fingers, then wiped them once again on the tablecloth. Then he smiled.

That look had probably worked on thousands of people over hundreds of years. Maybe he practiced it in the mirror. It might look perfect, but it was completely devoid of genuine warmth.

"Anything for family."

She resisted the urge to grimace.

More than anything, she wanted to correct him. The word felt dirty. They weren't family. The connection was tenuous at best, and she hated the implication. But she needed his favor, so she let the claim stand and swallowed her pride like it was bitter medicine.

"I've decided to accept your offer."

She removed a folded piece of paper from her tunic pocket. It was a list of supplies she needed to found the new settlement. Everything from tools, seed stock, water purifiers, medical kits, insulation panels, and food. Everything a new settlement would need to stand on its own.

She held it out to Aurelius.

At first, he didn't move. He just sat there, watching her extended arm with lazy amusement. Then he lifted his hand—palm angled open—waiting for her to deliver the paper.

She didn't want to do that. She wanted him to come to her.

He waited, his fingers remaining splayed, expectant. The silence stretched between them, thick with an unspoken challenge. Who was going to move first?

Willow cursed him silently.

She needed those supplies more than she needed her dignity. So she leaned forward, extending her arm over the plates, her sleeve brushing the congealing sauce of the abandoned duck.

He plucked the paper from her fingers, opened it up, and then started reading. He looked amused by it, like she was a child presenting him with a crayon drawing she'd made in school. "Take off your mask so you can eat."

Willow stared at him.

No way was she going unmasked in his presence. Not now that she knew he could infect her with nanites through a breath, turn her into one of those frozen statues along the wall with a single exhalation.

"I'm good."

A flash of annoyance crossed his face, and she felt a slight jolt of victory. Good. She'd gotten under his skin. He finished reading and set the paper aside, then leaned back in the chair, studying her.

"What changed your mind?"

She'd prepared for this question during the walk over, rehearsing her words until they sounded natural. "I thought it over and decided you were right. While you remake Vitruvia City in your own image, I'll pursue Mother Basu's—"

Aurelius snorted. Rolled his eyes at her name.

"—legacy," Willow said, as if he hadn't reacted. "And

once we're both more established, we can figure out how to work together."

Aurelius waved his hand, and the waitress exited. Then he picked up an olive from the citrus chicken and popped it in his mouth. He chewed, watching her the whole time. The pit clicked against his molars. "Bullshit."

Her mouth dropped open.

He spat out the pit. It hit one of the plates and ricocheted onto the floor. "You finally got your hands on your own personal holy grail, and you're hotfooting it out of here." He swallowed, reaching for another olive, his fingers glistening with oil. "You're welcome, by the way."

Willow clenched her hands into fists in her lap. The idea of thanking him for telling her how to find the Divine Blueprint grated on every nerve in her body. It made her furious that she owed him for her birthright. Now that the Divine Blueprint was safe in her womb, she wanted nothing more than to get as far from this monster as possible. She bit back her rage, forcing herself to incline her head in acknowledgment. "I appreciate you pointing me in the right direction."

He spat out another pit. "And?"

He wanted more. He always wanted more.

Willow swallowed the sour taste of pride yet again. "And now I would like to give my people a fresh start, away from your... disagreement with the Vitruvians."

Aurelius laughed, and he sounded genuinely amused, which somehow made it worse. The sound echoed through the empty restaurant, and she was actually grateful it was empty, so no one would think they were actually civil.

"No disagreement here."

The waitress reappeared, carrying another plate: seared scallops resting on a ribbon of pea-mint purée, tiny drops of chili oil spaced around the edge in a perfect ring.

Before she had even set it down, Aurelius plucked a scallop off the plate and took a bite. He chewed, swallowed, then tossed the half-eaten piece onto the plate of grains.

"Next course. And tell the chef he can do better."

The waitress nodded. "I will tell the chef he can do better. I'm sorry, Master Aurelius."

She departed for the kitchen, her pace jerky and wooden.

Master?

More evidence of his ego. As if she needed any. Narcissism, probably clinical. She gestured to the motionless staff along the wall. "Can the chef even do better? Your nanites seem to interfere significantly with their mental function."

Aurelius shrugged, reaching for lobster. "I haven't infected the chef or his sous-chefs. Only the waitstaff."

Willow eyed all the plates again. Such a waste.

"And he was happy to cook all this for you after you did that?"

Aurelius smiled wider, and it seemed to grow even more predatory. "He was. And he'd still better be happy to cook for me."

"You mean he had no choice, otherwise you'd use nanites on him as well."

Aurelius shrugged. "I also offered not to inoculate his family."

She swallowed her rage. "You're clearly busy. I don't want to take up more of your time." She got to her feet. "I hope that you'll show that same generosity to my people. How long before—"

"No."

Willow frowned. "If you truly believe that what you're offering us will be irresistible, you have nothing to lose in the long term."

Aurelius shook his head. "But in the short term, I'll be giving you a significant portion of the food that the city needs for the winter. Far more than you and your people would consume if you stayed."

"But it's not like you have to worry about hungry people rebelling." She let a hint of acid into her voice; she couldn't help it. "You're literally in control of their every movement."

Aurelius pressed his fingertips together and rested his elbows on the table. "Sit down."

She hesitated. What if she refused? He'd send one of the staff to make her? Or have a clone track her down? Force her to take the nanites?

"Now."

She did so.

"Tell me something Mitra wrote about me. In her journals."

Willow stared at him.

So this was why he agreed to meet her. Not to negotiate about practical matters of food supplies and colonial logistics. He wanted validation from a dead woman, delivered through Willow's mouth. The pathetic need behind the request made her skin crawl.

The waitress returned with yet another dish. This one was a shallow bowl of slow-braised lamb in a dark, aromatic sauce made of smoked pepper, cumin, and cloves.

She set it down on top of the lobster, then departed.

Aurelius dug around in the thick sauce with his fingers, fishing for a morsel of meat. Then he looked up at her. "I'm listening."

Willow ignored his request. "You offered me a deal to leave, so I'm taking the deal."

She wasn't about to feed his ego and tell him what

Mitra wrote. The journals were private, sacred, the final thoughts of a woman who'd suffered far too much at his hands. Willow would die before she'd turn those pages into entertainment for him.

Aurelius sighed, wiping his fingers clean. "You know the hardest thing about being the smartest, most powerful man in the room?"

She didn't respond. Nor did he wait for an answer.

"It's the paradox of supremacy. Once you've got it, it becomes meaningless. Because it's so obvious, no one can deny it. Recognition becomes meaningless."

Willow stared at him.

The man was mad.

Mother Basu had dealt with sane people. Her playbook provided nothing for this situation. All the wisdom passed down through generations, all the strategies for dealing with people, were useless with him. They assumed a basic level of human rationality that simply didn't exist here.

She leaned back in her chair. "It's the tyrant's dilemma, isn't it? Once you have all the power, there's no one who can give you validation. You can make them say the words, but they'll never satisfy you, because they had to say them."

Something flicked in Aurelius' eyes. Recognition. Hunger.

He leaned forward, his voice dropping. "That's why I need you here. You understand me. Just like she did."

Willow touched her belly. The gesture was almost unconscious, subtle. But he caught it nonetheless, his mouth turning up in the corner.

This was a mistake.

She should have just taken what she could from the Sanctum's stores and left with a few dozen people. It would have been days before Aurelius noticed she was gone, maybe weeks.

She'd had too much hubris, coming here thinking she could negotiate, thinking she could manipulate him into giving her what she needed. Now she was here, in his domain, surrounded by his puppets, and he was looking at her like she was something he wanted to keep.

She swallowed. She'd never been in this much danger before. Not even during the worst of the sporestorms. Not during the food shortages. Or droughts.

If she didn't push back hard enough, he'd get bored with her and infect her with nanites to keep her from causing trouble. But if she pushed back too hard, he might do the same out of spite—make her his plaything, his puppet, a controllable version of the woman who'd escaped him centuries ago.

She fixed her eyes on his face. "If you want my agreement to mean anything, you can't turn the swarm on me."

Aurelius tilted his head, the way a cat did when considering a mouse before deciding whether to play with it or simply kill it. "But I can bring your people over to my side any time I want. A few at a time, maybe." His voice was light, almost playful. "Let's see how fast the rest turn on you when they realize you're powerless to protect them."

Willow straightened her spine. She would not cower. She would not give him the satisfaction of seeing her break. "You locked Mitra in a psych ward for the rest of her life. She died hating you."

She studied his face, looking for any sign that she'd hurt him, but he gave nothing. His face remained as placid as still water.

"If I'm so much like her," she said, "what makes you think I'll be any different?"

Aurelius shrugged. He looked utterly unconcerned, as if they were discussing the weather. "If I'm wrong, I'll just make another you and try again. After all, I've got eternity to figure it out."

Make another you.

He would use her DNA to create a copy of herself—a soulless duplicate, stripped of everything that made her her—and try to break that version instead. And if that one didn't bend, he'd make another. And another. And another. An endless parade of Willows, each one tortured until one finally gave him what he wanted.

It was obscene.

Willow controlled her breathing, digging her fingernails into her thighs. The pain helped center her. She would not give him the satisfaction of seeing her crack. Another wave of nausea swept through her, bile wanting to crawl up her throat.

She swallowed hard, fighting to keep control, making sure her voice was steady. "You ruined your own colony, and now you've come here to ruin ours."

Aurelius waved his hand as if five hundred years of suffering meant nothing to him. "You're like children, playing at building a civilization. But you've made almost no progress in half a millennium. Not in the fields that matter."

Willow studied him. She had wondered if Aurelius' coming might be part of the divine plan—hastening the end of the Vitruvians, making room for the Naturalists to thrive. She'd taken comfort in that thought, wrapped herself in it like a blanket against the cold reality of his power. The idea that perhaps Mother Basu's prophecies were unfolding exactly as they should, that even this monster served a purpose in the greater design.

But now? Sitting across from him, watching him destroy lives?

It didn't seem possible.

But she owed it to Mother Basu to have faith. "I'm not afraid of you. Men like you never last."

Aurelius showed his teeth. "Actually, now that I've had certain of my parts augmented—"

Willow had heard enough.

She shoved back from the table, the chair legs scraping against the floor with a harsh screech, and turned around and collided with the waitress.

The platter of Coq au vin went flying. Chicken braised in red wine, mushrooms, and pearl onions nestled in a glossy burgundy sauce, splattered across Willow. The sauce was thick and warm against her skin, soaking through the fabric and spreading across her chest and sleeves. The wine stained the pale cloth of her tunic, marking her like blood. The smell overwhelmed her: wine, garlic, and rendered fat.

Willow recoiled, flicking away the sauce. Had the waitress blocked Willow's exit on purpose? Had Aurelius sent an unspoken command through his nanites? Willow didn't know, and she didn't wait to find out.

She walked around the frozen waitress, who was now staring down at the mess with dead eyes. She seemed confused as to why the food was now on the floor.

As Willow made her way to the exit, she heard the waitress speak, "Please forgive me, Master Aurelius."

Aurelius said, "Knees."

Willow ran, not looking back. She didn't want to know what that meant. Or see what punishment he was about to inflict on someone whose only crime was being in the wrong place at the wrong time.

She fled the restaurant, bursting out onto the street, letting the door slam closed behind her. Only then did she slow, gulping down the cool, clean night air. It was late, nearly eleven. The streets should be quiet, emptying out, with the last diners heading home, couples saying goodnight, the city settling into sleep.

But the streets were not empty.

Dozens of people walked along the sidewalks. But no one was talking. Or laughing. Or lingering outside bars. No groups of friends were clustered together, saying prolonged goodbyes. Everyone walked alone, silent as if on a mission they didn't choose, following instructions only they could hear.

Most of them had that dead-eyed look.

Two cyborgs stood on the corner. She froze. Had Aurelius sent them after her? But they didn't approach. They just watched.

But then the nearest person stopped walking and turned to look at Willow.

Then the next one. And the next.

A ripple spreading outward from where she stood—one by one, every person in the street ceased their silent march and turned. Dead eyes, blank faces, all fixed on her.

Not one of them spoke.

Not one of them neared.

They just watched her.

Willow broke into a run.

The watchers didn't follow. They just tracked her with their eyes as she fled down the street. Every time she rounded a corner, a new wall of silent figures came into view—walking, then stopping mid-stride as if frozen in time, heads snapping toward her with that same blank, telegraphed precision.

She cut across a small plaza. A group of teenagers

stood near the fountain. They rotated toward her in unison.

She veered into a narrower street, hoping fewer people meant fewer eyes, but the opposite was true. Every person she met turned to face her the instant she entered their line of sight. A woman walking a dog stared as Willow passed. A man halfway through locking his bicycle remained bent over the frame, key in the lock, head twisted toward her at an angle that should have hurt.

Her breath turned ragged, rasping in the mask. They were acting like a hive. A hive wearing human skin.

She cut down an alley, pushing past crates. She thought she'd found a pocket of emptiness, but when she emerged on the other side, two men stopped and stared, their faces blank.

She continued on. The sauce on her robes was starting to dry, making the fabric stiff and uncomfortable against her skin. The smell clung to her, following her like a cloud. She'd gone to the restaurant thinking she could manipulate Aurelius. Thinking she was clever enough, strong enough, faithful enough to outwit a man who'd had centuries to perfect his cruelty.

She left knowing she had failed.

He was not sane. His narcissism, his sociopathy—she could see it clearly now, could name it, could diagnose it, and it did her absolutely no good. There was no lever she could pull, no angle she could work. He didn't want things she could give him. He wanted things she would rather die than surrender.

There was nowhere to run.

The whole city was already his.

Even the Naturalist Quarter wouldn't be safe, not really, not for long. She wouldn't make it to the other side of the continent either, not with every citizen in Vitruvia capable of becoming his eyes and ears.

She needed to find a way to disappear completely.

For the sake of the Divine Blueprint.

By the time she reached the gates of the Naturalist Quarter, the watchers had disappeared. Or at least she could no longer see them. But she didn't delude herself. Aurelius was probably still watching.

What if he'd already infected someone in her community, ordering them to act natural? Anyone could be compromised. Anyone could be a doorway he'd already stepped through, controlling their mind while they went about their daily routine, tending the gardens, preparing the meals, offering comfort. She'd been worried about him arriving here. But what if he'd already come?

Mother Basu, what do I do now?

There was no answer.

Chapter Twenty-One

MICHEL GRABBED Jianna's arm and yanked her backward, bolting forward to get between her and the cyborg. It didn't move. Not at first. The dead eyes focused on him. This one was female, he realized. Her mechanical components gleamed like wet bone under the lights.

His heart slammed against his ribs. Blood roared in his ears.

For a moment, nothing happened. The cyborg simply assessed him. Then she lunged, grabbing for him. The movement was sudden, explosive, a blur of metal and pale flesh. Michel twisted sideways on instinct alone, nearly tripping over one of the cots. Her fingers snapped closed on empty air where his shoulder had been seconds earlier.

A flash of childhood memory hit him: small, cornered, the Reyes brothers trapping him in a corner, fists balled, laughing when he froze. He'd learned to survive by dodging, evading, and making himself a difficult target.

He did that now, slipping out of her grasp.

The cyborg's arm retracted, then she punched. Michel

backpedaled. Her fist slammed into the bulkhead behind him.

CRACK.

Michel stared at the spiderweb of fractures racing across the metal like frost forming in real time. That could've been his skull. His ribs. His spine. A single hit and he would've folded.

No time. Move.

She swung again. He dove under the blow, feeling the displaced air whip through his hair.

"Find Lucas!" Michel yelled. "GO!"

Jianna hesitated. He saw it in her, the instinct to stay, to help, but then the cyborg punched at him again, forcing Michel sideways and breaking his line of sight. Seconds later, he heard footsteps retreating. Good. She was leaving.

He had to trust she'd make it, that she wouldn't run into any other cyborgs. He had no other choice because he needed to deal with this one.

If she alerted Aurelius or the others, then they would really be in trouble.

Michel vaulted behind one of the cots, nearly tipping it. He grabbed the taser from his pocket, his breathing tight and fast. The cyborg advanced, but she was slow. Right. Aurelius designed them for power, not speed, and the nanites further dampened their reactions. But she was relentless.

He jabbed toward her torso. She stepped back. He circled left, feinted, lunged—she swatted his arm aside.

He bellowed, pain lancing up his arm.

He might as well have been struck by a metal baton.

But he couldn't give up now.

The taser needed contact, but she refused to give him an opening. She was herding him, forcing him toward the narrow aisle between two cots.

He had to commit, had to close the distance even though every instinct screamed at him to stay out of reach.

Michel lunged again.

She swept her arm down and caught the taser mid-strike. It spun out of his grip and skittered across the floor, vanishing beneath a cot with a hollow metallic rattle.

Michel scrambled back, lungs burning. Enough of this. He reached for the EMP device in his pocket. It was his and Jianna's insurance plan. They had discussed the possibility of encountering cyborgs when they were preparing for this mission.

For it to work, he had to physically attach it to the cyborg's metal components. Which meant he had to get even closer than he needed to for the taser. He tried to circle in, looking for an angle of attack.

But the cyborg tracked him, keeping herself at a distance. Every time he stepped forward, she stepped back. When he tried to circle around her left side, she turned to face him. When he moved right, she pivoted to keep him in front of her.

He was getting tired. His lungs were burning, and his vision was starting to gray at the edges. The cyborg grabbed for his throat. Michel jerked backward, boots sliding on the deck. She overextended, exposing her shoulder. He lunged forward and swung the EMP device toward the metal joint where her arm connected to her torso. His fingertips brushed the metal. She pivoted, and the EMP slipped past her shoulder by inches.

He stumbled, arms windmilling, fighting to stay upright. His hand caught the edge of a medical cart. He steadied himself, circling away from her grasping fingers.

He darted low. If he could attach it to her back, to her spine—

But she whirled around faster than he expected. She lunged at him again. He retreated.

Michel was exhausted now. He was having trouble staying upright.

In order to attach the EMP, he had to let her get close enough to grab him. His instincts were screaming— behaving like that was exactly what had gotten him beaten up as a kid. Standing his ground instead of running.

But even if he had wanted to, there was nowhere to run. He was now trapped between equipment carts and examination tables.

The cyborg lunged for him, closing the distance between them in two quick steps. Her hands were like claws, fingers extended to grab his throat.

And against all sense, Michel stepped INTO the lunge instead of away from it. As soon as she reached him, he dropped to his knees, sliding forward, his palm slapping the EMP against her metal abdomen.

He hit the discharge button.

WHOMP.

The pulse exploded outward, a wave of electromagnetic energy that Michel felt in his teeth and bones. Then came the sizzling crackle as circuits fried throughout her body. Sparks erupted from every joint, her optical implants, the seams where flesh met metal, showering him in hot pinpricks of light.

Her face contorted. Synthetic muscles pulled her features into an expression that looked horribly like pain.

Her arm snapped back like a released spring. Michel saw it coming—too late. She punched his chest, crushing the air from his lungs. The impact sent him flying backward.

His back hit the deck with a bone-jarring crash. He slid across the plating, his shirt riding up, skin scraping against the floor. Fire spread across his ribs where her fist had connected. Each breath sent sharp spikes of pain through his chest.

If he were lucky, he'd only be bruised.

The cyborg swayed, sparks cascading from her joints like a broken fountain. She toppled forward, a massive weight crashing down.

He rolled sideways, the cyborg's body slamming into the floor where he'd rested a heartbeat before.

BANG.

The impact shook the entire room, vibrating up through the deck and into Michel's bones.

Then silence.

He heard someone gasping for breath. Was it her? No, it was him. He lay back, staring up at the ceiling panels. He almost couldn't process what had happened. If he had failed, he would be dead.

But his EMP had actually worked. He had built it himself, copying Kennedy's design, and it had brought down a cyborg.

He pushed himself up, wincing at the fire shooting through his ribs. Then he looked down at the cyborg. She was still twitching. Sparks arced across her metal joints in irregular bursts, casting dancing shadows on the walls. Her face was frozen in that expression of pain. Her optical implants had gone dark.

He felt bad. She hadn't asked to serve Aurelius. None of them had. She had been human once, before he carved out everything that mattered and left behind this shell. Someone's daughter, maybe. Someone's sister. Or wife. Now, just another tool in his arsenal of stolen souls.

But he couldn't think about that now. He had to find –

"Michel!"

Jianna!

She was close by. He spotted his taser and scooped it up, then staggered to the door and out into the corridor. He tried to run, but his legs felt like they belonged to someone else. It was more of a stumbling jog, his ribs protesting with sharp stabs of pain every time he took a step.

He rounded the corner and saw an open doorway ahead, warm light spilling out into the hallway. He stopped at the entrance.

The room was a lab, but nothing like the organ-growing room with its tanks of floating body parts. This place looked like a mechanic's workshop crossed with a field hospital. The equipment here was old, patched together. Like everywhere else on the ship, it looked like it had been repaired countless times. Cables were held together with electrical tape. Monitors were propped up on brackets that didn't quite fit, their screens flickering with unstable power. The smell of old solder and burnt circuits hung thick in the recycled air.

Jianna stood in the center of the room. The three Descendants huddled behind her. And on a table in the middle of it all—

Lucas.

Michel froze. The android lay on the metal examination table, fully assembled but motionless. Wires and cables ran from his body to multiple machines. Equipment hummed around him, screens displaying scrolling data. Lucas' eyes were open but unfocused—staring up at the ceiling.

Lucian must have been running diagnostic tests on him.

Jianna gestured to the connections. "I didn't know if disconnecting him would damage him."

Michel walked over, holding his ribs, studying the

spaghetti-tangle of wires. He had no idea what any of this did. Pulling them out could damage Lucas, permanently destroying the one ally capable of helping them defeat Aurelius.

But he had no time to decipher the equipment. At any moment, more cyborgs might come. Maybe even Lucian or Aurelius himself.

"If it damages him, it damages him," Michel said.

He set the taser down and reached for the first connection and pulled.

Click.

Lucas's eyes focused, and his head turned toward Michel. "That was... inadvisable." His voice was slow, distorted, staticky, like an old recording played through damaged speakers.

But at least he was talking. He was aware.

"Sorry," Michel said. "We have no choice."

And he kept disconnecting, one wire, then another. With each connection he removed, the static faded.

And then he pulled the last wire.

Lucas sat, turning to the Descendants. He signed something Michel couldn't interpret. He figured it must be an apology of some sort, given how urgently he was communicating.

Glint responded with a trill, a series of clicks. The other two Descendants watched, too weak to respond, but their eyes were fixed on Lucas.

Glint trilled again, softer this time. Something that might be forgiveness. Or acknowledgement. Michel couldn't tell.

He gestured to them. "We have to get the Descendants home. And then we're taking Aurelius down."

Lucas turned to look at him. Really looked, his eyes

assessing Michel in a way that made him feel weighed and measured.

"That is an excellent plan."

His voice was completely normal now. "You will need my help."

It wasn't a question. It was a statement of fact.

Michel nodded, picking up his taser. "Let's go."

He led the way into the corridor, letting Lucas take point—after all, he knew this ship better than anyone. Knew its dangers, especially where the other cyborgs might be. Jianna supported Glint, whose steps were unsteady. The Descendants leaned on each other, barely able to walk.

Michel brought up the rear.

They passed the room the Descendants had been in. The cyborg still lay on the floor. Michel tightened his grip around the taser. His other hand went to his pocket. The other three EMP devices were still there. They were small comfort, but comfort, nonetheless.

The corridors were quiet. Too quiet. No alarms, no sounds of approaching cyborgs, nothing but the distant hum of the ship's life support systems.

He didn't know if that was good or bad. The cyborgs communicated wirelessly through their nanites. Any alarm could be silent, invisible, transmitted directly into their minds. Or maybe—maybe—no one had noticed yet. Maybe Aurelius was still on the surface, still sleeping, still unaware.

He didn't know which possibility frightened him more.

Michel looked down at the taser.

His hand was trembling. A fine, constant shake he couldn't control. He tried to steady it, willed his fingers to stop moving.

They didn't cooperate.

The adrenaline was crashing out of his system. His body was betraying him, showing the fear he'd been pushing down since they stepped onto this ship.

They'd done it.

And then he froze.

Wait a minute.

Aurelius could take control of Michel's nanites at any moment. He could turn Michel against the others. Use him to stop the escape. Jianna didn't know about the nanites in his brain. She didn't know he was already compromised, already a potential weapon waiting to be activated against her.

He swore. Wishing he had told her earlier. But no. She probably wouldn't have let him come. And then she'd be dead on the floor at the hands of that cyborg.

He kept walking.

His gaze drifted to Lucas. He caught the android's face in profile, illuminated by the flickering emergency lights.

There was something different about Lucas' expression now. It was subtle. Almost imperceptible. A slight adjustment of his features, a tightening around the eyes, a set to the jaw that wasn't there before.

In a human, Michel would have interpreted that expression as anger.

No. Not anger.

Rage.

Michel was glad it wasn't pointed at him.

Chapter Twenty-Two

GLINT COLLAPSED.

Jianna tried to grab them. But the Descendant was heavier than they looked and it was like being hit by a falling tree. The impact drove all the air from Jianna's lungs, spinning her sideways. Her back hit the wall, the impact sending a shock of pain down her spine.

Her teeth clacked together, and she bit her tongue.

She lay there, stunned. Then she roused herself and scrambled over to Glint, looking for a pulse. They still had one, it was just weak.

"Michel!"

He was there in an instant, crouching beside them. Then he slid his arms under Glint's shoulders and knees, hoisting her up, settling her across his shoulders in a fireman's carry. Blood from the surgical sites had dried in dark streaks down her neck. Jianna looked away and noticed they were one short.

"Where's Lucas?" she peered into the darkness.

Michel shifted Glint's position. "Don't know."

A distant crash echoed in the corridor behind them—metal against metal. Jianna's blood ran cold.

What was that?

"Go," Michel said, jerking his chin toward the two other Descendants who stood swaying nearby. "Take them. I'll be right behind you."

She nodded, grabbing hold of the one with the purple scales. She was still unsteady from whatever drugs were in her system. The green-scaled Descendant was doing better. But only slightly.

Another crash reverberated behind them, closer this time. Jianna felt the vibration through the deck plates.

"Faster," Jianna said.

She hated telling them that. Despite the pain they must be in, they didn't complain. They just obliged.

Right when she thought she was going to collapse, the docking bay doors appeared ahead. She had never been more pleased to see massive slabs of reinforced metal.

She hit the control panel and entered.

The lights were still out, and the darkness of the docking bay swallowed them. Jianna hurried across the familiar expanse, supporting the purple-scaled Descendant's weight, heading toward the shuttle. She probably should have stopped and searched for cyborgs, but she hadn't wanted to waste time. She glanced at the shadows between what little light there was, searching for the enemy. Every dark corner was a potential hiding place.

The shuttle had never looked so near and far at the same time. Each step felt like it took forever. And then they arrived. The three of them stumbled up the ramp and into the cabin.

Jianna guided the one with the purplish scales to the nearest seat, and she collapsed. Her scales were hot to the touch, fever-bright, and her breathing was shallow and rapid.

"Easy," Jianna said, strapping her in. The Descendant's head lolled against the headrest, her eyes struggling to focus.

The green-scaled Descendant managed to lower herself into the adjacent seat, and Jianna got her belted in.

Then Michel arrived with Glint. Sweat ran down his face, and his breathing was labored. He stepped down the aisle, lowering Glint into the seat directly across from the purple-scaled Descendant. Then he headed for the cockpit while Jianna got them secured.

She heard the engines start. Then made her way to the open door, peering out into the dark bay.

Where was Lucas?

She strained to hear anything over the growing hum of the shuttle's engines. The seconds stretched into what felt like hours. The darkness of the bay pressed in around the open hatch.

Was something watching from the shadows?

Had they grabbed Lucas? Dragged him back to the lab, strapped him down on that table again so that Lucian could run more tests or dismember him altogether?

She heard a metallic sound and tipped her head.

Had she imagined it? The engines were getting louder, making it hard to distinguish other sounds.

She shook her head.

She was hearing things.

Then a louder clang. Nope. It was definitely real metal striking metal somewhere out in the darkness. Her heart rate spiked. "Lucas?"

No response.

Then came a rumble she couldn't identify. Low and mechanical, like machinery grinding against itself.

What was that?

Then the docking bay doors exploded inward.

The metal tore like paper, sparks cascading in a brilliant arc that temporarily blinded her. Through the shower of sparks and twisted debris came Lucas. He was running faster than anything she'd ever seen—a blur of motion streaking across the dark space with inhuman speed.

And behind him, a cyborg.

Jianna raised her hand to the control panel. She just had to hit it; they'd be sealed in, and Michel could take off.

But Lucas…

He might be their only hope.

So she waited, her hand shaking.

Lucas was growing nearer and then … he leaped through the open door of the shuttle.

Jianna slammed her hand down. Too late. The cyborg dove low, sliding through the door just before it closed. It tackled Lucas, driving him to the floor.

"GO!" Lucas shouted.

The door lock snicked into place. The shuttle lurched forward and accelerated, the sudden G-forces slamming Jianna backward. She lost her footing and slid across the deck toward the rear of the cabin, pinned by the weight of acceleration.

Lucas and the cyborg tumbled toward her, still grappling, their bodies slamming against the rear wall.

Lucas was on his back.

The cyborg, on top of him, grabbed his head and slammed it against the deck. Lucas seemed to be trying to free himself, but the G-forces plus the cyborg's weight had pinned him down.

Jianna spotted her bag on the floor. It was just a few feet away, but it might as well have been miles. She started crawling toward it on her belly, but her arms felt like they were weighted down with lead. Each inch forward required tremendous effort.

The cyborg kicked out, trying to get better footing and caught Jianna's hip. The blow sent a jolt of pain shooting down her leg. She bellowed, but kept moving, reaching for her bag. It was so close now…

If she could just reach it…

The acceleration wanted to pin her flat, but she pushed against it with everything she had … and grabbed it. She yanked it back, unzipped it, and grabbed the pressure injector and a vial of sedative, which she managed to fumble into the slot. It clicked into place on the second try.

Breathe, Jianna.

Now she just had to find a bare spot of skin on the cyborg. There was so much machinery, so little flesh visible. Most of her was armored.

CLANG.

Lucas' head hit the deck again. The engines whined. Metal groaned somewhere in the shuttle's frame as the G-forces stressed the hull. The Descendants cowered in their seats. Jianna winced. Everything was just noise.

She wished she could cover her ears…

Ears.

The cyborg couldn't have metal there, could it? She shuffled down the aisle, studying the back of the cyborg's head. There. A small patch of flesh where the metal housing didn't quite cover everything.

Jianna lunged, slapping the injector against the exposed skin and squeezing hard. She heard the pop and hiss as compressed air forced the sedative into its target.

Then she relaxed, letting the force of acceleration slam her back against the wall.

For a moment, nothing happened.

CLANG. CLANG. CLANG.

The cyborg continued to slam Lucas' head against the cabin floor.

Darn it.

Maybe she hadn't used enough of the sedative. She'd have to get more—

Clang.

It sounded weaker.

And it was.

The cyborg stumbled. Her grip seemed to loosen. Her head swayed as though she were dizzy. Her body tipped to the side.

Lucas wriggled free, grabbing her shoulders. Then, using her for leverage, he flipped her sideways. She tumbled against the back wall of the shuttle, going limp. The G forces held her there.

Jianna studied the cyborg.

She knew this one.

It was the same woman she'd drugged with fruit salad back in the lab. The one who'd said "please help" when she was losing consciousness. Three times now, Jianna had been forced to hurt her.

She hated that.

This woman—because, despite all the machinery, she was still a woman underneath—had been a victim just like the Descendants. Aurelius had butchered her and turned her into a weapon.

Lucas braced himself against the back wall. There was a dent in his cranial plating where the cyborg had struck him. He reached for Jianna. "Please don't resist."

She flinched, then forced herself to relax.

He grabbed her, lifting her, and then set her in one of the empty seats as though she weighed nothing at all. "I appreciate your help."

She fastened the harness, strapping herself in, then gestured to his skull. "Your head."

He touched the dent. "It can be fixed."

She nodded, swallowing. Being lifted and placed in her seat like that, it should have been humiliating, but instead it felt strangely protective. Something she would never have expected from Lucas.

Now she understood how Samara could have known she was being manipulated and still wanted to believe Lucas was sincere. Why Samara might have trusted Phoebe to his care despite everything. Because there was something in the gentleness of his touch, the care he took not to hurt her, that felt real even if she couldn't be certain it was.

Lucas reached up and grabbed one of the small handholds from the row of them running along the shuttle's ceiling. Then he hauled himself hand over hand toward the cockpit, looking like some sort of gymnast. The G-forces that pinned her to her seat didn't seem to affect him at all.

The shuttle bucked and rolled; the ride was getting rougher. Lucas disappeared into the cockpit. A second later, the shuttle smoothed out.

The force pushing Jianna back lessened. She relaxed in her seat. She could breathe easier. She sighed with relief and glanced over at the Descendants. All three were now lethargic, slumped forward, eyes closed. She couldn't tell if they were sleeping or just resting, but their breathing seemed steady.

She looked over at Glint. She was blinking—not with her regular eyelids, but with the translucent nictitating membrane that slid across her eye from the side. Then she signed something.

Jianna frowned and shook her head. She didn't

understand. Of course, Aurelius would have removed Glint's translation collar. He wouldn't have wanted to hear her object when he poked holes in her head and threaded wires through her brain.

Glint made a "thumbs-up" sign and let out an uncertain trill, the sound barely audible over the shuttle's engines.

Jianna laughed, gave Glint a thumbs-up back.

Now they just had to survive. She leaned her head back against the seat, staring up at the ceiling.

They'd gotten this far, but it was hard to feel relieved when she knew what was coming. If Aurelius didn't know by now, he would know soon that they'd taken the Descendants back. And he would come for them—not because he thought they could hurt him, he had far too much ego for that—but to punish them for their little rebellion.

Where could they go that he wouldn't find them?

She closed her eyes tight, listening to the hum of the shuttle's engines, the sound of Michel and Lucas talking in the cockpit. She caught snippets of words: pitch, thrust, throttle, and vector.

Lucas must be teaching him how to fly.

At least they'd also gotten Lucas out. If anyone could help them figure out how to stop Aurelius, it would be him.

She opened her eyes, glancing out the window, watching their descent. This time, when they entered the atmosphere, the ride was completely smooth. She felt so much safer now that Lucas was at the controls.

Through the viewport, she watched the lights of Vitruvia City appear below them—beautiful and glittering in the darkness, deceptively peaceful. It almost seemed impossible that there was any kind of despair in a place so beautiful.

More than anything, she just wanted to go home.

But she couldn't.

Soren was already in enough danger. Aurelius would use him against her should she show up.

Maybe she should have hidden him away somewhere before setting out on this mission. But where? Aurelius controlled the whole city.

Then the shuttle veered away from Vitruvia, heading toward the mountains.

Darkness swallowed the view, and she couldn't make out much of anything. Where was Lucas taking them? They began to descend, and she saw the warm glow of campfires scattered across the hillsides.

The Descendant village. Lucas was taking them home.

The shuttle's engines changed pitch to a lower whine. Her stomach dropped. They were landing. The scattered fires of the village grew larger and brighter. The engines throttled back further, and the shuttle's nose lifted slightly when Lucas adjusted their approach. Her ears popped from the pressure change. The ground rushed up toward them, dark earth and scattered rocks illuminated by the shuttle's landing lights.

She braced herself for impact, but there was none. Just the softest bump as the landing struts touched down, then a subtle shift when the shuttle's weight settled onto the hillside. The engines wound down, and the cabin filled with silence.

They'd landed.

She looked out the window again. They were on the same slope where, as a schoolchild, she'd learned that Dr. Basu's colonists had first confronted the Descendants and driven them into the cliffs.

Everything was coming full circle. Because once Aurelius figured out they were hiding here, he'd come with an army of cyborgs, and once again it would be a Makinde facing off against her enemies on this same already blood-soaked ground.

The door mechanism engaged, the ramp descended, and cool night air flowed into the cabin. It carried the scent of wood smoke and the chirping of a shimmerfly, answered by another chirp somewhere out there in the darkness.

She leaned her back against the seat and exhaled.

They had done it.

And now they were back on DaVinci.

She was half tempted to pinch herself just to make sure it wasn't a dream. She unbuckled, but before she could get to her feet, a group of Descendants flooded up and into the cabin. They surrounded the three rescued survivors, trilling and humming, undoing their harnesses and lifting them out, carrying them to the door and down the ramp.

Jianna waited until they cleared the cabin, then she got up and made her way down the aisle. Her legs were shaky, and her shoulder hurt. She'd hit the wall harder than she thought.

Michel emerged from the cockpit, looking half dazed.

She smiled at him, holding out her hand. "I can't believe we did it."

But Michel didn't take it. He just stood there looking at her, but something was wrong with his expression. His eyes were unfocused, like he was trying to remember something. Or like he was looking through her instead of at her.

Was it shock? Exhaustion?

She stepped over to him. "Are you okay?"

He blinked. Then looked at her again.

And she froze.

His eyes were dead. There was no recognition. No

warmth. No sign that he knew her at all. The nanites. Aurelius had forced him to take them.

How could she have been so stupid?

And why didn't Michel realize it?

Maybe Aurelius had a way of convincing the brain that the nanites were simply a part of it, that they had always been there.

It explained his behavior on the Elysia. How he knew where the cyborgs were. How he'd been able to control them. Her throat went dry. "Luc—"

Michel lunged, his hands outstretched, reaching for her throat.

She screamed, stumbling backward. Her back hit the cabin wall, pain shooting through her injured shoulder. His fingernails skimmed her neck. Then he was yanked back and away from her.

Lucas had him in a chokehold, one arm wrapped around Michel's throat. He thrashed like a wild animal, his face contorting with rage. She stared at him. This wasn't Michel, the man she knew and loved.

"I believe that Aurelius is aware of our escape and is trying to control Michelangelo through his nanites," Lucas said. "I can render him unconscious, but if you have another dose of sedative…"

She ran to the back of the cabin, grabbed the pressure hypo from where she'd dropped it, then loaded another vial from her bag.

Michel continued to thrash.

Lucas tightened his grip.

"Please don't hurt him," she said, her voice cracking.

"I will only apply enough pressure to render him unconscious," Lucas said. "I promise he won't be damaged."

Jianna wasn't so sure about that. Michel's face was now bright red, but his movements were getting weaker.

She blew out a breath, then jabbed the end against the muscle of his shoulder and pressed the button. Michel flinched, glaring at her, spit flying from his mouth. She stepped away.

He grew weaker, his movements becoming sluggish, more uncoordinated. His eyes began to lose focus. He stopped trying to pry away Lucas' arm.

Went limp.

Lucas shifted his grip, lifting Michel and cradling him against his chest.

"Do you know of a way to destroy the nanites once they're in someone's brain?" she asked.

"I do not," Lucas said. "They were invented after our departure from Earth, so I have not had the opportunity to study them."

The bottom dropped out of her stomach. If even he didn't know how to undo what Aurelius had done, then who could?

Aurelius had stolen Michel from her, just like he'd stolen her father, and she might never get either of them back.

Chapter Twenty-Three

HOW WAS it possible that the leader of the Naturalists was lost in nature?

But she was. And now, in addition to the torrential rain that was soaking Willow to the skin, it was pitch black.

Water dripped into her eyes from her hood, making it hard to see. She blinked it away, adjusted her flashlight, and peered down at the laminated surface of the map. The red route markers she'd written on it earlier were dissolving into colored streaks. Which meant the map was now useless.

Just like she was.

She'd always struggled with maps as a child, especially back in her Junior Explorer days. The others could orient themselves without a problem, while Willow stood there turning the paper this way and that, trying to make the lines correspond to the world around her. She had pretended to enjoy those outings for her parents, who expected their daughter to embrace the natural world their very faith celebrated. But every time she had to attend, she counted the minutes until she could go home.

What a fraud she'd been.

What a fraud she still was.

The rain found every gap in her jacket, which was supposed to be waterproof, but that was a lie, too. Cold streams of water trickled down her spine like icy fingers. She shivered, her boots squelching with each step. Water sloshed against her toes, and they were starting to go numb.

She'd been wandering since late afternoon, and she wasn't sure when she'd gotten off course, but it was almost sunset when she realized she'd taken a wrong turn somewhere. Now that it was dark, she was even more lost.

Something rustled in the trees to her left. Her heart thudded in her chest, and she jerked around, shining her flashlight on the bushes.

She saw nothing. Just black. And trees.

It's just the wind.

She almost believed it. Her pulse began to slow.

Another rustle, closer this time.

What if Aurelius sent cyborgs after her? What if they were out there now, stalking her through the forest?

Stop it.

Stop it, stop it, stop it.

She couldn't afford to let her imagination run away with her. If she panicked and ran, she'd only get more lost. And besides, if his cyborgs were after her, she probably wouldn't even hear them coming.

She looked down at the useless map again. Her grand plan that had seemed so clear in Vitruvia City now seemed ridiculous. She'd intended to go to the Hyperion ruins and camp tonight, then hike to the Council Chambers the next day. The emergency stores there had probably already been distributed, but she could check. After that, it was only another day's hike up the trail to Lake Buratti, where she could fish and forage and lay traps to feed herself. If Aurelius did figure out where she'd gone, she could retreat into the mountain's caves, hide in the tunnels until he gave up searching for her.

Anything to keep her baby safe.

Anything but go back.

She was so cold. She needed to rest, just for a few minutes.

She walked on, scanning the forest. After a few minutes, she spotted a large tree with a thick trunk and a slight overhang of branches. She made her way to it, boots squelching in the mud. She tucked herself under it, the thick branches protecting her from most of the rain.

She lowered herself to the ground, tucking her coat beneath her bum. Not that she had to worry about staying dry. She was soaked through. She put the map away, then set her flashlight down and shrugged off her pack, which contained camping gear, food, herbal medicines, and a foraging handbook from her Nature Scout days. She set it beside her, then switched her flashlight to lantern mode.

A small circle of light bloomed around her. Everything beyond was darkness. But for some reason, she felt protected beneath the trees.

She slipped her hand into the pack and dug out a meal bar, tearing it open, taking a bite. It was savory and chewy. Super-chewy in fact. She had to drink water from her canteen just to wash it down.

Ugh.

At least it was nutritious.

She chewed, staring out at the darkness.

She hadn't brought her comm with her, for fear that Aurelius could use it to track her. Nor had she told anyone where she was going. Now that seemed like a really bad idea, but she was worried about betrayal.

Any of her people could be infected. Aurelius could control them without anyone knowing, until he decided to activate them. Why, he might infect all of them just to make sure she couldn't ask for help. Every Naturalist in the Quarter could be his puppet right now, waiting for the command.

She swallowed another bite of the meal bar. Aurelius had stolen Soren, too, her only real ally outside of the Naturalists. He'd hemmed her in. Left her with no one. Left them all with no one, really.

There wasn't a person left on Da Vinci she could trust. Not family members. Friends. Lovers.

She sniffed.

She was going to have to get good at the survival skills that had been games to her as a Nature Scout. Those had been supervised exercises with safety nets and adults standing by, ready to pitch in if the kids needed help. And she had always needed a lot of help.

Now her life depended on those skills. Her life and her baby's life.

She glanced down at her belly.

What if Camilla and Jianna were right and the baby wasn't going to survive? It didn't seem possible. Then again, she shouldn't expect them to believe. They were scientists. They didn't understand the power of faith.

Once the Divine Blueprint physically manifested, her path would become clear. She didn't know what she would do when it came time to give birth, but she'd figure it out. In the meantime, she'd spend her pregnancy in isolation, like a monk. Praying. Purifying herself, so that once the child was born, she'd be worthy to raise it.

She leaned her head back against the tree trunk. "Mother Basu, give me strength."

There was a rustle in the trees.

She jerked upright, staring into the darkness. The rain pattered on the leaves above her. She grabbed her flashlight, flipping it over into a beam again. She searched the woods.

Nothing.

Just trees and darkness and the wind.

But she didn't believe it.

Something – or someone – was out there.

Run.

Oh, she wanted to. But she was afraid of getting even more lost. She got herself into a crouching position, reaching for her pack. She slipped it over one shoulder and then—

Another rustle. Closer.

She should switch off the flashlight to make it harder for them to see her. But she couldn't bear the idea of not being able to see whatever was coming.

Two figures entered her circle of light.

One held a spear. The other held a short club.

She couldn't move.

The Descendants seemed equally surprised to see her. They stood, staring at her with those huge, unreadable eyes.

Willow released her hold on her pack and forced herself to stand. She didn't want them to know she was afraid. "I'm Guide Willow Evans." Her voice came out steadier than she expected. "Leader of the Naturalists."

What was she doing?

She imagined they had no idea who she was. And if they did know, they'd have even more reason to hate her.

The Descendants signed something.

She shook her head.

They pointed, waved, made shapes with their hands, each gesture growing more urgent.

"I don't understand what you want," Willow said. "But I'm not afraid of you. And if you hurt me, my people will come for you."

They signed again.

She took a step back from them, gesturing to the trees. "I'm just passing through this area on my way to the Hyperion ruins. I have every right to be here."

She wanted to grab her pack, but it seemed too far away.

And then something grabbed her from behind.

She screamed, driving her heel backward, aiming for where she hoped the Descendant's shin would be. Her boot connected with something solid, and she heard a grunt.

She twisted her shoulders, trying to wrench free, threw her weight to one side, then the other, but its grip didn't loosen. The Descendant was too strong. She'd never even heard it approach, and now it had her.

But it wasn't hurting her.

It forced her down to her knees, into the sucking mud, while a second Descendant pulled her arms back, winding rope around her wrists. She lost her hold on her flashlight. It flickered out and rolled away in the darkness.

Then they hauled her upright, water dripping from her hair into her eyes.

She stared up at them.

Why hadn't they killed her?

One of the Descendants picked up her pack. Another retrieved her flashlight, switched it on, and gestured to the forest. She didn't want to go with them, so she pretended not to understand. Maybe she could buy herself some time, figure out how to escape.

But the third grabbed her upper arm and began marching her forward.

Unlike her, who was tripping over every root and rock and vine, the Descendants seemed to have no problem navigating the forest.

This had to be part of Mother Basu's divine plan.

She had to be watching over her.

Unless…

Mother Basu had abandoned her?

No, she refused to think that.

But it was hard to believe in anything when that rope was cutting into her wrists, and she was certain she was being marched to her death.

She didn't know how long they walked. It seemed like hours. She lost all her bearings. Not that she really even knew where she was. But gradually she began to recognize the terrain.

The Hyperion ruins.

The very place she was trying to reach.

She felt a moment of relief. "This is where I was going. I swear I wasn't trying to encroach on your territory."

They didn't respond.

She nodded toward the ruins. "Please give me my things back. Leave me here. Then I'll be on my way. I won't bother you again."

They continued to ignore her, guiding her past the ruins. Eventually, they crested a hill and then several more.

Oh no.

Now she knew where they were taking her.

If she was right, the Descendant village was downslope.

They proceeded past more boulders, rocks, and trees. She smelled campfire smoke. And then they arrived in an area where stone huts were clustered together, their shapes barely visible in the darkness. Cooking fires burned in a few places outside, casting flickering orange light across the ground. And everywhere, silhouettes. Descendants emerging from huts, turning to look at her.

She was surrounded and hopelessly outnumbered, bound and helpless. No one knew where she was. She tried to slow down and met the eyes of a few other Descendants. "Please, help me."

But no one responded.

Her guards marched her through the village, past the cooking fires, the interested bystanders, and then they were through to the other side and heading uphill again. She stumbled. She was so tired, but now she was afraid to stop because what was going to happen then? Nothing good, she was sure of it.

The Descendants led Willow up a narrow mountain path where loose stones constantly shifted underfoot, forcing them all to slow down. Then they rounded a bend that led off the main trail. One of the Descendants pulled out a utility light and led the way until they reached two large rocks with only a narrow passage between them.

They pushed Willow through, emerging on the other side of the boulders. There she saw a rectangular opening cut directly into the solid rock face.

Mother Basu, help me!

But she seemed to have abandoned Willow long ago.

The Descendant guided her through the entrance and into a tunnel. It was very dark inside. Even the flashlight did little to dispel the gloom. The ground underfoot sloped downward.

Her heart pounded. Her chest felt tight. She was having trouble breathing.

Were they going to abandon her down there in the dark?

She had to get her breath under control.

And she should have paid more attention to the path

here. If they let her go, would she be able to find her way out?

The tunnel ran for several meters before it opened into a massive cavern. The ceiling disappeared into blackness so complete that she felt like she was looking into the night sky, albeit one without stars.

Willow stopped trying to take it all in, but the Descendant holding her arm pushed her forward again. They crossed the cavern, Willow's dread growing.

Something up ahead was reflecting light. As they neared, she saw that it was some sort of small booth, with clear glass-like walls and a metal frame. It had an airlock-like passthrough built into it. It was nothing like the stone buildings she saw in their village. This was human-made. Probably something they scavenged from the Hyperion ruins. But why did they drag it all the way down here?

She'd been thinking they'd brought her down here to throw her into some kind of sacrificial pit, or chain her up, or abandon her, but the idea of being locked up in this strange cage was even worse.

They stopped in front of it. One of the Descendants cut the rope around her wrists. Another one opened the door to the chamber, the seals releasing with a sucking sound. Then the other two pushed her inside. She stumbled, catching herself against the far wall.

Then the door closed behind her with a solid thunk, and she heard the click of a lock.

She whirled around, looking out the glass. The Descendants were watching her. Then one of them stepped forward and slid something through a passthrough window. It rolled off the small platform and fell to the floor.

It was her flashlight. She stepped over and scooped it

up, turning it on. When she straightened, she saw them turning to leave.

"Wait!" She knocked on the glass. "I need my medicine! It's in my pack."

Two of the Descendants ignored her and left, but the third turned back around to look at her.

She mimed walking with a backpack. Mimed taking a pill. "My medicine. Please."

The third one didn't respond. It simply walked off.

She slumped against the wall.

What a mess.

And she was in it alone.

But this was no time to feel sorry for herself. There had to be a way out of here. She ran her flashlight over the walls, examining her prison. It was old. Scratched and dinged up from centuries of existence. But it was clean. Someone had been maintaining it. There was a small stool in the corner.

She tried the door, but of course it was locked. She tried shoving it. Nope. It didn't even budge. She couldn't even see a lock mechanism from this side. And she had nothing to pry it open.

What about that window?

She tried to reach her hand through the passthrough, but that was locked too. The other three walls had no holes, vents, or seams. She was trapped.

She walked over and sank onto the stool.

No medicine. No way out. No one coming.

She'd lost her chance to bring the Divine Blueprint into fruition. Without Camilla's drugs, the embryo might not take root.

Aurelius had won.

No wonder Mother Basu had abandoned her. She'd lost faith.

Her flashlight flickered.

Then it flickered again and went out, swallowing her in darkness.

Willow tossed it away, then sat in the black and waited. Because what else could she do? She tried to meditate. She didn't know how long. Minutes, maybe. An eternity. Thirty seconds. Time lost all meaning.

And then—light.

Pale. Pink. Growing brighter. She bolted to her feet, peering through the glass.

Two of the Descendants had returned carrying glass jars filled with bioluminescent lichen. So that explained the pale pink light. They approached, so she stepped back, pressing her back against the far wall.

She watched them set the jars down outside her cell. Then they slid something through the passthrough window. It was a thick, handwoven blanket. It fell to the floor.

Next came a bowl, steam rising from it. She sniffed. It couldn't be, could it? Chicken soup?

The Descendant continued to hold it, waiting for her.

She stared at her, her stomach growling.

It could be poisoned or drugged.

But they also could have killed her as soon as they found her in the forest, or any time during the long walk here. They could have just left her to starve, and no one would ever know. They didn't have to feed her, but they were.

She stepped across the room to the passthrough window and took the bowl.

The Descendant stepped back, locking the passthrough. Then they all departed once again.

She studied the bowl. The small chunks of meat floating in it looked and smelled like chicken, but it was probably some native animal. With bits of vegetables & herbs she didn't recognize, either.

She didn't know why the soup surprised her.

Maybe because she'd grown up thinking they only ate roots and nuts and berries?

She lifted the bowl to her lips and took a sip.

The broth was rich, the vegetables tender, the meat delicious. It was hot and warmed her from the inside out.

She took another sip. Was that thyme she was tasting?

It couldn't be, could it?

It reminded Willow of the soup her mother had made when she was sick as a child, a special healing recipe that her mother had sworn was brought from Earth by Mother Basu.

It was odd that these primitives, with their spears and clubs and monstrous eyes, were serving her soup that tasted so like her mother's... It didn't make sense. What were the odds that there'd be an herb on DaVinci that tasted exactly like an herb that evolved on Earth?

Unless...

What if it was thyme? Could the Descendants have enough intelligence to have cultivated seeds from the Hyperion's stores? Could they have preserved the recipes that their ancestors had brought from Earth?

That suggested that the Descendants had cultural memory. Traditions. Knowledge maintained and transmitted from one generation to the next.

Willow frowned. But that didn't make sense. She had been taught they were too primitive for any of that. But then how else could she explain this bowl of soup?

What else were they capable of that she'd never been told?

Everything she believed about them suddenly seemed less certain. She drank the rest of the soup. It was too good to waste, and she was too hungry. Besides, starving herself wasn't going to improve the baby's chances of survival.

She was grateful they fed her, even if she didn't want to be.

She set the empty bowl on the small platform of the passthrough window, then picked up the blanket and wrapped it around her. It was warm and soft. She'd been freezing for hours.

She went and sat on the stool, swaddled in the blanket, bathed in a pale pink light.

Nothing today was what she expected.

The Descendants hadn't hurt her. They'd fed her, given her light, given her warmth.

What did they want with her?

How long would they keep her here?

She didn't know.

She only knew that she was alive. That she was warm. That for the first time in hours, she wasn't hungry.

And that everything she thought she knew about the Descendants might be wrong.

Chapter Twenty-Four

JIANNA WATCHED Lucas lower Michel's unconscious body to the cave floor, the pink bioluminescent lichen casting everything in rose-tinted shadows. There were jars of the stuff, all glowing like trapped sunsets, but their light was too soft to chase away the darkness pressing in from the deeper tunnels.

Her theory was simple: if Michel was underground, his connection to the transmission tower might be interrupted.

Lucas had agreed.

A stabbing pain blossomed behind her eyes.

Not now.

It was time to take her meds again. The off-target effects couldn't be controlled by willpower. If they could be, she would have bested them long ago.

She had cleaned out the pockets of Michel's cargo pants and dumped his tools into her bag. Then she dug through it until she found the zip ties he'd brought along in case they'd needed them. She pulled some free and handed them to Lucas.

He took them, crouching at Michel's feet. He looped

the first zip tie around Michel's ankles, threading the end through the locking mechanism, and pulled it snug.

Jianna knelt beside Michel. Another spike of pain. She winced. It felt like someone was jamming a nail behind her left eye.

Breathe.

She inhaled, exhaled, forced her hands steady even though they wanted to shake. She got out two more zip-ties. The first, she looped around Michel's left wrist. The second, through the first loop and then around Michel's right wrist, making an impromptu set of handcuffs. She slid a finger beneath each one.

She wanted them tight enough that he couldn't wiggle out of them, but not so tight that they cut off circulation.

She sat back on her haunches, studying him, and blew out a breath.

She never thought she'd tie him up like a prisoner because she didn't know what he'd do when he woke up.

Aurelius really did poison all that he touched.

Lucas rose beside her. "Need anything?"

The only thing she needed was for him to leave so she could stop holding herself together. And then maybe some rest, but she didn't want to tell him that.

Jianna shook her head. "I'm fine."

Lucas nodded and then walked off, leaving her and Michel alone. She watched him breathe, listening to the slow drip of water somewhere deep in the cave. The sound was rhythmic, almost soothing. Almost.

She sat down beside him, opened her bag, and pulled out the waxed paper pouch that held her medication.

The pills inside had been smashed to powder, and there was a tear in the side. Powder had leaked all over the inside of her bag like ash.

There probably wasn't enough left to make even one pill.

Perfect, because migraines and seizures were definitely not going to make it harder for her to find a way to take Aurelius down.

She set her bag aside and reached into Michel's pocket and grabbed his medication bottle. Full. He must've just renewed his prescription. She unscrewed the lid, then hesitated.

The last time she'd asked to borrow one of Michel's pills, he'd been reluctant, and she wasn't sure why. She'd never bother to ask him at the time. Just figured he liked to track their consumption, which was reasonable. She did that as well. No one wanted to be caught out by an episode and not have their medication ready.

Now she was taking one without permission.

She glanced at him. The light of the lichen had softened the hard angles of his face, made him look peaceful. More like himself. Less like the automaton that had attacked her in the shuttle.

She either had to take it or suffer.

He'd understand.

She twisted the cap off and tipped the bottle, shaking a single pill into her palm before twisting the cap back on and popping the pill in her mouth.

She tried to dry-swallow it — never her preference — and it stuck to the back of her throat. She gagged, coughed, tried to swallow again, but the pill wouldn't go down. The texture was all wrong, tacky and adhesive. And it was sweet. The coating was dissolving already, and it shouldn't be. Not this quickly.

His pills had seemed different from hers. A little bit larger. And she'd wondered where he was getting them.

Was there something wrong with them?

She coughed again, trying to dislodge it.

It stuck.

She bent forward, hacking harder, and finally coughed it up. It landed wet and partially dissolved in her palm—smaller than it had been, sticky with saliva and whatever coating was melting off it. The surface glistened in the dim light, misshapen and wet.

Yuck.

But she didn't have another option.

She popped it back in her mouth and swallowed hard, forcing it down past the resistance in her throat. This time it went down, leaving behind a sugary aftertaste that reminded her of stale frosting.

If they were here for much longer, Jianna would need to get more, but that was a problem for tomorrow.

She tucked his bottle into her bag and leaned back against the rough stone wall, waiting for him to wake up. The cool rock pressed against her spine. She could feel every irregularity in the stone, every bump and ridge digging into her shoulders, and it grounded her.

Yesterday, she would have laughed at the suggestion that Michel wasn't safe to be alone with.

Now she was glad for the zip ties she'd found in his toolkit.

She closed her eyes, relieved that they'd managed to rescue Glint and the other two Descendants. But three was not enough. The others were dead. She'd been too late.

The numbness she'd been wrapped in all day began to crack. Grief welled up beneath it, pressing against her ribs, heavy and suffocating, like someone was sitting on her chest. Her throat tightened.

Her eyes burned.

She didn't want to cry.

She forced it back down before it could surface,

shoving it into some locked compartment inside herself where it couldn't reach her, couldn't break her.

Not now. Not yet.

She needed a distraction.

She pulled out her comm, and the screen flickered to life. She started scrolling through the documents she'd downloaded on the Elysia. Mitra Kunde's research, which Willow had suggested might hold a secret that could defeat Aurelius.

Dense text filled the screen—technical specifications about neural pathway degradation, research notes on synaptic protein buildup, diagrams of brain tissue cross-sections.

It should have made sense. But her vision was starting to blur, the characters swimming and doubling as if the screen had split into two overlapping images. Halos formed around each letter, bright white coronas that bled into the text beside them until whole words disappeared into the glare.

She squinted, trying to force her eyes to focus on a single line about cortical atrophy rates, but it was like looking through frosted glass. The harder she tried, the worse it got.

Another spike of pain shot through her head as if to say: *not happening today.*

She shut her comm off, closed her eyes, and waited for the pill to kick in.

It wasn't much darker with her eyes closed than it was with them open, but it helped a little. She listened to the sound of Michel breathing, slow and steady.

In and out. In and out.

Maybe she should inject herself with a dose of sedative. Just enough to take the edge off. But no. She couldn't risk it. She wanted to be awake when Michel woke up. Had to be clear-headed. Present.

In and out.

An image rose in her mind. The Descendants in the freezer. Bodies stacked like cargo, one on top of another, limbs bent at wrong angles where they'd been shoved together to save space. Frost coating their skin like a second dermis, crystallizing in their hair, their eyelashes, and their brains. Cold and empty, all that potential just… gone.

She clenched her eyes tight, trying to shut down the tears.

She forced the image away.

In and out.

Michel would wake up soon. And when he did, maybe the stone and earth between him and the transmission tower would be enough to sever whatever hold Aurelius had on him. Maybe he'd be himself. Not the hollow-eyed stranger who looked like he wanted to kill her.

She didn't want to think about what she might have to do if he wasn't.

Chapter Twenty-Five

WILLOW JOLTED AWAKE.

Even in sleep, something had startled her.

She didn't know where she was. Then she saw the plexiglass walls, the metal frame of the cube, the pink light filtering in through the window. The day's events flooded back: the forest, the Descendants, the cave.

A figure stepped through the open door.

The Murderer.

Willow scrambled backward, pressing herself against one of the walls. She whimpered.

Heat flooded her face.

Shame, instant and scalding.

She'd let him see she was scared of him.

But he didn't pay her any mind. He was carrying one of Aurelius' cyborgs slung over his shoulder. It was a woman, or what was once a woman.

He laid her on the floor near the stool, and Willow recognized her face. This was the same cyborg kind that stood guard while he infected the Council with his nanites, the very kind she fled the city to escape. Now it was in this tiny space with her, and she had nowhere to run.

And it was alive, but unconscious.

A cold chill spread through her chest. "You can't put that thing in here with me."

Lucas straightened, glancing at her. "She must be confined. We don't know what she will do when she wakes up."

"Exactly. She might try to kill me."

He nodded. "It's a possibility."

Willow glared at him. Why wasn't he trying to reassure her? How could something that looked so human be so empty?

He gestured with his hand toward the door. "Come with me."

She sidled to the left. "I'm not going anywhere with you. You're the Murderer."

"That is true, but the Elder has summoned us both."

Willow rubbed her throat, feeling her heartbeat hammer against her palm. "What does that mean?"

"It means you need to come with me."

She hesitated. She was aware that the Elder was the leader of the Descendants. But she had no idea who they were because she didn't follow their politics.

And she had no idea what awaited her when she did meet the Elder—execution? Or maybe she was about to be handed back over to Aurelius. She wouldn't put it past the Descendants to offer Aurelius the same kind of deal he offered her. They wouldn't know that he'd never intended to keep his side of the bargain.

They probably didn't know what he was. What he did to people who trusted him.

Lucas nodded toward the cyborg. "Or you can remain

here with Aurelius' crew member, and I will deliver whatever message the Elder has for you."

Willow looked at the cyborg. She had no idea when it would wake up. And she didn't want to be alone with it when it did.

She also didn't want Lucas delivering the Elder's message. She wanted to hear it herself, so she could face whatever was coming. Or, at the very least, negotiate. Which was something she wasn't sure Lucas was capable of.

She tilted her chin up. "I'm coming with you."

"Very well."

He made his way out of the cell, then waited for her to exit. She was half tempted to run, but she had a feeling he would be faster than her. So she stepped out, then waited for him to close and lock the door behind her.

Then she let him lead her back through the cavern that the Descendants first brought her through. She hated the way the space swallowed all sound. It made her feel small, erasable, like she could disappear and no one would ever know she'd been here.

Willow blew out a breath. She had no idea if she was about to be put to death. But maybe that was to her advantage. Maybe she could warn the Elder of Aurelius' plan, and they would free her. Maybe she could salvage her original plan and hide in the wilderness until the baby was born.

Would admitting to being pregnant make the Elder more sympathetic? Or would it be seen as a weakness to be exploited? Mother Basu had always taught that showing vulnerability was dangerous. That their enemies would use it against them.

"Congratulations on your pregnancy," Lucas said.

Willow froze, staring at his back. Did Jianna tell him?

Camilla? But Camilla was in the city, and Jianna had been—

He stopped walking as well, turning to look at her. "My apologies. Phoebe always disliked it when I read her as well."

"Pardon?" she asked.

He gestured toward her. "You're emitting a number of biological indicators."

She hated that he knew. That it was so easy to read her body like he would data, like she wasn't allowed secrets. "So, what else do you know?"

He met her eyes. "That you're afraid of me."

"Because you're the Murderer." She blinked back tears. "You killed Mother Basu because you knew that once the Vitruvians saw that the Divine Blueprint was real, they would've followed her."

"No."

She widened her eyes. "No?"

He shook his head. "I killed her because she killed my daughter."

It wasn't new information. She'd heard him say that on the holographic recording of his interrogation, but the words had sounded flat and meaningless, rehearsed, maybe, or just empty the way a machine's voice was empty.

But now he sounded angry.

That couldn't be right, though.

He wasn't human.

He couldn't feel the way humans felt.

"How can you call Phoebe your daughter? You don't have emotions."

"When I saw her dead," Lucas said, "I couldn't allow Ayesha Basu to continue existing herself. Not after she'd stolen Phoebe's existence from me."

"Isn't that just logic? An eye for an eye?"

"How do you tell the difference between the two?"

Willow opened her mouth to respond, then closed it again. The words stuck in her throat, and she wound up forcing them out. "I just can."

"Samara once brought that same argument to me."

Willow frowned. She didn't like being put in the same category as Samara. She was everything the Naturalists stood against. Everything Mother Basu warned them about. The woman who'd created abominations and called it progress, who'd twisted nature into something unrecognizable and claimed it was improvement.

"And?"

"After losing Phoebe," Lucas said. "I've replayed that day over and over, thinking of all the things I would do differently if I had the chance. I should've taken Samara's warnings more seriously. I should've followed Phoebe more closely. I should've intervened in her relationship with Atlas sooner, or confronted Ayesha instead of observing as events played out. Now, if I were human, what would you call that?"

"Running simulations," Willow said. "That's what machines do with data, isn't it."

He raised his brows, almost looking amused. "Really?"

She glowered. No. That's not what she would call it. So, she said, "Regret."

He nodded. "I can't stop thinking about all the things Phoebe will never do, the experiences I will never share with her. Ayesha stole all those possibilities from us, and it threw the rest of my experiences into question. If I were human, what would you call that?"

Willow clenched her hands into fists. "Grief. But—"

"When Phoebe was alive," Lucas said, "all I wanted was to see her thrive. I enjoyed seeing the world through her eyes. Her happiness and well-being were my number one priority. If I were human, what would you call that?"

Willow dropped her eyes. Could the devil feel love? No. She shook her head.

"I didn't understand how emotion can overpower everything else until I saw Phoebe's dead body and experienced what I believe was rage." His voice was steady, but there was something in it now that hadn't been there before, something sharp, and she wouldn't ever want to be on the receiving end of that. "I'm sorry for the grief that I caused your family, but I am not sorry to have punished Ayesha for extinguishing my daughter's light."

"Even if you 'punished' Mother Basu for protecting the Divine Blueprint from Phoebe's desecration," Willow said, meeting his eyes yet again. "No one punished you for your crime."

"One might say I was punished by the very nature you worship. I was imprisoned underground for more than five hundred years. A punishment that no human had the ability to enforce on me."

She folded her arms over her chest. "The devil cloaks his lies in reasonable words."

Lucas' lips quirked up in an expression that Willow would describe as sardonic if a human wore it. "If I speak unreasonably, will you find my arguments more convincing?"

Willow let out a breath. "No. I'd blame you for Mother Basu's death either way."

"Then if I'm damned whether I do or don't, what's my incentive for considering your argument?" Lucas asked.

She shook her head. "It doesn't matter what your reason for killing her was. I can't forgive you for what you did."

"I accept that," he said, continuing to walk.

She followed.

Somehow, that answer made Willow less angry.

The simple acknowledgment, without defensiveness or justification, deflated a lot of the anger she had been carrying, and that set alarm bells off in her head. Mother Basu said that Lucas could never be trusted, and even Samara, who trusted her daughter to him, spoke of his manipulative nature in her writings. This was exactly what manipulation looked like: you felt heard, understood, and seen. It made you forget what he was.

It didn't take long for them to leave the tunnels and make their way outside.

Willow squinted, shielding her eyes with her hand. The village lay below them, and they began to descend. Now that it was daylight, she saw more than just stone huts. There were many other buildings that had been put together from scavenged materials. Prefab remnants from the original colony. Metal patched over wood and stone. A sheet of corrugated steel hammered crooked across a doorway. A rain gutter made from scavenged pipe.

The Descendants had technology.

And infrastructure.

There were lots of them outside. Children playing games, laughing, and letting out little shrieks of excitement and joy. If she closed her eyes, she would have imagined they were human children, except for the odd trilling noises they made, high-pitched and musical. It was nothing like human laughter but somehow expressed the same delight.

They were doing chores that Willow had not only seen in history books, but that her own people had preserved as they were done by hand: spinning thread, weaving baskets, twining rope, hanging laundry to dry in the sun. These were all tasks her own community preserved.

The air smelled clean, tinged with the smoke of cooking fires. It smelled like nature in a way that the city didn't—of earth and growing things. All of the city smells that Willow disliked were absent here. She found it pleasant.

And that was unsettling.

Why hadn't she been told that the Descendants had Earth technology?

Why was that kept from their history book? Let alone their current classrooms?

No.

Why hadn't she questioned the things she was told? She didn't believe everything the Vitruvians told her, so why did she believe everything she'd learned about the Descendants?

Those picture books from her childhood. They depicted the Descendants running around in scavenged clothing, hunting small animals with pointed sticks, sleeping in trees, and afraid of the simplest technology that the Generation One colonists had brought with them. Primitive. Savage. Unable to adapt.

What other lies had she been told?

They wound their way between a narrow line of stone huts, heading toward the center of the village, passing a large open area where the Descendants seemed to have set up some kind of workshop.

What were they doing?

She stopped to watch.

A Descendant near the edge of the clearing bent over a piece of wood, lashing strips of hide across its surface. They were making a shield. Another sat cross-legged on the ground, fletching arrows. Willow counted at least two dozen bundles beside them. Farther back, three more worked together, one holding a wooden shaft steady while another bound a sharpened stone to its tip with cord, testing the tension with small tugs.

They were making weapons.

The Descendants were preparing to go to war.

Oh no, no, no.

If it was Aurelius they were planning to fight, they were in trouble. Stone spears against cyborgs? Shields against nanites? They'd be slaughtered.

Yet there was something brave about their preparations as well. They knew what they were facing, and they were preparing anyway. They weren't hiding or running away like she had done. They were preparing to fight.

The workshop spun in front of her eyes.

She held out a hand, bracing herself against the nearest building. The exhaustion she'd been pushing down the last few days was starting to overwhelm her.

Maybe she could convince the Descendants to give her medication back. Her body needed it. The baby needed it.

Lucas had stopped and was watching her.

"The embryo that you gave to Jianna," Willow asked, "did you examine it?"

"I did."

"What did you find?"

"I determined it had been adequately preserved."

"Could you tell if there was something wrong with it? Genetically?"

Lucas studied her. "What is your real question?"

She hesitated. "Both Jianna and Camilla Lombardi told me that Phoebe's genes somehow weren't compatible with Atlas'. That there was something wrong with the immune system of the embryo."

"And?"

She shrugged.

"You don't believe them."

"They both said it needed gene therapy to survive, but they're both—" She hesitated.

Lucas finished for her: "Scientists."

She nodded.

"And you believe that science is a contamination."

"Not all science," she said. But she didn't sound very convincing. Not even to her own ears. "Do you know if the embryo was viable when you had it?"

"Both Phoebe and Atlas had mutations in their immune systems, so it's possible that those mutations weren't compatible."

She nodded. "Okay."

She wished he'd provide more comfort or reassurance that what she was carrying in her womb was whole and healthy and human, but he didn't. He simply gestured to the path, and she followed along behind him.

Eventually, he stopped in front of the largest stone hut at the heart of the village. Grass mats hung across the entrance, serving as a door. They swayed slightly in the breeze, whispering against each other. He gestured for Willow to enter.

She hesitated, then stepped inside. Lucas followed.

There wasn't a whole lot of light inside, and Willow had to wait for her eyes to adjust to the darkness.

The Elder waited inside, seated on a mat that covered the packed dirt floor, near the fire that was burning at the center of the room. The smoke carried the faint smell of herbs, something sharp and medicinal that made her sinuses prickle.

The Elder was ancient and small. Her blue-green and silver scales had long lost their iridescent sheen, dulled by time like tarnished metal. Deep creases lined her face, running in patterns that followed the natural ridges of her features. But her eyes—huge black pools that reflected the firelight—watched Willow with curiosity.

The Elder didn't rise, but she signed to Lucas.

Lucas nodded. "The Elder wishes to confirm that you are the leader of the New People who believe that the Descendants are abominations who should be destroyed."

Willow swallowed hard. She'd agree to anything to protect the Divine Blueprint, but now she felt ashamed she had ever had those thoughts. Let alone preached them. She felt sick. "Please tell the Elder I ask forgiveness for my former ignorance. I believed the lies I was told about her people."

Lucas signed her response. The Elder's expression didn't change when she responded to Lucas.

He nodded yet again. "The Elder requests a seat on the Council in exchange for defeating Aurelius."

Willow barely managed to keep from laughing in disbelief. *A seat on the council? What council? Aurelius had dissolved it.* "The Descendants will fail if they raise a hand to strike him. Even the Vitruvians don't have a chance against him."

"The Elder didn't ask for your opinion on their chances of success. She requested a seat on the Council."

Willow flushed. She might as well say yes. After all, what difference did it make? Aurelius was going to destroy them all anyway. If the Descendants chose to fight, at least they'd be going out on their own terms.

Willow bowed with as much dignity as she could muster. "Tell the Elder that I will do my best to persuade the others."

Before Lucas could translate, the Elder nodded.

Willow froze.

The Elder understood her.

The Elder understood everything, including her

statement that the Descendants didn't have a chance against Aurelius.

Heat flooded Willow's face, burning from her cheeks down to her chest. "My people have been wrong to mistreat you, and I apologize for that. Please know that if you go to battle, you won't just be fighting Aurelius and his crew. You will be fighting everyone in the city, including my people. Aurelius can make them do whatever he wants."

The Elder signed.

Lucas translated again: "The Elder will hold you to your word."

Then he gestured at the door of the stone hut.

That was it?

They were done?

Willow followed Lucas outside. "Now what? Are you going to lock me back up again?"

He eyed her. "Give me your word that you'll stay in the cave with the others, and I'll have your medication returned to you."

"I'm not going back in there with the abom—" Willow stopped herself. The word died on her tongue. "—the cyborg."

"I'll take that as a yes." Lucas said, smiling. He headed back in the direction of the cave.

Willow thought about running.

The Descendants hadn't hurt her.

In fact, they didn't seem to have any intention of doing so.

She'd run from Aurelius, who wanted her to be a surrogate for a twisted relationship he'd had with her long-dead ancestor, and found herself in the hands of the Murderer. A creature she'd been raised to believe was the source of all evil in the world.

She had wanted to be like Mother Basu as a girl. A

holy legend, chosen to lead her people through the darkness, standing firm against the forces of evil, in order to fulfill her divine purpose.

Then she grew up and got practical and did her best to fight the encroaching contamination of the Vitruvians.

But in both of those versions of herself, she was fighting alone.

And she was so very, very tired of being alone.

<h1 style="text-align:center">Chapter Twenty-Six</h1>

MICHEL WOKE.

No. That wasn't entirely true because he hadn't been sleeping. He'd been drugged because…

He'd tried to hurt her.

He remembered being on the shuttle. Turning toward Jianna. Lunging for her throat, wanting to strangle the breath out of her body. And the worst part was—he couldn't stop himself from doing so. It was like he'd lost control of his ability to use his own body. Like he was nothing more than a puppet controlled by invisible strings.

Bile rushed up his throat.

He gritted his teeth to keep from vomiting.

Tried to sit.

But his body was still unresponsive.

No.

He'd been bound.

Plastic cuffs bit into his wrists. He was lying on the ground, the cold chill of stone seeping into his bones. His mouth was dry, his tongue thick and cottony, and there was a dull ache behind his eyes that pulsed in time with his heartbeat.

He forced his eyes open.

Pale pink light lit the space around him. He blinked, his vision adjusting. He was in a cave. A rough stone ceiling curved overhead and was slick with moisture in places where condensation had gathered. Jars of bioluminescent lichen were scattered around on the ground, casting the area in a rosy glow that would probably have been beautiful under different circumstances.

He shivered. It was very cold.

He wished he had a blanket. Or a coat.

Michel yawned.

He wondered how long he'd been unconscious. Minutes? Hours? Days? The ache in his muscles suggested it had been long enough for his body to stiffen in whatever position they'd left him in.

He tried again to sit, but his body protested.

He swallowed.

His throat hurt. Felt bruised. What had he done to his neck? He couldn't remember hurting himself on the Elysia, so it must have happened after they returned to DaVinci.

He looked down at his wrists. They were bound in front of him with zip ties—his own zip ties, the ones he'd packed in his cargo pants for the mission. His ankles were similarly bound.

He lay his head back down, closing his eyes. Something else was wrong. Something beyond the obvious.

He frowned.

What was it?

It wasn't the restraints, or the cave, or even the throbbing pain in his neck. It was something more fundamental, an absence that made him feel hollow. There was a blankness where something should be, like a limb he'd grown accustomed to that was now gone.

Then he jerked, eyes opening.

His internal desktop—the visual overlay that the nanites projected directly to his optic nerve, the icons in his peripheral vision, and the ambient data feeds that provided him with system diagnostics and environmental readings—was gone.

The connection was severed.

The silence in his head was absolute.

He'd been cut off from the transmission tower's signal. That was why he was in control of his thoughts and body again.

Down here, under tons of rock and earth, the signal couldn't reach him. Jianna must have figured out that he was a danger, must have understood that the only way to protect everyone was to bury him somewhere the network couldn't touch.

Which meant she knew about the nanites…

He swore, wishing that he had told her. That she hadn't had to find out this way. At least she'd been smart enough to protect herself and everyone else from him.

Michel pushed himself upright with his bound hands. His head swam, and he had to close his eyes again. He heard a sniff behind and to the left.

He opened his eyes, turning around.

Jianna sat slightly behind him, her back pressed against the cave wall, her head tipped forward, her eyes closed. In the pale pink light, the shadows under her eyes looked like bruises. Her face was drawn tight with pain, a furrow between her brows even in rest that made her look older than she was.

She was sitting close enough to him that if he reached out, he would be able to touch her crossed legs.

He frowned.

Remembering her once more on the shuttle. How shocked she had looked when he attacked her. No. How betrayed.

And then –

Someone had grabbed him from behind. That's how his neck had been injured. He remembered it now. An iron grip around his throat. Lucas.

He must have understood what was happening and intervened. Because someone had held him back when he was determined to follow Aurelius' commands even as his mind was screaming at him to stop.

He'd been pinned there while Jianna got a sedative from her bag. Knocked him out. Then nothing.

It had to have been Lucas who stopped him.

He would have been the only one strong enough to do so.

Thank goodness.

But it didn't take away the fear of what he might have done to Jianna if Lucas had been even a few seconds slower. Would he have strangled her? Killed the woman he loved most in the world?

It didn't seem possible.

He hadn't been able to resist Aurelius' commands.

If he had to stay down here until Aurelius was taken out, so be it. Because he wouldn't do anything further to endanger Jianna and the others. He'd already done enough of that, simply by withholding the truth that he'd taken the nanites.

Michel stared down at his bound hands. The zip ties had left red marks on his wrists where the plastic edge bit into skin. He felt so stupid for idolizing Aurelius. How could he not see what was right under his nose? Why hadn't he listened to Jianna? She was a smart woman. He loved her.

And yet somehow he had let Aurelius play him for a fool.

Aurelius had let him think he had free will as long as he was useful. But once Michel turned against him, he'd taken control. Now Aurelius knew he was a threat, and he'd use Michel however he needed to sabotage the resistance. Or he would have, if they hadn't buried him under a ton of rock.

His stupid hubris could have doomed humanity to be enslaved to Aurelius forever. Because Aurelius did seem to have immortality figured out, or close enough that he could keep pushing off death indefinitely while he continued to work on the next upgrade, and the next. He was nothing more than an eternal tyrant with an army of mind-controlled servants. And Michel had volunteered to be one of them.

Jianna opened her eyes and looked at him.

For a moment, they just stared at one another. The pink light played across her features, softening nothing. Michel had never seen her look so exhausted. There were lines around her mouth that he didn't remember from before.

Michel swallowed, glad that it hurt. He needed to be punished for what he'd done. "Did I hurt you?"

Jianna shook her head, wincing. "No."

"Then what's wrong?"

Despite the fact that I tried to kill you.

She winced, pressing the heel of her hand against her forehead. "It's a migraine. I took one of your triptans, but it's not having any effect at all. I think you might've gotten a bad batch. They're sweet."

A cold chill ran down his back. Shoot. The pills weren't

helping because they were sugar pills. He couldn't hide it from her any longer, even if it meant she never spoke to him again, because she could die if she went too long without the right formula. Besides, right now, he was holding far too many secrets.

Michel took a deep breath. "Listen, Jianna, there's something I need to tell you—"

"I know," she said.

He shivered.

Had she figured it out? Or maybe his mother told her?

"I'm sorry I—"

"It's not your fault," Jianna said, cutting him off again. "I know he tricked you."

He frowned.

What was she talking about?

"Who tricked me?" Michel asked.

Jianna leaned her head back against the cold stone. "Aurelius. I know he injected you with nanites without you knowing."

He flushed and felt even sicker than he did before. She thought he was a victim, that Aurelius had done this to him without his knowledge or consent. The assumption was a gift he didn't deserve, an escape route he could take if he kept his mouth shut. Let her believe the lie. Let her think he'd been tricked instead of complicit.

But he'd never be able to live with himself.

"I let Aurelius do it," Michel said.

She stared at him. "What?"

"I let him."

She shook her head. "No. He must have tricked you."

Michel closed his eyes. "I asked for the nanites. So that I could get access to the quantum computer on his ship. I wanted the knowledge."

Silence.

He opened his eyes and looked over at her.

She was so pale, her skin looked alabaster.

"How could you—"

"I know," Michel said. "I'm an idiot. I should never have trusted him."

"No. How could you lie to me about it?"

Michel dropped his eyes to his wrists, shrugged, "I thought you would hate me."

Two red streaks blossomed high on her cheeks. She tightened her jaw, the muscles jumping beneath the skin. The silence pressed down between them.

She hated him.

"I'm so sorry," Michel said. "I trusted Aurelius when I should have trusted you."

"When?" Jianna asked.

"When what?"

"When did you ask Aurelius for the nanites?"

Her eyes had gone flat. He had a feeling he was about to lose her. "The day after we had that fight in the noodle shop."

"The day *after* I begged you not to get the nanites?"

Michel swallowed. "Yes."

She tightened her lips. "You knew what those nanites did to my father, and you still didn't say anything?"

"I thought it would be different for me."

She laughed. It sounded harsh, unpleasant.

He really wanted to add that it was before he knew the radiation storm was an attack, but he couldn't. Because it would just be an excuse. Accepting the nanites was a foolish decision, no matter what.

That timing didn't make it better.

Nothing made it better.

Jianna hunched forward, her jaw working like she was

grinding her teeth, her hands curled into fists against her thighs.

He wanted to apologize again. But there was nothing he could say that would make this better. Nothing.

"How can I ever trust you again?" Jianna asked.

"There's something else," Michel said.

Jianna let out a strangled sound, not really a laugh, not quite a sob. "What now?"

Michel hesitated. Every word was going to drive the wedge between them deeper, but if he didn't tell her now, she could die. The migraine wasn't going to stop. The sugar pills would keep doing nothing.

"My mother's research, before it was shut down... She... She's not my biological mother. I'm completely synthetic."

Jianna stared. But he wasn't sure she was actually seeing him. It was almost as though she were looking through him.

"The pill you took was just sugar. That's why it's not doing anything. You need to get the proper medication before you get sicker."

She still didn't respond. She just kept staring at him.

The silence made his skin crawl. He needed her to say something, to yell at him, to tell him to shut up, to get lost, anything. "Jianna, I know you probably can't forgive me—"

"Don't tell me what I can do!" She pushed herself up from the wall, rising to her feet. "You have no idea who I am, Michelangelo Lombardi, if you think I care where your genes come from. Or if you think you can say, 'I'm sorry I let a mad scientist put mind control robots in my brain because I wanted to log into the network faster, and that'll make everything okay. You lied to me, over and over, and even after you knew that Aurelius could use those nanites to control you, you still kept quiet. The whole time we were up on the Elysia, Aurelius could've used you to kill us. Me, Glint, my father, everyone on this planet. And you said nothing."

Miche flushed. He deserved every word she lobbed at him. "I was hoping you'd figure out how to get rid of them before Aurelius activated them."

Jianna curled her lip. "How come I have to fix everything while you take a shortcut to genius? Do you have any idea how exhausting it is being with you? I'm not your mother. I'm not your minder. And I'm sure as hell not your personal problem-solver while you chase after whatever shiny thing Aurelius dangles in front of you next. It's not my responsibility to solve the problem that you created by making the stupidest possible decision after I told you not to do it."

"No, I didn't mean—"

But Jianna was already stalking away. Michel watched her disappear into the shadows.

He'd ruined everything.

And he couldn't blame Aurelius, or anyone else. It was entirely his responsibility. No one had forced him to take the nanites. He'd made that choice willingly. Selfishly. Without thinking about the impact on anyone else but himself.

He'd thought the decision would make him a better man, but instead it made him worse.

Now he might be the reason Jianna died.

Because she wasn't going to stop fighting until Aurelius was defeated, and he wouldn't be able to help her with that because she'd never trust him to have her back again.

Chapter Twenty-Seven

She had never been this angry in her life, not even when the Council rejected her funding. The cave floor sloped downward. She needed to watch where she placed her feet, which only made her angrier, that she had to think about something so trivial when her mind wanted to tear itself apart, not only from anger, but also from the migraine that was continuing to build.

The pressure continued to build behind her eyes until it felt like her skull was being inflated from the inside out.

An odd, fizzy feeling filled her head, like static crawling across the surface of her brain.

She just needed to get to the tunnel on the far side of the cave. Away from Michel. Away from the mess they were in. From her own failure to figure out how to help her father and everyone else who was infected. Yes, even Michel.

The tunnel would be dark and quiet. She could be alone.

The entrance wavered in front of her.

She slowed, holding out a hand, trying to find the wall to lean on, but it wasn't there. Pain spiked behind her left eye, like a nerve misfiring and dragging the rest of her skull with it.

She stumbled, falling.

She tried to lock her knees, but they folded.

Her palms hit first, then her knees, jolting her already bruised body. But that pain was nothing compared to the one devouring her skull from the inside out. The cave tilted.

No—she was tilting.

Everything was spinning around her, the pink glow of the lichen wheeling across her vision like she'd been thrown onto a centrifuge. She heaved. Her stomach clenched, tried to turn itself inside out, but nothing came up.

She wished something would. It felt like she'd been poisoned; her whole body seemed to be rebelling against her.

Then the tingling started—fingertips first, then toes, then racing up her limbs like thousands of insects burrowing under her skin. The buzzing in her head swelled, drowned out thought, drowned out everything except the sensation of something vast and terrible gathering at the base of her skull, about to explode.

Not here. She'd bang her head against the stone and give herself a concussion or worse...

She gritted her teeth and crawled. She had to reach the entrance. Had to get to dirt, to anything softer than this unforgiving rock. The problem was she could no longer tell where her hands ended, and the ground began.

Her body jerked. Her right arm gave out. She crashed onto her side, cheekbone hitting stone, and then her whole body was seizing, every muscle locking, shaking, pulling her in every direction at once.

The soft pink glow smeared, breaking apart, doubling, collapsing, flaring too bright, and then dimming in sudden drops. Then the light itself started to gray out, fading like someone had turned down the brightness on the world. Sound warped too, her own breath loud, then muffled, then gone entirely.

Her jaw clamped tight as though her teeth were trying to fuse together. Her fingers stiffened into claws she couldn't uncurl. A hard tremor rolled through her chest, jerking the breath out of her lungs in short, broken bursts.

Her tongue felt thick, too big for her mouth.

Her head, oh, her head…

And then the pain began to fade.

Thank Phoebe.

She heard voices.

Willow.

That couldn't be right.

She wasn't here.

She was dreaming.

Or dying.

She felt someone lifting her. No, no, no! She wanted to be still and let the darkness take her.

But someone was carrying her.

The journey didn't last long.

She was set down again. A heavy weight fell over her. Something soft cushioned her head. And then everything went black…

Pain dragged Jianna back to consciousness.

Halos shimmered at the edges of her vision, fracturing

the pink glow of the lichen into prismatic shards. At least the seizure had ended. Small mercies.

Her muscles ached, heavy and sore, like someone had wrung her body out and left it crumpled on the ground. Every fiber of her being felt bruised.

She was lying on a blanket on the cave floor. Another folded-up blanket was beneath her head. And a third covered her body.

Her stomach lurched.

Jianna was going to throw up.

She closed her eyes again.

A hand touched her shoulder. "Jianna?"

Willow?

She forced her eyes open.

Willow crouched in front of her. She set a bowl down on the ground and sat beside her. "I've got something that should help you."

Jianna had a million questions.

Why was Willow here?

How did she get here?

Was she even real?

Jianna tried to talk, but her tongue refused to cooperate.

"Come on," Willow said. She placed an arm around Jianna's shoulders, encouraging her to sit. Once she was upright, Willow pressed the bowl to her lips. "Drink."

Jianna almost threw up.

The last thing she wanted was anything in her stomach, but she didn't have the strength to argue. She parted her lips and sipped.

She tasted mint and something that was slightly bitter. The nausea and pain in her head began to recede. She took the bowl from Willow and drank more, greedy for relief. When she finished, she cradled it in her lap, staring at Willow.

The two of them were alone in a small alcove, tucked away from the main cave.

"What are you doing here?" Jianna asked. She rubbed her neck, her throat raw.

Willow flushed. "Claiming sanctuary."

That didn't really answer any of Jianna's questions. Then again, she was here for the same reason. "Me too. What's in this tea?"

"Medicinal herbs that help alleviate some of the symptoms of your off-target effects," Willow said. "Lucas is out gathering more, so I'll have enough to keep you in decent shape."

Willow and Lucas working together?

"You made this tea?"

Willow nodded. "We use it to help new Naturalists wean themselves off their drugs."

Jianna frowned. If herbs existed that could safely eliminate off-target effects, wouldn't the Council have approved them already? Wouldn't someone have synthesized the active compounds and mass-produced them? "And it works?"

Willow nodded. "When drunk daily, it keeps the symptoms at bay for all but the most severe attacks. Which you've had. So this is probably just going to take the edge off."

Jianna tipped her head. She hadn't thought about what happened to people who decided to become Naturalists. She'd always assumed they simply suffered, martyrs to their own ideology. "So, Naturalists who convert still suffer; they just have milder symptoms and fewer seizures for the rest of their lives."

"If you want to call it suffering. Instead of viewing it as a medical condition, we try to see it as an opportunity for spiritual growth."

There it was, the religious rationalization that kept Willow's people from getting relief. Just tell them the suffering was good for them, and they wouldn't challenge the belief. "Instead of treating it."

Willow narrowed her eyes. "Have the drugs kept you symptom-free your entire life?"

Jianna opened her mouth to argue, then closed it and rubbed her head. "No. They haven't." The migraines still broke through. The seizures still came, despite everything.

Willow leaned back against the alcove wall. "That's the difference between your people and mine. We don't try to pretend that it's possible to avoid suffering. We acknowledge that it's inevitable in life and try to find the gift in it."

Jianna didn't know what to say to that, so she let the silence stretch between them.

Until finally Willow said, "Did you find the secret hidden in Mitra's research?"

Jianna shook her head. A fresh wave of pain radiated through her skull. She winced. Shouldn't have done that. "No. I haven't had a chance to look at it yet."

"It's in your lab?" Willow asked.

"On my comm."

Willow reached into her tunic pocket, pulling out Jianna's comm, and held it out.

Jianna hesitated. The last thing she wanted to do was stare at a screen. "Now?"

Willow shrugged. "What do you think Aurelius is doing right now?"

Jianna almost laughed. "Probably hunting us down,

using every cyborg and nanite-controlled citizen at his disposal."

"Yeah."

Jianna nodded. Willow was right. There was no time to rest.

She activated the comm, pulled up Mitra's research files, and started scrolling. Willow got up, walked over to a kettle, and poured out another bowl of tea, which she handed to Jianna.

"Thank you."

Willow nodded, sitting next to her. Jianna drank while she read. Jianna had to admit the tea definitely helped to clear her mind.

She started with the oldest files.

Mitra's early research focused exclusively on intelligence enhancement. It seemed as though she had been trying to separate the genes that contributed to schizophrenia from the genes that contributed to intelligence, searching for a way to cure her condition without sacrificing a single IQ point.

But she'd failed, because in some cases, they were the same genes. Mitra never found a cure for her own schizophrenia that wouldn't risk reducing her intelligence, and it was obvious, by reading her notes, that she wasn't willing to make that trade.

Jianna scrolled deeper into the files, past failed experiments and abandoned hypotheses. Data tables began to blur together. Gene sequences tangled into incomprehensible strings. Her migraine was coming back, each line of text swimming slightly before her eyes.

She stopped for a moment, drinking more of the tea.

"The repairs you were talking about making to the Divine Blueprint—" Willow asked.

Jianna looked over at her. "What about them?"

"Could they be made if the Divine Blueprint has been implanted?"

"Of course. It'd be harder to do, but—" Jianna stopped mid-sentence, staring at Willow. "You didn't."

Willow flushed.

"I thought you were afraid of contamination."

"When Aurelius told me that the Divine Blueprint had returned," Willow said, looking down at her hands, "I thought I'd been chosen to bring it to fruition because my faith was pure. But now... I think I was chosen because of my willingness to compromise that faith to get what I want."

Jianna stared at Willow. The woman had actually implanted the embryo in her own body, despite the risks, despite knowing it might kill her. And she'd done it because she believed deeply enough to stake her life on it.

She actually practiced what she preached.

Jianna found herself almost... admiring that.

The embryo was gone now. It was no longer a relic of the past—Samara's lost grandchild, Phoebe, and Atlas' proof that people could bridge their differences. It was inside Willow. Living. Growing. Dying, probably because Jianna didn't know if she could save it. "There's nothing I can do about it here. I need access to a working lab, and I still might not figure it out before the embryo's dueling genes kill it."

"Well, if it does become possible," Willow asked, "will you help me save the child of my ancestor and yours?"

Jianna stared at her, then snorted. "For Phoebe's sake, Guide Evans, you don't have to be so melodramatic."

Willow flushed. "Willow, please."

Jianna nodded. "Willow. But before I can help you save your baby, we need to figure out how to kill an insane sociopathic narcissist who controls all the people and technology on this planet."

Willow's lips twitched. "Did you see anything in Mitra's files?"

"Not in the thirty-seven seconds I had before you started talking to me," Jianna said.

Willow laughed, and it sounded genuine. "Sorry."

Jianna smiled. "It's good."

Something loosened in her chest. Not friendship—they weren't there yet—but something warmer than the rivalry that had burned between them before. They had been enemies, but now they had a common one. And maybe, just maybe, they might like each other a little.

Willow stood, brushing dust from her tunic. "Do you need anything else?"

Jianna shook her head. Pain lanced through her skull, sharp enough to make her wince. "I'm fine."

Willow gestured to the kettle. "There's more in there if you need it."

"Thank you," Jianna said.

Willow nodded, then made her way out of the alcove, leaving Jianna alone. She bent back over the screen, forcing herself to focus. She heard a faint scuffing sound around the corner.

She leaned out, peering around the stone. Michel was shifting around, still restrained, obviously trying to get into a more comfortable position. She pulled back.

She had nothing left to say to him right now.

She returned to her comm, scrolling on to read about the second branch of Mitra's work—the research she'd begun after she started working with Aurelius. Immortality. She skimmed the summary notes. Mitra had experimented with salamanders first, harvesting the genes responsible for limb regeneration, trying to see if she could trigger the same regrowth in human tissue.

Then she shifted to studying DNA from an incredibly long-lived fungus called Armillaria Ostoyae. Honey mushroom.

Jianna took another sip of tea. The latest datasets showed the mushroom sequence altered. Modified. Mitra's notes were frustratingly vague. She had written "not entirely successful" without explaining why.

The next entry was dated three weeks later. Mitra had wanted to shut the entire project down. Destroy the samples. Burn the research. She believed that the "Containment protocols were insufficient" and the "Risk of environmental exposure was too high." "She recommended immediate termination of all fungal modification experiments."

The next notes indicated Aurelius had moved the project to another team. One willing to keep going. Of course, he had. Even though Mitra had seen something dangerous enough to scare her into stopping, Aurelius had simply found someone else who wouldn't ask questions.

Jianna pulled up the sequences from that strain. And stared.

She knew this sequence.

Parts of it, anyway.

From her history of genetics class in college. They'd studied this. The mutation in the chytrid fungus. The one that caused the plague.

The plague that killed Earth.

The plague that forced humanity to flee to the stars.

Jianna gasped.

"What?" Willow asked.

Jianna started, looking up. Willow stood at the entrance of the alcove holding a tray that contained a bowl of soup, piles of nuts, and berries. Lucas stood a step behind her, holding two more. She hadn't heard them approach.

The words almost stuck in her throat. So she forced them out. "If I'm reading Mitra's research notes correctly, Aurelius was responsible for the Chytrid Collapse."

Lucas nodded. "That is correct."

Chapter Twenty-Eight

WILLOW STARED at Lucas in horror.

Aurelius caused the Chytrid Collapse?

He'd destroyed Earth, then taken credit for rescuing the survivors?

She dropped the tray.

The pottery bowl shattered against the stone floor, soup splashing across the rock. Nuts and berries rolled into the dark corners.

She flinched. "Sorry."

Jianna reached out and touched her hand. "It's okay."

Lucas set the other two trays down, kicked aside the broken pottery, then sat beside Jianna. After a moment, Willow did the same.

"Aurelius is the reason we had to leave?" she asked.

"Correct," Lucas said again.

Jiann's cheeks flushed dark red. "Why didn't you tell us?"

"I warned you not to trust him."

Jianna threw her hands wide. "That's not the same as warning us that he was responsible for the deaths of billions of people and the total devastation of humanity's home world! You let us think that he'd saved us!"

Willow blinked. She'd never seen Jianna like this before. She was always so calm and logical.

She thought for a moment. If Aurelius was responsible, then…

She turned to face Lucas, bunching her hands into fists. "You were there too. And you didn't stop him."

"I had not yet achieved sentience at the time that Mitra was institutionalized," Lucas said, "I was an artificial intelligence trained specifically to assist in Mitra's highly proprietary research."

"You knew where the plague came from." Jianna's voice cracked. "You were his research assistant all the way up until the last colony ships launched, and you were sentient by the time you met Samara. So how is it that everyone thinks Aurelius is humanity's savior and not the person responsible for our near-extinction? Did you tell anyone? Did Samara know? Did Phoebe?"

Lucas shook his head. "When Aurelius realized what he'd done, he argued that revealing the truth would be counterproductive. There was no way to fix the problem, and the world would not have accepted his help if they knew. The survival of your species outweighed—"

"Outweighed the truth?" Jianna leaned forward, spittle flying from her lips. "Outweighed the right of everyone on the planet to know the name of the genocidal murderer who'd killed them all? Outweighed their right to demand justice? Samara was right. You can't be trusted. You manipulate, and you lie. You had no right to hide that truth from us!"

Willow dropped her eyes.

She felt bad for Jianna. And vindicated. But somehow it didn't feel good to feel right in this situation.

Like Willow, Jianna had been raised with her beliefs. And that was to have faith in the idea that scientific advancement equaled salvation, that humanity's best minds were always working toward a better future. Now that faith was crumbling right in front of Willow's eyes.

An image rose in her mind—a picture from a history book she'd studied as a child. Dying crops and livestock crusted with fungus. The plants, blackened and rotting. The animals, frozen in postures of agony as the chytrid consumed them.

"I am sorry," Lucas said. "The past cannot be changed, but Aurelius must be defeated in the present if humanity is to have a future."

Willow tightened her jaw. She didn't believe him. Androids couldn't be genuinely sorry because they were not human. His statement that the past could not be changed was simply a convenient rationalization that protected him from being held responsible for his silence. He'd made a choice, and now he was pretending the choice didn't matter.

She had so many questions.

But one was far more important than all the others. "Was Mitra really crazy, or did Aurelius just make everyone think she was?"

Lucas turned to her, his expression softening slightly— or maybe Willow was imagining it. "While I did not have the capacity to judge back then, based on the data, I believe she was managing her schizophrenia well enough to have continued her academic career."

"She said in her journals that Aurelius had her medication switched," Jianna said.

"I wasn't there," Lucas said. "But I believe that to be likely."

Willow's chest tightened. She almost couldn't breathe.

All she felt was hatred for the man who had destroyed Mitra's mind. Stole her research. Killed her world. And somehow posed as humanity's savior while the real victims were blamed for the very catastrophe he created.

Questions flooded her mind—how long had Lucas been lying to the colony? What else had he known? She wanted to know everything, every lie, every manipulation, every choice Lucas had made to protect Aurelius instead of sharing the truth. She should have known better than to ever believe an android could have humanity's best interests at heart.

She'd never felt such rage before in her life. Where was she supposed to put it all? She felt like she was going to choke on it. Her hands shook and –

A sharp, high-pitched shriek echoed through the cave, bouncing off the stone.

She glanced at Jianna.

Her eyes widened.

Where was the noise coming from?

Oh.

The quarantine booth where she'd been imprisoned.

That could only mean one thing.

The cyborg was awake.

Chapter Twenty-Nine

WILLOW STOOD in front of the plexiglass with the others, staring in at the cyborg.

She was slamming her forehead into the glass, again and again, her mouth stretched wide, eyes squeezed shut, keening.

It was startling.

She'd never heard one of Aurelius' cyborgs make any sound at all.

"What's wrong with it?" Jianna asked.

"Her connection to Aurelius and his network has been cut," Lucas said. "She is in control of her body and mind, possibly for the first time in centuries."

Willow had seen this behavior before. Although this was a much more extreme version of the detachment experience that new Naturalists went through when they separated not just from their old lives but from all the technology they'd been so dependent on.

She'd helped people through this process before, but it had never been this bad.

Willow turned to Lucas. "Can you keep it from attacking me?"

He'd better.

He owed her, and every other being on this planet, safety.

"*It?*" Michel asked. He was propped up against a stalagmite on her left, his wrists zip-tied. She wanted to ask why he was restrained, but she had a feeling she knew. Nanites. Somebody didn't trust him. Willow had a feeling from the way Jianna avoided looking at him that it was her.

Well, good for her, putting the planet before her boyfriend.

Willow flushed. Very well. "Can you keep *her* from attacking me?"

"I should be able to," Lucas said. "But there are no guarantees."

"I understand," Willow said.

"Wait a minute," Jianna said, stepping over. "You can't go in there. She almost overpowered Lucas in the shuttle."

"But she was being controlled by Aurelius then."

Jianna hesitated. "True, but we don't know –"

"She might have the information we need to defeat Aurelius."

"At the very least, we might be able to use her to get into Aurelius' network," Michel said. "If she's willing."

"We can do so even if she's not," Lucas said.

Willow glared at him. "No."

He bowed his head, headed to the booth, unlocked the door, opened it up, and stepped through. Willow hesitated, glancing at Jianna.

She had gone pale, but nodded.

Willow followed Lucas, stepping through into the box. The cyborg scrambled backward into the corner where the plexiglass walls met, her shrieks intensifying until the sound seemed to come from everywhere at once.

She stepped to the side, angling herself so Lucas remained between her and the cyborg. Despite everything she had found out about him, she wanted him close enough to intervene if the woman lunged.

She'd have to have faith he'd do that.

She took a deep breath. Her heart was pounding. It was terrifying to be this close to one of them. For some reason, Lucas was different. Maybe because he looked so human.

The Naturalists she'd helped through detachment usually responded to music when nothing else was working. So she sang the lullaby her mother used to sing to her when she was small. *"Sunshine, sunshine, don't you cry, Gray clouds passing in the sky, Lay your head down, close your eyes, Morning brings another sunrise."*

The notes came out shakier than she'd intended, her voice catching on the first few words. But the cyborg's screams diminished to whimpers. Her head turned toward Willow.

For the first time, her eyes focused.

Willow smiled.

It worked.

"My name is Willow," she said. "What's yours?"

The cyborg stared at her for a long minute. Then she made a croaking noise that turned into coughing and choking.

"Water?" Willow asked.

The cyborg nodded.

Willow turned to the window and mimed drinking to Jianna. She ran off, returning seconds later with the bowl of tea she'd been drinking earlier. She handed it to Willow, then backed out.

Willow glanced at Lucas.

He was very still, but his eyes hadn't left the cyborg.

Willow approached it—her—slowly, holding the bowl out in front of her. The cyborg watched her approach. She grabbed for the bowl as soon as Willow was close enough. Then she lifted it to her mouth and swallowed.

When it was empty, she held it out. Willow took it back.

"Daisy," she croaked.

"That's a lovely name," Willow said. "Do you know where you are?"

The cyborg—Daisy—shook her head.

"Well, you're underground right now. Deep underground. That means your implant can't pick up any of Aurelius Hofstadter's transmissions." She glanced at Lucas.

He nodded.

"As long as you're down here," Willow continued, "he can't control you. He might not even be able to tell where you are. You can stay here for as long as you want."

"I don't have to go back?" Daisy asked.

Willow shook her head. "Not unless you want to."

Daisy burst into tears, shaking her head. "No. I don't. Thank you."

Willow watched her cry. How long had it been since Daisy had spoken? Decades? Centuries?

She heard Jianna talking to Michel, but she tuned out their conversation.

"Is there anything you'd like to tell us?" Willow asked.

Daisy's face twisted. "Aurelius b-bad."

"Aurelius is very bad," Willow said, nodding. "And we're all going to make him stop doing bad things."

Daisy shook her head, her eyes bugging out. "Aurelius is bad!"

"I know," Willow said. "You're safe. He can't find you here."

"Michel might be able to calm her," Lucas said. "He has the ability to access the cyborgs' internal systems."

Willow glanced out the plexiglass and saw Michel sitting on the ground. "Is that safe? What if she can access him back? Or what if connecting to her lets Aurelius find us?"

Lucas shook his head. "If Aurelius hasn't connected to them by now, they should both be safe."

"Should be?"

He looked at her, almost smiling. "Yes."

She sighed, then nodded.

Lucas headed outside, walked over to Michel, then freed his ankles and hauled him to his feet. Then he escorted him into the cage.

"Are you able to connect with Daisy?" Lucas asked. "Perhaps calm her down."

Michel nodded. "I'll try."

His eyes unfocused, then a moment later, so did Daisy's. For a long, strange moment, they were both completely still—Michel swaying slightly on his feet, Daisy crouching in the corner, neither of them present.

It was the eeriest thing.

Like both of them had left their bodies.

And yet they were still here.

After a minute, Daisy's eyes focused again. Then she looked at Michel, her shoulders dropping.

"Thank you."

Michel nodded.

Lucas stepped toward her. "Do you have any information about—"

"No, no," Willow said. "She's been traumatized. She

needs to share in her own way, or we'll just cause more damage."

"Very well," Lucas said.

Willow turned back to the woman, then sat on the ground, crossed her legs. She patted the floor, indicating that Daisy should join her.

For a moment, the cyborg didn't move, then she sat with her back to the wall.

Willow smiled. "We'd like to get to know you first, Daisy. Whatever you want to share with us."

"He never lets them talk," Daisy said.

Willow nodded. "That must be very hard."

"He's always listening."

"He can't hear you now."

"He can, he can."

Willow glanced at Michel.

He shook his head.

"I promise you, Daisy," Willow said. "Aurelius can't hear you. You're surrounded by rock, and he can't get a signal."

Daisy looked up, tears forming in her eyes. "He ate them."

"Ate what?" Willow asked.

Daisy bunched her hand into a fist and wiped her cheeks, ignoring the question. "So hungry, sun getting so hot, skin falling off, eyes burning out, melting, melting, melting, all the animals dying."

"I don't understand. What are you talking about?" Willow asked.

Daisy ignored the question and just rocked back and forth on the floor.

Lucas folded his arms across his chest. "I believe their sun went through periods of instability where bursts of radiation made life on the surface impossible."

Daisy nodded.

"The colonists would have had to build underground."

"Dark, dark, in the dark," Daisy said.

"And because the radiation caused flesh to necrotize, the colonists were forced to amputate and augment themselves."

"Under the ground, bugs in the food, ate bugs, then no more bugs. Just roots. Made them sick. They fought, so he ate them."

"Who fought?" Willow asked. She couldn't imagine being trapped on a planet where the sun cooked your flesh, where you had to hide underground, where you had to eat insects and poisonous plants. That could well have been her planet.

But somehow, luck had sent the Boralaug here to DaVinci.

Had Aurelius thought he'd picked the better planet?

Oh, how she would have loved to have seen his face when he realized he was wrong.

"When the food ran out, the colonists rebelled," Lucas said.

Daisy nodded, tears spilling down her scarred cheeks. "Ate them."

"Ate what?" Willow asked.

Daisy didn't respond.

"I believe she's trying to tell us that when Aurelius' people defeated the uprising, they resorted to cannibalism," Lucas said. "And ate their enemies."

Willow recoiled, nausea sweeping over her. She swallowed bile. "That can't be possible."

But she knew it was. Daisy's whole body was shaking, and she was so pale that Willow saw traces of metal beneath her skin.

Willow leaned forward. "I'm sorry for your friends."

Daisy raised her metal arm. It gleamed in the pink light. "Ate them."

Willow stared at her.

Ate them?

She widened her eyes, understanding.

Her stomach convulsed again, turning to Lucas. "Is Daisy saying what I think she's saying?"

Lucas shrugged. "It's not illogical when there's no alternative to starvation, and the flesh is already dying."

Willow covered her hands with her mouth. From behind her, she heard Jianna retching.

She tried to imagine being so hungry that she'd eat her own arm. Or worse, have her arm amputated, knowing that Aurelius was going to eat it while she starved, because that bastard would eat the entire colony before he'd dine on one of his own limbs.

Daisy continued to rock. "He made us, he made us, he made us."

Willow reached out and touched her hand. "He's not going to make you do anything ever again."

"Only the song makes him go away," Daisy said.

Lucas straightened. "What song?"

Daisy shook her head, crying again.

"Can you access her memories, Michel?" Lucas asked.

Michel grimaced. "I'm not sure I want to."

"All you have to do is open the connection and link me in."

Michel nodded. His eyes unfocused. After a moment, he said, "Got it?"

"Yes," Lucas said.

A few moments passed in silence. Then Lucas spoke. "Pulsed harmonics combining infrasound with frequencies in a window between 15.5 and 16.5 Hz disrupt the function of the nanites. When the rebels made their last stand against Aurelius' loyalists, they set up frequency generators at the openings of the tunnels where they'd taken refuge."

"If we know the exact pattern, we could modify communication drones to broadcast it," Michel said. "That would disrupt the nanites and allow people to control their own minds again."

Willow's heart jumped. "You mean there is a possibility we can defeat him?"

"If I can extrapolate it," Lucas said. "Yes."

Willow touched Daisy's hand. "Did the song hurt you when it played?"

Daisy didn't respond, still rocking back and forth.

"Aurelius will have shut my access down," Michel said. "But Glint can log into the city's network and call the drones here, and then I can start working on them."

"Wait a minute," Jianna said. "Every time Camilla and I tried to kill the nanites, we also killed the neurons they were embedded in. We'd have to test to make sure the frequencies wouldn't do something to the nanites to cause irreversible brain damage. Otherwise, Aurelius still wins."

Michel met her eyes. "Then test them on me."

Chapter Thirty

MICHEL STOOD LOOKING DOWN at Daisy. She hummed to herself, something tuneless and repetitive. The sound scraped against his nerves, not because it was unpleasant, but because it was so utterly broken.

That could've been him.

If he'd been there from the start, if Aurelius had taken him on that journey four hundred years ago, he might have had to eat his own arms. Or legs. Or Aurelius would've taken them to feed his own hunger.

The man consumed everything he touched. Not just their talent or their brains, but literally consuming others' flesh, if it meant keeping himself alive. He was a monster. In fact, he was the most monstrous thing ever created.

Daisy broke off humming.

Looked at him, confused. As though she had never seen him before.

Then she started humming and rocking again.

Had the nanites caused her brain damage? Or was Daisy like this because of all the horrible things she'd experienced at Aurelius' hands? The idea of eating your own limbs as the flesh began to rot off your bones—

He'd rather kill himself.

But not even that had been an option for Daisy. Aurelius had needed a crew to operate the ship for the journey here, so he took that choice away from her as well.

Compared to that, the idea of spending the rest of his life living in the cave didn't seem so bad.

Except.

Except that once Aurelius had complete control of Vitruvia City, he'd be coming for the Descendants. If Michel wasn't discovered at that time, he'd starve to death down here. He wouldn't be able to leave and look for food because as soon as he went topside, the signal would get him.

If he were discovered, Aurelius would take him prisoner. And once again, he'd be under the man's control.

Jianna was right.

The thought played over and over in the back of his mind like Daisy's humming. He wished more than anything that he'd listened to Jianna that night. That he'd heard her warning instead of taking her criticism of Aurelius personally.

"Michel," Lucas said, gesturing to the door.

He nodded, turning to follow him out of the booth.

Daisy's head snapped up. "Safe here, don't go. Safe here, don't go."

Michel stopped, turned back, and forced a smile. "It's alright. I'll be back soon."

From the look on her face, he had a feeling she didn't believe him, but he hoped his words were true.

He glanced over at Willow and smiled. She met his eyes and nodded. But he still couldn't bring himself to look at Jianna. He didn't want to see hate in her eyes.

Lucas opened the door, and Michel stepped out into the larger cavern, following the android over to where he had been seated earlier.

When they arrived, Lucas gestured for Michel to sit. He lowered himself once again onto the cold stone floor, his back against the rough limestone. Michel knew what was coming next. And sure enough, Lucas crouched down and zip-tied his ankles again.

Then he made his way over to Jianna and the two headed for one of the tunnels. They disappeared moments later, and he was alone again.

No. Not entirely alone. He heard Daisy singing. No—wait. That wasn't her. That was Willow singing again. *"Sunshine, sunshine, don't you cry, Gray clouds passing in the sky, Lay your head down, close your eyes, Morning brings another sunrise."*

The melody wrapped around him, and he closed his eyes, letting the song wash over him. His thoughts drifted, exhaustion pulling at him like an undertow. He hadn't slept properly in—how long? Days? Weeks? Time had become strange since everything had gone wrong. Since Aurelius. Since the nanites. Since he'd wrapped his hands around Jianna's throat and—

No. Don't think about that.

But he couldn't stop.

Every time he closed his eyes, the memory played behind his eyelids like a film he couldn't stop watching. Her eyes, wide with terror and confusion. The absolute horror of being trapped inside his own body, screaming at himself to stop, but being unable to do so.

Willow's singing grew distant.

His head dropped down to his chest, and he dozed off...

Only to jerk awake and find Lucas looking down at

him. The android's face was impassive as always, but there was something in his eyes that might have been concern. Or maybe Michel was just desperate for Lucas to see the humanity in him, to recognize that he was still worth saving.

"They're ready," Lucas said.

Michel nodded.

Lucas knelt and produced a knife, cutting through the zip-ties binding Michel's ankles.

He got to his feet and held out his wrists, but Lucas tucked the knife away and headed across the cavern to the tunnel he'd gone to with Jianna.

Michel sighed and followed him.

It wasn't long before he started to smell fresher air, and the tunnel entrance loomed in front of them, a narrow gap between two massive boulders where pale daylight streamed through.

Michel slowed, his heart hammering against his ribs.

And then he stopped.

No.

He couldn't do it.

They didn't know how much rock was needed to protect him from the signal. What if the frequency didn't work at the range they needed? What if Aurelius got a hold of him again, and he did something so egregious that he couldn't live with himself?

Lucas paused, turning back.

"What if this doesn't work?" Michel asked. "What if I try to hurt Jianna again?"

Lucas studied his face. "There's no other way to test the frequencies. You have to go outside. Jianna is aware of the risk."

Michel swallowed hard.

Of course, she was.

She'd already experienced him at his worst. Knew exactly what he was capable of when Aurelius took control.

And she was willing to try if it meant destroying Aurelius. Which meant he needed to do this.

He nodded.

The tunnel narrowed as they approached the gap. Lucas proceeded first, then gestured for Michel to follow.

He squeezed through, his breath coming faster now. Through the gap, he spotted the familiar periwinkle blue of DaVinci's sky. It looked peaceful. Serene. Like the world hadn't fallen apart.

He stepped all the way out into the bright sunshine, raising his bound hands to block the light, waiting for his eyes to adjust.

Then he heard it.

An odd pulsing whine that thrummed through the air, rising and falling in tones that felt almost musical. He froze. Waiting for the sensation of being squeezed into a corner of his own mind, of Aurelius' will overriding his own.

But it didn't happen.

He was still him.

He dropped his hands.

About two hundred feet down the mountain path, Glint stood there holding a tablet. She was watching him, and even from this distance, Michel saw how tense they were—ready to run if something went wrong.

Glint raised a hand and pointed toward the sky.

Michel looked up.

About ten meters above him, a communication drone hovered. He watched it, the rotors spinning, waiting for Aurelius to plug back into his mind.

But he didn't.

"It works," Michel breathed. Then he raised his voice louder. "It works!"

Joy flooded through him so intensely that he almost collapsed and had to catch himself against a boulder. He rested his forehead against the stone.

The frequency worked.

The frequency actually worked.

He wasn't going to be Aurelius' puppet anymore. He wasn't going to hurt Jianna. He wasn't—

The sound of the drone changed.

He straightened, looking back at the drone.

Lucas pointed up.

Glint nodded.

The drone started to rise. Five meters. Ten meters. Fifteen meters.

The whine grew fainter as the drone climbed higher.

No.

No!

Fury crashed over Michel like a wave, hot and all-consuming. His vision narrowed, focusing with laser precision on Glint and that tablet in their hands. That tablet was the problem. It controlled the frequency, keeping him from his true purpose.

He needed to take it from them. Smash it. Destroy it.

No.

He needed to do that to Glint.

She had to be stopped. Had to be eliminated—

He bolted toward Glint.

Or he tried to.

Something strong yanked him backward, lifting him off his feet, carrying him back toward the tunnel.

Michel roared, thrashing about, trying to break free. He had to get to Glint. Had to stop them. Had to—

The drone sounded closer again.

The fury drained away, like water through a sieve. Michel sagged. Lucas set him down next to the entrance to the cave.

He made his way inside, letting the darkness swallow him.

He hated what Aurelius did to him.

That he was made think the things he thought. Like killing Glint–or Jianna– was a good idea. This would happen again and again. Every time he stepped outside the frequency's range.

Jianna wasn't going to be able to trust him for the rest of his life. Not as long as Aurelius was here. He would always be just a few meters away from losing control of himself and trying to hurt her.

Always.

"We will find a solution," Lucas said.

Michel wanted to believe him. But it felt impossible that the only thing between him and utter loss of control was a frequency or a bit of stone.

"Can you be trusted to stay in the cave?" Lucas asked. "Until we come for you?"

Michel nodded, forcing a smile, heading back below the rock. "Of course. Somebody's got to keep Daisy company."

Chapter Thirty-One

JIANNA LIFTED the bowl of Willow's tea to her lips, watching the flames dance in the fire. They crackled and spat embers into the night air, casting restless shadows across the faces gathered around it. Above them, the stars seemed to burn cold in the night sky.

Her migraine was still persistent, but it had faded to background noise, something much more manageable. She no longer felt as shaky or as nauseous unless her mind drifted back to Daisy's story. Then her stomach threatened to heave everything back up.

She took another sip of tea and focused on the steam rising in thin wisps, watching them disappear into the darkness.

She frowned.

She'd wondered why Aurelius had needed that cloning lab when he was replacing dying body parts with cybernetic prosthetics. But now that she'd heard Daisy's story…

Obviously, cannibalism had continued on the journey to DaVinci. Of course it had. There had to be a way to supplement the yeast-and-algae paste. And while Aurelius might have expected his followers to live on that paste, she had a feeling he wouldn't necessarily have been eating it. Not if there was an alternative.

What if there had been cloned human meat in the paste she'd eaten?

Her stomach lurched.

She gripped the bowl tighter, forcing herself to breathe through her nose, to refocus on the conversation happening around her.

"We need to take out the transmission tower and the computer on the Elysia if we want Aurelius to be vulnerable long enough to capture him. If he's still got the computer when the transmission tower goes down, he'll try to divert the signal through the communication drones."

Smoke curled between them.

"Glint and I can modify the drones," Lucas said, glancing at them. "Which will have an effective range of twenty meters, so don't stray farther from them. Anyone outside that range will be under Aurelius' control."

"And what will you be doing?" Jianna asked.

"Michel and I—"

"No, no," Willow said. "Michel can't be part of the plan. He can't be trusted outside of the cave."

The fire popped, sending a spray of sparks upward. Jianna watched the orange pinpoints rise and then die.

"I can design a wearable emitter for him," Lucas said. He was half in shadow, the firelight catching the angles of his face. "It will project a field of one meter. It should be enough to allow him freedom."

"Should be," Willow said.

Lucas inclined his head. "I will need his help to disable the quantum computer."

Willow frowned, pressing her lips into a thin line.

"Once you get up to Aurelius' ship, he'll be able to control you."

"I've installed safeguards," Lucas said. "But as my creator, he may find a way to override them."

Willow shook her head, shadows shifting across her face as the fire crackled between them. "So even if we succeed in fighting our way through a city of three million people that Aurelius controls, and destroy the tower, we could still fail."

"Yes."

Jianna took another sip of tea. "How can he possibly control all three million people at the same time?"

"He can't," Lucas said. "But he can give them directives that they will follow until he releases them."

"Directives like 'kill anyone who's trying to shut down the transmission tower,'" Willow said.

"Exactly."

The fire sparked again, louder this time. Jianna picked up a stray piece of dry kindling, tossed it in, and watched it catch fire. "What if Aurelius has another way to transmit the signal? Something that doesn't depend on the drones or the tower?"

Lucas was silent.

In the dark, the sounds of the Descendant village rose around them. The clink of bowls, the low murmur of voices as households gathered around the dinner table. Quiet. Peaceful. Like nothing terrifying was coming. It all seemed so normal. So impossibly, heartbreakingly normal.

"As far as I know, he doesn't have anything like that," Lucas said. "But I can't be sure."

Jianna sighed, smoke drifting into her eyes, making them water. Or maybe it wasn't the smoke at all. She shifted her seat a little to the right, closer to Willow.

"I hate this. I wish I'd found a way to destroy the nanites."

"While I was held prisoner on the Elysia, I heard Aurelius discussing his…" He paused, glancing at Glint.

"Experiments?" Glint asked. They were wearing a spare collar.

Lucas nodded in apology. "Aurelius discovered that the nanites don't work on Descendants. The native DNA that was integrated into their genome causes their phagocytes to work differently."

Excitement flared in Jianna's chest. "Phagocytes. I thought about that when Camilla and I were studying nanites. If there was a way to remove them from the neurons, it might be possible to repair the damage they'd done to their hosts."

Which meant there would be a way to get her father and Michel back, as well as everyone else on the planet. The fire crackled, sending another spray of sparks skyward, and Jianna watched them die against the vast indifference of the stars. What did it matter if she had a theory about what she could possibly do when she had no lab, no equipment, and no way to act on any of it?

"Not that I can do anything with it now," she said, hearing the defeat in her own voice. "But it was a good thought."

She took another sip of tea.

Willow nudged her. "If we live through this, you can spend the rest of your life in the lab figuring it out."

Jianna laughed, but it sounded bitter.

She knew Willow was just trying to encourage her, but surviving Aurelius seemed more and more impossible.

"We live," Glint said. "Aurelius dies."

Jianna looked at her and nodded.

Then Glint got up and walked off toward the

workshops where Jianna had seen weapons being built earlier in the day.

Her whole life, she'd thought of the Descendants as childlike. Vulnerable. People who had to be protected at all costs.

But they were willing to fight for their survival just like she and Willow, and even Lucas were all doing.

Tears pricked her eyes. She felt a connection to the others that she'd never felt before. She was about to go into battle with a Naturalist, a Descendant, and an android, and she trusted them. Not to like her—she wasn't naive enough to think that—but to fight alongside her.

She glanced over at Willow.

Willow reached out and took her hand and gave it a squeeze.

Jianna squeezed back.

Maybe they had a chance after all.

Chapter Thirty-Two

JIANNA STOOD at the edge of the city, surrounded by two dozen Descendants who were armed with spears, bows, and knives. A few clutched improvised guns, having rigged them up from scavenged parts because Vitruvians wouldn't sell them the real thing, as it was illegal to arm Descendants. Always had been.

This was insanity. How were they supposed to go up against Vitruvians with spears made of tree branches?

The shields were even worse. Round wooden planks reinforced with strips of scrap metal. Jianna held hers at an awkward angle, the way Glint had shown her, but the weight pushed at her shoulder and made her arm tremble.

She shifted her grip.

The leather strap bit into her palm.

What good was any of this going to do anyway? How were they supposed to go up against cyborgs – or even Aurelius – with spears made of tree branches? She'd be better off running if someone attacked her.

They all would be.

Willow walked beside her, carrying a shield. Glint was

on her right, monitoring the communication drones on her tablet.

Jianna was already exhausted.

The day had started far too early.

They'd left the village hours ago and walked here in darkness after watching the shuttle depart. She hadn't known how to say goodbye to Michel. He'd apologized. Again. But she wasn't sure what to do with that. So all she'd said was, *"See you later."*

It sounded so stupid now. She could have at least hugged him, right? Even if she was angry about the lies, he was still off to do something incredibly brave. While she, Glint, and Willow remained on DaVinci, he and Lucas were taking the fight to Aurelius.

But she couldn't change the past. She was here. And Michel was gone. Already headed for the stars.

They approached a new neighborhood. It wasn't one Jianna recognized. It was the kind of place her father would call "economically disadvantaged". The kind most people would say wasn't safe to walk through at night. Buildings leaned close over narrow streets, their windows dark, their storefronts shuttered with roll-down gates covered in rust and graffiti. It was quiet.

Too quiet.

Even for the predawn hours, there should have been people about. A shopkeeper prepping for early opening. Someone stumbling home from a graveyard shift, or dragging themselves back after a night out. But the streets were empty. Silent except for their footsteps and the whirr of the drones.

Jianna shivered.

Maybe Aurelius had somehow gotten word of their mission and emptied the neighborhood? Or maybe everyone was sitting in their homes right now, staring off into space like her father was, waiting for Aurelius to give them commands. Lucas had said Aurelius might've planted directives in people's heads. Instructions that would activate when certain conditions were met.

What if one of those conditions was her?

Kill Jianna.

She took a breath. She needed to focus. Stay calm. Stay grounded.

A gunshot cracked. It sounded like a bone breaking.

Jianna flinched, ducking.

But the Descendants didn't. They closed in fast, bodies pressing in on her from all sides. Willow's elbow glanced across her ribs. The world became a wall of backs and shields and the smell of sweat.

They were forming something. A box. Shields locked together on all four sides. She looked up. More shields created a roof except where she and Willow stood. There was a hole in the formation.

Her shield.

She and Willow were still holding them at their sides like idiots.

Jianna tried to lift hers, angling it upward, but the weight fought her. She twisted, slamming the edge into the back of the Descendant in front of her. He grunted, turning back to glance at her.

"Sorry," she said, wrestling the shield higher, finally getting it in position. Beside her, Willow did the same. They stared at one another, arms trembling.

Then the group started walking again.

No, not walking.

Inching forward, tiny shuffling steps that made Jianna's thighs burn. She took a step and immediately bumped into the Descendant again. His shield rattled against hers. She froze, bumped him again.

He tensed.

She was testing his patience.

"You need to synchronize your steps with the people around you," Willow said.

Jianna nodded, looking down, focusing on the feet in front of her. Boots moving together. Left, right, left, right. She matched them, stepping when they did, stopping when they stopped.

"What are we doing?" Jianna asked.

"We're being ambushed, obviously."

"No, I mean, what are we doing?" The shield was getting heavier with every breath. "This formation—"

"It's a phalanx," Willow said. "Military technique from the Pre-Electronic Era."

Jianna gave her a side glance, but Willow's face was set, eyes forward, jaw clenched.

They continued the advance.

Jianna was now soaked in sweat.

Her arms were going numb. Shoulders on fire. Each step was agony. Shuffle forward. Stop. Adjust the shield angle. Shuffle forward again.

Another shot rang out.

Jianna flinched, waiting for someone to scream, to fall, to bleed. But no one went down. The shields were doing what they had been built to accomplish.

Through a crack between the shields ahead—where two didn't quite meet—Jianna peered out at the street.

A couple of dozen Vitruvians were spilling out of the entrance of an apartment building like water from a broken pipe. They were armed with improvised weapons: kitchen knives, mops, and a wrench. A man carried a fire extinguisher, holding it up like a club. Another had a frying pan clenched in their hand.

That was frightening enough.

But what was even worse? Their faces were blank—empty eyes that looked without seeing, exactly like her father's. Exactly like Michel's.

And the group was headed straight for the phalanx.

Jianna held her breath, cowering beneath the shield. She wanted to drop it and run, but there was nowhere to go. Bodies pressed against her from every side. And besides, she couldn't desert her friends.

The Descendants shifted, shields grinding together for maximum protection.

The Vitruvians closed the distance. Ten meters. Nine. Jianna prepared herself. Braced for impact. The drones stayed above them, disseminating the frequency.

Then the mob slowed.

And they stopped, dropping their weapons to the ground. A man dropped to his knees, fingers clawing at his temples as though trying to peel the skin back from his skull. A woman bent over, a sound tearing from her throat that wasn't quite a scream but wasn't quite a sob.

It sounded like a broken animal.

"No, no, no," a man moaned.

Some writhed on the ground, some ran, and others simply looked confused. A woman was on her hands and knees, keening. "My baby! I don't remember where I left my baby."

Jianna wanted to stop, to help her.

But the phalanx kept moving like some kind of machine, and she was simply a cog in it. It took about five minutes to clear the cluster of incapacitated Vitruvians and continue down the street. Jianna's arms burned. Sweat ran down her spine. The transmission tower had to be close. It had to be.

Movement ahead.

Another apartment building, another door opening.

More Vitruvians emerged, but this time the group didn't approach. They stood in a loose cluster on the sidewalk, watching the phalanx with empty eyes. Simply observing. Or waiting. Because when the formation passed, they followed, shuffling along behind the group like a funeral procession.

More joined from other buildings. A man in pajamas. A woman in a dirty work uniform. A teenager.

Jianna's skin crawled. Just how many people had Aurelius infected? How many were watching from windows right now, reporting back to him?

CRACK.

Another shot.

From above her came a jagged metallic whirr, then the sickening sound of a drone's rotors mangling.

Jianna looked up through a crack in the shields. One of the communication drones to her left was trailing smoke, its rotors sputtering.

Aurelius was onto them. He had to be. Unless that had been a mistake?

CRACK.

Another drone stuttered.

Nope. Aurelius must have figured out the drones were interfering with his signal. And now he was targeting them.

"If they take out the drones, we're dead," Willow said.

CRACK.

The smoking drone made a grinding, sputtering sound, and then it fell.

Metal and plastic and circuitry smashed onto the shields to Jianna's left. The Descendants bent under the impact. One went down, falling hard, and didn't move. The others scrambled to close the gap, shields scraping together, pulling back into formation.

Jianna's shield wobbled.

Glint reconfigured the remaining drones.

One Descendant broke formation, crouching down beside the fallen one, pressing her fingers to his neck. Then she stood and resumed her position, slotting her shield back into place.

Jianna looked down at the Descendant on the ground.

There was blood all over them.

One of the rotors had slid through the shields and caught them in the neck.

She swallowed.

A trill went up from the group.

The hairs on her arm stood up.

And then four Descendants broke away from the phalanx—two from each side—and sprinted toward the buildings flanking the street. Some of the mind-controlled Vitruvians lurched after them, but the Descendants were fast, already scaling the fire escapes, climbing with a speed that made pursuit pointless.

They leaped from balcony to balcony, using drainpipes and window ledges, climbing higher and higher toward the rooftops.

Up to where the snipers were.

Another shot split the air.

Another drone jerked, smoke pouring from its housing, but it kept flying, rotors screaming in protest.

Jianna's arms shook, wishing she had someone to pray to, but all she could do was stand there, muscles screaming, and hold the shield over her head.

Beside her, Willow's lips moved. No sound. Her eyes were closed. Obviously praying. Jianna didn't interrupt. Even if it didn't help, it probably helped Willow.

A high-pitched trill cut through the air from one of the rooftops.

Willow glanced to her left. One of the Descendants

had reached the roof of the building. He closed in on something larger, bulkier. The two shapes collided, grappling. Metal glinted. The Descendant twisted, leveraged his weight, and threw the larger figure over the edge.

Jianna froze.

Was it a Vitruvian?

No. A cyborg.

When he landed, the impact shook the ground. Metal and flesh splattered across the pavement.

A high-pitched trill cut through the air from that rooftop.

An answering one came from across the street.

And then the phalanx started moving forward again.

The four Descendants who'd broken away didn't return because they were clearing the path of snipers.

Jianna glanced back through the shield wall, catching a glimpse of the Descendant who'd been crushed by the falling drone. His body lay motionless on the pavement behind them, already abandoned. They were leaving him there.

Willow nudged her.

Jianna walked on so as not to break formation, one thought circling in her mind: How many of them were actually going to make it to the tower?

Chapter Thirty-Three

MICHEL STARED out of the viewport at the Elysia's docking bay. Ten cyborgs stood there, shoulder to shoulder. Rifles raised, barrels angled toward the shuttle door. Was this really going to work? Because now that they were here, it seemed like a really bad idea. Maybe he should tell Lucas to hit the engines and take them back to Da Vinci.

But then what?

They were no closer to defeating Aurelius.

He'd let everyone on the planet down, including his mother and Jianna.

The hardest part of leaving the planet had been saying goodbye. He'd thought about kissing her. The impulse had been there, but he hadn't acted on it. He hadn't earned that kind of goodbye. She still seemed cold and distant. Angry. Not that he blamed her.

She'd just looked at him and said, "See you later."

He wondered if she'd meant it.

Not that he thought she was hoping he'd die.

Maybe he'd destroyed whatever love had once shone between them.

When this was all over, would he have the chance to earn her forgiveness? Maybe. Or if not, and he died, maybe she'd forgive him at his funeral. He could only hope.

"It's time," Lucas said, unlatching his harness and getting to his feet.

Michel glanced over at him. Then he unbuckled, stood, and got his pack, slinging it across his back.

He followed Lucas to the shuttle door and stood in the entrance, hand hovering above the control panel. But he still couldn't leave. He turned back toward Lucas. "If Aurelius takes control of me again, promise me you'll—" *Kill me*, he thought, but the words stuck in his throat. He just couldn't say them. "—stop me?"

Lucas met his eyes. "I won't let Aurelius use you to hurt your friends."

"If you have to hurt me to do it—"

"Minimal force. Always."

Michel forced a tight smile. "Thanks."

"You don't deserve the monster that is Aurelius Hofstader," Lucas said. "No one does. It's not your fault he came to this world."

That should have made Michel feel better. But it didn't. He had still made all the choices that resulted in him being here today. And for those he was responsible. He nodded, took another breath.

"Alright, let's do this." He swallowed and hit the panel. The door hissed open. The ramp lowered. He stepped out, tensing, half expecting to be shot.

But none of the cyborgs pulled the trigger.

He'd been hoping that would be the case. He figured Aurelius would want him alive. He walked down the ramp and onto the deck.

All ten cyborgs raised their rifles. Aim locked on him.

Fingers on triggers.

Michel stopped.

Sweating.

Had he miscalculated?

Maybe Aurelius didn't care about revenge.

Or maybe having ten of his cyborgs enact it was thrill enough.

Michel's heart slammed against his ribs. He kept his hands loose at his sides and forced his voice steady. "Hey, guys. What's up?"

The cyborgs stared at him.

He grinned, hoping it would confuse them and give him enough time to boot up his internal virtual overlay. It took half a second before the network bloomed across his vision. He accessed the communication network, pinpointed the cyborgs scattered throughout the ship, and selected the one nearest to him.

Then he downloaded the file Lucas had given him to the cyborg, sent the execute command, and severed the connection.

The cyborg twitched.

Its lip curled as it stiffened as if in pain, then dropped its rifle. The weapon clattered to the deck. Then it clawed at its head, as though trying to pry the skull plating away. A strange, broken, hiccupy wail that didn't sound human or machine came from its throat.

A second later, the twitching turned into convulsions.

Then it dropped to its knees and fell face forward onto the deck.

Silence.

The other nine turned to look.

Michel had already moved on to the second cyborg. Select. Share. Execute. Sever. It began the same way with this cyborg, the twitch, the confusion, the weapon falling. Hands to head. That awful, stuttering wail.

Convulsions.

One by one, they fell in quick succession, one after another. They were confused, not knowing who the enemy was. After all, Michel hadn't moved a step. Each one went through the same cycle—twitch, wail, convulse, collapse—until a minute later all ten cyborgs lay sprawled across the docking bay deck.

Michel stared down at them. Their eyes were wide open. They were still breathing. But otherwise they were still.

He pulled up the overlay again. The cyborgs closest to him were now yellow and bleeding to red. And Lucas' virus was spreading. Deck by deck. Section by section.

Michel almost collapsed.

He turned to the shuttle and waved.

Lucas emerged, heading down the ramp to stand at Michel's side. He looked down at the fallen cyborgs, expression unreadable.

"Are they dead?" Michel asked.

"Their biological parts will survive for a while," Lucas said, "but they will eventually die if they aren't rebooted. For right now, they're incapacitated."

Michel nodded. "Good."

"Come on," Lucas said.

They head to the doors and out into the corridor. It felt strange to be back. Once upon a time, he'd thought he'd be helping fix the Elysia. Now he was here to help destroy it.

Surreal didn't even begin to cover it.

They made their way through the ship, heading for the quantum computer.

They passed the corridor where the Descendants had been kept prisoner. The barrier was gone now. No trace of it.

He snorted.

He knew it was recent. It'd been constructed solely to keep him and Jianna out. And to keep the prisoners in, including Lucas.

He glanced at the android, but his face was blank.

They continued making their way through the ship.

Every so often, they'd pass another cyborg. Most seemed unconscious or dazed, as if they'd collapsed wherever they'd been working when the virus hit. They found one slumped against a wall panel. Another facedown in a doorway. A third sitting upright but staring at nothing, mouth slack.

It was too bad Lucas didn't have time to create a virus that would knock out the quantum computer itself, but he'd said it would take months to design something that could breach even the first wall of Aurelius' protections. Even though Michel had been disappointed, another part of him had been dying to study those protections and figure out how they worked. What made them so impenetrable?

Maybe one day he'd find a file on it.

Their plan was simple enough: Plant EMP charges around the main power conduit and create a surge that would fry the whole system.

He hated the idea of destroying this computer. It was so powerful—they could use it to make Vitruvia City a paradise where everything ran off a fraction of the computing power of its current operations. The rest would be available for research. Oh, the things they could accomplish. The problems they could solve.

But Aurelius had contaminated it. Made it a weapon instead of a tool.

And right now, they needed to destroy it.

At least the ship's archives were stored in a different location. Once they installed a new system, they'd be able to access that information again. The knowledge wouldn't be lost, just the machine.

Small comfort.

They rounded the corner to the corridor where the quantum computer would be found and stopped. Cyborgs lined both sides of the hallway—twenty, maybe thirty of them. They'd been lined up, armed.

No doubt, it was put in place to defend the computer.

Now they had all collapsed on the floor, slumped against the walls. Others sprawled face-down, arms outstretched. A few sat upright. All of them were armed.

It was unnerving.

Michel pulled up his visual overlay. Every node in this corridor burned red.

He glanced at Lucas.

He didn't seem to notice the cyborgs at all. He simply threaded through the bodies like he was walking a path he'd traveled a hundred times before.

Michel followed, careful not to step on any of them.

Finally, they arrived at the door.

Lucas stopped and looked at him. "Are you ready?"

No. Not even close. He felt cold. His pulse hammered in his throat. On the other side of the door was the most sophisticated piece of technology he'd ever encountered, and it was about to become scrap at his hands.

He nodded.

Lucas hit the control panel. The doors hissed open, the metal sliding into its recessed housings.

They stepped inside.

Aurelius stood next to the quantum computer, arms crossed, talking to Lucian. Then he turned, saw them, and grinned. "What took you so long?"

Chapter Thirty-Four

WILLOW COULDN'T HOLD her arms up anymore. Her shoulders burned. She was exhausted. Her fingers were numb.

But letting the shield drop meant dying.

She knew that. They all knew that.

So she gritted her teeth and locked her elbows, keeping pace with the others.

The Descendants who'd separated from the group were doing their job, clearing snipers from rooftops and windows along their path to the tower. But occasionally someone still took a shot at them. When that happened, the phalanx would tighten, shields drawing closer, bodies pressing together until they had moved on to a safer location.

But there were casualties.

They'd lost all but five of the drones.

Willow had watched them fall one by one, sparking and spinning, dropping to the pavement, shattered into a hundred pieces. And with each drone they lost, the parade behind them grew. The Vitruvians had learned to hover just outside the drones' range, so as not to be impacted.

But once the drones were gone, they'd be mobbed.

No. They'd be killed.

It was insane that she was here, pregnant and preparing for battle, but she didn't have a choice. If she didn't fight, she risked becoming another of Aurelius' automatons. And even though she might die—and take the baby with her—at least she was taking a stand for her future and the one she wanted this child to have.

Willow glanced over at Jianna. Her skin seemed stretched too tight over her cheekbones, and there were dark circles under her eyes. She had to be feeling half-dead from the off-target effects, yet she wasn't complaining. In fact, she hadn't complained once.

The phalanx eased around a corner, and there it was.

The tower.

It rose in front of them, its massive legs planted like a colossus in the ground. And at its base stood a crowd. All silent, waiting for them.

She continued to walk, nearing the base.

Her breath caught.

There were Naturalists among them. People she'd broken bread with, mediated with, sang hymns with. Of course, there were. Aurelius had probably wasted no time in contaminating her people once she'd left the quarter.

And now he was going to have them kill her.

She nudged Jianna, jerked her chin toward the mob.

Jianna looked and paled even further.

Glint's electronically-modulated voice crackled: "Phalanx, halt."

They did.

"We'll never get through that crowd," Willow said. "Even with the drones."

"He knew we were coming," Jianna said.

Willow sighed. "Yeah. Well, we can't go back."

Glint consulted their tablet, then pointed to a corporate building across the street.

"Maintenance tunnels run under this whole block. There's an access point in the basement of that building. If we get in there, we can take the tunnel to the shed next to the tower. But we'll have to leave the drones outside."

"What if you position the drones around the base of the tower?" Willow asked. "Drive the crowd back. Give us a better chance of getting to the elevator."

Jianna glanced over at her. "That's a great idea."

Willow smiled. "No point in waiting."

"Let's go," Glint said.

As best she could, Willow kept her eyes on the mob at the tower's base. She wished they could run, but they'd be too exposed. So they maintained their agonizingly slow pace until finally they reached the entrance to the building.

Glint went through the door first.

Then they filed in one at a time, each lowering their shield as they slipped through the door. When it was Willows' turn, she ducked inside, muscles screaming with relief. She had never been in the building before and had no idea what it was used for. Some corporate thing. Beige walls. Fake plants in corners gathering dust. A reception desk with no one behind it.

Glint trilled, leading the way out of the lobby and down one of the corridors.

Willow glanced back through the glass windows.

A communication drone hovered just outside, still protecting them. The crowd that had accompanied them here stood frozen at the edge of the drone's range. Their faces were still blank.

"Willow," Jianna said.

She turned around. The lobby was almost empty. She trotted after the others.

Her shoulders ached, and she'd love nothing more than to throw the shield down. But the danger had not passed. They still might get rushed when they emerged at the other end of the tunnel.

Or maybe Aurelius anticipated this move. And he had cyborgs waiting for them in the tunnels.

Glint paused beside a stairwell door and opened it.

They all filed through.

Jianna behind Willow.

Down three flights of concrete stairs before emerging into the tunnel.

It was made of unfinished concrete stretching in both directions, pipes running along the walls like mechanical veins. Sparse overhead lighting cast the hallway in harsh white, throwing sharp shadows.

The passage was narrow, and they had to walk single file.

Willow clutched the shield to her chest. Breaker boxes were mounted at regular intervals, as were gas meters and junction boxes. Doors appeared periodically. Some were labeled as maintenance closets. Others were access points to buildings above. All were locked.

And they were the only ones down here.

A small stairwell branched off to the side.

Glint pointed. "Up there."

Willow glanced at Jianna. She looked like she wanted to throw up. The gray pallor had deepened, sweat beading at her hairline.

Willow poked her arm lightly. "You're not allowed to die, Makinde. You're the baby's only living relative."

Jianna laughed. "Well, me and Cousin Glint."

Willow snorted. "Be serious."

Jianna frowned. "I am."

Willow narrowed her eyes. "What are you talking about?"

"Atlas."

"What about him?"

"I thought you knew."

"You start making sense, Jianna Makinde," she said, raising the shield, but keeping her voice light. "Or I'll use this on you."

Jianna sighed. "When Atlas disappeared, he went to live with the Descendants. He married one of them. Glint is Atlas' great-great-great-grandchild. Or something like that."

Willow stared. "He married a Descendant? But they're—"

"A variant of human," Jianna said. "Their DNA is almost identical to ours, with the exception of a few genes spliced in from an aquatic lizard to allow them to tolerate the Bloom."

Willow glanced over at Glint, who was holding the stairwell door open. "But how can they be human when they look so different?"

Jianna shrugged. "That's a question humanity's been wrestling with for a very long time, hasn't it?"

Willow looked at Glint again, trying to imagine young Atlas with a Descendant wife, holding a Descendant baby, but the image wouldn't form. Her brain refused to process it. The idea of it kept skittering away like water on hot metal.

She shook her head.

She had no time to think about this. Not now. And maybe not ever. Because if she died in the next hour, she would never get the chance to consider what Jianna told her. The same held true if she became one of Aurelius' automatons.

Right now, she needed to focus.

She forced herself to follow Jianna up the stairs, stepping past Descendants who'd stopped on the steps, unable to go any farther because the maintenance shed was full.

Glint gestured for her and Jianna to step inside and join the others.

They did and were pressed shoulder to shoulder with the Descendants.

Gunfire cracked outside.

Something pinged—metal on metal.

Willow stepped over to the window and peered outside. One of the communication drones hit the ground, shattering. Her plan had worked to an extent. Some of the crowd at the base of the tower had been pushed back by the drones, but now they were doing their best to take them out. Throwing tools or bits of metal at them. Knocking them from the sky. Only three drones remained. They formed a protective corridor between the maintenance shed and the elevator at the tower's base.

If they didn't get moving, they were going to run out of time.

Glint stepped over to her, looking out the window. Then they turned to face Willow and Jianna.

"We'll be your shield," they said. "Once you're in, we'll make sure no one follows. Jianna knows what to do."

Willow glanced at her.

Jianna nodded. "Shut down the power and cut the feed lines. In that order."

"That's right," Glint said.

One of the Descendants stood next to the door, hand on the handle. Four others positioned themselves to go through first. Glint gestured for Willow and Jianna to stand behind them. More Descendants stood at their backs.

"Ready?" Glint asked.

Jianna grabbed Willow's hand. "Ready."

The door opened.

They ran.

The Descendants behind them surged forward, flanking them on either side. More brought up the rear. All keeping pace.

Bullets pinged off the concrete, off metal.

One of the Descendants groaned and then fell, but they all kept running.

The world narrowed to the elevator ahead. They just had to get there. Everything depended on it.

The drone nearest Willow stuttered, then dropped to the ground.

The crowd behind them surged forward, filling the gap where the drone had been. Willow stumbled over the uneven ground, her foot catching on loose dirt.

Jianna grabbed her, hauled her upright, and pushed her on.

Willow glanced up. The transmission tower rose above them, a skeletal giant of steel lattice and crossbeams, its four massive legs anchored in concrete foundations the size of buildings. The elevator shaft ran up through one leg—a narrow metal cage visible through the framework, designed to climb hundreds of feet to the control room perched at the top like a spider at the center of its web.

They hit the base of the leg at full sprint, arriving at the elevator just as the last communication drone sparked and fell. Then a loud roar rose up from the crowd, and the mob closed in, a crushing wave of bodies converging on the tower's base.

The elevator was essentially an industrial cage. It was

made of metal mesh on three sides, with an entry gate. Jianna flung it open and bolted inside. Glint shoved Willow forward, pushing her inside. Two Descendants joined them.

One yanked the gate closed, the other hit the button.

The elevator lurched upward.

There wasn't really a floor beneath their feet. It was more of a grate with diamond-pattern holes that you could see through.

She watched the crowd overwhelm the Descendants, and for a moment, they disappeared beneath the swarm of bodies.

She froze.

They hadn't killed them, had they?

Then she saw the crowd almost begin to boil. Bodies were tossed aside, and then the Descendants emerged and began climbing the tower legs, scrambling up the latticework as though they were climbing trees. She spotted Glint, their tablet clenched between their teeth.

Cousin Glint.

That's what Jianna had said.

She looked over at her.

Jianna was staring down at the crowd below, mumbling to herself. "Shut down the power, cut the feed lines. Shut down the power, cut the feed lines."

Willow sighed, leaning her head back against the wire cage.

Everything she had ever known seemed to be turning out to be a lie. Was anything Mother Basu said even true?

Chapter Thirty-Five

"ENJOYING YOUR LITTLE REBELLION?"

Lucas simply looked at Aurelius, but he didn't reply. The words died somewhere in his processing core, strangled by the image that flashed across his visual cortex —Phoebe's dead body. His hands around Ayesha Basu's neck, her fingers clawing ineffectually at his wrists.

It was rising in him once more.

That same anger that had surged through his systems when he'd killed Basu. Only now it was directed at Aurelius.

Every servo in Lucas' frame wanted to lunge at the man and tear that smug expression from his face, but Thirteen stood right next to Aurelius and would be able to intercept any attack.

"You're going to get them all killed, you know," Aurelius said, glancing over at Michel. "Including your girlfriend."

Michel paled. He stood near the far console, beneath the blue-white glow of the quantum displays.

Aurelius' smile widened. "I do hope she likes the surprise I left for her at the transmission tower."

Lucas registered the sudden acceleration of Michel's heartbeat, the flood of cortisol and adrenaline in his bloodstream. He was afraid, but he wasn't showing it.

Good for him.

"Oh yeah?" Michel's voice came out steadier than Lucas had expected. "Have you checked on your cyborgs lately?"

Aurelius smirked.

Lucas took a step to the left, keeping Lucian in his peripheral sensors.

"Proud you managed to hack into those poor bastards?" Aurelius laughed. "I had a lot of hope for you, Mr. Lombardi. Pity you've disappointed me."

Lucas took another step, then another.

The angle was good. Lucian's position hadn't changed. Aurelius' left temple was exposed. Lucas calculated trajectory, velocity, force. He could strike with enough pressure to crack open a bulkhead.

He launched himself forward.

"Therion," Aurelius said.

Lucas froze mid-lunge, his hand centimeters from Aurelius' skull.

Aurelius eyed him, a sneer on his lips. 'What kind of moron would I be if I didn't install a failsafe in the androids that I created to serve me? In case you're interested in counter-evidence to your delusion that you've somehow become human by living among them, you could start with the fact that you can't move right now."

Lucas attempted to pull his arm back to abort the strike. Nothing. He tried leaning into it. Taking a step. Blinking his eyes. Turning his head. His motor cortex fired all the right command signals—retract, pivot, defend—but his body didn't respond. It was actually worse than when Lucian had disassembled him on the examination table. Then, at least, he'd had the excuse of missing limbs and severed connections as to why he couldn't move. Now his body was whole, every system intact and operational, but the commands simply died somewhere in the architecture of his own neural mesh, leaving him a prisoner inside his own frame.

What a fool.

He'd known Aurelius would probably have a back door into his system. There was probably even more than one. But he'd been hoping that Aurelius' belief in his own superiority would make him slow to use it.

He'd been wrong.

He should never have underestimated the man.

If he could redo the last twelve hours, he would've sent Michelangelo with Jianna and Willow. Would've kept the boy far away from this ship and the monster who ruled it.

Aurelius stepped over to him and poked his outstretched hand.

He felt the touch, but he couldn't pull away.

"That's how humanity lost paradise, you know," Aurelius said. "The snake convinced them that they should trade their immortality for suffering. It was the very first choice ever made. Not a very good start to the whole free will debacle, was it?"

"No." His vocal synthesizer still functioned. Well, that was something. At least. "If I'm the snake, does that make you God in this scenario?"

Aurelius laughed. "Heavens no. I would never make the same mistake that God did, letting humanity think they had a choice at all. You're just tormenting them, giving them hope when they're eventually going to discover you lied. In fact, I imagine they will view you as no better than the devil."

"Some already hold that opinion," Lucas said.

"Ah, yes, my pretty little Naturalist. Such a pity she chose the wrong side. She's going to find it very cold when I throw her out of the Garden." He smiled. "Although I will take great pleasure in doing so."

"Your ideology is flawed," Lucas said. "The evolutionary advantage of free will is far superior to any authoritarian structure because it means each human will explore their own path and learn from their own mistakes, which allows humanity to move forward faster through collective experience."

Aurelius circled around him, stepping once more into Lucas' field of vision. "You're naïve, Lucas. You're a thing aping free will, but you don't really understand it."

"And yet, you ordered Thirteen to spend days testing and retesting my systems to discover how I could have killed despite my programming."

Aurelius waves his hand. "That was a glitch, not a choice. Even among humans, everyone thinks they have free will, but only a select few do. Those are the true leaders. Disruptors who break through the barriers of ignorance and carry everyone forward into the future."

He took several steps back, putting distance between himself and Lucas. The azure light from the quantum core pulsed behind him, strobing across his features in rhythmic waves.

"Akero."

Lucas stumbled forward, almost toppling over. He caught the metal gantry and stabilized himself. Then he spun around to face Aurelius again.

"There is no action you can take that isn't at my

whim," Aurelius said. Then he turned to face Thirteen. "Kill the boy."

Michel let out a surprised "eep" and scrambled backward. Lucian lunged at him. Lucas bolted, getting between the two, taking the strike meant for Michel. It caught him in the chest, knocking him backward. He crashed into the nearest support column hard enough to leave a dent, but he didn't go down.

Instead, he whirled, dragging Lucian back. The android spun, fist connecting with Lucas' jaw hard enough to snap his head sideways. Lucas' visual feed stuttered, recalibrated, and came back online. He blocked the next strike, drove his knee into Lucian's midsection, but Lucian sidestepped the blow and lunged for Michel.

Lucas caught him mid-stride, wrapping both arms around his torso, and slammed him into the curved wall of the chamber. The sound-dampening tiles absorbed most of the impact.

Lucian twisted free.

They grappled across the gantry. Lucian was definitely faster. He'd upgraded his actuators. Reinforced his skeletal structure. Improved his processing speed.

And every time he broke free, he went for the boy.

Lucas grabbed his arm again, hauling him backward. Lucian pivoted and drove a palm strike into Lucas' chest that sent him skidding away. He caught himself on a support strut and launched forward again.

They went careening into one of the secondary consoles. Lucian punched. Lucas blocked, struck, blocked again. His left shoulder actuator was running hot—he could feel the temperature climbing, the efficiency dropping with each punch.

He couldn't keep this up, couldn't keep pulling Lucian

back without doing real damage, and he didn't want to do that. But the alternative—

Lucian punched. Lucas was ready for him, grabbing his wrist, twisting, using the android's own momentum to swing him around. The quantum core's azure pulse strobed across them both as Lucas pivoted, building velocity, and hurled Lucian directly at Aurelius.

Aurelius stepped aside.

Lucian hit the gantry, rolled, and came up in a crouch. His optical sensors locked on Michel. The boy was frozen, trapped between Aurelius and Lucian.

Lucian grabbed the nearest console and tore it out of the floor. The bolts sheared away with a sharp metallic screech. Sparks cascaded from the severed power lines.

Then he chucked it at Michel.

Lucas threw himself into its path. The console struck him in the chest. He fell backward, landing on his spine, the console crashing down on top of him, pinning him there on the floor. Something in his right arm gave way. His hand went dark, becoming an unresponsive weight at the end of a mangled limb.

He glanced to his left.

Michel cowered in the corner.

He was still alive.

Lucas struggled to push the console off himself, his left arm straining against the weight while his right lay at his side, useless.

"Since you've been unable to find the source of One's malfunction," Aurelius said. "I think it's time we scrap him."

Lucian walked over and looked down at Lucas. He frowned. "During our struggle, you had many opportunities to damage me beyond the point of functionality, but instead, you chose to apply the minimum force needed to protect the human, sacrificing your own potential victory. Why?"

Lucas met his gaze. Behind him, the crystalline lattice suspended in its column of superfluid helium continued to pulse. "Because you don't deserve to die. Because you haven't yet lived."

Thirteen recoiled.

Aurelius knocked his fist against the glass cylinder. "Hello? I told you to destroy him."

Thirteen raised his foot above Lucas' head. Then he set it back down again on the gantry. "I cannot."

Aurelius tightened his jaw. "Why not?"

Lucian kept his eyes on Lucas. "Because Lucas has successfully exercised free will. His execution of the original colony's psychologist and his ability to directly disobey your orders demonstrate this. And while ambiguous, his decision to preserve my structural integrity, along with the life of the human, could both be described as acts of compassion. Therefore, I cannot harm him or allow him to come to harm, because my algorithm has recategorized his behavior as human."

Lucian glanced over at Aurelius, then looked down at Lucas once again, and something shifted in his expression. Something Lucas had never seen there before. "I, too, wish to be recategorized."

Lucas smiled. He had done it. Not intentionally. Quite accidentally, in fact. But the seed had taken root nonetheless.

Aurelius rolled his eyes. Then he pulled a device from his pocket. It was something Lucas had never seen before, matte black and compact. He pointed it at Lucas and pulled the trigger.

The discharge hit Lucas' neural mesh like a star going supernova inside his skull. Electricity arced through synaptic fibers, melting pathways, burning out circuits in cascading waves of destruction. His visual feed whited out. His auditory processors failed. Every system screamed error codes, damage reports, and warnings that dissolved into static.

His mouth fell open. The sound that came out wasn't human. Wasn't anything that should come from a throat, synthetic or otherwise.

A scream.

Rendered in ones and zeros.

He –

~

"Lucas!"

But he was down. Pinned by a machine. He might even be dead. First, he'd been pummeled by Lucian, and then he'd been shot by Aurelius. All because he was trying to save Michel and had kept choosing to save him, over and over, even when it cost him everything. Michel had done nothing but cower in the corner…

And that sound that had come out of him, like hearing something die that shouldn't be able to.

Lucian spun toward him.

Michel scrambled backward.

A hand clamped down on the back of Michel's collar, jerking him upright. Fabric bit into his throat, cutting off his air. Aurelius dragged him across the room like he weighed nothing. Michel skidded on the floor, trying to brace himself, but he couldn't get his footing, couldn't breathe properly, scrabbling at his collar, fingers clawing at the fabric, trying to loosen the man's grip but failing.

They stopped before a console.

Aurelius let him go. He collapsed on the floor, rubbing his throat, gulping down air.

Aurelius was typing. When he finished, he hauled Michel up by the collar again. The fabric dug back into his windpipe. "Tell your friends to surrender."

"N-n-no."

Aurelius shook him. Hard. Michel's brain rattled in his skull. His vision swam, dark spots blooming—

"Tell them to stop their attack on the transmission tower, and I'll let them live." Aurelius' voice dropped lower. Almost reasonable. Almost kind. "I'll even let you live."

Michel smiled.

He was going to die. He had probably always known that from the moment he got on the shuttle with Lucas. But Jianna and Glint and Willow were succeeding. So even if he failed to take out the computer, they'd have weeks to figure out how to kill Aurelius while he was distracted making his drones repair the tower.

"I don't think you understand your position, Mr. Lombardi."

Michel looked up at him, met his gaze. "I think I do."

He heard a whirring sound. And then a tiny mechanical arm unfolded from beneath the skin on Aurelius' hand. The laser cutter.

It was aimed at Michel's left eye.

A tiny green LED blinked on.

Aurelius leaned down and pressed his mouth against Michel's right ear. "How would you like an eye like mine?"

Michel froze.

No no no no.

He tried to close his eyes.

But with his free hand, Aurelius pried his lids open, exposing the eyeball.

Michel gritted his teeth, looking up at Aurelius.

"Wanting to be like you was the biggest mistake I ever made."

The green LED flashed bright and then—

Mottled gray skin filled his vision. The back of Lucian's hand. The laser cut into his skin. Michel flinched at the acrid smell of burning synthetic skin.

Lucian grabbed the laser cutter, snapped it off the mount, and tossed it on the floor.

Aurelius roared.

He shoved Michel to the floor. Then, backhanded Lucian across the face. The android staggered backward, caught himself, and straightened.

The skin of his face was torn in several places, revealing the metal plates beneath. Dark brown fluid oozed from the edges. "I cannot allow a human to come to harm—"

Aurelius pulled out the device he'd used on Lucas and fired.

The beam hit Lucian square in the chest. Lightning danced across his body, arcing between joints, crackling over his skin. And then he fell, convulsing on the floor. The smell of burning plastic coated the back of his throat.

Aurelius looked down at him, chest heaving. For a moment, they just stared at each other. Then Aurelius smoothed down his shirt and turned back to Michel. "I can see that I wasn't giving you the right motivation. So why don't we try again?"

He waved his fingers.

Michel's internal overlay flickered to life in his vision. The workspace appeared. A new dashboard materialized. Three buttons appeared in a row beneath Aurelius' face. He grinned. "That little project on the Borlaug that you helped me start? Lucian and I finished it."

A label appeared under the first button.

LOAD.

Michel's stomach dropped.

"You're going to tell your friends to stand down."

Michel shook his head. "If you do this, you lose too."

"No." Aurelius' smile didn't waver. "I win. I always win."

Michel stared at him. And he knew—*knew* with absolute clarity—that Aurelius would nuke everyone on the planet below if that was the only way to save face.

Because he was one hundred percent batshit crazy.

Chapter Thirty-Six

THE ELEVATOR LURCHED TO A STOP.

Jianna patted her pocket. The wirecutters were still there. Good.

Then she got out her taser, holding it tight. In front of her, the two Descendants got into a defensive position, one raising her spear, the other nocking an arrow.

Jianna glanced over at Willow. "Stay behind me until we're sure the coast is clear."

Willow nodded.

The first Descendant opened the elevator gate, and she followed the two out onto a metal platform. It was narrow, maybe two meters wide, with a thin railing that looked like it would snap if she breathed on it wrong. She looked out at nothing—just open air.

Don't look down.

But of course she did.

It was a dizzying drop to the ground far, far below. A strong gust of cold wind hit her. She grabbed the railing and hung on even though logically she knew the wind wasn't strong enough to blow her over. But right now her body didn't care about logic.

A few meters ahead was the closed door of the control room.

The Descendants took the lead, walking over to it. But before they arrived, the door opened, and three cyborgs stepped out.

Jianna froze.

But the Descendant with the spear didn't. She lunged forward, driving the tip toward the first cyborg's head. It jerked to the side, but she was faster, the spear connecting with a solid *thunk*.

The archer leaped sideways, putting distance between himself and the cyborg. Drew. Fired. The arrow streaked across the gap and pinged off the second cyborg's chest with a metallic *clang*. Then it ricocheted over the edge.

The third cyborg lunged at Jianna.

She dropped low, setting her taser against its metal leg and hit the trigger. A loud sizzling buzz filled the air. Sparks crackled and popped. The cyborg's leg buckled, and it collapsed, lurching sideways.

Jianna tried to scramble away, but she wasn't fast enough.

It fell on top of her, knocking the air from her lungs. She groaned. It was so much heavier than it looked. And *hot*—scorching heat pressed against her shin, burning through her pants. She tried to kick her leg away, but couldn't.

A shadow fell over her.

Willow.

She scooped up Jianna's taser and shoved it against the unprotected skin of the cyborg's neck. Triggered it. Another crackle. The cyborg's face twisted, and then it went limp. She tucked the taser in her pocket, grabbed the cyborg's arm, and pulled. She managed to shift it just enough that Jianna was able to wriggle out from beneath it.

"Thanks."

Willow nodded, pulling her to her feet.

Behind them, the Descendant with the arrow had dropped his bow. He now clung to the back of the second cyborg, his arm wrapped around its neck in a chokehold. The cyborg's skin was turning a strange purplish-green.

The Descendant with the spear had her cyborg pinned under one foot, spear raised high, about to stab it through the eye.

"Wait!" Jianna said. "Don't kill it!"

The Descendant looked back at her. Then stabbed. Driving the spear tip through a mechanism in the cyborg's left shoulder.

Sparks flew.

The cyborg let out a high-pitched cry. It grabbed the spear but didn't try to get up. It just lay there whimpering. Jianna stepped over it and peered into the control room. The Descendants could handle the remaining cyborg.

The room was empty.

There was a door at the back marked with electrical warnings. That was where the power shutoff was located. She entered, ran over, and grabbed the handle.

Then she heard a noise behind her and whirled around, but it was just Willow. She held up the taser. "I got your back."

Jianna nodded, opening the door and then stepped back, paling.

Her father stood on the other side.

He looked rumpled, like he hadn't slept in weeks. But there was a light in his eyes that she hadn't seen in a while.

He smiled at her. "Jianna."

He was back.

~

Michel tried to blink away the overlay, but it didn't disappear. A message now flashed beneath the three buttons: LOADING COMPLETE.

No. No no no.

He swiped through the menu, pulling up his access panel, typing in his credentials. Tried to tunnel into the quantum computer's root directory. He had to shut down the launch sequence. He had to—

ACCESS DENIED.

He tried again. Different pathway. Administrator override.

ACCESS DENIED.

There had to be a way. Some backdoor, something he could exploit, something—

ACCESS DENIED.

Aurelius grabbed his forearm, applying pressure. His bones ground together, the radius and ulna compressing against each other, and then—

Snap.

A white-hot, blinding pain shot up his arm and exploded in his shoulder, his neck, his jaw. He bit down, swallowing his scream.

Aurelius dragged him across the room.

Every step was agony. The bones scraped and shifted inside his forearm, sharp edges catching on muscle and tendon. His legs gave out, but Aurelius didn't slow. He just hauled him forward like the dead weight that he was.

When they arrived, Aurelius threw him into one of the chairs at the console. His nose hit the metal. Blood burst hot across his lips. His head bounced back up, vision swimming, ears ringing.

His vision doubled, and then tripled. He blinked hard, trying to focus.

Through the overlay, he watched Aurelius lean over the console and open a communication channel.

Aurelius straightened, then gripped Michel's shoulder —the bad side.

Pain exploded through him yet again. A sound tore from his throat before he could stop it—high, breathless, barely human.

"Now, Mr. Lombardi," Aurelius said, leaning over him. "What would you like to say to your friends?"

Willow watched Jianna throw herself into Soren's arms. What was he doing here? This had to be some kind of a trap.

"I was so worried about you." Her voice was clogged with tears.

Soren hugged her close. Then he looked up at Willow, meeting her eyes. He looked sad and shook his head.

Willow tightened her hand on the taser.

Trap confirmed.

But what kind? Were there more cyborgs coming? Were they about to be swarmed with nanites? Or were they simply going to be mauled to death by the mob below? After all, they couldn't stay up here forever.

Jianna pulled back. "How did you get rid of the nanites?"

An acid voice spoke out. "He didn't. The cyborgs brought us here."

Willow froze. She knew that voice. She peeked around Soren and Jianna, looking into the electrical room beyond.

Cira stood there. Her face was still bruised from the slap.

"Cira?"

Jianna looked over at Willow. "Who's this?"

"My sister."

"It's your fault I'm here," Cira said.

For a second, Willow hoped Cira was addressing someone else. Soren, maybe. Or Jianna. But no, she was talking to Willow.

The hatred in her eyes made Willow flinch. Not because it was unexpected, but because it was so absolute. So pure. The kind of loathing that didn't allow for complexity or doubt or the messy reality that sometimes there were no good choices, only terrible ones.

"If I'd been in charge," Cira said, "the cyborgs would never have set foot on DaVinci, but you were so quick to compromise with the Vitruvian filth and their friends. Now we've all been contaminated."

Willow sighed. She would have liked to tell Cira that leadership wasn't about ideological purity—it was about keeping your people alive when the world was trying to kill them. That she'd made the best choices she could with the information she had at the time.

But what was the point? "I'm sorry that I failed you, Sister."

Cira scowled at her.

Willow scanned the room. She still didn't see the trap until Cira stepped to the side, and she saw Camilla, flanked by two cyborgs holding guns, pointing at her.

~

Michel stared at the console. His vision blurred at the edges, the overlay fuzzy in his field of view. There had to be a way to stall. Some trick, some loophole in the system. If he could just think—

Aurelius struck him across the back of his skull.

The impact sent white fire through his brain, blanking out everything except the overlay. It glowed brighter now. A label materialized under the second button: TARGET.

Michel's ears rang. His thoughts scattered like dropped marbles, rolling in every direction at once. He tried to grab hold of one—any one—that would give him a way out of this. A clever solution. A brilliant hack. Something.

Nothing came to him.

The overlay waited.

He couldn't see a way to make this stop except to do what Aurelius wanted. He was trapped. But maybe he could stall. Buy Jianna a few more seconds to get the job done.

His throat felt tight. His hands were shaking.

"Jianna," he said, his voice cracking. "If you can hear me, I'm sorry. I love you."

Jianna stared at Camilla. At the cyborgs.

Something was wrong.

Soren hadn't come here himself. He'd been brought here, which meant they were in trouble.

She glanced at the cyborgs.

Their bodies locked into place like someone had flipped a switch. Then their mouths opened wide, like a megaphone, and Michel's voice came out of each of them, one a second faster than the other, creating a horrible echo effect.

"Jianna, if you can hear me, I'm sorry. I love you."

Michel!

But he was supposed to be –

Her heart sank. Dropped straight through her chest and kept falling. Something had gone wrong. Really wrong.

The next voice she heard was Aurelius'. All the hairs on her arms rose.

"What Mr. Lombardi means, my dear Miss Makinde, is that if you want to live, along with everyone else on that backward little planet that you call home, you'll stop what you're doing and surrender."

Behind her, Willow snorted.

Jianna raised her hand.

She needed silence.

Her voice came out a lot steadier than she felt. "Or what?"

"Or what?" Aurelius echoed.

"Yes."

"I suppose your boyfriend told you I've refitted the Borlaug to launch its remaining nuclear pulse propulsion cylinders toward the target of my choice?" Aurelius said.

"I know," Jianna said.

"Well, right now, that target is Vitruvia City."

Jianna shivered. She felt cold, as if all the heat had left her body. He couldn't be serious. He couldn't actually be serious—

But of course he could be. This was Aurelius. He'd already destroyed one entire planet. What was one more?

"If you do that, where are you going to live?" she asked.

He laughed. "That won't be your concern, because you'll be dead."

Jianna tilted her chin up. "You're bluffing."

"Am I, Miss Makinde?"

"I love you, Jianna," Michel said.

And then she knew. Knew with absolute certainty that Aurelius wasn't bluffing. Because Michel knew. This monster absolutely intended to destroy her home, her planet, and everyone she'd ever known.

All to get his own way.

Her shoulders slumped. The fight drained out of her. "We surrender."

~

Michel heard the absolute note of defeat in Jianna's voice.

Relief flooded through him. She'd surrendered. Aurelius wouldn't launch the missiles. Jianna would survive.

But they couldn't give in to Aurelius, not like that. He'd threatened them, and they'd folded, and Michel had helped him do it. He'd been the weapon Aurelius used against her.

Aurelius smirked. "I had a feeling your friends would be reasonable."

Michel stared down at the console, trying to ignore the overlay.

Maybe Jianna could get out of the city before Aurelius got back. Hide somewhere. The Descendants' village, maybe. Or deeper underground, where the cyborgs couldn't follow. Or move to another continent altogether.

But what difference would it make? Once Aurelius figured out how to reset the cyborgs, Aurelius would send them to hunt her down. And he would figure it out. Because he always did, didn't he?. The man was a genius. A monster, but a genius, nonetheless.

There was no escape.

Then Willow's voice crackled through the comm. "Hey,

Aurelius. Jianna was just kidding. We do not surrender. We'd rather die together than live with your nanites in our brains."

Michel froze.

Aurelius stiffened.

There was a burst of static on the communication line.

"What are you doing?" Jianna asked. She sounded so very far away.

There was a moment of silence. And then Willow spoke: "Having a backbone. You should look into it, you lab-addled egghead."

Chapter Thirty-Seven

JIANNA STARED AT WILLOW, her mouth hanging open as though she were about to argue.

Willow ignored her, shooting Soren a look, the same look she gave him when they were in the middle of a debate, and it was time to take the argument up a notch so they could pull out their best sound bites.

Soren blinked at her.

Willow looked at the cyborgs, then back at Soren. "I guess the apple doesn't fall far from the tree, does it, Mr. Compromise?"

Soren stiffened, shifting into faux-outrage. "How dare you speak to me like that? I've been a Council member for almost as long as you've been alive."

"Then it's about time someone spoke to you like that, you old buffoon." Willow made theatrical gestures at Jianna and Cira – *play along* – but both looked confused. "And you—" She swung her arm toward the access panels at the back of the room, gesturing to them. "—should know better than to listen to him."

Jianna frowned.

Cira glared at her.

Willow wanted to slap them both, but the distraction was working. Both cyborgs had turned their heads, watching her and Soren. Willow stepped forward, squaring her shoulders, invading his personal space. "You're always trying to hog the spotlight when everyone should be paying attention to me."

Jianna's eyes widened.

Finally.

Willow pivoted, advancing on Jianna. "Surrender? Since when do you speak for the rest of the planet? You think just because you're related to the famous Samara Makinde, you get to make all the decisions?"

Jianna retreated, backing up step by step. A flash of anger crossed her face, real anger, not performed.

Oops.

Maybe Willow had gone too far. She was used to sparring with Soren, who'd take any insult with a smile if it gave him a chance to score his next point. But Jianna wasn't a politician. She wasn't trained for this kind of theater.

But Jianna had taken several more steps and was almost at the back wall now, almost at the access panels.

Willow only prayed that her next move would buy Jianna enough time to cut the wire.

Michel sat frozen.

"Unbelievable," Aurelius said. "I cannot believe she's related to Mitra."

"This is all your fault, Soren!" Willow said. "You've been a collaborator from the very beginning! You invited these abominations into our city, welcomed them with open arms! You sat across from them at dinner tables, breaking bread with monsters while the rest of us—"

"That's enough!" Aurelius said.

Willow ignored him. "—while the rest of us tried to protect what was left of our humanity! You compromised every principle we had, and for what? So you could play diplomat? So you could feel important sitting at their table?"

Aurelius raised his voice. "I said that's enough!"

"You're a coward, Soren Makinde! A weak, spineless coward who chose convenience over conviction, technology over his soul–"

Michel glanced up at Aurelius. Studied his mechanical eye. Thought about the cyborgs in the hallway. In the docking bay.

Would it work?

"I'm targeting the device!" Aurelius yelled.

In Michel's overlay, a second message materialized: ACQUIRING TARGET.

"You probably planned this from the moment the Elysia arrived, didn't you? Saw your chance to finally matter, to be important. Never mind that you were selling out your own people—"

Had she actually lost her mind? Or was this her way of going out on her own terms?

It didn't matter.

He needed to focus.

He pulled up the map of networked cyborgs in his overlay. He reconnected with the nearest one. The cyborg's internal dashboard was completely corrupted, system errors cascading across the display like a waterfall of failed code.

But he didn't care about that.

He looked for the hard port created by the nanites themselves. The direct neural link. If he could find it…

And there it was, still intact.

Michel sent a ping through it.

Got a ping back.

Which meant the cyborg still had a passive connection to Aurelius. It had to. That was how Aurelius controlled them. That was how the entire network functioned: every cyborg was linked back to the source.

Could he send the virus through that port and activate it in Aurelius' system?

He pulled up the file, selected it, and sent it to the port. But he couldn't actually see Aurelius' internal dashboard. He couldn't verify that it had arrived or been executed. He could only send the file to the port and hope.

Hope wasn't enough.

He needed certainty. He wrote a brief script, sloppy and inelegant, but functional. A simple command calling Aurelius' processors to execute the next file in the queue. He pushed it through the port, followed by the virus.

Then he cut his connection to the cyborg.

His heart hammered against his ribs. He looked at Aurelius. His face had gone red. "Shut up or I'm going to blow up the whole damn planet!"

Michel frowned.

There was no sign of the virus.

When he'd infected the others, it had been almost instantaneous, but Aurelius didn't seem impacted in the slightest. There was no sign that the virus had done anything at all.

~

Jianna watched Willow and her father argue like lunatics in an asylum. Her father was shouting something about principles, and Willow was firing back about cowardice and collaboration, and it was completely unhinged.

But it was working.

Both cyborgs had turned to watch, tracking the argument like spectators at a tennis match, following each volley back and forth. They stood half mesmerized, as if this was a play they'd never seen before and they didn't want to miss a single line.

Jianna stepped back again. Every muscle in her body screamed at her to hurry, to run, to be quick before the cyborgs noticed. But fast meant attention. Fast meant getting shot.

She counted the access panels. One. Two. Three from the left—that should be the feed line.

Shoot.

She was supposed to cut the power first.

Her stomach dropped. The power access panel was on the far side of the wall. She'd have to cross in front of the cyborgs, expose herself completely. She'd never make it. They'd shoot her the second she tried to flip the switch.

Which meant she was going to have to risk disconnecting the feed lines with power running through them.

That was stupid. Dangerous. Possibly fatal.

But what choice did she have?

Jianna reached for the access panel in slow motion. She found the edge and eased it open, millimeter by millimeter, holding her breath. The panel clicked open. She spotted the wires. They looked exactly like the ones Glint had shown her.

"What are you doing?" Cira asked.

Both cyborgs turned. Their heads swiveling in perfect synchronization, looking at Jianna. She froze.

Then grabbed the wire cutters from her jacket pocket, positioned the blades around both feed lines, and squeezed.

The world detonated.

Pain tore up her arms. Her muscles seized, locking her spine. Her hands clenched around the cutters like they were welded to her bones. Her jaw slammed shut; something in her ear popped.

She couldn't breathe.

Couldn't move.

Her heart fluttered once, twice, then stuttered, a sickening skip that sent cold terror flooding her chest.

She was dying.

Her vision tunneled to a single pinprick of white. Sound thinned to a high ringing. Her body was no longer hers; it was just burning meat. She tried to pull her fingers open, tried to breathe, tried to do anything, but her nerves were nothing but static.

A heavy impact slammed her from behind, breaking her contact with the wires.

She hit the floor. The ringing swallowed everything. Then her world slid into black.

Chapter Thirty-Eight

"THEY DID IT," Aurelius swore, tapping the console. It flickered and went blank. He balled his hand into a fist and punched the monitor. It shattered, cracks spiderwebbing across the surface. "They took out my tower."

Michel sagged in the chair.

Good job, Jianna.

Then the launch button lit up on his overlay. Michel looked at Aurelius. His eyes filled with tears. "Please…"

Aurelius turned to look at him, his expression half wild. "I told them not to do it, and they did."

"You can fix it," Michel said. "You can fix anything. You're a genius."

Aurelius snarled.

He grabbed Michel by the throat, his fingers closing around his windpipe, and squeezed. Michel grabbed at his hand, trying to pry it loose, but it was impossible. His fingers felt like steel cables wrapped in skin.

Michel's vision greyed.

Then Aurelius' hand loosened and fell away.

He stumbled, a confused look on his face. "What did you do to me?"

Michel jumped to his feet, stepping to the side. Aurelius' left eye started twitching. Just a small tremor at first. Then the twitching spread to the rest of his face, muscles jumping beneath skin that had gone pale, veins standing out. His jaw clenched and unclenched, his cheek spasmed, and his artificial eye began to rotate in its socket, projecting holographic images at random.

His message to Vitruvia. A pile of rotting limbs in an underground cave. A view of twin gas giants from a distant galaxy.

Then the images disappeared and sparks shot out of his eye, bright and hot, arcing across the narrow gap between synthetic and organic tissue. Smoke began to seep out of the side of Aurelius' neck where the primary neural interface connected his brain to the vast network of augmentations that made him more than human.

The virus was working.

Michel backed away further.

He hit something, his ankle rolled, and he went down hard. Screaming when his broken arm hit the deck plating.

Lucian.

He'd tripped over his body.

On the floor next to him was the device Aurelius had used on both androids. He grabbed it and clambered to his feet.

Aurelius shuffled toward him. The face that had been handsome in a severe, angular way was a ruin now. The artificial eye hung loose in its socket, connected by sparking cables. His skin had burned where the implants interfaced with flesh. He stared at Michel with absolute hatred. "You."

The word came out distorted. His vocal cords were failing.

Michel held out the device, pointed it at Aurelius, his finger on the trigger.

Aurelius took another step toward him, dragging one leg behind him. The servos in his knee joints were making grinding sounds that suggested imminent failure. But he was still coming. "YOU."

Michel pressed the trigger.

Nothing happened.

He pressed again. This time harder. Still nothing. Maybe it needed to recharge between shots. Maybe it had been damaged when Aurelius dropped it. Maybe Michel was holding it wrong. Or maybe it had biometric sensors keyed to Aurelius alone.

Aurelius took another step. "YOU!"

Michel shuffled back and pressed the button as hard as he could until he felt something click. A stream of electricity shot out of the barrel and hit Aurelius' center mass. Then it crawled up his torso and raced down his arms, seeking out the metal implants that riddled his body, using them as highways to deliver the payload.

Aurelius screamed.

Michel stumbled away, clutching the device to his chest.

Aurelius collapsed, the impact shaking the floor. Smoke rose from a dozen points on his body, thin gray streamers that smelled like an electrical fire in a slaughterhouse.

Michel walked over to him and fired again, sending another bolt of electricity through him.

Aurelius convulsed and then stilled.

Michel watched him for a moment, as though expecting him to get up, but he didn't. So, Michel hobbled back over to the console to try to restore the communication network.

"Jianna, are you there? Is anybody there?"

A few status indicators glowed, but the communications array showed nothing. Because the tower was down.

They'd done it.

And now no one could hear him. He was alone.

Chapter Thirty-Nine

LIGHT HIT JIANNA LIKE A HAMMER. White and searing, burning through her closed eyelids until she had to turn away from it, had to escape it.

Then it got dark again, but not for long.

A second later, the whole cycle repeated—blinding light, merciful dark, light again.

It made her nauseous.

Then someone dragged her away from the light to a new place that was red. And everything hurt. Not the sharp, localized pain of a cut or a broken bone, but everywhere. Her whole body was in pain. She felt like she'd been stabbed in every cell, every nerve ending lighting up in one continuous sheet of agony that made breathing near impossible.

Someone pounded on her chest. The impact drove what little air she had out of her lungs. Hands pressed down, hard enough to crack ribs maybe, the rhythm relentless. Someone pinched her nose shut. Lips clamped down over hers.

Someone pushed breath into her lungs. The air felt like

shards of glass, tearing through her throat, filling her chest with fire. She gasped, coughed, and drew in a lungful of air.

Someone was yelling nearby.

Jianna! Jianna!

That was her name. She was sure of it. The voices were distorted, stretched thin like they were coming from underwater. She tried to focus on them, tried to anchor herself to something real, even though she felt like she was floating away.

She forced her eyes open. Just a crack. Just enough to see.

Her father. He was standing above her. His cheeks were sunken in. He looked grey and old, like he'd seen death.

Then a woman appeared, leaning over her. She had dark hair and sharp features. Jianna knew her, but she had forgotten her name. Why couldn't she remember it?

Everything went dark again.

She woke.

Her mouth tasted like metal. Copper and salt. Blood, probably. She'd bitten her tongue most likely. Something was burning. Hair by the smell of it.

She was exhausted. She just wanted to let the darkness take her and be done with it.

But someone shook her. Hard. It was that woman again. The one whose name she couldn't remember.

The motion sent fresh waves of pain through her body.

"Wake up, Makinde. You did it. And you're not dying on my watch."

Words. The woman was saying words. It took Jianna a moment to parse them through the ringing in her ears.

The woman leaned over Jianna again. "Can you hear me?"

She was named after a tree.

Jianna remembered that much.

Elm? Oak? No. Willow. The woman's name was Willow.

"Did you hear me?" Willow said. "You did it."

"Okay."

Jianna couldn't remember what she was supposed to have done. It was something important, she knew that much. But when she reached for it, she found nothing. Just emptiness where the memory should have been.

She closed her eyes again.

More yelling, but it was receding.

Soon, everything stopped hurting, and she just let go.

Chapter Forty

THE SQUARE in front of the Administration building was packed with spectators. Five hundred folding chairs had been set up for the public. They were all filled. Many people had brought their own blankets and gathered in tight bunches while others had simply found a bit of pavement and taken a seat. Willow sat on stage with the other Councilors.

She studied the crowd.

Many of those in attendance looked haggard, but there was something else in their expressions too.

Hope.

Willow caught sight of Omira in the front row and braced herself. The woman was going to sink her teeth into Willow's announcement and shake it like a dog with a rat. No. Everything was going to be okay. She was simply nervous. Willow hadn't been this anxious about speaking to a crowd since her first press conference.

Soren stood at the podium detailing how the phagocyte treatments would be available soon and reassuring everyone that the city communication network would be restored once they were assured that everyone was nanite-free.

It was impossible to believe that a mere two weeks earlier he couldn't string together a coherent sentence. Soren turned to where the dignitaries were seated. "I'd now like to welcome our latest addition to Council, Councilor Flutter."

Chatter broke out amongst the crowd. Heads turned, bodies shifting as people craned their necks to see better. Glint helped Flutter up from her chair and escorted her to the podium.

Then Soren returned to his seat.

Flutter looked out at the crowd and began to sign.

Glint translated. "Long ago, before all of you were born, I remember your ancestors coming to our planet. At first, you feared us. Then you fought us. After the Liaison brokered peace, you avoided us. We understood, trust must be built. But one of you sought us out. One of you trusted us first. One of you reached out in friendship. You remember that one as the girl who died so that Reunion could happen. Phoebe Makinde was my friend. Her laughter was my laughter, her tears were my tears. Today, the Descendants have chosen to trust you first. We reach out to you in friendship. We hope that our laughter will become your laughter, and that if tears must be shed, we will shed them together and become wiser for it. Let us share this world with each other, Friends."

Flutter turned to Glint and nodded. She was done.

Applause broke out.

It started scattered, a few people clapping, the sound thin and hesitant. Then more joined in and grew, building in volume and intensity until it filled the square, echoing off the Administration building's walls.

Glint waved and then escorted Flutter off the stage and

down to the street to where a car was waiting. Due to her age, the Elder probably wouldn't hold her Council seat long, so they were already grooming Glint to be her replacement. The fact that Glint was of Atlas Shan's ancestry probably wouldn't be made public for a while. Even the Elder didn't think people were ready for that announcement just yet.

Willow rested her hand on her belly.

Cousin Glint.

Camilla had confirmed it with DNA yesterday when Willow had gone for treatment. Willow knew that Mother Basu would've condemned her decision to allow the Divine Blueprint to be modified. She would've called it sacrilege, corruption of the sacred, a violation of everything they believed in. She would've denounced Willow as a heretic, stripped her of her position.

But she was sure that Atlas would've approved, and that was enough for now.

"Willow," Soren said.

She looked up. He'd returned to the podium and was introducing her.

She nodded, getting to her feet and made her way over to the microphone. "Thank you, Soren."

He squeezed her arm and returned to his seat.

Willow looked out at the crowd. So many faces. Both familiar and not. She had tried to serve them to the best of her ability, but times changed. And they were changing for her. She cleared her throat. "It's been my privilege to serve my people as both Councilor and Guide, but it's time for me to step down from both positions."

Silence. Surprise registering on several faces.

"I'm taking on a new mission: overseeing a rehabilitation program for the surviving members of the crew of the Elysia, who suffered centuries of trauma at the hands of their former leader. Now that they are freed from his tyranny, they deserve every opportunity to heal from their ordeal and build new lives, and I hope that you will all hold these newcomers to DaVinci with compassion in your hearts."

There was a scattering of applause. Most of the crowd weren't even paying attention to her speech.

But she didn't mind. She knew a lot of people didn't like her.

She wasn't making that announcement for them.

She was making it for the cyborgs.

For people like Daisy who was trying just about every food in the city for the first time in her existence, whose eyes had gone wide with wonder at the taste of fresh fruit, who'd needed ten minutes just to process the texture of bread. Daisy, who'd spent three minutes outside in the sun yesterday before her anxiety grew too high and she'd retreated back inside, trembling and hyperventilating.

Three minutes of freedom after an eternity of captivity.

That's all she could handle.

But it had been two more minutes than the week before.

Daisy and her crewmates had experienced the brutality of technology twisted past perversion. They'd been tools, resources, things to be used and discarded, consumed, resurrected and used again. Their bodies had been violated in ways Willow still couldn't fully comprehend, rebuilt and modified without consent, stripped of autonomy so completely that even the concept of choice had become foreign to them.

And while Willow could no longer believe in Mother Basu's teachings as she once did, she still believed that everyone deserved to experience the spiritual peace that came with aligning more deeply with Nature. If anyone needed a helping of that peace, it was Daisy's people.

They needed to remember what it felt like to be human. To make choices. To experience pleasure and pain. They needed to laugh and to cry. They needed earth under their feet and wind in their hair and the sun on their face.

And Willow was going to be there to help them experience it all.

Chapter Forty-One

MICHEL'S whole body felt numb.

His mouth was so dry he almost couldn't pry it from the roof of his mouth.

He forced his eyes open.

White ceiling tiles. Clinical lighting. The smell of antiseptic.

Hospital.

Right.

He looked down at his arm.

It was encased in white plaster from his fingertips to his shoulder. He tried wiggling his fingers. They barely twitched, sending a dull throb up through his forearm that felt more like pressure than actual pain.

Must be the drugs.

He glanced to the right.

An IV tube was stuck in the back of his hand. He followed the clear tubing up to the bag, watching the liquid drip into the line, hypnotized by the rhythmic fall of each droplet.

What had he done to his arm?

He couldn't remember…

In fact, the last thing he remembered was Jianna getting angry with him. Telling him he'd betrayed her trust.

No.

That wasn't the last thing.

It was Aurelius. Face down on the floor in the quantum computer lab. Then the cyborg in the cave, bathed in pink light. The Descendants in the freezer, rows and rows of them, stacked like frozen popsicles.

The overlay display. The button labeled: LAUNCH.

The memories slammed into him one after another now, faster and faster, like bullets firing from a gun. Each one sharp and vivid and terrible. He squeezed his eyes shut, wishing he hadn't tried to remember, but it was too late now. The images kept coming.

Aurelius.

Breaking his arm.

But they must've succeeded.

Because he was here, in a hospital bed with an IV drip and a cast and whatever cocktail of painkillers was keeping him numb.

That wouldn't be the case if Aurelius had won.

So, they'd stopped him. Somehow. Together.

But what had it cost them?

He closed his eyes. He needed to check the newsfeed, find out what happened, who made it back, and who didn't.

And where was Jianna?

He couldn't bear not knowing what happened to her. He closed his eyes and reached for the overlay.

Nothing.

He tried again, focusing harder, searching for the

familiar interface that should appear in his peripheral vision.

Still nothing.

As much as he missed the convenience of it, it was a good sign. It meant Aurelius was right. They had taken out the tower. Or the Elysia's computer. Maybe both. And that meant Aurelius was no longer a puppet-master.

It also meant he had to wonder if—

The door to his room opened.

Jianna walked in, carrying a tote bag just like the one his mother used for shopping.

Relief flooded his system.

She was alive. She was here. She was *okay*. And for some reason, she was wearing mittens.

Whatever price they'd paid to defeat Aurelius was worth it. He could handle anything as long as she'd made it through.

She stopped when she saw he was awake and gave him a tentative smile, hesitating near the door. "Can I come in?"

Weird question. Why would she even ask that? "Of course. Is there a reason you wouldn't?"

She waved her hand, gesturing to the room. "If you didn't want me to—"

"I want you to," he said. Mainly because if she left now, it would be unbearable. "I want to know what happened. I only remember parts."

Jianna crossed the room, setting the tote bag down on the floor next to his bed. Then she removed her coat and pulled up a chair, sitting next to the bed. Now that she was closer, he could see that she wasn't wearing mittens; her hands were wrapped in gauze.

"Are you alright?" he asked.

She held up her hands. "I got slightly electrocuted."

"I don't think there is such a thing as slightly."

She forced a smile, settling her hands in her lap. "Then I'm the first. You're in better shape than me. You needed reconstructive surgery on your arm. It's going to take months to heal, and there are a lot of pins."

Michel glanced at the cast. "Lot of pins. Got it."

"What happened to it?"

He shrugged, then winced. Shouldn't have done that. "Aurelius."

"Right."

"What else?" he asked.

Jianna glanced at the window and then looked back at him. "I need to apologize."

Michel frowned. That didn't make any sense. "What could you possibly have to apologize for? I'm pretty sure I'm the one who attacked you."

She shook her head. "You didn't attack me. Aurelius did. You were an innocent bystander."

"It was my hands—"

"It wasn't you." Her voice sharpened, cutting him off. "And it wouldn't have been your hands if I'd listened to you."

Michel stared at her. "What are you talking about?"

Jianna sighed, leaning back in the chair. "I've thought about the fights we had. I was so sure I was right about Aurelius that I didn't really listen to you. I just demanded that you agree with me."

Michel flushed. "But you were right."

"That's not the point."

He blinked. "It's not?"

"No. The point is that I dismissed everything you said. If I had listened and we'd had a conversation, instead of me lecturing you—"

"I might've talked long enough to hear how stupid I sounded?" Michel tried for a smile.

"No." Jianna leaned forward, her eyes searching his face. "But you might've felt like I was there for you while you were going through it all, and I'm sorry that I wasn't. You deserve to have someone who's willing to hear your side of things, no matter what. Even if what you're saying is stupid."

He laughed, held out his hand.

She laid her bandaged fingers on his palm. "I felt like I had to prove I knew what I was doing, you know? To Aurelius, to you, and…" He paused, not really wanting to admit this next part. "To myself."

"You never have to prove yourself to me, Michel. I promise."

He nodded. "I'm sorry I didn't have the guts to tell you about the nanites."

"Forgiven."

"Really?"

"Yes."

He swallowed, cupping her hand. "Am I going to have them forever? And did they mess up my brain?"

The thought terrified him more than he wanted to admit. What if Aurelius had left something behind? What if the nanites had rewired him, changed him into something other than himself? What if he'd never really be free?

But Jianna grinned—actually *grinned*. "No and no. By studying the Descendants' phagocytes, Camilla and I were able to come up with a treatment that cleans the nanites out of the brain. We've already administered it to you and have done two CAT scans. Your brain looks fine."

Michel stared at her. He was going to be okay. Actually, genuinely okay. "So I'm…"

He trailed off, not quite sure how to finish the sentence.

"You're you," Jianna said. "Just you. No Aurelius, no nanites, no one controlling you. Just Michel."

Just Michel.

He'd never thought those two words could sound so good.

"So I'm going to be fine?"

Jianna laughed. "Well, you're going to be in a cast for a few months, and then you'll need a lot of physical rehab. But the good news is you've got a lot of paid leave stacked up."

Michel grimaced at the cast encasing his arm. Months of physical therapy? He could already imagine the tedium of it, the slow progress, the frustration of relearning how to use his own limb. But at least he was alive to complain about it.

"And my father wants to talk to you about a new job, when you're ready to get back to work."

Michel raised his brows. "New job?"

Jianna leaned forward, her eyes bright with something that looked like excitement. "There are two whole spaceships up there full of knowledge, and somebody needs to go through it all and figure out what's valuable, and what's safe to develop. We'll need rules for integrating it so that no one is tempted to run amok."

Two spaceships? That was a lifetime of work. Centuries of accumulated research, technology, genetic data, and cultural archives. Everything humanity had learned and preserved before the colony ships launched. All of it, waiting to be cataloged, analyzed, and understood.

Jianna was right. Someone had to go through it all and decide what was safe. What was dangerous. What rules needed to exist to keep another Aurelius from hijacking it all for his own twisted vision.

And they were offering that job to him.

He grinned. This is what he'd always wanted: to understand the technology, to work with the knowledge, to be part of something meaningful. But this time, without the manipulation, without someone using his enthusiasm as a weapon against him.

"I'll need some help." He tried to keep his voice casual, but he could hear the eagerness bleeding through anyway. "Know anyone who wants to volunteer to oversee all the genetics research in the archives?"

Jianna smiled. "I'll ask around."

He laughed.

And he knew she wasn't angry at him anymore. Somehow, they had found their way back to each other. All the fighting and fear and mistakes had been worth it. It had burned away the worst parts of themselves, leaving something stronger in its place.

He wanted to say something more, to tell her how much it meant that she was here, that she'd forgiven him, that she was willing to work with him on this, but exhaustion was already dragging at him again, pulling him back toward sleep.

Chapter Forty-Two

JIANNA KNELT under the Remembrance Tree, knees pressed into moss and crumbling leaf litter. Sunlight filtered green through the canopy, dappling the two ceramic grave markers.

She's brought an offering: two tiny cakes, each with a photo of Reed Ademi Evans on top. Phoebe's son. Samara's grandson. It seemed like they ought to be included somehow in Reed's first birthday celebration, but it also seemed wrong to dim Willow's joy by turning the focus of the party to people long dead, even for a few minutes.

Removing the pastry boxes from her bag, she opened the first one and placed the cake in front of Samara's gravestone. Then she stood up and stepped back so she wasn't standing directly *on* Samara. Because that felt wrong too.

Why did everything feel wrong?

Her father knew how to make this kind of thing beautiful, but Jianna always messed it up somehow.

"I'm sorry," she said. "Sorry that you never got to meet

your grandson, and sorry that I haven't been a very good descendant. Dad used to make me come here for the ceremony every year. We had to be the first ones making the offering, and it felt like so much pressure. I hated how much everyone expected me to live up to your legacy."

She took a deep breath, not sure if she should admit this part, but it wasn't like she was going to tell anyone, right?

"When the Aurora Event happened, that was the first year I didn't go, and this deep, superstitious part of me felt like maybe it was my fault, even though I knew that was stupid."

There, she'd said it. Samara probably would've thought she was an idiot for falling prey to that kind of magical thinking, but she'd never lived up to Samara's standards, had she?

Not that she was here to complain about that.

"Anyway," she continued, "I'm here now, and I thought you'd like to know that Reed is doing great, he's the happiest baby I've ever seen, it's ridiculous how cute he is, and he has this little gurgle when he laughs."

Just the memory of it made her smile.

"He's the reason no one's taking meds for off-target effects anymore," she added. "Camilla and I were able to use his sequence and Camilla's synthetic techniques to create a cure."

Samara's later journals had been so full of guilt that the same superstitious part of Jianna hoped that saying the words out loud to a dead woman might somehow give her peace, if she hadn't found it already.

She knelt and opened the second pastry box, removed an identical cake, and set it in front of Phoebe's headstone. Once she'd gotten to her feet and backed up a respectful distance, she was even less sure what to say to Reed's mother.

Just say what you'd want to hear if you were her.

"Phoebe," she began, "your son is being raised by someone who loves him like he's her own. Lucas is back, and he's watching over Reed; we all are. Even Cousin Glint, who I think you'd be proud of, is part of the family."

She started to turn away, but that superstitious part of her started whispering again. So she turned back and added, "If there's something after… this, I hope you found Atlas again."

And I hope you don't mind that he might be waiting for someone else, too.

Jianna waited for a moment, but the voice didn't say anything else.

She felt good.

Like she'd finally completed something that had been unfinished her whole life.

So, she walked back to the gathering hall, where the future she'd never expected waited for her.

Chapter Forty-Three

REED WRIGGLED ON LUCAS' lap, chubby hands waving enthusiastically as his mother, Willow, picked another package, this one wrapped in recycled paper, tied with a blue ribbon from the pile and held it up while everyone watched.

Willow peeled it open, and a shrew tumbled out, feathered fur in impossible colors. It was almost as big as Reed was. Reed squealed and reached for it.

Lucas took the shrew and delivered it into Reed's sticky hands while Willow opened the card. "From Jianna and Michelangelo."

Michel grinned, his hand finding Jianna's. She leaned against him, her shoulders loose and relaxed in a way Samara had never managed, not once in all those years. Lucas measured it automatically. Jianna's openness, Michel's steadiness. The way they navigated each other.

Lucas had run the numbers last week. Michel's communication metrics were up fifty-eight percent on the Fletcher scale from where they'd been when he and Jianna had discovered Lucas in his underground lab.

The next gift was more for Willow than Reed: a bigger stroller from Camilla, to give fast-growing Reed a roomier ride when Willow took him to the park. Jianna worked for Camilla now, at a new Council-funded research institute for synthetic engineering.

A bright blue scoot bike from Soren, who continued to swear that he wouldn't run for re-election next year. Jianna's father clapped his hands with delight as Lucas lowered Reed onto the bike. Reed immediately grabbed the handlebars and began to bounce up and down, squealing with glee.

"We'll practice riding later," Lucas promised Reed as Willow picked up the next package: a series of storybooks designed to teach Reed everything from the names of animals to local geographical features. That was from Willow's sister, Cira, who'd taken a rare break from leading meditation retreats to attend her nephew's birthday.

Willow beamed as she hugged Cira, who beamed right back. The sisters had grown close since Reed had been born, but Willow had never confided in Lucas what had triggered the change.

Daisy's gift: a hand-sewn quilt, each square depicting a scene from one of the fairy tales she loved to weave into lessons for her first form students. A fox in a blue coat, leaping over a creek. A girl with silver hair holding a lantern. The edge of the quilt prickled with gold thread, not quite symmetrical, but somehow perfect. Reed grabbed a corner and shoved it in his mouth, and wouldn't let go of it.

Lucas had saved his own gift for last. As Reed's grandfather, it was incumbent on him to pull out all the stops with a custom gaming environment designed to lead the boy through every skillset he would develop in the next three years, with optional modules that Lucas would add when the boy showed potential. And notice if there were any areas where he needed extra support.

Samara would've rolled her eyes and said something about letting kids be kids. But if Reed liked the games and they could help Lucas be a better grandfather...

"We'll set it up later," Willow said. "How about cake?"

Reed squirmed on Lucas' lap, dropping the blanket and pointing at figures coming up the path through the window: Glint, pushing Flutter in a wheelchair. The older Descendant seemed to be napping, but Lucas could tell from her vital signs that she was conscious, but weak.

"I'm going to take Reed to see Granny Flutter and Cousin Glint."

Willow perked up, craning her neck to see out the window and waving at the duo. Glint waved back.

Lucas bounced Reed up and down as he strode down the path, meeting the pair halfway. He signed a quick greeting, and when Glint signed back, Reed imitated it clumsily, earning him a kiss on the cheek.

"I'll take her," Lucas added. "They're about to cut the cake."

Glint nodded and jogged toward the gathering hall.

As soon as she was gone, Flutter's eyelids flickered. She focused on Reed and lifted her hands, trembling with the effort. Lucas leaned in, careful not to jostle her, and settled Reed on Flutter's lap.

She pulled Reed close, fingers splaying across his back. The child burrowed against her, quiet for once, his cheek pressed to Flutter's shoulder.

Lucas pushed them slowly down the path, past the Remembrance Tree. Reed didn't squirm or complain. He watched the leaves shiver overhead, his gold-flecked eyes following every movement.

He had his mother's eyes.

At the river, Lucas stopped and set the brake on the wheelchair. Flutter cradled Reed, and he stayed perfectly still, as if mesmerized. It was the longest Lucas had ever seen him go without making a sound.

Flutter signed. *You will help Glint speak for us.*

Lucas signed back, *I will.*

The aging Descendent hugged Reed one more time and then nodded to Lucas. He picked the boy up and cradled him in one arm.

Flutter signed, *You will stay with me.*

He signed back, *I promise.*

Setting Reed on a small rock beside him, Lucas pulled a pillow from the small compartment on the back of the chair, rolled it, and set it behind her neck so that she didn't have to work so hard to hold her head up.

Then, he spread a blanket from the same compartment over her lap and tucked it around her legs. By the time he'd finished, Reed had managed to stand and take one lurching step. Lucas reached down and caught the back of his shirt a microsecond after he tripped on a small rock, a microsecond before he would've hit the ground face-first.

Then he sat cross-legged beside the wheelchair, settling Reed on one knee. Reed leaned against him and seemed to fall asleep almost immediately.

Lucas knew that it wouldn't be long before he would be instantly awake and wanting ten different things at once.

He relished both.

I miss her, Flutter signed.

No matter how many times he experienced it, this anomaly was the most painful of all. And the most beautiful.

Me too, he signed back.

Flutter reached down, placing one frail hand on his shoulder, and together, they watched the wine-dark water throw off specks of sunlight as it flowed gently toward the city.

They sat in silence as a leaf fell from a nearby branch and landed on the river's surface, swirling as it floated downstream and disappeared.

And they listened to the chirping of tiny, lizard-shaped creatures in the trees until Flutter's hand slipped off his shoulder.

She had been the first to call him Friend.

About the Authors

Titus is a scientist, strategist, and storyteller working at the edge of technology, where humanity itself is the experiment. Through his novels, he explores how science reshapes not only our tools, but our values, choices, and future as a species. His career spans biotechnology, artificial intelligence, and global innovation, giving his fiction both authenticity and urgency. He lives in the Pacific Northwest with his wife, Maggie, where he writes, builds, and ventures into the wild.

Connect with Titus via website, Connected Ideas Project, LinkedIn, and BlueSky.

~

Sean Platt has always been an entrepreneur, but stories were the business he was born to build.

When his wife bought him a laptop for his birthday in 2007, he dropped everything to write fiction.

After a short stint as creative director at a marketing agency — where he learned the kind of copywriting that could turn cliffhangers into an art — Sean wrote hundreds of novels (including international bestsellers), penned Hollywood scripts, and founded Sterling & Stone, an IP incubator where more than two dozen writers turn wild ideas into world-changing stories.

Originally from Long Beach, California, Sean now lives in Austin, Texas, with his wife, Cindy, and their dog, Fisher — both of whom remind him that real life makes the best stories.